SWEET REWARDS

LORI BEASLEY BRADLEY

O livia Thibodeaux Montgomery sat on the veranda outside her second-floor bedroom at her father's home and watched jagged forks of the lightning spear the sky to the west. She hoped a late spring storm would do something to diminish the oppressive heat. She fanned herself vigorously as Magdalena, her maid, friend, confidant, and her blood half-sister, brushed her raven hair up off her porcelain-skinned neck to twist into a tight bun on the top of her head.

"If it rains," Olivia asked, fanning away a petulant mosquito, "do you think Daddy will call off this horrid party tonight?" Since the loss of her husband, William Montgomery, at Vicksburg in a violent clash between Union and Confederate troops, Olivia had resumed residing with her parents on their palatial sugar plantation, Sweet Rewards, west of New Orleans. Her father spent lavish amounts of money on parties trying to lure suitors for Olivia's hand in marriage. Armand Thibodeaux was desperate for a male heir to Sweet Rewards that only

Olivia could give him now that her mother was in her late forties and past her childbearing years.

"Daddy ain't gonna cancel this party, Miss Livvy. He bettin' the farm on this riverboat man catchin' your fancy. He done brung him all the way out here from St. Louis to meet up with y'all."

"Magda, don't go calling me Miss Livvy here in my own room. You know I don't hold with that old slave nonsense. You are not my slave. You are my sister, and everyone in this God-forsaken Parish knows it."

"That may be, but Daddy still do, and if he heared me callin' you anything but Miss Livvy, he'd be whoopin' my black ass for sure."

"Yes, but Daddy isn't in my bedroom at this minute, and your ass is about as black as mine." She jerked her head and yelped when one of Magdalena's pins stabbed her scalp. "You did that on purpose, and you can stop talkin' like an uneducated cane-field nigger. You had the same tutors I did and can speak better than I do most of the time."

"I most certainly can, but I did not do that on purpose. You won't hold still." Magda laughed. "I may be an educated house nigger, but Daddy isn't out there looking for some rich riverboat man for me to marry, is he? He'll marry me up with one of them dumb cane-field niggers of his and call it good."

"He will not," Olivia protested, "you are a free woman and can marry any man you please. Daddy can't force you to marry anyone you don't want to anymore."

"You mean like he can't force you to marry up with no rich riverboat man?" Magda snorted indignantly. "He still treats me like a house slave. He made me bed with that fat old bastard Remus last week when he was here."

Olivia stood and jerked the tie of her dressing gown

tight at the waist in anger. "Why didn't you come to me, Magda? I would have put a stop to that nonsense. He's got no right to do that. You have not been a slave for almost ten years now."

"It's alright, Livvy." Magdalena walked to the wrought-iron railing around the veranda to try and catch a cooling breeze. She ran a hand the color of heavily creamed coffee over her black hair, twisted into a tight bun at the back of her neck, and wrapped with a cotton cloth, denoting her place as a house servant. "Mammy says that if I'm nice to Remus, he might ask her to come work for him, and she'd like that. She loves your mother, but she's gettin' too old to put up with Daddy's depravities anymore. Anyhow, old Remus just rolls over and goes to sleep after I suck his little cock."

"Magda, don't be crude," Olivia chided and then asked with a giggle, "Is it really all that little?"

Magdalena stuck her thumb into the air and smiled. "Not much bigger than this. With that belly of his, I bet he ain't been able to see it in years unless he's in front of a mirror."

Olivia giggled along with her sister.

She took Olivia's hand and tugged her toward the bedroom. "Come on in now, and let's get you into the bath. Daddy's going to want you smellin' all fresh and sweet for tonight." They went through the glass-paned French doors into Olivia's opulent bedroom, where a servant had filled her white enameled tub with hot water.

"What am I wearing to this little circus tonight?" Olivia asked as she dropped her dressing gown to the floor, revealing a tall, slim body with raven hair falling nearly to her shapely behind. She stepped gingerly into the tub, testing the water's temperature with her toes before climbing in and sitting.

"I think you should wear that new orchid gown your mother brought back from N'Orleans last month. It is so pretty and looks just like one I saw in a color plate of Empress Josephine. Nobody wears that old-style anymore, and the color is almost the same as your eyes. I'm sure it will impress that riverboat man." Magdalena went to the wardrobe and brought out the orchid silk-chiffon dress with its high empire waist and short puffed sleeves. She laid it out across the bed and went on to pull clean undergarments from the heavy oak bureau.

"I'm gonna fix that pretty little diamond tiara in your hair and," Magdalena went on pulling things from the bureau drawers, "this diamond choker and dangling earbobs. You will look just like a princess from the court in France."

"I'm certain that is exactly what this man is looking for," Olivia sighed as she squeezed warm water from a sea sponge over her face to run down her throat and over her pale white breasts, "a plantation princess with two hundred acres of cane fields *and* a processing plant for sugar."

"What difference does that make if he can give you the babies Mr. William couldn't?"

Olivia thought of her sweet William and how their hopes had been dashed every month when her flux had come. "I don't think it was William's fault. I'm the only living child Mother ever bore. Daddy says she comes from bad blood. Maybe I'm the same. William and I were married for two years before he went off to the war, and I never conceived once."

"Livvy, you were young. Lots of girls don't conceive until they get into their twenties. You are twenty-four now, and maybe this riverboat man will have a huge set of ballocks to make lots of good strong seed. Mr. William, he was a small man. Did he have small ballocks too?"

Olivia's face flushed in her tub. William's were the only human ballocks she had ever seen. She had no idea if they were big, small, or otherwise. She knew Magdalena had much more experience with men than she did, having been passed around to her father's friends on many occasions and having had dalliances with young men on the plantation over the years.

"I am quite certain William's ballocks were more than sufficient for the task." She stood and pulled a large cotton towel from a brass hook on the wall and wrapped herself in it before stepping out onto the long, oval, braided rug.

They both gave a start when someone tapped on the door. Olivia pulled the towel tight around her as her mother came into the room from the hall, aided by her silver-handled cane to walk. Marie Thibodeaux saw the orchid dress lying out on the bed and smiled.

"Thank you for choosing that one, Olivia. Your father will be ever so pleased." Marie picked up the dress and held it up, admiring the soft, ethereal fabric that fluttered in the breeze coming through the open French doors from the veranda.

"Thank Magda," Olivia told her mother bluntly. "It is not what I would have chosen."

"I'm not gonna let her wear another one of them old black dresses to any of her father's parties no more, ma'am," Magdalena declared, giving Olivia a petulant grin.

"Thank *you* then, Magdalena." Maria laid the dress back onto the bed. "Would you mind giving Olivia and me some time alone, dear?"

"Of course not, ma'am." Magdalena gave Marie a quick curtsey and left the room.

"Olivia, William has been gone for seven years now. It's time for you to move on with your life." Marie rested her frail frame on the bed and leaned her cane next to her. "I was hopeful when you took off your mourning clothes two years ago, but you have spurned the advances of every man your father has presented to you since."

"Mother, no man will ever be able to replace William in my heart. His grasp on it is still strong. I can think of no other." Olivia's gaze fell on the silver-framed photo resting upon her nightstand of the man in a starched gray captain's uniform of the Confederate Calvary. The image was all in muted tones of black and gray, but Olivia swore she could see the bright blue twinkle in those silent, fixed eyes.

"*Ma Cherie*." Marie took her daughter's hand. "I know you loved William very much, and he loved you very much too. That is something most women never experience in a lifetime. You are a very lucky woman, but it is time to carry on with your life and find another to father your children."

And there it is. The reason Father wants me to marry. All he cares about is a male heir for Sweet Rewards. I'm nothing more than a damned broodmare, in his opinion.

"Tell me, Mother, is this man a friend of Father's with all of his same distasteful proclivities? Does he frequent whores and abuse women for the fun of it?"

Marie reached to touch the silver handle of the cane at her side. "Your father was not always the man he is now. We come from different times, Olivia. Your father and I had our slaves and our French culture. Armand was an extremely handsome young man, and I was overwhelmed by his charms and that he chose to ask for my hand out of all the debutants presented that year." Marie sighed sadly and took a deep breath. "Then he was involved in that foolish duel that scarred his face, and he changed. Your father is a vain man, and the loss of his looks affected him more than I could ever have thought. In the end, he blamed me because he'd called the man out for insulting my virtue. Then when I failed to provide him with a living male child to carry on the Thibodeaux name, he blamed me again."

"Mother, none of that was *your* fault," Olivia protested to her sad mother. "Father had no business calling out a man to duel with blades when he didn't have the skill to do so, and women lose children out here in this miserable swamp all the time. He should have taken you into New Orleans, where there are good doctors and midwives. He should have taken you to the townhouse in the city instead of leaving you out here in this filthy swamp."

"I had good care here, Olivia. Georgia took very good care of me, just like Magdalena takes good care of you." Marie stood and hobbled with her cane out onto the veranda, where a cool wind had picked up, blowing clouds heavy with rain up from the Gulf. Olivia bit her lip and followed her mother. "New Orleans in the summer is a terrible place to be. It is hot and has miasmas. Yellow fever takes hundreds every year. Sweet Rewards was the only place I ever wanted to be during my pregnancies."

"So tell me about this man Father has chosen for me to marry this time," Olivia said, changing the subject. "Have you met him?"

"We have dined with him on occasion in New Orleans. He is quite handsome and owns a shipping line on the Mississippi and Ohio Rivers. He has offices in New Orleans, but his main office and home are in St. Louis, I believe."

"Why has he not married already? Is he widowed, or does he simply prefer paid women in his bed?"

"There is no need to be crude, Olivia Marie. From what I have seen of him, he is a hard-working man who has put many years into building up his business on the rivers. I think he has simply chosen to wait until he could offer a woman security before looking to marry. I think that is commendable."

"I think he is simply looking to add a sugar plantation and a processing plant to his holdings by marrying the widowed daughter of the plantation's owner," Olivia sneered.

"Olivia, I could not give your father a proper heir to Sweet Rewards, so that responsibility now falls upon you." Marie limped back into the room and sat upon the chaise lounge by the doors where she could enjoy the breeze while watching her daughter dress.

"Mother," Olivia dropped her dressing gown on the bed and began pulling on her bloomers. "I will not make you any promises, but I will meet this man and listen to what he has to say."

"I cannot ask for more, *Cherie*. Your father will be ever so very pleased." Marie took her daughter's hand again and smiled. "And I am very pleased about the dress and the tiara. Make certain you wear the white opera gloves with it. You will look *tres chic, ma petite*. You will look just like Josephine herself in all her royal splendor."

❧ 2 ❧

From her room, Olivia could hear the noise rising from the parlor below. The orchestra warmed up, and the knocking at the door announced new arrivals to the night's soiree. Magdalena fussed over her, fitting the tiara perfectly straight upon Olivia's head, and slapped her shoulder every time she fidgeted in the chair.

"Will you please hold still, Livvy? I want to get this pinned in nice an' tight, so it doesn't go slidin' off your hard head into the punch bowl."

Olivia let her sister have her way and sat perfectly still. They heard another knock on the door from below. "Do you think that might be him?" Olivia asked with a twinge of nervous energy. "The orchestra won't begin to play until he gets here. Then I can make my grand appearance on the stairs."

"You're going to take that rich riverboat man's breath plum away, Livvy." She patted the diamond choker down flat around Olivia's white throat. When they heard the orchestra, she pulled Olivia to her feet. "Now, walk carefully, so you don't knock that tiara off."

"How can I possibly when you have it tacked to my skull with horseshoe nails?"

From the top of the stairs, Olivia could see the regular swamp-rat gentry from the neighboring plantations. They never passed up an opportunity to show off their Paris fashions ordered from the shops in New Orleans. The women wore the slimmer skirts with all the frilled aprons and ridiculous big bows on their backsides. They simply couldn't pass up the free food and drink offered by her father on these occasions, and it irritated Olivia to no end.

Between her parents stood a tall man in an elegant black silk waistcoat, trousers, and top hat. He stood almost a head taller than her six-foot-tall father, and his tanned face was extremely handsome in a rakish sort of way. Above his full lips, he wore a pencil-thin mustache, and his eyes were slate-blue like the tiles on their townhouse in New Orleans. They weren't a bright, sparkling, playful blue like William's had been but a darker, smoldering, brooding blue, giving him an air of coldness, distance, and mystery. His broad shoulders were well-defined in the jacket and his waist trim in the perfectly pressed trousers. Although this man was easily ten years her senior, Olivia found he aroused her.

Perhaps Mother is right. Seven years without a man between my legs has been long enough.

Olivia was happy for the confining corset because thinking about being with the man had caused her nipples to harden and become erect under the heavy brocade fabric. It also embarrassed her to admit to the throbbing between her thighs and the wetting of her neglected womanhood.

Olivia gracefully descended the winding staircase into the Sweet Rewards plantation house's wide foyer and through the crowd of admiring onlookers. She heard the sighs of women as they saw her in the exquisite dress, and she smiled, knowing her mother would be pleased. She walked directly to her parents and their guest. Olivia raised her head to reach her father's scarred cheek and plant a light kiss before bending to her mother's. She started to raise her hand to the tiara but decided against it. Magdalena, she was certain, had secured it.

"Olivia," her father said, taking her hand and passing it to the tall man next to him. "I would like to present you to Mr. James Devaroe of New Orleans and St. Louis."

Olivia curtseyed with her gloved hand, absorbing the heat from his through the cloth. "So very nice to make your acquaintance, Mr. Devaroe," Olivia said, holding his hand just a bit too tightly for convention but reluctant to break the connection.

"And I to make yours, Mademoiselle Thibodeaux." He brushed her fingers with his lips, and Olivia momentarily regretted the gloves.

Olivia yanked her hand back. "Mrs. Montgomery," she snapped. "It is Mrs. William Montgomery."

"Of course," he amended. "Pardon my ignorance. I meant you no disrespect, Mrs. Montgomery."

"Of course you didn't, James." Armand Thibodeaux slapped Devaroe's shoulder while he gave his daughter a disapproving glare. "Let's all go into the dining room and be seated. I believe the cooks have been working their fingers to the bones for this fine dinner."

James Devaroe offered Olivia his arm, and she reluctantly took it. They followed her parents into the dining room where Georgia and Magdalena had set the twelve-foot cypress table with the Thibodeaux family china, fine crystal and, gold-plated flatware upon bright white linen. Brass candelabras, gleaming like gold, sat every few places apart, giving a brilliant, glittering effect to the elegant table.

Her parents took their places at either end of the long table. Olivia found her place card sitting next to Devaroe's near the center while others found theirs. Some were seated at the main table with the hosts, while the hostess relegated others to smaller tables situated around the room. One of those was Simon Montrose, the arrogant son of a neighboring plantation owner and an ardent suitor for Olivia's hand for many years. Olivia could tell by his narrow-eyed stare that he felt slighted by this insult, and she smiled inwardly at his displeasure. Simon Montrose would have been her last choice as a husband, and her father knew it. They had rebuffed Montrose's offers for years, refusing to allow Sweet Rewards ever to fall into the hands of the Montrose family.

Simon's irritated glare at her father tempered Olivia's ire at James Devaroe, and she lifted her champagne glass to her slightly rouged lips and sipped. This vintage she found more to her liking than some, with a sweet rather than dry taste. She emptied her glass in one long swallow.

Armand Thibodeaux stood with his stemmed glass in hand when waiters in white waistcoats and black trousers made certain everyone had champagne in their glasses. An impressive figure of a man, even with the hideous scar that marred and twisted the right side of his face, he raised his glass and tapped it with his fork. The room quieted.

"I would like to thank you all for coming tonight," he said in a clear, deep Creole-accented voice. "I would like us all to drink a toast to my lovely daughter, Olivia, and my dear friend James Devaroe of Devaroe Shipping and Cartage. Many of you know him, I am sure, and do business with his fine company." Thibodeaux raised his glass toward the couple and then drank, signaling the others at the tables to also begin enjoying the fine vintage before them.

At one of the satellite tables, a chair scraped across the polished marble floor, and someone cleared his throat. Everyone looked over to see Simon Montrose standing and looking pointedly toward Olivia and Devaroe, while his stoic white-haired father, Sterling Montrose, sat looking on with an aggravated frown. His glass sat on the table untouched. He only stood a few inches taller than Olivia's five-foot-six but was of a muscular build. He wore his stringy brown hair long to his shoulders and had a long whip-thin twisted mustache and pointed goatee.

"Monsieur Thibodeaux, I find it revolting that you would offer your lovely daughter to this pirating scum when I, a man of long-standing, local blood, unashamed of the spelling of my good French name, have made numerous offers of an honorable marriage and a joining of our two fine houses."

Olivia saw her father's and Devaroe's faces darken with Montrose's insults. She placed her gloved hand over James Devaroe's clenched one and gave her head a slight shake. He eased a little. Olivia saw the tension leave his shoulders, and his hand relaxed beneath hers.

"Simon," her father said, deliberately using the less formal first name of his offending guest, "while your offers have been sincerely received, my daughter has on regular occasion refused them. She is a grown woman and, I fear, has a mind of her own. She will take a husband again when she sees fit and not one minute before. It has ever been beyond my ability to change her mind on that accord."

"Perhaps that is true, Armand," Simon Montrose said with a doubtful smirk, "but I still cannot believe you would countenance this *nouveau riche* pretender to soil your fine bloodline. His parentage is that of pirates, for God's sake."

Olivia felt Devaroe tense again like a cat about to spring on its prey. She held tight to his hand, hoping to keep him from leaping over the table and attacking the odious Simon Montrose.

"Furthermore," Montrose continued to bait her father, "I always assumed you kept a tighter rein on the women of your family. If you told the girl to marry, she should, as an obedient daughter, feel it her familial duty to obey her father and wed the man of *his* choosing. She *is* obedient under your roof, is she not, Armand?"

Simon Montrose walked to the table directly across from Olivia, who stood to face him but kept a hand on Devaroe's shoulder to keep him in his seat. "Olivia Thibodeaux Montgomery," he said, holding out his own gloved hand over the table to her. "I again offer you my hand in marriage to unite two good Louisiana families and two prosperous plantations into one."

The tension in the air hung as heavy as the humidity on the hot June evening hung over the steamy bayou. "Simon Montrose, you officious little fool, I wouldn't have your hand in marriage if you were the last man of any bloodline in this mosquito-infested swamp," Olivia seethed. "Now, please sit back down like a good little boy and stop insulting my father and his guest or get out of our home so we can enjoy the rest of our evening." Several ladies in the room, including her mother, stood and clapped while Simon Montrose, followed by his father Sterling, stormed from the dining room, slamming the door behind them as they exited the mansion.

Olivia took her seat along with the other ladies, several giggling at Montrose's humiliation. Armand Thibodeaux tapped his wine glass with a fork again and stood.

"Thank you, daughter, for ridding us of that buzzing mosquito," he said and smiled at Olivia with pride. "I told him she had a mind of her own." The room broke out in loud laughter. "Again, a toast to my lovely, mule-headed daughter, Olivia Thibodeaux Montgomery."

"Mrs. Montgomery," James Devaroe said to her as he forked up a slice of succulent roast pork from his plate, "you certainly know how to put a man in his place."

"Does that bother you, Mr. Devaroe?" she asked him between bites of potatoes dripping with savory pork gravy. The mood in the room had become much lighter after Montrose's exit. The orchestra took up playing once more, and conversations buzzed all around them.

"*Au contraire*, I find a strong woman very intriguing," he said with a smile. "I suppose you have to be strong to survive out here in this wilderness."

Olivia's eyes darted around the lavish room, where the light sparkled off the crystal goblets, gold flatware, and expensive china, and she smiled. "I would hardly call Sweet Rewards a wilderness outpost, but managing any business builds one's character. I'm sure it's the same with your shipping line. Is it not?"

"I suppose it is," he agreed and sipped from his champagne glass. "I have four riverboats, twelve barges with tugs, and a whole fleet of cartage wagons with teams.

Keeping track of it all can be quite unnerving at times. I have managers in New Orleans and St. Louis, of course, but I still try to keep a tight rein on things."

Olivia admired his strength and his ability to contain his obvious anger during Montrose's rant. She also admired the fact that he had allowed her to take the lead in rebuffing Montrose. Some men would surely have felt belittled by that.

"Your father seems to have a pretty good handle on things here at Sweet Rewards."

"Everything except his mule-headed daughter," Olivia said and laughed. "Father has been trying to marry me off since William's death at Vicksburg. But I suppose you already knew that." Olivia finished her plate and dabbed her linen napkin at the corners of her mouth to make certain none of the brown gravy remained there.

"Your father," Devaroe said after emptying his champagne glass and setting it aside when the waiter offered a refill, "is a very astute businessman. He wants to make certain Sweet Rewards is in capable hands should his health fail him, or he suffer an accident." Then he added, "The good Lord forbid," and crossed himself.

Armand Thibodeaux stood again at the head of the long table. "I believe we gentlemen will adjourn to my study for cigars while the ladies retreat to the parlor with my good wife before we have our dessert and coffee at the end of the hour. I believe Cook has prepared us a lovely orange marmalade cake."

To approving chatter, the two sexes moved to their respective domains, except Olivia and James Devaroe. He followed her through French doors onto a brick patio where candles made from the aromatic mosquito-repelling tansy plant were lit and sitting on round wrought-iron tables. The air wafted cool and damp from the earlier rain, and the tails of lightning bugs flickered over the manicured lawn beyond the short brick wall separating the two areas.

"It's a lovely evening," he told her as he took a seat upon the low wall, which would, undoubtedly, dampen the seat of his expensive trousers. He took no mind of it, and she caught him staring at her in the flickering glow of the candles.

Olivia luxuriated in the cool breeze left in the aftermath of the earlier storm. Now, with the clouds gone, stars twinkled in the black heavens above where only a sliver of moon hung to illuminate the night. Tree frogs squeaked in the nearby woods, and the musical calling of night birds replaced the stringed instruments of the orchestra inside.

"Yes," she replied and took a seat close to him. Olivia could feel the heat from his body and smelled his masculinity.

I've gone too damned long without a man between my legs.

The throbbing of her womanhood began again as she breathed in his aroma. The scents, a combination of Bay Rum shaving tonic, cigars, liquor, and man-sweat, dizzied her senses. The excitation more than she could bear, Olivia stood and stepped away from him. The tingling in her nipples attested to her arousal and added to her discomfort.

Devaroe followed her across the patio and laid his strong hot hands upon her bare shoulders between her diamond choker and the sleeves of her elegant dress. Although it was a bold, ungentlemanly action, Olivia found herself leaning back into his embrace, allowing the heat of his touch to flow through her very being and melting into him like the wax of the candles around her.

Olivia felt his lips brush the top of her left ear, and the heat of his breath there released a hot flow of passion between her thighs. She wanted more than anything to turn around and taste his mouth. She wanted to feel those lips upon hers, and she wanted him to feel hers. Goose flesh broke out upon her arms, and the tiny hairs rose in anticipation of another touch.

Devaroe turned her around and brushed her cheek with those hot full lips, trying to get to her mouth, but she pulled away. She wanted his touch more than anything she'd wanted in a long while, but she resisted for convention's sake.

"This is unseemly, Mr. Devaroe," she said, backing reluctantly away. "We don't know one another nearly well enough to be spooning on my father's patio."

"Pardon my misassumptions, Mrs. Montgomery," he told her and walked stiff-backed past her and into the house.

Misassumptions? Does he think I lured him out here to do illicit things in the dark? The throbbing in her groin persisted. *Did I?*

A mosquito buzzed around her ear, and she slapped at it. She could still feel his hot breath on that ear, and the thought of it only caused her throbbing discomfort to intensify. Olivia had not felt this way around a man in years. Did it mean her love for William had waned away? Could that possibly be?

"Livvy, what you doin' out here in the dark alone?" Olivia jerked her head up with a start at the sound of Magdalena's voice. "You better be comin' in," she told her, and Olivia noted Magdalena wore a serving maid's uniform. "We gonna start servin' dessert in a few minutes. Why that riverboat man go stormin' through the house the way he did? You say somethin' to make him mad already? Daddy ain't going to like that none if you did."

"I just wouldn't kiss him," Olivia sighed.

"Lord have mercy, girl, why not? That man looks sweet

as honey on cornbread," she giggled, "and hot cornbread at that."

"Magda, I am going to swat you if you don't stop being crude." Olivia stormed past her half-sister, who stood giggling as she passed, and returned to her seat in the dining room. All the ladies sat in their respective seats, waiting for the men to return. Her mother gave her a hopeful smile and arched an eyebrow as if in question. Olivia returned the smile but did not know or care what it conveyed.

Devaroe returned to his seat next to her, and she could smell the strong scent of tobacco and brandy on him. He had joined her father and the others in the study for a smoke and a drink. His nearness brought about another flush to her face, and when she glanced at her mother, she knew Marie Thibodeaux saw it from the satisfied grin on her pale, thin face. Olivia suspected her mother already had the guest list and wedding invitations in mind as she sat there smirking at her red-faced daughter.

After dessert and coffee in the dining room, the guests chatted and mingled for another hour before beginning to filter out of the mansion. Only James Devaroe remained. He would be ensconced in the guest suite just down the hall from Olivia's room. The thought of him sleeping so near brought up her color again, and she poured another glass of champagne in an effort to quell it.

A butler escorted Devaroe to his room, and Olivia bid her parents a good night soon after.

"Thank you for a lovely party, Father," she said and kissed his scarred cheek.

"What do you think of him, Livvy? Do you like him, or should I send a note of capitulation to Simon?"

Olivia rolled her eyes and slapped her father on the

shoulder. "That's up to you, Daddy. I am ever your obedient daughter."

"That will be a cold day in Hell," her father said and laughed. "I'm proud of you, girl, for putting that officious fool, Simon Montrose, in his place, though. You are of true Thibodeaux blood."

"Even if I'm just a lowly female Thibodeaux?" Olivia kissed her mother and walked to the stairs with the orchid silk swishing about her legs as she stepped.

"You looked beautiful tonight, *ma Cherie*," her mother called after her.

"*Bonsoir, ma mere.* We will talk about this in the morning. I'm exhausted."

In her room, Olivia stripped out of the lovely dress. With Magdalena's help loosening the cords of her corset, she finished undressing and took down her hair.

"So, Miss Livvy," Magdalena teased, "how do you like that rich riverboat man? Did Daddy finally find you, someone you'd consider fit to marry?" She pulled out the final pin, and Olivia's hair tumbled down like midnight rivers to fall below her shoulders and cover her firm white breasts. Just thinking about James Devaroe's hot, strong hands on her bare shoulders brought her nipples to attention once more and a throbbing between her thighs.

"He is, indeed, an interesting man." She ran her fingers through her hair and scratched her scalp with her nails. The relief at having her hair released from the confining, tight bun paled against the relief of being able to breathe again with the escape from the confining corset.

"Interesting and handsome." Magdalena giggled. "Mammy told me to dress nice and gave me some silk stockings and fancy garters to wear to his bed tonight. I am supposed to entertain the riverboat man in his room."

"What?" Olivia stood and stormed out the door of her

room. First, she intended to speak with her father about this ridiculous house-slave bullshit but changed her mind and marched down the hall to the guest room. She found herself in front of the door and resolutely knocked.

"Come in, my dear," she heard him call from inside the room and pushed open the heavy oak door. James Devaroe lay naked on the bed, stroking his large, erect penis. When he realized who stood there, he scrambled to cover himself with the quilt folded at the foot of the bed.

"My sister will not be joining you in your bed tonight, Mr. Devaroe, or any other," Olivia growled.

"Your sister?" Confusion contorted his handsome face, and he continued to pull at the quilt that lay over his erection and his bared loins. "I have no idea what you are talking about, Mrs. Montgomery. Your father said he was sending up a house girl to take care of this condition you left me in." He pulled at the quilt over his erection. "What do you mean about a sister?"

"That house girl just happens to be my father's daughter, too. She is my half-sister and my maid." Olivia turned when she realized he gaped at her wide-eyed. Wearing only her flimsy summer dressing gown, she realized it now hung open down the front, exposing her naked breasts, belly, groin, and legs.

"You came in her place then?" He smirked, not taking his eyes off her body. "How very gallant of you, Mrs. Montgomery." He pulled the quilt from his body to reveal his erection to her. Olivia, to her shame, imagined it sliding between her legs or lying throbbing against her belly, and her nipples stiffened again along with the wetting of her throbbing groin. In her mind, she could feel his tongue brushing over those nipples and his teeth grazing them.

She pulled her dressing gown together. "I'm afraid you are going to have to service yourself tonight, Mr.

Devaroe." Olivia turned red-faced and stormed from his room. This man infuriated her. He intrigued her, but he also infuriated her.

Storming back into her room with her hair hanging loose about her head and her gown falling open again, Magdalena met her laughing in snorting fits. "You went down to that riverboat man's room and made a damned fool of yourself, didn't you, Livvy Montgomery? You are besotted with that man. Just admit it."

"I may be interested, but that doesn't mean I'm going to let him use you the same way he might use a paid woman in a cat house," Olivia told her sister. "And I'm going to speak with my father about this. You are no longer a slave in this house, and he can't pass you around at his discretion. You are a free woman who can decide for herself who she does and does not want to bed with."

"Maybe I *wanted* to bed with that rich riverboat man," Magdalena teased her. "You aren't the only one who hasn't bedded with a handsome man in a good long while."

"That may be, little sister, but I'm laying claim to this one," Olivia said and giggled.

❦ 4 ❧

The morning after the party at Sweet Rewards dawned sunny and hot. While eating their breakfast on Olivia's veranda, she and Magdalena watched James Devaroe walk off across the grounds.

"Where you think he's goin'? Magdalena asked as she poured honey into her tea.

"Probably going out to inspect his prospective holdings," Olivia sneered and took a bite of her buttered croissant. She watched the man cross the green lawn and slip down a path through the woods surrounding the property that led toward the swampy bayou area around the cane fields.

"Why don't we take a walk today?" Olivia sipped her tea as she watched Devaroe disappear into the brush and palmetto at the edge of the lawn.

Magdalena followed Olivia's eyes and smiled. "It's a bit warm for a walk, Livvy, but if you insist."

They finished their meal, dressed, and left the house. Magdalena took the lead and headed across the lawn in the same direction they had seen Devaroe go. "I assume this is the direction you wanted to stroll this mornin'."

Down the path, shaded by the overhanging branches of oaks and cypresses, thick with Spanish Moss spilling over them, they walked until they heard splashing. Olivia pulled Magdalena behind the thick trunk of a giant cypress and looked around to see James Devaroe swimming in one of the shallow ponds on the property.

"That riverboat man might be rich," Magdalena snorted, "but he's plenty stupid goin' swimmin' out here in this swamp. He's gonna be gator bait if he don't get out of that pond."

As if hearing her, James Devaroe pulled himself up on the narrow dock built out into the water by the plantation's fishermen. He wasn't wearing a stitch. His tall, tanned body glistened with water as he stretched out his lean, hard-muscled limbs on the boards. He balled his clothes up and tucked them under his head. As they watched, his hand moved down over his tight, flat stomach to his groin and began fondling his penis into a massive erection.

"Hellfire," Magdalena said and giggled, "this might be an interesting walk after all."

Olivia smiled at her sister and peeked back around the big tree. Devaroe busied himself, stroking his cock with his right hand, running it first down to its base and then back up over the purplish bulb at the top. He repeated the action and watching the act brought a tingling throb once more to Olivia's groin. She shivered as she imagined that beautiful thing slamming into her, and she moaned with the thought.

"I hear that, sister," Magdalena concurred. "I wouldn't mind me a little of that slidin' into my black cunny. Maybe we could share him. It sure looks like he got more than enough for two."

Olivia ignored the mosquitos flitting around her sweaty head and watched the naked figure on the dock pleasuring himself. She imagined ripping off her skirts, running to him, and straddling that beautiful, stiff cock. She closed her eyes, swallowed hard, and imagined how it would feel lowering her body onto the hard staff, rising from between his well-defined thighs, and riding it until she exploded with those exquisite waves of pleasure between her thighs.

When she opened them again, she saw him massaging his large, dark ballocks with his left hand before arching his back up off the old gray boards as his fisted hand slid over his cock faster, and he groaned loudly with the explosive shot of thick white fluid that squirted up and onto his hard, tanned belly. She watched and wished she had been the one eliciting and receiving that thick milky deposit.

"Yes, I most certainly think he's got plenty for two, Livvy," Magdalena sighed. "I ain't never seen a man pleasure himself like that before. Have you?"

"No," Olivia admitted, absently brushing a mosquito away from her head and trying to ignore the annoying throbbing between her thighs.

Look at me, skulking behind a tree, spying on a man in his most private moment. What have I become? Mother is right. Seven years is simply too long to have kept me from a man. Perhaps I should visit the guest room tonight and give James Devaroe a try. Maybe if he thinks I'm a disrespectable wanton woman, he'll go away and forget about this marriage nonsense.

"Be quiet, Magda. I don't want him to hear us. He'll think we're spying on him."

"But we *are* spying on him and that beautiful cock of his," she whispered with a giggle. "I'd sure like me some of that pretty white cock between my legs. How 'bout you, Livvy?"

"I've been thinking the same thing, Magda." She glanced back to the dock where Devaroe lay, seemingly asleep with one muscular arm across his face and the other hand still clenching his ballocks. "It has been too damned long."

Olivia pulled Magdalena away from the tree and back up the path toward the house.

"Daddy's gonna be happy to hear that."

Remembering the sight of Devaroe naked in his bed and picturing herself naked and crawling in with him, she doubted her father would appreciate her plans for the night. Olivia shushed Magdalena again and continued to pull her up the path until they found themselves on the green lawn adjacent to the house's back patio, where her mother lounged in the shade, fanning away mosquitos and stirring a breeze.

Marie Thibodeaux waved when she saw them and motioned them over to join her. Olivia released her hold on Magdalena's arm and joined her mother in the cooler shade.

"Whatever have you girls been doing out there in the brush?" She fanned with more vigor and picked up a heavy glass tumbler of sweet tea. "Olivia, make certain you check yourself for ticks. The dogs have been absolutely infested with them this summer, and I don't want you coming down with tick fever." She sipped her tea as Olivia joined her, and Magdalena went into the house. "I heard the LaRue boy died of it last week. I don't know how I am going to abide another funeral of a child."

"Mother, they had his funeral mass the next day. It's too hot to keep a body for more than a day after death during this heat."

"Yes, of course, they did, *Cherie*. It has my mind all in a jumble. Now tell me," her mother asked, fanning away another annoying mosquito, "what did you really think of our Mr. Devaroe?"

Olivia's mind flashed back to the scene she had just witnessed on the dock, and she felt the heat flushing her cheeks. Like the touch of a ghostly lover, the breeze caressed the damp, bare skin of her arms. Just the thought of the man's naked form made her entire body sensitive, and her nipples hardened and ached for the touch of his lips upon them.

"He is quite a magnificent specimen," she blurted before thinking about to whom she spoke.

"Yes, he is," Marie replied and smiled with satisfaction at her daughter. "Your father will be pleased to hear you are not completely dismissing him out of hand."

"Mother, I've only just met the man. Don't go putting us into a marriage bed quite yet." Olivia picked up her mother's glass of tea and took a sip, somewhat surprised to taste more than just tea in the sweet concoction. She replaced the glass hastily, hoping her mother hadn't seen her take the drink. Since her *riding accident* the year before, requiring her use of the cane to walk, Marie was known to partake of the liquor cabinet's contents more than just occasionally.

Olivia and everyone residing in the Sweet Rewards plantation house knew Marie had not ridden in years. Her *accident* had occurred in her bedroom at the hands of her drunken husband while on one of his lecherous binges when he beat and abused her, cracking her pelvis and keeping her in her bed for weeks afterward. Such had been the marriage bed of Marie and Armand Thibodeaux for as long as Olivia could recall. According to Magdalena, he used her mother, Georgia, in much the same fashion.

Perhaps that was one of the reasons Olivia had loved William so. He had been a sweet and gentle lover, always attentive to her needs and desires before his own. She was thinking of her sweet, gentle William when James Devaroe came walking onto the lawn from the woods. Marie looked at her daughter and raised an enquiring eyebrow.

"Good afternoon, ladies," he greeted them, wiping sweat from his forehead with a silk handkerchief. "This is a lovely, shaded space." He pulled up the legs of his wrinkled trousers and sat in one of the cushioned wrought-iron chairs.

Marie rose, picked up her glass, and hobbled back toward the door to the house. "I need a refill," she told them. Devaroe jumped out of his seat to open the door for her. "Thank you, James. I will have Georgia bring you both a glass." Marie disappeared into the house, leaving Olivia alone with Devaroe on the shady patio.

He took the liberty of sitting in the chair at the small round table next to her. Olivia picked up her mother's discarded silk fan and began waving it in front of her face.

"Did you enjoy your walk, Mrs. Montgomery?" he asked with a sly smile.

"Excuse me?" Olivia asked and felt her cheeks flushing once more.

Did he know we were there watching him? Was he putting on a show for us?

"You and your sister would not make very good scouts, I'm afraid." He chuckled. "You made enough noise to scare up every rabbit and small bird for a mile, and that perfume you wear is quite distinctive. Orange blossom, I believe?"

"You knew we were there, and you still …" Her fan moved even faster, and her head told her to stand while her throbbing loins told her to stay put.

"That scent brings something out in me that I can't seem to control. Did you and your sister enjoy the show?"

Olivia took a deep breath and smiled. "Indeed we did, Mr. Devaroe. And as my Mother was telling me earlier, you should make certain to check yourself for ticks. They are bad this year." She laid the fan down and stood. "You should also check yourself for leeches. That little pond is positively full of them."

Devaroe reached out and took her free hand, pulling her close. "Perhaps you'd like to come to my room tonight and make the inspection yourself." From her skirt, he picked off a tiny brown thing, holding it so she could see its tiny wiggling legs. "You see, I just saved you from one. Now it's your duty to return the favor."

His strong hand holding hers ignited one fire in her, but his arrogant attitude ignited another. "You presume too much, Mr. Devaroe," she said, jerking her hand from his.

He stood, took her arm, and raised it until he had her wrist under his nose. He inhaled deeply over the spot where she applied her neroli oil, made from the blossoms of bitter oranges.

"I told you that scent makes me lose all control." He inhaled again before dropping her arm. "It's absolutely enchanting," he told her with a grin, "just like the beautiful woman who wears it."

They were interrupted by Magdalena coming through the door with a pitcher of tea and two glasses. "I have y'all's tea, Miss Livvy." She set the tray on the table, poured tea in the two glasses, and gave Olivia a little wink and a smile. "Enjoy," she told them and returned with some haste to the large house.

"That's your sister?" Devaroe asked as he picked up one of the tumblers to hand to her. "I don't see the resemblance."

"Luckily, we both look like our respective mothers and

not our father, although Father was considered a very handsome man before his unfortunate scarring."

Devaroe took her head by the chin and turned it from side to side, examining her face. "I think you must be correct, but with Armand's scar, it's hard to tell. You do have your mother's fine features, though. They remind me of those on the marble statues of Greek goddesses, very delicate and perfectly proportioned. I saw some at the museums in Paris."

"You have visited Paris?" she asked with awed enthusiasm.

"Yes, I went to school there in my youth and stayed until just before the War. I came home when there was a certainty of a conflict. My father required my help with the business."

"The pirating business?" she asked, referring to Montrose's insults of the night before.

"Privateers," he corrected. "My father had ships that ran the Union blockade of New Orleans. We've had ships doing business with the Islands for decades, though."

"Why do you not spell your name in the French fashion then?"

"When my ancestors came to Louisiana from Canada in the last century, they'd already changed the spelling. Something to do with their business dealings with the British back then, I believe." He took a long drink of his tea. "My mother said it is spelled this way in the family Bible, so it's the way it is written on the baptismal and marriage records. I suppose I could go to a magistrate and have the spelling changed, but it would cause all sorts of problems with business contracts and the like."

Olivia nodded. "I can see where that could be a problem. Father has a whole floor of lawyers doing his business in New Orleans. I can just imagine the ruckus it would raise if he went in and told him he wanted to change our name's spelling. It would take clerks months to go through all the paperwork."

"And you only have the sugar plantation," he told her with a chuckle as he stretched his long, lean body and yawned. "I have the boats and barges on the rivers, the schooners that run to the Islands, and the cartage division. I have contracts with hundreds of different businesses from Jamaica to Minneapolis."

He watched her face, and Olivia thought he must be looking for signs of her being impressed with his extensive holdings. She smiled and watched his eyes as he continued. "I just commissioned a shipbuilder in San Francisco to build me three frigates to start sailing into the South Seas and to China. Devaroe shipping will be an international concern very soon."

"That is very impressive, Mr. Devaroe. You have been to San Francisco?" The thought of that exotic city enthralled her. Olivia only dreamed of escaping from the Louisiana swamp. She and her family had visited Martinique once on a business trip, but that was as far away from Sweet Rewards as Olivia had ever been. Before marrying William, she had attended finishing school in New Orleans and dreamed of visiting Paris someday like all the other girls. William had promised to take her to Virginia to meet his family and visit their horse farm, but the war had put an end to that.

"I have not yet had the pleasure," he replied. "My business there was done over the telegraph and through intermediaries. When the ships are complete, I plan to be there to watch them set sail," he said and took her hand. "I am hoping to have a wife to be there with me to launch their maiden voyages."

❀ 5 ❀

They dined privately that evening, using the common china and the silver flatware. They ate spicy shrimp and rice with biscuits and butter. A delicate white wine accompanied the meal, and they chatted amiably over their food. Olivia sat close to Devaroe at the table, the heat from his body radiating into her from his nearness. She could smell his Bay Rum over the spices of the dinner, and it aroused her beyond belief. It was all she could do to keep from reaching for him under the table, but she managed to control herself and kept her hand respectably in her lap.

"So, James," Armand Thibodeaux said between bites, "my daughter tells me you are stepping up your shipping empire and moving into the Orient."

"Yes, that seems to be where the future of trade is coming from, and the Celestials pay huge sums for transport here to the States."

"Fools," Olivia sighed. "They pay huge sums to come to this country to be taken advantage of and treated no better than slaves when they get here by unscrupulous mine owners and the railroads."

"Perhaps you can bring some of them down here to Louisiana, James," her father said and laughed. "I understand most of them are accustomed to our climate and understand the farming of rice. We could use that good cheap labor here."

"Father, you already have a plantation filled with Negro indentures who work for almost nothing."

"Child, just leave the matters of business to the men. You have no concept of what it takes to sustain a profitable business."

"Father, I've been shadowing your footsteps here on Sweet Rewards since I could walk." Olivia stabbed a shrimp in her shallow bowl with such vigor that it splashed sauce out onto the tablecloth. "I understand the economics of this business better than you think. I may just be a silly, weak-minded female who you consider nothing but a broodmare for your heir to Sweet Rewards, but I guarantee you that if you dropped dead tomorrow, I could step in and run this plantation just as well."

"Olivia, *ma Cherie*," her mother interrupted, "let's not air our laundry in front of our guest."

"*Ma mere*, y'all intend this man to be my husband. Shouldn't he become accustomed to our laundry?"

"Olivia Marie," her father stormed, pounding a fist on the table. "Do not be insolent." He turned to James, his face red with anger and embarrassment, "Please excuse my daughter, James. I'm afraid I've indulged her overmuch throughout her life. She has not learned any respect. Perhaps *you* will be able to teach her some."

"So, have you settled upon terms for my breeding services to Mr. Devaroe, Father?" Olivia stormed and darted her eyes between her father and Devaroe. "What kind of price did you get for my hand, Daddy, free shipping for a lifetime?" She stood, knocking her chair over, and turned to leave the room.

"Olivia, my dear." James Devaroe grabbed her hand before she could escape from the table and out of the room. "I want you for my wife. I'll not deny that, but if you choose to reject me, I can respect that. You're not a bale of cotton to be bartered over in the marketplace." He dropped her hand, but she did not leave.

Instead, she righted the chair and sat. "So, have you agreed-upon terms?" she asked without looking at any of them. The strong grasp of Devaroe's hand on her skin brought back the memories of the morning, and desire rose in her like the boiling of water in a pot.

Her father cleared his throat. "Yes, we have agreed upon a bride price, and all you have to do is agree upon a date for the wedding."

"So how much did he squeeze you for?" Olivia asked Devaroe as she watched her parents squirm in their chairs. "I'm sure he didn't let me go cheap even though I'm *used* goods and have never conceived a child to prove my worth as a breeder."

"No, he certainly did not," Devaroe laughed. "I had to promise him ten years of shipping contracts for the plantation and to reduce my business contracting with the other plantations he competes with."

"Well, after we have wed, you can forgo that silliness." Olivia glared at her glowering father. "You cannot ignore business opportunities for something you already possess, and if you ignore business opportunities, you will deny me the funds I'll need for travel to places like Paris and San Francisco."

"Nonsense, daughter," her father said, "you'll be staying right here on Sweet Rewards unless you're traveling with your husband."

"I will travel wherever I please. This plantation will be the death of me if I don't get away for a while. I can't very well conceive an heir to this palace in the swamp if I'm locked up here, and my husband is off in San Francisco or St. Louis," Olivia said calmly as she wiped her mouth and stood again. "Mother, you can choose a date." She scowled at her father. "Getting away from here can't be soon enough." She turned and left the room this time, clacking her wooden heels on the marble floor as she walked.

James Devaroe watched her storm off and listened to her shoes as she mounted the stairs. He glanced at Armand's face and smiled to himself. Even if he didn't appreciate her for more than a female to carry his heir for this plantation, the man had raised an amazing daughter.

I think this is a woman with whom I could spend the rest of my life. Armand may be correct, and she needs a bit of taming, the way a prize mare needs to be tamed by its new master, but I see that as a challenge I'm willing to accept.

Armand cleared his throat and lifted his glass. "Shall we toast then to the nuptials of the happy couple?"

Marie lifted her glass. "Has the contract been signed then?" she asked hesitantly.

"It has," Armand said in reply, "and I'd suggest you go to her room tonight, James, and consummate the contract now before my headstrong daughter takes it into her fool mind to disobey me."

"Armand," Marie gasped, "they have not been wed by a priest yet."

Armand Thibodeaux glared at his wife across the long table. "I spoke to a priest some time ago about this, Marie, and he told me that in the eyes of the church, once the betrothal has been made and I agree to the terms of a marriage contract, and a ring has been offered and accepted, the couple may consummate the bond." He grinned. "The good Father said it was a way to make certain the prospective bride does not then try to renege in some way. Once consummated, they are as good as married in the eyes of the Church."

Marie's eyes went wide. "But no ring was offered or accepted," she said.

Devaroe took a pearl ring from his pocket and showed it to Olivia's mother. "I swear she will wear this ring before I consummate this marriage contract, Madam Thibodeaux. I would do nothing to shame you or my intended bride in your home."

๛

Olivia kicked her shoes off in her room, sending one clattering into the wall beneath the window.

I am escaping this God-awful swamp if it is the last thing I ever do. I should have stayed in the townhouse in New Orleans after the Yankees killed my William. Yankees and war be damned. If I'd died, at least I'd be with William, even if it meant being entombed here forever on Sweet Rewards. I'd be dead rather than dying a lingering death as I am now.

Olivia unbuttoned her dress and let it fall to the floor. She wanted to open the French doors in the hopes of a breeze, but it would mean allowing hordes of mosquitos into her room for the night. Olivia poured water at the washbasin, dipped a cloth, and wiped down her sweaty brow, neck, and bosoms. She slipped out of her camisole and dropped her bloomers, wiping the cool rag over her naked body. Unable to get comfortable, Olivia dropped onto the bed and stared at the doors to the veranda.

Maybe if she lit some of the tansy candles, it would dissuade the little buzzing beasts so she could get some air. Then again, the heat from the candles would only make things worse.

Olivia stood again, naked before the washbasin, cloth in hand, when she heard the door from the hall open. She turned, expecting to see either Magdalena or her mother there, but her mouth fell open in shock to see James Devaroe standing there, turning the key to lock the door behind him.

Grabbing up her dressing gown, Olivia tried to cover herself. In two strides, Devaroe stood in front of her. He tugged the gown away and tossed it on the floor. Unbuttoning his silk shirt one silver button at a time, he held her gaze. She watched the thick black hair on his broad, tanned chest begin to peek through the gap in the white silk. Olivia grabbed his black vest and pushed it off his shoulders like a brazen woman.

Devaroe wrapped his arms around her white body, glistening with sweat from her arousal as well as the sticky Louisiana heat.

"You sparkle like the icy snow on the banks of the Mississippi in Minnesota, but you are far from cold, Mrs. Montgomery." She felt his hands running down her back to settle upon the cheeks of her derriere. He pulled her into his hot body and buried his face into the hair on the top of her head. His hot breath there sent shivers of excitement down her spine and ignited a fire in her groin.

Olivia let the excitement of the moment carry her away and lifted her face to meet his. She allowed his hot, soft lips to take her mouth and jumped back a little when a spark like lightning in the air ignited as their lips touched for that first time. He must have experienced it too and smiled down at her, baring his glistening white teeth.

"We are betrothed now, Mrs. Montgomery. It is allowed by the Church for us to couple as husband and wife without sin. Your parents have given their consent." Devaroe reached into his trouser pocket and brought out a gold ring set with a pearl resting between two bright yellow diamonds. He took her left hand in his and slipped the ring onto her finger. "This ring has been worn by the matriarchs of the Devaroe family since well before they sailed to Canada over two hundred years ago. I declare us betrothed and claim you as my own, Olivia Marie Thibodeaux Montgomery if you have me."

Olivia met his lips again and melted with the heat of his chest on her erect, aching nipples. She brushed his lips and breathed, "Yes, James Devaroe, I will take you as my husband."

Devaroe pulled her naked body closer and kissed her with a deep passion Olivia had not experienced in years. His tongue, which he'd snaked between her wanton lips, tasted like liquor and tobacco, but she didn't care. She slid her arms around him inside his unbuttoned shirt, returning his embrace.

Olivia shivered with excitement as his hands ran up and down her back and squeezed the firm cheeks of her behind. Using her fingernails, she scratched his back not with eagerness but with languishing and gentle teasing. He shivered under her touch, and goose flesh erupted over his body as he turned her toward the bed. Bending a little at the knee, he lifted her onto the mattress and laid her, so her head rested upon the white chenille-covered pillows. Devaroe shed his shirt, unbuckled his belt, and let his trousers fall to the floor around his bare feet.

Olivia looked at his hard, toned body with muscles rippling in his arms and thighs and smiled in anticipation of becoming one with it. The thick, coarse black hair on his chest narrowed below his hard nipples but continued in a line over his rippling belly to connect with that around his erect penis and dark brown ballocks. She reached out and caressed the testicles, which elicited a groan of pleasure from the man, who joined her on the bed, bending over her to kiss one of her hard nipples. That brought about a pleasurable groan from her, and her body quivered.

Olivia moved her hand up from the hanging sack to encircle the erect shaft above it; the girth was such that her fingers barely met her thumb. Devaroe moved closer to her so she could get a good hold and reached a hand down to knead her breasts, pinching her nipples. Those pinches made her moan with delight as her womanhood moistened, awaiting his entry. He ran his hand from her breast down over her flat belly to probe the throbbing wetness between her thighs, which brought more pleasurable moans from deep in her chest.

Devaroe took those moans as a cue and moved down to straddle her thighs and thrust himself deep into her. After going seven years without a man, she must have been tight. He groaned as if in pain, but she watched him smiling and knew it to be a pleasurable pain.

"You are like a virgin, *ma Cherie*," he panted as he continued to thrust into her, causing Olivia to pant as well. She ran her hands over his taut thighs and pulled him into her. He bent and kissed her neck, sometimes sucking hard at her tender flesh or nipping it with his teeth. He reached under her backside, dug his fingers into her, and pulled her body up to meet his, causing some pain to her. She groaned and flinched, but he gripped her harder.

Olivia tried to wiggle free, but the movement appeared to intensify his pleasure, and he dug his nails into her as if trying to get her to do it some more. She did, and he soon groaned out his release and fell on top of her, just short of her release, which frustrated Olivia. William had always held his until he was certain she had achieved her pleasure.

"Olivia, my dear, that was outstanding." He rolled off her and gave her thigh a hard slap, causing her to flinch. Her little jerk excited him, and soon he licked her breasts again. Then he rolled her over onto her stomach and began massaging her backside. Devaroe probed her cunny, wet with his fluid, and brought some of it up to massage between the cheeks until he probed the other cavity there, inserting first one finger, then, to her dismay, another.

"Didn't your last husband ever temper his sword in this?" he asked as she flinched when he shoved two fingers into her anus, eliciting a yelp of pain and displeasure from her, which again seemed to excite him. He wet himself inside her cunny, then brought his hard penis up and used it to massage her anus.

"Did he?" he demanded as he shoved into her backside with his hard, thick manhood.

"No!" She yelped with pain and tried to crawl away from beneath his weight. That scream excited him more, and Devaroe pushed into her completely. Olivia could feel his ballocks slamming against the cheeks of her backside as he thrust in and out of her, causing unbearable pain, but each time she winced or yelped with the pain, he got more excited and used her with more force.

"Let the pain amplify your pleasure, my dear," he whispered into her ear. "Here, let me help." Olivia felt his hand slide beneath her belly and down between her legs. He found the throbbing knot there and began to massage it in time with the thrusts onto her backside. To her surprise, the combination of the pain in her anus and the pleasure of his massaging brought about an astounding release, and Olivia found herself meeting his thrusts until her groin exploded with waves of intense, throbbing pleasure.

"Oh, my god," she moaned as her body stiffened, and she rode the throbbing bursts of pleasure in her groin.

Her excitement brought about his release, and he shoved into her hard and groaned before rolling off her, panting and sweaty.

Devaroe turned to look at her and brought his hand up to brush a finger across her lips. "Is that virgin too?" He chuckled when he saw the horror in her eyes. "Don't worry, *Cherie*, I will be gentle with it."

Olivia could feel his fluids oozing from her and rolled off the bed. She wet the washcloth and wiped him from between her legs and butt cheeks. When she brought the cloth back to the basin, blood spotted it. Horrified, Olivia rinsed the cloth and wiped again. This time the cloth came away with more semen than blood from the tender orifice, which relaxed her.

"How is it that soldier-boy husband of yours never broke you in properly? You have three doorways to pleasure, and he only ever took the one?" he asked her, watching her clean up and fondling himself into a semi-erection.

Olivia glared down at the man she'd just agreed to marry and frowned. "I will not speak to you about what William and I did in our marriage bed. It is none of your business."

"I beg to differ," he said with a scowl, "but I will not speak of him again if that is what you wish."

"It is," Olivia said as she bent and retrieved his clothes from the floor. She pitched them to him on the bed. "You should leave now and return to *your* room." She picked up her dressing gown, covered her naked body, went to the French doors, and opened them. The cooler night air washed over her sweaty body as she walked out onto the veranda. At the railing, Olivia looked up at the night sky, sparkling with stars and a sliver of a moon.

William would never have used me like that. It would have gone against his very nature to inflict pain on me or to take his pleasure before I had mine. This relationship is a mistake. I can't spend my life with a man like this. He is just like Father, and I refuse to become a simpering victim like Mother.

Olivia glanced back into her room to see Devaroe sitting on the edge of the bed, tying his shoes. She walked back into the room, slid the pearl ring from her finger, and handed it to him. He looked up at her in dismay, furrowing his brow and opening his mouth to speak.

Olivia did not wait to hear what he had to say. She dropped the ring into his lap, went back through the French-doors, and closed them behind her. When Olivia peeked back into the room, she saw Devaroe dressed and bent over her writing desk. Shaken by the ordeal she had just endured in her bed, Olivia pulled the soft cotton dressing gown tight around her abused body, not against a chill in the night air but rather one running through her very being.

The stars sparkled brightly in the sky over mist-covered grounds Sweet Rewards, but Olivia heard distant thunder. With the feeling of a dark foreboding, she tread lithe as a cat over the boards of the veranda to peek again into her room. Finding it empty, Olivia opened the doors and entered. She ran a hand over her scalp to feel tender spots where Devaroe had pulled her hair. She did not remember him doing that, but he must have because when her hand came away, strands of tangled black hair came with it. Olivia let the hair fall to the floor, closed her eyes, and allowed tears of rage, pain, and disgust to slip down her cheeks.

Fearing his return, she went to the door to the hall and locked it. To reinforce the lock, she took the chair from her desk and propped it under the knob so the door, if unlocked somehow, could not be pushed open. Finally feeling safely barricaded in her private fortress, Olivia returned to her bed. The white chenille spread had blood spots on it, and she immediately went to the basin to get the wet cloth to try and clean it away.

She then saw a piece of her private stationery writing in a neat flowery script upon her pillow. On the sheath of paper lay the pearl ring. Olivia hesitated to pick up the paper, but she finally did, sliding it off her pillow, so the ring remained.

My Dearest Wife, Olivia,

You may choose to wear the ring or not. It is of no great care to me. But make no mistake; we are now, in the eyes of God, The Church, and any parish magistrates you may wish to approach, man and wife. I have a binding marriage contract with your Father, who accompanied me tonight to your room to hear the consummation of our union through the door. You accepted my proposal and my ring, and then you accepted me into your bed and your body. We are, by law, husband and wife now. The public ceremony is simply a formality that we can forego if you wish, but I believe it would comfort your mother some to have the ritual with a priest, dress, cake, and candles. Your father and I will be very happy if you have conceived a son tonight, but there will be many more nights here for us to accomplish that. You make a most pleasing bedmate.

Your Husband, James Eduard Devaroe

Olivia read the words on the page several times, allowing their meaning to solidify in her brain. Then she took it to the lamp, set it to the flame, and watched it catch. Before the crimson light reached her fingers, Olivia dropped the paper, more black ash than not, into the water of her basin and watched it float and fizzle out in the liquid stained pink with her blood.

❧ 6 ❧

Olivia woke to frantic pounding on her door and, for a moment, feared Devaroe had returned. Then she heard her mother's panicked voice from the hall.

"Olivia, *ma Cherie,* are you ill? It is almost noon, and we have not seen you all morning. Let me in," Marie Thibodeaux pled in a frail voice, still rapping on the door.

"In a moment, *ma mere.*" Olivia rolled over and felt pain shoot through the lower half of her body. The cheeks of her backside ached when she put pressure on them, and Olivia could tell James Devaroe had bruised them. She grabbed up her dressing gown and wrapped it around her as she stumbled to the door and removed the chair, securing her privacy.

As soon as Olivia turned the brass key in the lock, her mother burst through the door, supported by her silver-handled cane. "Are you ill, *ma petite?* You never sleep this late."

"I am fine, Mother. I simply did not sleep well last night." Olivia went to her bed and sat gingerly on the edge. Her mother joined her and took her hands and studied the left one as if searching for something. Olivia glanced at her side table, and her eyes fell upon Devaroe's ring. It still lay there where she'd dropped it before burying her head into her pillows in the early morning hours, sometime just before dawn.

"Your father and Mr. Devaroe told me you had accepted his ring and consummated your betrothal last evening." Olivia saw Marie eying William's picture lying face down on the table and her daughter's red and swollen eyes. "Are you not happy, daughter? Your William would want you to be happy, would he not?" Marie looked desperate, her hands shaking as she held her daughter's. She smiled then, trying to lighten the mood. "I have spoken with Georgia, and we will begin preparations for the wedding ceremony to be held here in the garden. We can take a carriage into New Orleans to have you fitted for a dress later this week." Marie continued to ramble on about invitations, flowers, and guest lists, but Olivia ignored her chatter. Her mother seemed to be so happy planning her only daughter's wedding. How could she ruin that for her? Instead of speaking, Olivia stood, walked away from the bed until her back was in full view of her mother, and let her dressing gown drop to the floor.

"*Mon due,*" she gasped when she saw the bruising and swelling on her daughter's body. "Devaroe has done this to you?"

"Yes, Mother, this is how he consummated our betrothal." Olivia knelt and retrieved the discarded robe. "I cannot marry a man like that. I will not be like ..." She let the words fall away into silence.

"You will not be like your beaten and crippled mother?" Marie stood and clutched at her cane for support. "You needn't be, daughter. Give him a son to inherit all of this," she waved her cane around the room and out the veranda, "and you needn't suffer him any longer."

"You can take your child and go where ever you please. Move yourselves to New Orleans or Paris. Educate your son to take over here when the time comes, but get yourself away from the depravities of your husband." Marie hobbled out onto the veranda, where a cool breeze blew inland from the Gulf, promising more severe weather later in the day. "I could never accomplish that. All my sons were born dead or dying. Had I been able to bear your father a living son, we would have left this place long ago."

"Mother." Olivia followed her mother out and took her frail hand. "I thought you stayed because you loved Father and wanted to please him."

"I loved your father with all my heart when we married, and I was certain he loved me, but I was a young and foolish girl then." Marie walked to the railing and leaned there looking out over the vast property of Sweet Rewards, the thin skirt of her light cotton day dress blowing in the breeze. "When you were born a girl, Armand was disappointed, but I thought I would have no problem giving him a son. You were conceived in our first month together, and the pregnancy went well. I had no idea you would be my only living child. I had to fulfill my duty as his wife and bear him a son and heir. Your father was a kind and loving man until that duel took his looks."

Marie tapped her cane against the railing and continued to gaze out across the dense green swamplands. "Then he became mean and took to drink. He began to blame himself when Georgia and his other dalliances produced only female children, too. I swore to myself that if I ever bore him a living son, I'd take us away from here." Marie reached into a pocket of her skirt and pulled out a small leather-bound book. She handed it back toward her daughter without looking away from the horizon.

"It's a bankbook for an account at the Lafayette Bank in New Orleans. I have been secreting funds there for decades now. You will find the account is also in your name, *ma Cherie*. When the time comes, there is more than enough money there to support you and your child handsomely. The townhouse in New Orleans is also deeded in your name. My father saw to that before his death." She smiled sadly as she stared out over Sweet Rewards. "He wanted you to have a legacy other than this mosquito-infested bog land, as he liked to call Sweet Rewards."

Olivia had little memory of her Grandfather LaMonte. Before her tenth birthday, he had died of yellow fever, but she and William had taken up residence in his townhouse in New Orleans soon after their wedding. Olivia loved the place that shared a courtyard with three other townhouses and stood close to the market square. From the veranda over the street, they could see the Gulf and smell the sea. Memories of coffee there with William, listening to the sea birds, and the bustling of the waking city were some of Olivia's most cherished.

Clutching the small book, a sliver of hope stabbed Olivia's heart. She could see herself living in the townhouse again with Magdalena. The family townhouse had survived the war with little damage, and her parents had paid to have the place renovated to use when the family went into the city. Now it sat waiting for her to return.

"*Ma Cherie*," Marie said and took her daughter's trembling hand, "your father thinks we sold the townhouse after the War when you came home. There is no way Devaroe will ever know of its existence. I arranged through a friend to make it appear as though the property had been sold and took money from that account to give to your father as proceeds from the sale. He paid for the renovations after the war so we could sell it."

"But you, Georgia, Magdalena, and I have stayed there many times since the war," Olivia said, looking at her mother with a new appreciation. "Where did he think we were staying?"

"He always gave me money to stay at a hotel. That money went directly into the little book there for you. Armand does not deal with that bank and has no idea I have. My father banked there, and he was well respected."

"Mother," Olivia gasped and giggled. "I had no idea you could be so devious."

"My father's people came originally from Scotland, *Cherie*. It has ever been a hotbed of deception and intrigue." Marie laughed and turned back to face her daughter. "Now, we must begin planning this wedding and pray to God in Heaven that you conceived a son last night. You need not share your bed with the man again until after the wedding. As a matter of fact, I will protest to your father that I do not condone such activity under this roof. Your father may have betrothed you to the man, but you are not legally wed to him yet."

Olivia told her mother about Devaroe's note, and she scoffed at it. "Mr. Devaroe may protest all he likes, but he is still a guest under my roof and will abide by my wishes if he plans to remain here."

"And what about Father's wishes?" Olivia joined her mother at the railing and enjoyed the cool breeze. The scent of hot molasses carried on the wind from the processing plant reminded Olivia that she had not eaten yet today, and it was getting well into the afternoon. "Will you join me for lunch, Mother?"

"I've already had lunch, *ma petite*, but I will join you for tea and cakes on the patio. We can start a guest list for the wedding. When would you like to go to New Orleans for a dress? It may take a month to have one made." They both walked back into Olivia's room, where Marie picked up the pearl ring from the bedside table and handed it to her daughter. "Perhaps you should at least play the part of the hopeful bride." She arched a delicate eyebrow and grinned at her daughter.

Olivia rolled her eyes but took the ring and slid it onto her finger. "To Hell with buying a dress," Olivia hissed. "I will wear the Josephine dress for my wedding and say it holds fond memories for me because it was what I wore when I first met my betrothed." Olivia dressed quickly in a light cotton day dress.

Her mother smiled slyly. "I suppose if he can betroth you with a used ring, you can marry him in a used dress." Mother and daughter laughed together as they supported one another down the wide stairway to the Sweet Rewards mansion's foyer. Magdalena met them there just as Armand Thibodeaux and James Devaroe came through the front door.

"Magdalena, dear," Marie said to Olivia's maid, friend, and sister, "I am having your bed moved into my Olivia's room until the wedding." She gave her husband and Devaroe a withering glance and continued to the patio. "I will not have my daughter accused of being unchaste under my roof before her wedding." She winked at Olivia before turning to the two men. "Will you gentlemen care to join us for tea and cakes on the patio?"

Magdalena gave Olivia a questioning look before heading back to the kitchen to help her mother with Marie's tea, and cakes served on the patio. Olivia smiled, followed her mother out through the heavy French doors, and took a seat at the round wrought-iron table.

You have more backbone than I gave you credit for, Mother.

Olivia watched her mother leaning on her cane as she walked.

It's a shame you never showed it sooner.

James Devaroe took the seat to the left of Olivia and lifted her hand to his lips, brushing it lightly. Noting she wore the ring, he smiled. "This ring belonged to my great-great-grandmother and is said to have been made from one of the first pearls to be brought to France from the Orient." He lifted Olivia's hand to show off the ring to her parents. "And these yellow diamonds come from a mine in India. They were gifts to the king himself from some potentate there."

"And what were your family's ties to the Royal House, Mr. Devaroe?" Marie asked as Magdalena brought out a tray laden with delicate porcelain cups. Saucers, a pot of tea, and a plate of cakes coated with a fine orange glaze also filled the tray. They would make her fingers sticky, but Olivia was ravenous and scooped up two of them to balance on the edges of her saucer next to her teacup.

Devaroe also took two of the sticky cakes and bit into one immediately. "My grandfather's grandfather on my father's side was a retainer to the king," he said with his mouth full, and he blew crumbs onto the table as he spoke.

"And how did your family, with their ties to the French royal family, manage to keep their heads during the Revolution?" Marie asked, furrowing her brow at his poor table manners.

"Like many families here in Louisiana, they had fled to the new world before the heads began to roll into baskets in France. Yours, I believe, Mrs. Thibodeaux, fled to the Islands, while your husband's came here to the fertile swamps to produce the sweet gold we feast upon now." He popped the last bite of cake into his mouth and licked his fingers noisily.

"My great-grandfather moved down here from Canada to further his shipping concerns from the lakes and the rivers to include the high seas and the Islands," Devaroe said and sipped his tea. He furrowed his brow at the taste, took a silver flask from his pocket, and added something to the tea.

"Mr. Montrose was correct, of course, when he said I come from a family of pirates," Devaroe continued with a grin. "Much of my family fortune came from taking English and Spanish transport ships in the Caribbean. It was all quite legal and sanctioned by the government. We held privateering licenses from first the French and then from the real pirates in Washington." Armand joined him in a chuckle.

Devaroe smiled and bit into another cake. All the while, he held tight to Olivia's left hand with his right. She tried a few times to move it, but he held it in a vise-like grip. He seemed to be trying to let her know she belonged to him now and could not escape. He rotated his thumb over the iridescent pearl on the betrothal ring until the band cut into the soft flesh of Olivia's finger.

She finally relaxed her hand in his, and he took the pressure off the ring and her throbbing finger. Georgia brought out another pot of tea and bent to whisper something in Marie's ear. Marie smiled up at her. Georgia nodded and left.

"The boys have moved Magdalena's bed and bureau into your room, *ma Cherie*. *Y*our honor is now safe," she said, giving Devaroe a black stare. "I will not have the neighbors slandering you at your wedding." Marie smiled sweetly at her husband, who sat glowering at her across the small table. "Olivia has decided to wear the beautiful Josephine dress that she met our Mr. Devaroe in as her wedding dress, so we will not need to wait for a seamstress to take weeks. I think we can have all the preparations made for a wedding two or three weeks from Saturday if that is agreeable with you, Mr. Devaroe."

He jerked his head around to look at Marie in surprise. "Of course, it is absolutely agreeable, Mrs. Thibodeaux." He lifted Olivia's hand to his lips and kissed it with a triumphant smile in his eyes. "I would wed her tomorrow if I could."

"I'm sure you would, Mr. Devaroe," Marie said and winked mischievously at her daughter. "I'm sure you would."

James's mind roiled as he sat at the table with Olivia's hand in his. What had she told the old crone to ban him from her room and move her mulatto sister into her room?

We'll marry that little bitch off to one of the field hands and find Olivia a proper maid once we are married. I have no idea how Olivia can countenance her father's nigger git like that. It has to be humiliating, and I'll not have it in my home.

7

Two weeks after the hand-scribed invitations were delivered by house stewards of the Thibodeaux household, Olivia and Magdalena, who were rarely separated now, walked down the path together through the shady woods toward the pond with the dock. The hot late spring had turned into a hotter early summer in the Southern Louisiana bayous, and the only relief that anyone could find outside the sweltering house was in the open air of the shaded woodlands.

Olivia and her sister fanned away relentless hordes of buzzing mosquitos with their silk fans, to not much avail. Olivia slapped at her neck and Magdalena her arms.

"I hate these damned little bastards," Magdalena swore as she slapped Olivia's back, squashing a blood-filled insect going in for another bite. "The summer has just started, and I'm already wishin' for winter."

"I most certainly agree." Olivia swatted another with her fan as they neared the dock on the small pond, swollen from its normal banks by the recent rains. "I hope it cools a little for the wedding next weekend." On the dock, Olivia kicked off her slippers and hiked up her skirts above her knees before squatting to sit on the old boards of the pier. She dropped her feet into the green water of the pond and sighed as the cool water engulfed her legs.

"We're gonna be gator bait swingin' our legs in the water like this." Magdalena dropped down next to her sister and splashed her feet in the water, sending up a cooling spray of droplets onto both of them.

"Roy says he hasn't seen signs of a gator in this pond in years. Do you see any wallows or slides?" Olivia swung her arm around to indicate the pond's banks that showed no tell-tale signs of alligators sliding from them into the water. The big beasts tended to have regular spots where they sunned themselves and left a muddy trail where they went in and out of the water.

"Ouch!" Olivia suddenly jerked her left leg up out of the water to reveal a tiny circular welt on her calf. "Damned perch."

Magdalena began laughing but pulled one of her legs up with a welt of her own. "We just food for everything today, it seems, Livvy. Keep your legs movin', and they won't get ya." Magdalena dipped her hand into the pond and sent an arc of water flying up toward her sister, who jumped and squealed with delight when the cool liquid hit her face and shoulders. She bent and did the same. Soon both young women sat wet from head to waist and laughing like little children.

In the throes of their playful distraction, they did not see or hear James Devaroe come down the path to the pond. It was not until they felt the treads of his boots on the wooden planks that they knew they no longer had the pond to themselves.

"I see you ladies have found a relief from this miserable heat. May I join you?" He kicked off his short boots, rolled up his trousers to his knees, and sat down next to Olivia, using her shoulder as a crutch until he was down. He slid his hand down to encircle her waist and pulled her closer to him. They'd had little time to be alone or close to one another since the night of their betrothal.

"I have missed you," he whispered into her ear before nipping the lobe hard enough to make her jerk away. That made him laugh, and when Olivia glanced over, she could see a bulge growing in the front of his trousers. "Why don't we really cool off?" He laughed and pushed her into the water.

Magdalena, sitting close to her sister, grabbed for her when she heard Olivia give a startled gasp and begin going off the weathered old boards. Olivia's momentum pulled Magdalena with her as she went off the dock into the murky green water of the little pond. They could hear Devaroe laughing wildly as they sank into the pond. Their skirts became heavy in the water and pulled them both down until their naked toes touched the slippery muck at the bottom of the shallow pond.

Olivia held her breath and blew air through her nose to keep the water out. She pushed up with her toes but rose slowly in her heavy, wet skirt and petticoat. Magdalena did the same, and soon their heads broke the water, and they reached for the edge of the dock to pull themselves up. Devaroe, still laughing maniacally, offered Olivia his hand. She took it, but instead of using it to pull herself out of the water, she gave it a mighty tug and sent the laughing Devaroe head-first into the pond with them.

Magdalena heaved herself up onto the dock and tried to help Olivia. Still, before she could get her sister up, a strong hand grabbed Olivia and pulled her back into the water, leaving Magdalena alone, open-mouthed, on the old planks.

In the water, Devaroe pulled Olivia to him and kissed her mouth hard. He shoved his tongue between her lips and teeth until it found hers and twined around it with ferocity. He tasted of stale tobacco and whisky. He held her tight around the waist with one hand while with the other, he pulled up her wet skirts until he found her bloomers, which he ripped away so he could get his hand between her legs and find his prize.

I have been longing for this. It has been too long since our night together. You need a reminder that you belong to me now.

Olivia did not struggle against him, allowing wandering fingers into her beneath the green waters of the pond while Magdalena looked on from the safety of the old dock. Devaroe pushed her toward the pilings until Olivia's back rested against old wood, slick with green slime. He continued to kiss her with her hair getting tangled and pulled in the splintered old cypress posts holding up the dock. He took his hand out of her, and Olivia could feel him unbuttoning his wet trousers to release his hard cock into the water.

She felt him pushing her skirts up again and pulling her legs up until they encircled his waist. With one quick shove, he was inside her. He broke the seal he had on her mouth and gave a loud grunt of pleasure as he entered her. He tried to get to her breasts, but her bodice's fabric clung tight to her, and no matter how hard he tugged, the buttons fastening her dress in the back would not give. In mad frustration, he bit into her neck and sucked at it painfully while he pounded into her under the water. He shoved her bare butt cheeks against the old wood of the slime-coated piling.

Your mother may have thought to keep you from me, but you are mine now, Olivia, and she'll not deny me.

Though she felt violated, Olivia's body reacted of its

own accord, and soon she found herself clenching his cock inside her and arching into his thrusts. She reluctantly invited him into her and shivered with pleasure as he slid over that tender spot between her thighs, and she exploded with a loud gasp of released, frustrating pleasure. She could not help herself, pulled him into her, and returned his kisses until he too groaned and shoved her one last time into the old post.

Withering out of her, his cock and most of his fluids floated out into the murky waters of the pond. "You see, *Cherie*, we are excellent together," he breathed into her ear before releasing his grip on her legs and back-paddling into the water as he rebuttoned his trousers.

Olivia, her torn bloomers long gone somewhere at the bottom of the pond, turned to heft herself back up onto the dock. Magdalena bent and tugged at her shoulder to help her up, and soon Olivia sat, a soggy mess, on the edge of the pier. Devaroe swam over to her and reached up for her to take his hand.

Unsure if she could trust him not to pull her back into the water, Olivia stretched out her left hand to him. He grabbed it but did not get a good grasp, and with both their hands still wet, he slipped free. In doing so, Devaroe pulled the pearl ring from Olivia's wet finger. The three of them watched it fall into the green depths of the pond. Devaroe's eyes went wide with the loss of his valued family heirloom, and he immediately dove in after it.

Olivia did not know what to feel. She felt sorrow at the loss of a treasured family jewel but not sorry for any loss to her. The ring meant nothing to her. She watched Devaroe come up for air and dive down again a dozen times before he finally gave up and pushed himself up on the deck next to her. She did not say anything, and neither did

Magdalena, who sat next to her wringing out her drenched hair.

After a few silent moments, Devaroe grabbed Olivia's shoulders, turned her toward him, and scowled into Olivia's eyes. "You did that on purpose, you little pampered bitch," he seethed. "If you wanted a new ring, why didn't you just say so?" He swung his arm and hit the post of the old dock with such force. Olivia flinched away from him and went flying off the dock into the water. She hit her face on the post and landed in the water with a splash that drenched both Devaroe and a wide-eyed, stunned Magdalena.

Devaroe turned and stormed off the dock and back up the path toward the house carrying his boots and leaving Olivia flailing in the water.

I can't believe she allowed my ring to drop into the pond. She's a foolish, spoiled child. Armand's business and this horrible swampland are not worth her foolishness.

Magdalena stretched an arm out to her from the old wooden dock. "Come on, Livvy," Magdalena called, reaching for her flailing sister. Olivia righted herself in the water, still stunned by Devaroe's ridiculous accusations and dizzy from hitting her head. She swam slowly through the water and took Magdalena's outstretched hand. Olivia let her sister assist her back onto the old dock, where she slumped against her in silence.

"You alright, Livvy?" Magdalena wiped a trickle of blood from the corner of Olivia's mouth with her skirt. "That lip's gonna be a frightful mess for a day or two, and your face is gonna be bruised somethin' fierce for a while. We better get you back to your room and keep you hid from your Mammy for a while."

Magdalena helped Olivia unsteadily to her feet. They walked with a shaking Olivia being held by her sister, both fighting sodden skirts up the slippery path and shooing away mosquitos with their fans. "That woman might take this kind of treatment by Daddy, but she's not gonna 'bide it for her daughter even if it be from the rich riverboat man Daddy wants you to marry. She's probably gonna shoot that riverboat man if she sees you like this."

Olivia gave her sister a half-hearted laugh at the thought of her mother going after Devaroe with her gun. "That's not Mother's style. She's more likely to spike his bourbon with ground castor beans or sprinkle it on his cakes at tea time."

"That'd do it for certain." Magdalena laughed as she slowed at the edge of the lawn to see that the way was clear, and Marie Thibodeaux was not sitting in her chair enjoying the shade of the patio. "You got any of them castor beans in your medicine box, Liv? I might just pound me up some and dose that riverboat man myself. He ain't nothin' but a foul-mouthed son-of-a-bitch. He the one that pulled that ring off your finger and dropped it, not you."

They entered the house without speaking and slogged their way up the stairs in their clinging, wet skirts to Olivia's room, where Magdalena now also resided. She locked the door after they entered, and they began shedding their wet clothes. She wrapped herself in a dry dressing gown, took her wet things out, and draped them over the railing of the veranda to dry before going back in and picking up Olivia's and doing the same with them.

Olivia went into her privy closet and stared at her aching face in the mirror over her vanity. Her lip bled from a swollen split on the right side, and her cheek looked blue and swollen, as well. Olivia touched it gingerly and winced. She knew there would be no hiding it for a few days until the swelling went down and shook her head in disgust at James Devaroe.

He's no better than Daddy, and I'll not have it.

At the little cabinet where Olivia kept her supply of medicinals, she took out a blue glass jar containing yarrow salve and dabbed some of it on her split lip. The balm would help heal the wound and ease the swelling. After returning the salve to the cabinet, Olivia went out to the veranda with her comb to attempt to untangle her hair and comb out all the slimy, green moss from the dock's pillar.

As she combed her hair, Olivia could not keep from thinking of Devaroe between her legs. The man satisfied her that she could not deny. The sting of the salve on her lip reminded her of his brutal nature, however.

He's just like Daddy, and I will not be treated the way Mother has been treated all these years. I know that all men are not this way. William was so gentle and kind. Are there no more like him in this God-forsaken Louisiana?

Olivia sat, combing her hair up and over her head, when her father began pounding on her door and demanding she open it to let him in. Magdalena opened the door, and he shoved his way past her to join Olivia on the veranda. He grabbed Olivia by the hair she had combed forward and yanked her head back to look at her face.

"What in Hell's name did you go and do, Olivia Marie? Your husband is packing his clothes to leave Sweet Rewards before your damned wedding ceremony."

"I didn't *do* anything, Father," Olivia retorted hotly. "We were cooling off in the pond, and when he grabbed my hand, the ring came off and fell in the water."

Armand Thibodeaux twisted and pulled his daughter's hair harder. "He says you took off the ring and *threw* it at him in the water."

"She done no such thing, sir," Magdalena said from inside the room.

"You stay out of this, girl." He pulled Olivia's hair again, bringing hot tears to her eyes. "This is between my fool daughter and me."

"Well, just you look at your fool daughter's face and see what that riverboat man done to her, and he be the one that pulled off that ring and let it drop, not Miss Livvy," Magdalena uncharacteristically stormed at their father.

Armand Thibodeaux walked around to take a good look at Olivia's face and noted the bluing of her cheek and the swollen, bloodied lip. "I suppose you've already gotten the throttling you deserve, Olivia," he said and let go of her hair, allowing it to fall once more to cover her battered face. "Stay in your damned room, though." He stalked through the room and yanked open the door. "I don't want your mother seeing you in this state. She is already in a fitful state over this whole wedding business," he told Olivia and slammed the door behind him.

Olivia sat in the chair with her hair a mess around her face and tears washing down her bruised cheek. She cried just like she had when her father had scolded or whipped her as a child.

If that son-of-a-bitch is leaving Sweet Rewards, then so am I. I'll go to New Orleans to the townhouse. What a bastard, Olivia thought, but she didn't know if she thought it about Devaroe or her single-minded father.

❧ 8 ❧

James Devaroe did leave Sweet Rewards, even with her father threatening breach of contract lawsuits against him. The man left in a huff, cursing Olivia with every breath. She and Magdalena heard him go as they leaned over the railing of the veranda and laughed at their father chasing after Devaroe, screaming and waving his arms in fury.

I can't get away from this misbegotten place fast enough.

Devaroe eased his horse into a walk after he was out of Sweet Rewards' sight, and certain Armand was not following him. It would be dark in a few hours, but he remembered passing a couple of inns just south of the main highway back to New Orleans. He was certain he could make it to one of them before nightfall.

He slowed his mount when he saw a gang of men crossing the road from a stand of cane to another. A man on horseback followed them and stopped in the road when he saw Devaroe. As he drew closer, the man behind the workmen recognized him, and Devaroe saw a smirking grin spread across his face.

"Did Olivia finally come to her senses and send your pirating ass on its way, Devaroe?" Simon Montrose said with a chuckle. "I'm sure Armand will press her to marry me now. He wants an heir." Montrose smirked. "And the wedding invitations have already been sent out. I'll ride over there this very afternoon and make my case. There's no sense wasting all the wedding food. I'm sure he's already laid by." Montrose cackled.

Anger and jealousy surged through Devaroe as he scowled at the pudgy man astride the white horse. He knew the man was right, and Armand would probably force Olivia into a marriage with this fool if he made a good case. Devaroe saw Olivia's gentle eyes and suddenly couldn't bear the idea of this fool atop her.

"I'm just going into my offices in N'Orleans to deal with some business matters before my wedding next weekend." He smiled at Montrose. "I have to make a quick trip of it," he said and brought a hand down to his crotch. "I've got to get back to attend to Olivia. Armand is, indeed, in a hurry for that heir. My betrothal night and every night since have fairly worn my little man out in the attempt."

"You're a cad, Devaroe," Montrose sneered. "She deserves better."

"You mean you?" Devaroe said in a mocking tone. "You wouldn't last a night under Olivia Montgomery's tender mercies. That woman would wear your little cock down to a nub." It was now Devaroe's turn to cackle as Montrose's face went pale with rage.

"You'll pay for that, pirate," Montrose seethed. "Take him," Montrose yelled and motioned to his field hands. "He's yours to do with as you please, and then leave him in the ditch for the scavengers."

Negroes rushed toward Devaroe and pulled him from his horse. They delivered punches and kicks, spit on him, and pulled off his boots and his jacket. Devaroe could hear Montrose's cackling laugh until a kick to his head sent him into a black abyss of painless relief.

###

"Well, I guess we gonna have to send out uninvites to that wedding," Magdalena said with a giggle.

"That suits me just fine," Olivia snapped as she dried her tears, combed back her hair, and stood up. "Pack our bags, Magda. We're going to New Orleans."

"That sounds like fun," Magdalena sighed. "How many days you want me to pack for us, two or three?"

"Pack it all," Olivia stormed. "We're leaving this God-forsaken swamp for good." Olivia walked to her wardrobe and began tossing dresses onto the bed. She emptied it except for the chiffon Josephine gown. That she left hanging and slammed the wardrobe doors.

When they finished, there were four cases stuffed almost past the point of buckling shut. The keys to the townhouse and the leather bankbook rested at the bottom of Olivia's satchel along with her jewelry, her personal stationery, a corked bottle of ink, her pens, and her silver-framed photo of William.

Olivia sent Magdalena to tell the groom to have the old buggy hitched and ready for them at first light in the morning. She wanted to get as far away from Sweet Rewards as she possibly could tomorrow.

Magdalena brought their supper up to their room, and Olivia gingerly ate the ham, green beans, and cornbread with the enthusiasm of an inmate to be released from her prison. Magdalena, who had told her mother about their departure, did not enjoy her meal quite as much.

"My Mammy ain't none too happy about this movin'

away and not tellin' the Misses about it. She thinks it cruel and mean not to let your Mammy say a proper goodbye."

"My Mother will understand completely. I've left a detailed note for her."

"A note," Magdalena scoffed, "ain't no proper kiss and hug goodbye."

"It will suffice," Olivia said and tossed her dressing gown on the bed. "I am going to have a bath. The water should be cool enough by now. You didn't pack away my soap and sponge, did you?"

"No, ma'am, Miss Livvy, ma'am, they be right there with your tub." Magdalena laughed as she put the dirty dishes on the tray to take back to the kitchen.

"Oh, hush up," Olivia snapped, surly, at her sister as she stepped into the tub. "You know I don't condone that kind of talk in my room."

"Yes, ma'am, Miss Livvy, ma'am." She laughed and ducked out the door as Olivia's wet sponge came flying at her to land with a wet squish on the closing door and slide to the floor with a plop.

Olivia smiled at her sister's sarcastic nature and rested her head on the edge of the white porcelain tub, relaxing. The thought of Devaroe leaving in a huff amused her, and she smiled. Then the thought of him pumping into her there in the pond kindled overwhelming warmth between her legs again. There was no getting around it, that man set her loins on fire.

Well, he is gone now, and life will go on at Sweet Rewards, but it will have to go on without me.

Olivia lowered her hand down between her legs to massage the throbbing bulb until she experienced those delicious explosive waves of pleasure that made her groan and shiver in her warm bath. Olivia could not ignore his violent tendencies when her lip started throbbing too. The vicious punch on the dock had both surprised and stunned her.

We had just made love. How could he possibly have been so vicious toward me after that?

She shook her head and slid under the water to wet her hair for washing. The orange blossom-scented soap both relaxed and soothed her. Olivia used the sweet-smelling bar to lather her head until she'd piled all her black locks in a huge coil on top of her head. Her head, still tender from her father's assault, ached and stung. She massaged it and made certain the soap got down to the scalp to dislodge any of the slimy green moss that may have been deposited there earlier.

Olivia slid down beneath the tepid water again and ran her fingers through her hair to get out the soap, though she loved the scent it left behind if she didn't get it all. With her hair free of soap, Olivia pulled herself up in the tub and jumped with a start to see her mother standing over her.

"Did you honestly think you could sneak away from here without me knowing about it, *Cherie?*" Marie handed her daughter a towel and gasped when she saw the swollen lip and blue cheek. "Devaroe?"

Olivia nodded, stepped out of the tub, and fell into her mother's arms sobbing. "I am so very sorry, *ma mere.* I know you and Georgia have been working late into the nights to put together this wedding, and now I have gone and ruined it." Olivia wrapped her arms around her mother and rested her wet head on her shoulder.

"Hush now, daughter, nothing has been done that cannot be undone." Marie led her sobbing daughter to the bed to sit. Olivia saw her looking at the pile of bulging cases and choked off a sob. "I am not here to stop you," Marie said in a soothing whisper. "I am here to tell you that you need not worry about your father in this matter. I have sent him off to drink and play cards in St. Johns. He will be there all night and well into tomorrow morning with one of his whores."

Marie used the towel to dry Olivia's back and wrapped it around her dripping hair. She kissed her daughter's cheek with soft, warm lips that Olivia remembered from her childhood, soothing her after a skinned knee or a spanking from her father.

"I will tell him you have gone off in shame over losing Devaroe and disappointing him. That will feed his over-sized ego until you can get safely away and ensconced in the townhouse. I will tell him you have gone to stay with your school friend in Shreveport."

"Thank you, Mother," Olivia said, wiping her face with the end of the towel. "We will leave at first light and hope-fully make it into New Orleans before it gets too dark. If not, there are several good inns along the way."

"You must be cautious of bandits along the way, *ma Cherie*. I have heard there are roving bands of freed slaves lying in wait for unsuspecting travelers. Here, take this," Marie said and put a small Derringer into Olivia's hand. "I have loaded it, and here is more ammunition and the thigh holster." She laid a leather drawstring bag in Olivia's lap. "You remember how to load it?"

"Yes, Mother," Olivia sighed, "you've spent hours with my loading and reloading the damned thing."

"I know," Marie said uneasily, "but promise me you will keep it on your person and not in some bag packed in the back of the carriage. Wear your special traveling skirt." Marie stood, leaning on her cane. She reached out, lifted her daughter's head with small, frail hand, and planted a kiss on Olivia's damp forehead. "I love you, *ma Cherie;* you are my only living child. I cherish you in my heart, but it is time for you to move on. Go to New Orleans, make a home for yourself in the townhouse, go to parties and the opera, meet a man you can love, and perhaps give me a grandchild to hold before I die." Marie brushed tears from her cheek, turned, and left her daughter sitting on her bed quietly weeping.

❧ 9 ❧

Olivia looked out over Sweet Rewards from her veranda for what she hoped would be one last time. The early morning fog, not yet burned off by the relentless summer sun, crept across the grounds, wrapping its wispy tendrils around trees and bushes. The fog mixed with the Spanish moss hanging from the old trees gave the place an ethereal glow that had scared her as a child after hearing Georgia's stories about the ghosts of witches and murdered women who haunted the bayou.

This morning Olivia stared at the vast grounds with its creeping fog and hanging moss and felt excited to be leaving it. She looked out over the acres of Sweet Rewards to etch a picture of it in her mind. The early morning breeze carried the scent of summer jasmine, honeysuckle, and molasses. Olivia closed her eyes and inhaled that memory too.

The sound of Jimbo coming in to pick up the last two cases to take to the buggy jolted Olivia out of her silent vigil.

"These is the last two cases, Miss Livvy. The buggy be

ready when I get them stowed," the burly groom told her and picked up the heavy leather cases. He walked out the door to carry them down to the waiting buggy below.

Olivia followed him in her dark red poplin traveling suit. She carried a straw bonnet to put on when the sun came out and her personal leather bag that she would stow by her feet as it carried what cash money she had, the bank book, her jewelry, and the key to her lovely townhouse. The little gun she had strapped to her thigh in a holster, concealed by her skirt but easily fetched through a false pocket.

The design had been crafted by her mother years ago for long trips on the road. The swamps bred their own pirates. The wild men's boats, just little skiffs that they could easily maneuver through the trees in the shallow waters, were pirate ships. The men would pilot their small boats close to the roads and silently lie waiting for unsuspecting travelers.

Olivia remembered hearing tales of travelers being robbed, beaten, and murdered along the muddy track from St. Johns to the main highway into New Orleans. Olivia's mother worried about roving bands of freed Negroes, but Olivia had heard these stories long before the Negroes had been freed. She knew these scoundrels were white and always had been. She ran her hand over her skirt and felt the security of the little Derringer secreted there.

Olivia walked through the meandering mist still clinging to the ground and climbed into the old buggy, heavily laden with her and Magdalena's luggage. She heard the wailing of Georgia and knew Magdalena would soon be joining her. In a coffee-brown traveling suit much darker than her skin and carrying a folded parasol, Magdalena climbed up into the seat beside Olivia.

"Let's get this travelin' act movin'," Magdalena said as

she wiped tears from her face and blew her nose on a clean cotton handkerchief.

Olivia took the reins hooked to Old Blue, the dappled-gray horse she and William had bought as a colt soon after marrying. William, who knew his horse flesh, had said the colt would serve them for many years. As it turned out, he never really served William, but Olivia loved and pampered him. Blue was one of the only things she had left of William, and after the past few days, she needed to feel close to her late husband again. After Devaroe's departure, Olivia had returned the narrow, gold wedding band placed there by William all those years ago to her finger. She was Mrs. William Tyler Montgomery and always would be.

I don't know; whatever gave me the idea I could ever be anything else.

They traveled steadily along the muddy, rutted track from Sweet Rewards toward the main road north to the King's Highway that led into New Orleans. The fog burned off by nine, and the sun came out to scorch them through bright cloudless, cerulean blue skies.

Olivia pulled to a stop, got her bonnet from behind her seat, and tied it on. Thus far, they had driven directly into the bright morning sun for most of their trip, but soon they would reach the track north, and she could stop squinting. Luckily the road was overhung, for the most part, by big trees that shaded the women, but the northern track was edged by cane and rice fields, with scant relief from the hot Louisiana sun.

About a mile from the intersection of the two roads, Olivia noticed something strange in the weeds ahead of her by the road. As she neared what looked like a roll of cloth, Olivia pulled gently on Blue's reins to slow him.

"Will you go and see what that is, Magda," Olivia asked her sister, who sat on the side of the buggy where the object lay. They neared it, and Olivia swore she saw movement. Perhaps it was nothing more than an old tarp with an animal nesting beneath it.

Olivia scanned both sides of the track, looking closely into the thick brush along the way. The road agents were said to entrap travelers passing by with something laid out to slow them down. As they neared the object, it became clear to Olivia that it was no discarded tarp. The distinct form of shoeless male feet and legs in trousers lay there motionless in the thick weeds.

Olivia stared intently into the bushes but saw no signs of humans there. She even looked up into the high limbs of old oaks in case they hid there, ready to jump down on them. She pulled Blue to a halt, and Magdalena jumped down out of the buggy and ran to the body.

With a startled expression, Magdalena shouted up to her, "It be that riverboat man, Livvy, and he's in a bad way. You better come take a look. I don't think he dead, but he beat up really bad."

Olivia jumped down and ran around Blue. She gave him a quick pat on the muzzle as she passed to reassure him. Lying there in the mud and weeds, Olivia saw, was James Devaroe. Evidently, he had not been as vigilant as she while traveling down this lonely path. Along with his boots, he was also missing his hat, jacket, and gold cuff links. That silver flask probably was not in his vest pocket either.

Magdalena knelt on one side of Devaroe and Olivia on the other. Purple stained his eyes, which were swollen shut, and he had bruises and knuckle scrapes on both his cheeks.

His lips trickled blood down his stubbled chin and looked like a rose blossom. They were red from his broken and bleeding nose and swollen. Olivia could see boot prints on his white silk shirt, and she knew he had suffered several vicious kicks and stomps to his torso.

She and Magdalena managed to roll Devaroe over onto his back, and Olivia, who had helped in a hospital during the war, carefully ran her hands over his bruised sides to check for broken ribs. They all felt intact, but that did not mean there were not cracks she couldn't feel.

"From the look of these bruises," Olivia said to her sister as she felt for breaks again. "I bet he has some cracked ribs. They are too bad to have not done some serious damage."

Now it was Magdalena peering into the wooded hedges for bandits. "We better get him up in the buggy, if we can, before the bastards come back."

"James." Olivia patted his bruised face to tried and wake him. "Magda, get me the canteen, please." When it came, Olivia put the opening to his mouth and tried to get some water through his swollen lips. She took the opportunity and ran her hands over his face to check for broken bones there as well. The nose definitely felt broken, and she eased the notch of the damaged cartilage back into place and cringed at the sound of the gristle scraping together beneath the skin.

The pain of that brought Devaroe around, and his eyes fluttered open as far as they could through the swelling. Olivia could not tell whether he recognized her or not, but she repeated his name and offered the canteen again. This time he parted his lips with a painful moan and accepted the water. Olivia warned him to swallow carefully so he wouldn't choke.

"James, do you think you can get up? We need to get

you into the buggy." Olivia and Magdalena helped him to sit, but his head fell over as he swooned again from the pain of his many injuries. They couldn't just sit there holding him all afternoon, so Olivia began dumping the contents of the canteen over his head.

That revived him enough that they could get him, unsteadily, to his feet and walk him to the buggy. Both held him up by the waist of his dirty, torn trousers.

"Let's gets him up in the seat with you, Livvy. I'll ride in the back on the cases," Magdalena said and helped heave the heavy man up into the seat of the buggy. She then climbed up into the crowded back compartment with their luggage. Olivia returned to her seat and reached over to make certain Devaroe sat securely on the buggy's padded bench seat before picking up the reins and getting Blue moving once more.

"Where are we gonna take him?" Magdalena called from the back.

Olivia turned the buggy around in the narrow track. "Back to Sweet Rewards, I guess. The only other place nearby is Montrose's house, and I am *not* going there," Olivia said. "Hold on tight, Magda. I'm going to run Blue as fast as I can to get us back before too long. I don't know how long he can remain sitting up."

"Give Blue the reins, Liv. I'll hold on." Magdalena secured herself amongst the luggage and held tight to the back of the seat and the outer edge of the little buggy

Olivia slapped the reins on Blue's dappled behind, and the horse took off at a trot. He bounced everyone and everything in the buggy. A few times, Olivia had to reach out with her right arm to pull Devaroe back from the edge of the buggy. Finally, she let the man slump over onto her shoulder while she did her best to keep them out of major mud holes and ruts. Blue did an excellent job of steering them around the dangers, but after almost half an hour at the fast pace in the hot afternoon sun, the horse began to lather.

Just past the turn into the Montrose estate, Olivia had to slow Blue. A group of people stood in the road ahead, blocking her way. They didn't look like highwaymen. Olivia thought they must be field workers on their way home, but they did not part for her, and she had to stop.

Behind the dozen Negro men surrounding the buggy now sat a stout, pale man wearing a wide-brimmed straw hat on a white horse. When he began laughing, she recognized Simon Montrose.

"Well, Olivia dear," he sneered in a high nasal voice, "I see you've found and collected your wayward fiancé."

"You did this to him, Simon, and just left him by the side of the road to die like an animal?" Olivia raged at the scurrilous man on the horse, trying to look taller in the saddle than he actually was.

"Now, don't get your bloomers in a twist over some worthless pretender." Montrose chortled. "My proud family can trace its roots back to the throne of Louis XIV."

"What were they, groundskeepers, stable hands, or muckrakers in the midden pits at Versailles?" Olivia sneered.

Montrose rode up to the buggy, grabbed Olivia by the hair, and pushed off her wind-blown bonnet. "How dare you insult my family name, you spoiled little puffed-up tart." He pulled his booted foot out of the stirrup and kicked Olivia solidly in the chest between her breasts. She gasped as the vicious kick surprised her and temporarily knocked the breath from her lungs.

When her breathing came back to her, Olivia could hear Magdalena screaming curses as she fought from behind the buggy. Men laughed and called out lascivious comments to their fellow attackers. Olivia could hear fabric ripping and the sound of hands slapping bare flesh.

Soon Magdalena quieted, but the hooting and laughing of the men behind the buggy continued. Olivia could only imagine the defiling her sister must be enduring at the hands of Montrose's band of field hands.

Montrose sat watching what was going on in the road behind the buggy and laughed maniacally. "I hear that nigger bitch is your sister, Olivia." He laughed at Olivia, who was snaking her hand into the false pocket of her skirt. "If you fuck as nice as it looks like she does, you and I will have a fine marriage indeed."

"I seriously doubt that," Olivia said as she raised the little pistol and aimed it at Montrose's midsection. His eyes grew wide at the sight of the little double-barreled gun, and he began backing his horse away. "Call off your dogs, Simon, or I'm going to blow a hole in your belly big enough to jump through."

Devaroe, who still had his head on her shoulder, whispered hoarsely in her ear, "Shoot the snarling bitch, and the pups will run away."

"Call them off, Simon, or I'll shoot you. I swear, I will."

"Now Olivia, my sweet, you wouldn't harm your future husband before he gets a chance to taste that sweet cunny of yo …"

He didn't get the chance to finish his crude sentence as his guts began falling out of his belly onto his saddle from the double-barreled shot from the little gun. The laughter from behind the buggy turned to silence after the loud pistol blast and then to the sound of running feet as Olivia jumped from the buggy and stood, waving the pistol in their direction.

She watched the Negro workers go running off toward

Montrose House, some of them struggling to hold up their pants as they fled. Olivia rushed from the buggy to kneel at Magdalena's side. She lay practically naked in the soupy red mud of the road, her clothes torn and haphazardly pushed around so the men could touch her bosoms and get between her wide-spread legs.

"Magda." Olivia wept at seeing her beloved sister in such a state.

Magdalena pushed herself up on one elbow and glanced around at her ripped clothes. "I'm gonna kill me some cock-sucking cane-field nigger sons-of-bitches." She rolled and pushed up onto her knees in the mud, and Olivia stood to help her up. When Magdalena got to her feet, her muddy petticoat fell from her waist, where her attackers had pushed up to reveal her curly black nest.

Magdalena picked up her torn, muddy camisole and put it back on. Unable to button it because the men had popped all of them off to get to her bosoms, she just tied it at the top and held it together with her muddy, shaking hands. Her fingers were bloody where the nails had broken off to the quick in the struggle with her attackers. Olivia picked up the remnants of the brown suit and handed them to her sister, who had climbed awkwardly back into the cramped rear of the buggy.

"I see you done got *your* cocksucker," she snorted a laugh, referring to Montrose slumped and bloody but still mounted in his saddle.

When she walked back to get in the buggy again, Olivia slapped the white horse, now streaked red and brown with dribbling blood and gore down its sides. She smacked it hard on its rump, and it headed back toward his stable at Montrose House at full gallop.

Olivia watched Simon Montrose's body shift and bounce in the saddle with trailing entrails, flinging blood and filth about the frightened steed as it ran. Somehow, the body managed to stay on the horse as it rounded the turn to the plantation.

Run on home to daddy, Simon. I don't think he'll be able to fix this one for you.

Olivia took her seat and set Blue to a trot once more. With still an hour until dusk, the buggy stopped in front of Sweet Rewards, and Jimbo, their groom, came running at the sight of Blue in a lather. He began yelling, and soon it seemed like the whole plantation milled around their buggy.

Jimbo rushed to help Magdalena down from the buggy's back with great care and carried her into the house and up the stairs. Some of the hands unharnessed Blue and walked him back to the stables, where Olivia knew he would be rubbed down until he was dry and then be rubbed with liniment to ease his sore muscles.

Devaroe was helped out of the buggy and taken into the house, where Olivia knew he too would be well attended. Her bleary-eyed father and anxious mother met her on the porch.

"What is this all about, Olivia? I thought you were going to Shreveport. How did your sister end up in such a state?" her father asked, surprising Olivia with the concern in his voice for his other daughter. "And what are you doing with James?"

"I *was* going to Shreveport," Olivia said with dry sarcasm, "but Mother said you were ever so distraught over losing yet another prospective husband for me. I went out and found the son-of-a-bitch and dragged him back here. As you can see, he put up a bit of a fuss, and I had to get a little rough with him." She winked at her mother, who stood behind Armand Thibodeaux, doing her best to hold in a giggle.

"I had to be a little forceful with him when he put up a fight about coming back," Olivia continued as she walked up beneath the columned balcony of the shady porch. "It may be all for naught, though," she said as she pulled open the heavy oak front door. "I killed Simon Montrose." Olivia handed her mother the little Derringer while her father stood looking on in shocked amazement with his eyes wide and his mouth opening and closing like a catfish lying on a dry bank.

❧ 10 ❧

The next two weeks blurred in Olivia's mind. Magdalena recovered in Olivia's room. She woke many nights listening to her sister sobbing into her pillows. After her first attempt to console her and Magda slapping away, Olivia just let Magdalena cry it out. Rage and a sense of helplessness possessed her poor sister that Olivia could do nothing to assuage. Olivia hoped none of those men ever got near Magdalena, who now carried a large knife strapped to her waist.

James Devaroe recovered slowly in the guest suite down the hall. The doctor brought out from St. Johns had diagnosed him with severely bruised and several cracked ribs. He'd lost a couple of teeth, and his attackers had cracked his jawbone on the right side of his head. The old doctor told them the men had severely bruised one of Devaroe's kidneys with their many vicious kicks as well. The white-haired doctor wrapped Devaroe's torso tightly and recommended a soft diet and lots of water. Devaroe did not like his restriction of alcohol for two weeks, but Olivia brought a flask to him anyhow to help ease his pain.

She slipped into his room on the fifth night after their return and sat down in the chair next to his bed.

"I told you before that you'd never make it as a scout," he whispered with a hoarse laugh.

"I didn't mean to wake you, but I brought you a gift," she said as she handed him the flask she'd bought in St. Johns the day before to replace the one he'd lost.

"You are truly an angel sent to me from Heaven, Mrs. Montgomery," he said and clumsily uncorked the flask he put immediately to his very swollen pink lips. Much of the bourbon never made it into his mouth, but Devaroe seemed to enjoy what did.

"Is your sister alright?" he asked her between painful sips.

"I don't know," Olivia sighed. "She cries at night and won't talk to me about it." Olivia sat quietly for a moment, thinking. "I think she is angry with me because I got to kill Montrose, and she didn't get a chance to kill any of the men who hurt her."

"She will work it out in time," Devaroe said confidently. "She's a strong woman and doesn't strike me as the type that chews on something for any length of time."

"She's carrying a really big knife now," Olivia told him as she took the empty flask from his hands.

He grabbed her hand, brought her wrist to his nose, and inhaled deeply. "Orange Blossom. Thank you for wearing it, Olivia." He kissed the wrist gently before dropping it. "And I hope none of those sons-of-bitches ever find themselves in a dark alley with your sweet sister."

"Hell," Olivia scoffed, "I hope she ends up in a dark alley with all of them, one at a time. I might even see if I can arrange it somehow."

"You're a hard woman, Mrs. Montgomery," Devaroe said with a painful chuckle.

The following night, Olivia returned to his side with another flask. "I probably shouldn't be doing this," she whispered as she handed it to him. "The doctor said you should have no liquor, but you are in so much pain. I don't think this little bit to help you sleep will hurt you overmuch."

"Neither do I," he said as he tipped up the flask and drank deeply. Olivia watched him and was relieved that she could ease his pain just a little.

Should I even give a good God damn after he hurt me the way he did? He is still a human being in pain. After spending all that time in the Army hospital, watching those boys suffer, I can't bear to see it.

Olivia walked to the bed and straightened the blankets around him. The heat in the room was stifling, so she did not cover him with them. The window stood open with cheesecloth tacked over it to keep out the mosquitos, but no breeze refreshed the hot room.

Devaroe took her hand, inhaled the fragrance at her wrist again, and gently kissed it with his bruised and swollen lips.

"Have they come for you over Montrose's death?" he asked with her wrist at his nose.

"Yes," Olivia whispered, "they came for me the next day, and we had to go into St. John's to see the magistrate. Father made them come up here and look at you and," Olivia continued sadly, "Magdalena had to go in and give her testimony as well, though I don't think they cared overmuch for the suffering of a lowly house nigger.

"After hearing our stories and the doctor's testimony about the boot print on my chest from Montrose's kick, they called it self-defense and let me come back home," she said with a soft smile on her lips.

"Simon's father is still threatening to take it to higher authorities, but with Simon's long list of past offenses against women of gentle birth, father doesn't think it will go very far up the ladder." She brushed a strand of hair from Devaroe's brow.

"No matter how much money the Montrose family has put into the Democrats' political coffers, none of them will stand up for a known abuser of women whose father has always bought him out of trouble."

"I will testify in your defense," Devaroe said as he squeezed her hand. "I was awake for most of it. He assaulted you, then you allowed him to call off his pack of hounds, and he refused," Devaroe sighed. "No jury in the country would convict a woman in that situation when she has two witnesses, even if one of them is just a Negress."

His comment, referring to her sister, irritated Olivia, and she pulled her hand from his grasp, took the flask, and left the room. "Goodnight, Mr. Devaroe," she said before shutting the door.

This man is driving me insane. One minute he is the sweetest, most charming man in Louisiana, then he opens his mouth, and I simply want to thrash him.

Olivia went to her room, undressed, and crawled into her bed. Magdalena slept soundly, and that made Olivia happy. The past two nights had been filled with fits of weeping, thrashing in the sheets, and cursing.

Olivia closed her eyes, and in what seemed like only a few minutes, strong hands on her shoulders woke her. She gasped in frightened surprise, but Devaroe whispered a hush in her ear.

"Quiet," he breathed. "I can stay away from your bed no longer, wife." He nudged Olivia over and scooted in beside her, kissing her neck all the time. He ran his hand up and down her naked body and gasped in pain a few times when he moved closer to her.

A hand came over to caress her breast, pinching the

nipple into a hard, throbbing button of flesh. His hand went down and kneaded her backside before finding its way between her thighs and exploring her wet, throbbing center.

Why can I deny this man nothing?

"Get back to *your* bed," Olivia scolded in a whisper but shivered under his hot, strong touch and ached for more. "You're in no condition to be taxing yourself in my bed." She reached a hand behind her and touched the hot skin of his hard-muscled thigh, raising goose flesh on his skin too.

"I'll never be in too bad a condition to ignore this," Devaroe breathed into her ear from behind her. "You are irresistible, my beautiful Olivia."

He pulled Olivia's body closer into him, and his hard cock rubbed against her behind. It found its way into the crack and slowly pushed into her.

I will never understand this fascination he has with my behind. It's unnatural.

Devaroe sighed heavily when the meaty head pushed inside her. Olivia did her best not to flinch or squeal, though she wanted to.

First, she did not want to excite him into something more, and she especially didn't want to wake Magdalena and make her think she was being attacked again. Devaroe might find himself missing some very vital parts of his anatomy should that happen.

Soon he pulled out of her ass and found her moist cunny. "I just wanted to get a little taste of that," he whispered to her softly as he entered her hot, waiting cunny. He pushed it in slowly so she could feel every inch of his girth, stretching her open and brushing her throbbing pleasure knot.

"If you insist on continually seeking your pleasure

there," she whispered with a quiet giggle, "you will never get me with child."

"Quiet, woman," he chided as he thrust in and out of her with a slow, steady rhythm, bringing on shivers of pleasure Olivia could not deny. He excited her wet cunny until she could stand it no longer and began meeting his slow thrusts with those of her own.

This pirate excites something in me William never did.

Olivia clenched the muscles of her womanhood around his thick, throbbing cock, and he groaned with pleasure. His thrusts quickened, and he panted heavily into her ear. Olivia's explosion of pleasure came with his, and they both tried to stifle their groans without much luck. They craned their necks around to see Magdalena sitting up in her bed with her lips pursed and an eyebrow cocked.

"Miss Livvy, your Mammy, put me in here to protect your virtue against this riverboat man, and here you are ruttin' with him like a damned bitch in heat." She plopped back down on her pillows and pulled the sheet up over her head with a loud sigh of exasperation.

"Does this mean the wedding is back on, Mr. Devaroe?" Olivia whispered as she rolled flat on her back to look up into his ruggedly handsome face.

"Keep wearing that orange blossom perfume and plying me with bourbon, Mrs. Montgomery, and I will take you to Paris and marry you in *Le Notre Dame.*"

"Oh, good Lord," they heard Magdalena mutter from beneath her sheet.

"Very well, ladies," Devaroe said as he slipped out of Olivia's bed. "I will bid you both a very good night," he said and let himself out the door and into the dark hall, buck naked and tightly clutching at his bruised ribs.

"It sounds like he fucks nice," Magdalena quipped as she pulled the sheet back down off her head.

"Yes, that he does," Olivia sighed and rolled to face her sister, who was now sitting up and staring at Olivia. "When he takes his time and gives me a chance to get my pleasure as well, it is *very* nice."

"Yeah, it's nice when they take it slow and easy. When I was fuckin' Jimbo," Magdalena said casually, "he took it slow like that and made me shiver like I was naked in the winter cold."

She was quiet for a minute, and Olivia saw her smile fade again. "Not like those bastards on the road…" She did not finish but rolled over and began to sob into her pillows. Olivia got out of her bed and crawled in next to Magdalena. She wrapped an arm over her sister's quaking body and rested her cheek on Magdalena's shoulder.

"I'm so sorry, Magda," Olivia wept. "We shouldn't have done that here with you in the room. I just can't resist that man's touch."

"It's alright, Livvy." Magdalena rolled onto her back to look up at her sister. "I love you, sister, and I think this riverboat man makes you happy."

Magdalena reached out to take her sister's hand. "It's time for you to be happy again, Livvy. Mr. William's been gone a long time now." She raised her arm and touched Olivia's porcelain cheek with her latte-colored hand. "You should marry that riverboat man and be happy again." Tears trickled down Magdalena's cheeks, and Olivia brushed them away.

"You should be happy too, Magda. We will take you away from here with us and live in New Orleans. You can find a good man there." They fell asleep together, embracing one another the way they had as children, and woke the next morning tangled in the sheets and laughing.

The wedding of Olivia Thibodeaux to James Eduard
Devaroe promised to be the social event of the year
in the Parish with everybody who was anybody invited to
attend, except the Montrose family, of course.

On the day of her wedding, Olivia sat in her room
being attended to by Magdalena, who fussed with her hair,
continually readjusting the tiara affixed to a white lace veil
for the occasion. Olivia stood staring at herself in the tall
oval mirror in the door of her wardrobe.

"This dress is almost the color of my eyes, isn't it," she
said as she held up a bit of fabric from the Josephine dress
and ran her hand over the skirt delicately.

"I told you it was the first time I saw it," Magdalena
said and stepped back, admiring her work in the mirror
from behind her sister. "That riverboat man is gettin' the
most beautiful woman in the entire Bayou." They heard
the orchestra begin to play, and Olivia rose on wobbling
legs.

"Girl," Magdalena chided, "just take a deep breath

and calm yourself down. Why you so nervous? You've done this gettin' married thing before with Mr. William."

"Oh, I know," Olivia said and slapped Magdalena's hand away. "But not to him." She gathered up the swishing chiffon skirt and felt the long lace veil trailing behind her. She could feel the weight of the fabric pulling the tiara tight against her hair, wrapped in a tight bun on the top of her head. The lace draped over her shoulders, and Olivia felt like a princess in one of the storybooks from her childhood.

Stepping with grace and care, Olivia walked out of her room and down the flower-festooned staircase. In a formal black waistcoat and top hat, her father stood at the bottom, waiting for her. Olivia thought she saw a hint of pride in the eyes above his scarred cheek as he smiled up at her.

Olivia took his arm, and they walked together through the parlor and out across the patio to a large white canvas canopy erected for the occasion. All the backwater gentry sat in wooden folding chairs on either side of an aisle scattered with rose petals cut from the same flower garden as those in her bouquet. Olivia wondered if her mother had cried at sacrificing so many of her precious blooms for this occasion. When Olivia saw the glow on Marie Thibodeaux's cheeks as she walked down the aisle, Olivia knew her mother had not.

Armand Thibodeaux left her at the side of James Devaroe with a quick kiss on her cheek and took a seat next to his smiling wife, who sat awash in pink silk. *Pere* Dominic from the church in St. Johns stood before them in his priestly robes, sweating, no doubt, in the July heat. The day before had been cloudy, and everyone had feared rain, but the morning had dawned clear and bright. He performed the shortest version of the marriage mass as he could and proudly introduced the new Mr. and Mrs. James

Eduard Devaroe to the cheering onlookers beneath the canvass canopy.

Olivia suspected they cheered more for the ending of the long service than the beginning of the lives of the newlywed couple. During the ceremony, servants had set up tables on the patio with bowls of punch and silver trays of finger foods. Inside the house, more tables held trays of delicacies, both sweet and savory.

James, still sore from his pummeling, wore a black silk waistcoat, trousers, and top hat. He kissed his bride at the altar and walked with her hand in hand down the aisle and out onto the green lawn. Magdalena and her mother, Georgia, and the other Negro staff stood outside the canopy's shade to listen to the ceremony and cheered them as they came out onto the lawn.

Olivia, going against all the conventions of the day, broke free of her new husband and went to the crowd of servants and hugged Magdalena, Georgia, and even Jimbo. She considered most of those people who worked on Sweet Rewards her family as much as her mother and father.

Georgia had mothered her more physically than Marie ever had, and Jimbo, who'd taught her how to ride and forage for wild berries in the swamp, was like an older brother to her more than Armand Thibodeaux had ever been fatherly.

Olivia did not care what any of the backwater gentry trash thought about her kissing a Negro in their presence. She ignored the astonished gasps from some in the crowd and continued to hug and kiss others of the household staff, just to amuse herself and Magdalena, who stood with a huge smile as she shook her head when she too heard the gasps.

When she returned to her husband's side, one of the

stewards rushed forward with a bowl of water and a rag, expecting her to clean the Negro off her face and hands before joining the clean, white guests at the party.

"Thank you, but I am perfectly clean, Jacob. You can take that away." She held out her hand to her husband, and he took it without reservation.

"That little stunt may cost you," he whispered to her with a laugh.

"Do you think I give a good God damn what this bunch of backwater cane kings think about me?" She laughed and leaned her head on his broad shoulder as they walked into the cooler shade of the big brick plantation house.

Her mother came up and unpinned the tiara and veil so that Olivia could move around the room with ease. "I am so very proud of you, *ma Cherie.*" She kissed her daughter on the cheeks and hands.

Many in the receiving line refused to shake Olivia's hand or accept a kiss. Olivia just smiled as they passed with their noses in the air and made a note in her mind of each one who snubbed her. None of them mattered to her in the least, but someday *she* would be running Sweet Rewards, and when that time came, Olivia Thibodeaux Montgomery Devaroe would remember those snubs.

As the afternoon passed, Olivia, tipsy from champagne and full of shrimp, thought about retiring to her room for a short rest but knew that would not be proper. She did not want to embarrass her parents, so she continued to mingle and chat about meaningless courtships and the problems of grubs or snails in the flowerbeds.

Just after the clock in the hall chimed four, there was a loud pounding at the door, and one of the stewards answered it and admitted Sterling Montrose into the gathering. Olivia heard shocked gasps as the tall white-haired man in his mid-sixties entered the parlor carrying a small, wrapped package.

"Hello, Sterling," Armand Thibodeaux greeted the unexpected guest.

"Hello, Armand," the man said, slurring his words from too much drink. "I have a wedding gift for your murdering, nigger-loving bitch of a daughter." He threw the package at Olivia, who stood nearby. She looked on in astonishment at the white-headed man dressed in a white linen suit fit for the celebration. "Go on, open it up," he demanded without moving from where he stood at the entry to the festively decorated parlor.

Olivia bent and picked up the package carefully wrapped in silver and gold foil paper. She pulled the ribbon on the bow holding the wrapping on, and found a small wooden box. Olivia opened the hinged lid with trembling hands to see two bits of contorted metal lying on a bed of cotton. She peered up at Sterling Montrose in confusion.

"Those are the two slugs they dug out of my Simon's gut," he said angrily, clenching his fists. "I thought you might like them as a reminder of his murder. I don't know what my boy ever saw in you, bitch, but you bewitched him and then refused his hand repeatedly before you killed him."

He took several steps toward Olivia, and both Armand and James moved to block his path. "You can't protect the witch forever, Armand. I have influential friends in New Orleans. I even have more influential friends in Washington. If it's the last thing I do in this life, I'll see the little nigger-loving whore hanged for murdering my sweet boy."

Sterling Montrose, red-faced and ranting, took two more steps toward Olivia. He abruptly stopped, however, and grabbed at his chest. Montrose took a strangled breath, clawed at his pale face, and then fell to the floor. He reached out a clawed hand toward Olivia before he took his final gasping breath with an accusing finger pointing at Olivia.

The silent room broke into an immediate buzz, and those who heard the commotion from outside came crowding into the parlor as the doctor bent over Sterling Montrose and pressed fingers on his neck. He stood and shook his head, indicating the man on the floor had passed from this life.

Olivia, still clutching the little box, buried her face into James Devaroe's chest before swooning into his arms.

Olivia woke in her bed with her mother bathing her forehead with cool water. She felt sick to her stomach and thought for a brief moment that she might vomit. She tried to sit up, but her mother held her shoulder down.

"Stay put, *Cherie.* You have been through a terrible ordeal." Marie wrung the rag in the washbasin and returned to sit on the edge of Olivia's bed.

"I cannot believe the nerve of that foul man to come here like that on your wedding day with such an awful thing and call it a wedding gift. Then he up and dies in the middle of the festivities. We didn't even get to cut your beautiful cake."

Her mother continued dabbing Olivia's forehead, but with every sentence, the dabbing became more like pounding until Olivia finally reached up and took her mother's hand to still it.

"Mother, I am fine." She sat up and realized she no longer wore the Josephine dress, and that darkness had fallen outside her window. "What time is it? Has everybody gone?"

"Yes, *ma Cherie,* your wedding day has been ruined by that horrid Sterling Montrose and his monstrous gift.

Everyone fled in terror after you fainted, fearing Sterling had cursed the entire gathering."

Tears slid down Marie's face at the destruction of the beautiful wedding she and Georgia had worked so hard to put together. "Even *Pere* Dominic fled, crossing himself and muttering prayers against demons. I have never felt so insulted in my life. None of them even cared enough to ask about your condition. Your husband carried you up here and helped Magdalena undress you. By the time he came back downstairs, they all had fled, even the damned doctor," Marie said, shaking her beautifully coifed head. "*Mon Deux,* such a bunch of superstitious fools out here."

"Mother, they are just a lot of backwater swamp rats who've been hearing Voodoo stories since they were children. It makes no difference to me. I am still married. The ceremony was over, and the fools all ate and drank themselves full before Montrose showed up." Olivia wrapped her arms around her mother and kissed her cheek. "It was a beautiful wedding, *ma mere.* I could have wished for nothing better."

Olivia swung her feet out of bed, stood, and wrapped herself in her dressing gown. "Let's go downstairs and cut that cake. I am hungry." Olivia gazed around the darkened room. "Where is James?"

Marie broke into wracking sobs once more. "He is gone, Olivia."

"What?" Olivia gasped, stunned by her mother's announcement. "What do you mean he's gone?"

"I suppose he too was frightened by what happened. He just came back down the stairs, spoke with Armand for a moment, handed him his wedding ring, and left the house. I heard him riding away sometime later." Tears slid down her mother's pale cheeks, and her thin hands shook in her lap, still holding the wet cloth.

Olivia then saw the gold band resting on her bedside table. Shocked and confused, Olivia put an arm around her mother's trembling shoulders and lifted her to her feet. "I'm still hungry," she whispered to her sobbing mother. "Let's go have some damned cake."

12

Marie took to her bed for three days after the wedding fiasco. That gave Olivia time to get all the reminders of it cleared from the house and grounds. The men took down the canopy, folded the chairs, and returned them to the place from which Marie had rented them.

All the food leftover was sent home with the staff or sent out to the tenant farmers' homes on Sweet Rewards. None of it would go to waste. Olivia took the floral garlands and bouquets down to the cemetery to decorate the graves of soldiers who'd been killed and didn't have family nearby. Her wedding bouquet, she took to William's grave on the property, where she cried and begged him for his forgiveness.

"I promise you, my love, I will never think to love another man. Perhaps this was God's way of telling me that you are my one and only husband."

Tears streamed down her face as Olivia walked from the family plot at the rear of the lawn behind Sweet Rewards. A priest had blessed the tiny fenced area decades ago to make it consecrated ground where the family could be buried.

A large mausoleum stood out there, built by some long-dead grandparent, but they had put William in the ground. In a letter to her after he went off to fight, William asked to be buried in the earth like his many comrades. He did not want it said that he thought he was better than the soldiers serving under him by being laid to rest in a clean, dry building while they moldered away in the cold, damp ground.

William's family wanted his body sent back to Virginia to rest in their family crypt. Still, the Army had sent it back to Sweet Rewards, as William had directed in his military paperwork. Olivia received several angry letters from his parents and even one from a lawyer who said the family had filed suit to have his body dug up and sent back to Virginia. Nothing ever came of it, and William rested here on Sweet Rewards, where she planned to rest next to him someday.

When all the telltale signs of a wedding ever having taken place at Sweet Rewards were removed, Olivia went into her mother's room to try and lure her out of her bed.

"Good morning, *ma mere*, it is a beautiful cool morning. You should come breakfast with me on the patio while it is still nice."

"I am not well, daughter, just leave me be," Marie said, propped up on pillows in her thin, sweat-soaked cotton dressing gown.

"Mother, you need to come out of this stifling room and get some fresh air. Georgia says, you have not eaten. Join me for breakfast, even if it is nothing more than tea and a roll. Georgia has made some of those lovely cinnamon rolls you adore."

"Olivia," her mother sighed and held out a pale, frail

hand. "I have not been well for some time now. I saw the doctor, and he tells me I have a cancer in my womb." Olivia's knees went weak, and she collapsed on the bed, gripping her mother's pale, trembling hand.

"Why didn't you tell me?"

"*Ma Cherie,* there is nothing to be done for this ailment. The good doctor has given me laudanum for the pain, but I have taken it infrequently. In these past weeks, however, I find myself turning to it much more often." She gripped Olivia's hand. "It is why I gave you the bankbook and the key to the townhouse. I do not want you to see me in my decline. I would like you to go to New Orleans. Forget about making an heir to this God-forsaken place and make a happy life for yourself. You are the heir to Sweet Rewards, and if your father cannot deal with that fact, then he can sell the place or burn it to the ground for all I care." Marie fell back on her pillows again. "Your things are still packed, are they not?"

They were. When Devaroe agreed to go ahead with the wedding, Olivia assumed she and Magdalena would be going off with him afterward and left their bags packed except for a few essential things. "Yes, but I don't want to leave you, Mother." Tears began sliding down her cheeks, though she tried her best to stop them. She buried her face in her mother's chest. "What kind of daughter leaves her mother in her time of need?"

Marie put her hands on either side of her daughter's head and lifted it off her chest. "A daughter who obeys her mother's wish that she not watch her suffer and waste away. Go to New Orleans now. You have a place to stay and the means with which to live comfortably.

"I will speak to *Pere* Dominic about having this ridiculous marriage annulled, my sweet girl. Everyone knows the man ran off after the ceremony without consummating it. There will not be any difficulty, I'm certain."

Marie reached for a glass of water on her bedside, and Olivia handed it to her. She took a few halting sips and handed it back. "Go to New Orleans and find a good man who will stand by you, *ma Cherie*. I know I will never see a grandchild," she choked on a sob, "but I will know you are living a life free of this horrible place, a life of parties, cafes, and the opera—a life that I could never live because of your father—and I'll not see you tied to this place because of his desire for a male heir."

Marie fell back on her pillows again and closed her eyes. "I think I will sleep for a while now. You needn't wake me when you go," she whispered before falling asleep.

Olivia picked up the glass of water and sniffed. She recognized the sickly-sweet aroma of laudanum. Marie would sleep for a while without pain.

Olivia sat there for a long while, holding her mother's hands and watching her breathe steadily in deep, restful sleep. When she began to snore softly, Olivia smiled. Her father always laughed while accusing her of snoring, but Marie would vehemently deny it. Olivia smiled down at her sleeping mother, aware they all knew she snored regularly and loudly sometimes. She let go of her mother's hand and left the room, closing the door behind her. In the hallway, she met Georgia, who brought her mother a tea tray and a bowl of hot grits.

"She has told you?" Georgia asked, knowing her mother had. She set the tray on a hall table and wrapped her arms around Olivia. "You and my girl need to go now before your Daddy gets back from the fields."

"How long have you known?" Olivia asked the woman who'd changed her dirty diapers and helped her take her first steps. Georgia was as much a mother to her as the woman she'd just left.

"From the first, when she started having pains and her belly bloated up. I figured what it was and told her to go see that white doctor in St. Johns, but I knowed."

Georgia put a hand on each of Olivia's shoulders. "I been with Miss Marie since we was girls on her daddy's plantation. Like my girl, her daddy was my daddy, too. I will stay with her and see her out of this world, Livvy. I love her just like you love my Magda, and I won't never leave her."

Olivia looked at the woman she now knew was her aunt, as well as the mother of her sister, with wide eyes. "Does Magdalena know that? Does she know she's my cousin as well as my sister?"

"She know. That why you two be so close. She almost close enough to be a true sister." She squeezed Olivia's arms and pulled her close. "Now you and my girl get goin' before your daddy gets back. Jimbo done got Blue all hitched up, and your things is gettin' loaded in the buggy."

She waved a hand when Olivia gave her a questioning look. "I thought it might be today. Magda's got your things packed, and Jimbo is loadin' them in the buggy now." She turned to pick up the tray but gave Olivia a swat on the backside first. "Get yourself goin' now. Your tavelin' clothes be laid out on your bed." Georgia picked up the tray of grits and tea, opened her mother's door, and left Olivia open-mouthed in the hall.

The next thing she knew, Magdalena tugged at her sleeve, pulling her toward the stairs. "Come on, Livvy, we got to hurry. Mammy and Miss Marie want us a good ways down the road before Daddy gets home."

She led a silent Olivia up the stairs into her room and helped her change into her red traveling suit. Magdalena wore a long-sleeved day dress and her straw bonnet on her kerchiefed head. She handed Olivia her case that still contained the cash, bank book, and keys. Since their return, it had sat untouched in her wardrobe. She put Olivia's straw bonnet on her head, and Olivia pushed her aside and tied the bow.

"I'm not a child, Magdalena," Olivia fumed. "I can dress myself."

"Well, you are as slow as a pregnant sow," Magdalena said as she led Olivia out of the room and down the wide, marble stairs. They halted in the foyer, and Olivia looked back toward her mother's silent room. "She done said her goodbyes, Livvy. Don't cause her to suffer through it again." Magdalena pulled her through the door and out to the loaded and waiting buggy.

13

Olivia climbed up and took the reins. When Magdalena had seated herself, she urged Blue with a flip of the leather straps, and he took off toward the road at an easy trot. The breeze caused by the moving buggy felt good on the warm morning, but Olivia saw dark clouds to the south and hoped they didn't get caught in a storm before they could get to an inn for the night.

"How long have you known that we have the same grandfather as well as the same father?" Olivia finally asked after sitting quietly for an hour.

"I've knowed for a long time, but Mammy didn't want me to tell it. She said it was for Miss Marie to tell and not me."

"And did you know about my mother being sick too?"

"Mammy said Miss Marie or Daddy would tell you when the time come. It wasn't my place to tell you." Magdalena reached a hand over and put it on Olivia's shoulder.

Olivia wanted to shake it free, but the comfort she felt from her sister's touch made her leave it. "This has been a

Hell of a week. I get married, my husband leaves me, I learn my mother is dying, my nurse is my aunt, and my sister is also my cousin. If it weren't so pathetic," Olivia coughed out a laugh, "it would be funny."

"I s'pose when you spell it all out that way, it is kindly awful." Magdalena squeezed her sister's shoulder a little harder. "You can add to it that you're takin' me away from Sweet Rewards just when I an' Jimbo start talkin' about jumpin' the broom."

"I thought you didn't want to marry a cane-field nigger," Olivia said, surprised by her sister's announcement.

"I don't. But to be in the rights about it, Jimbo ain't no cane-field nigger. He's a groom."

"And a damned fine one too," Olivia agreed as she rolled her eyes and smiled. "He could come to the city and get a job in any livery. I'd be more than happy to write him a reference or go in person and vouch for him."

"Jimbo don't want to leave Sweet Rewards. It's his home. His mammy and pappy were both born and buried there. He doesn't know any different and doesn't want to change."

"He's twelve years older than you, anyway, Magda."

"I don't care none about that. Jimbo's sweet and gentle," Magdalena took a long breath and smiled, "and he fuck nice."

"I suppose that *is* important." Olivia laughed, glad the mood had lightened again between them.

"Damned right it is. Jimbo said that if I found myself with a child from that bunch of bastards of Montrose's, he'd be proud to marry up with me and raise my child as his own."

Olivia had not even given thought to the possibility that Magda could be pregnant from their encounter with

Montrose's field gang. Then it struck her that she could very well be pregnant with Devaroe's child. At least she had a ring on her finger, for all that was worth.

"If you *are* pregnant, we'll just say your husband got killed in the same accident as mine." The two women looked at one another and broke out laughing.

"Or mine went off with yours on his riverboat and got himself drowned."

That was something Olivia had not considered. Should she change her name to Devaroe or keep Montgomery? The people in the neighboring townhouses knew her as William's wife, but they also knew he'd died in the war. If she started growing a big belly, how would she explain that?

Olivia took a deep breath and let it out. She would cross that bridge when she came to it. Until then, she was Mrs. William Montgomery and would stay that way until matters forced a change.

As they neared the spot in the road where Montrose had stopped them, Magdalena started fidgeting in her seat and brought her knife out onto her lap. Olivia glanced away from the road to see her sister looking around and peering intently into the brush at the sides of the narrow track. She also sat clutching the big knife to her breast with both hands so tightly her knuckles were white.

"I don't think anyone is going to bother us, Magda," Olivia said, lifting the little pistol she had retrieved from her thigh holster as they had neared the Montrose property.

"I sure hope you remembered to reload that damned thing after you unloaded it into Simon Montrose's fat, white belly."

"Mother did as soon as I tried to give it back to her,"

Olivia said with a sad smile. "She reloaded it and told me to keep it as a wedding present."

"I bet she never thought your husband would leave you before you ever got a chance to use it on *him*."

"I'm certain she didn't." Olivia snorted a laugh and urged Blue to pick up his pace until they were completely clear of the Montrose holdings. She didn't like the way Magdalena fingered that knife. "Jimbo give you that pig sticker?"

"Yeah, he did," she said with a broad smile and stared off into nowhere, sliding her fingers over the shiny, wide blade. "He told me he'd show me how to use it so long as I promised not to cut his ballocks off with it. He got nice ballocks."

"Really? I heard that the wild Indians in the west cut white men's ballocks off and tan the leather to make gri-gri bags from."

"I bet that'd shrink 'em up some," she said with a mischievous grin, "but Jimbo's would still hold a powerful lot of charm powders."

"How long have you and Jimbo been—" Olivia didn't know quite how to phrase the question. She saw the granite stone denoting the Montrose property's edge and pulled back on the leather reins to slow Blue once more. In the distance, she heard the rumbling of thunder and groaned inwardly.

"How long we been fuckin'? Since the Christmas Party last winter. I drank too much of that Muscatine wine they make out there in the barn, and one thing led to another, and I woke up naked in his bed. I think he was as surprised to wake up with me as I was." She giggled and settled into a more relaxed posture. "We nuzzled a little and decided we liked it and been beddin' together out there now and then. At least when I'm not holed up in your room

guarding your precious virtue. For all the good that done."
They both laughed until the first light spattering of rain
forced them to pull over and put up the top to the buggy.
They both lifted the folded leather cover and hooked it in
place to keep the worst of the rain off them.

"Jimbo covered our bags with an oilcloth," Magdalena
said as she took off her straw bonnet and ran fingers
through her black ringlets. "I am sure glad to get that hot
bonnet off my head. I'm sweatin' like a whore in Church."

"Me too." Olivia untied the ribbon holding her bonnet,
put it on the seat with her sister's, and shook out her long
black tresses, letting them fall over her shoulders. The
cooler air brought up with the rain felt good on her bare
head, and she reveled in it, shaking her hair back as far as
she could to allow the breeze to get to her sweaty neck.

The already damp track became a muddy mess, and
Olivia had a hard time keeping them in an upright position. The buggy slid and tipped this way and that with
Blue doing his best to keep them on solid ground. The rain
began falling in heavy sheets, and Olivia could hardly
make out the road. Thankful that Blue could see, she gave
him the reins and allowed him to plod along at his speed.
The wind blew rain into their faces at times, and before
long, both of them looked like drenched kittens.

By eleven, they reached the spot where they had found
Devaroe the last time they were on this journey. The rain
had eased some, but they still slid about on the soupy track.
Finally, they turned onto the north and south road to the
King's Highway. The wider road made of harder packed
earth and red gravel meant the ruts were fewer, and engi-
neers built the road, so it rose in the center, so the water
ran off into ditches on the roadside, allowing less standing
water. Blue could safely pick up speed, and within an hour,
they reached an inn near the King's Highway.

"I think we'll stop here for the night even though it's still early," Olivia told a wet and bedraggled Magdalena.

"Sounds good to me. I think we've stayed here before with Miss Marie on the way to the city. Their cook makes good grits an' greens if I remember rightly."

They turned into the cobbled way to the inn's front, and a groom immediately came for their horse. A boy in a slicker coat came out to ask about their bags, and they told him they would just take in their private cases if he thought their other luggage would be safe and dry in the livery.

"Oh, yes, ma'am, it will be plenty safe. The King's Inn has a good reputation. Ain't no thievin' goes on here." He assisted Olivia out of the buggy while the groom helped Magdalena. They grabbed their bonnets, wrung out their dripping hair, and stowed it up under the concealing straw, ribbons, and frills. Magdalena reknotted her hair and covered it with her white kerchief. Olivia shook out her skirt and straightened her jacket before following the young man to the door and entering the smoky common room of the King's Inn.

Olivia remembered the place as soon as she walked in and smelled the combination of tobacco smoke, stale liquor, and mildew. White-trash share-croppers, fishermen, and crabbers filled the room. They whiled away a rainy day on cheap alcohol and paid women, a few giving her and Magdalena leering stares and a few crude whistles. Olivia saw Magdalena fingering her knife and gave her a little shake of her head. The one thing they did not need was trouble with the locals.

As they walked up to the fat proprietor's counter, strewn with torn and crumpled pieces of paper, empty plates, and half-full mugs of beer, more people came jumbling through the door. Olivia thought she recognized the woman but could not be certain. When her brood of caterwauling children came bursting through the door behind her, she recognized them as the Pulliers, a shrimping family from the north end of Bayou Tesche. The woman tried to put on airs, bragging about her trips to the opera in St. Martinsville and her grand house. There were some very elegant houses around St. Martinsville, but Emily Pullier's would never come close to any of those.

"We need a room for the night, please," Olivia told the proprietor, raising her voice to be heard over the four boisterous children.

"Yes, ma'am, but your nigger girl there will have to sleep on one of the benches in the common room."

"Excuse me?" Olivia asked, exasperated, tired, and on edge because of the raucous children. "The Thibodeaux's and their retainers have been frequenting this inn for years. My maid will share a room with me."

"I suppose that will be alright," the fat man behind the counter said, eyeing the woman behind her and Magda nervously, "but she has to sleep on the floor using her own bedding."

"Do we look like we have bedding? If you do not have a cot available for her, Magdalena will share my bed," Olivia told him hotly.

From behind them, Olivia heard a surprised gasp and then felt someone push past her to the counter. Emily Pullier slapped a hand on the wooden counter and cleared her throat loudly. "I hope you are not going to allow this nigger to sleep in a bed and use a chamber pot that decent white women and children will have to use after her." She looked back at Olivia and smirked.

"Well, if they allow filthy shrimper trash to stay here, why would the retainer of a genteel family like the

Thibodeauxes be a problem," Olivia returned. "The rotten shrimp stink on this lot is turning my stomach already."

"If you are gonna allow this nigger to sleep in a bed in this establishment, I will be taking my business elsewhere, and everyone is gonna know from me that the King's Inn is nothin' but a filthy nigger-lovin' establishment."

The proprietor looked from the bedraggled woman in an ill-fitting, home-spun dress and her ragged, muddy, snot-nosed children to Olivia and Magda in their wet but well-tailored clothing and said to Olivia, "Your maid is most welcome to share your bed, ma'am. The Thibodeaux family have been good customers of this inn, and *their* patronage is much appreciated."

Olivia edged Emily away from the counter without looking at her. "Thank you, sir. How much will that be, and could we order a meal sent to our room? We need to dry these clothes before coming to eat, and I fear that won't be before morning."

"Yes, ma'am, that will be two dollars for the room and fifty cents each for a tray. The wife has a nice ham, greens, grits, and cornbread if that will be alright."

"That sounds delightful," Olivia told him and opened her case to take out her cash. She unfolded the stack of twenty-five one-dollar notes and handed him three. She returned the bills to her case, clasped it, and waited for the man to get a key from a row of hooks behind him.

When the clerk turned his back, Emily Pullier turned to Olivia with narrowed eyes. "I s'pose you're runnin' off in shame for shootin' poor Simon Montrose, then killin' his daddy at your weddin' to a man who run off from ya as fast as he could."

"I see the swamp-rat gossips have been hard at work," Olivia replied coolly. She took the key and shoved past

Emily. "You really should teach these little brats some civility in public. They're an embarrassment."

"How dare you insult my children," Emily snapped and grabbed Olivia's shoulder with rough, red, clawed fingers. "You and your family look down on mine because you live in a big house on a sugar plantation and can buy off the law even after committin' cold-blooded murder." Olivia heard the room behind her quiet as the onlookers listened to the women's exchange.

"I don't look down on you, Emily *Casper* Pullier. Like my peers, I don't look at you at all." Olivia emphasized Emily's maiden name because everyone in the bayou knew her father and brothers spent more time in jail than out for petty crimes. Two of the brothers had spent time in a military prison for desertion during the war. The Caspers were the lowest of the low in the bayou, and though Emily had tried to claw her way up, she would never fit in with the backwater gentry.

Olivia and Magda climbed the stairs to find their room with Emily Pullier screaming profanities at them. When they found the room, they could still hear the woman screaming.

"You most surely pulled on her tail, Miss Livvy." Magdalena laughed as she shut the door behind them and turned the key to lock it.

"The bitch deserved it." Olivia fell back on the bed and sighed. "It sounds like the story of my beautiful wedding has traveled all around the bayou. Mother was right. It's time for me to go to New Orleans and get the hell out of this swamp."

14

Nothing of merit plagued the rest of their trip into New Orleans, and they arrived at the townhouse on Basin Street well before dark the following afternoon. Olivia parked the buggy in the alley next to the block of four townhouses to unload their bags before taking it to a nearby livery where she could leave it and Blue.

Magdalena undid the oilcloth tarp and pulled it back to reveal their bags open and riffled through.

"Damnit," she exclaimed, and Olivia came hurrying back to see what the problem was. "The thieving sons-of-bitches went through every bag and then just left them open. Weren't nothin' in mine of any account. How 'bout yours, Livvy?"

Olivia looked at the jumbled mess and sighed. "My silver vanity set, but that was all. I had my jewelry in my satchel I took in with me."

"Well, you can sure count on them bein' gone. "I'm going to write Mammy and tell her about this and to spread it that the King's Inn has thieves workin' there. She'll make sure all the families know about it right quick."

Although it had been illegal to educate slaves, both Georgia and Magdalena had been educated by their respective mistresses in their homes on the plantations. Some tutors flatly refused, but most needed the money and overlooked their young pupils' skin color.

"If we hadn't been wet and hungry, I'd have traveled on past that place, but the next good inn would have been hours away." Olivia began stuffing garments back into the cases and buckling the straps to carry them into the house. Some garments they just draped over their arms to carry around the corner of the building to the front door on the cobbled street side of the townhouse.

Walking back into the townhouse brought back so many memories. Olivia's eyes began to tear as soon as she looked across the room to the French doors leading out to the courtyard. She and William had spent so many happy hours out there reading to one another or sharing meals with the neighbors, cooked over a fire pit in the center. She remembered the laughter and the merriment of those times, and the tears slid down her pale cheeks from her violet eyes to drip onto her jacket.

"Oh, Livvy." Magdalena saw the tears and wrapped an arm around her sister's shoulder. "Don't be thinkin' 'bout the old times. Think about all the new times."

Olivia blinked back the tears, wiped her face with the sleeve of her jacket, and took a deep, cleansing breath. "You're right, Magda." She wiped the dust from the round oak table separating the kitchen from the parlor area. "We need to clean this place up. I don't think anyone's been here since we visited before the workmen finished."

"No, me and Mammy came with Miss Marie last fall before Christmas to shop. You were off visitin' that friend of yours in Shreveport."

"She was still well then? My mother?" Olivia asked as she started up the stairs to the bedroom.

"Miss Marie just had found out from the doctor. She wanted Christmas to be extra special that year."

A moment of grief and pain struck Olivia. Christmas had been extra special with a huge loblolly pine, cut from one of the forested areas north of Sweet Rewards. Georgia, Magda, and Marie had festooned the stairway and mantle with garlands and bright red potted poinsettias brought up from the Islands. Georgia had baked her delicious fruit cakes, and she had hung the tree with cookies decorated with colored sugar and frosting. Gifts wrapped in brightly colored foil paper and tied with marvelous bows piled around the tree for everyone, including the stables' household staff and grooms. Marie had included everyone in the festivities. War widows and orphans filled the house for a huge dinner of goose, turkey, and ham with all the fixings.

Olivia could not remember a grander Christmas at Sweet Rewards. It would be one she would remember for the rest of her life. Her mother had certainly thought it would be her last with the family and went all out to make it a festive and memorable occasion.

Olivia remembered her father griping about the cost of it all, but her mother, to Olivia's dismay, had told him to hold his tongue and enjoy the season. In most cases, Armand Thibodeaux would have slapped his sassing wife, but he had not. Olivia smiled, remembering him dressing up as Father Christmas to hand out stockings to the children and baskets of food to the widows before the big dinner. He kept on the costume, complete with the white beard covering his scar so the children would not be frightened.

Glancing back down at the townhouse's parlor, she

remembered Christmases with William there, and tears stung her eyes once more. Here she was back in their home without him, and the thought saddened her so.

She trudged up the stairs to their bedroom, complete with a privy closet. The smaller bedroom, where Magdalena would sleep, only had a chamber pot, but it had a full bed, a nice wardrobe, and a vanity with a mirror. Olivia made certain her sister lacked none of the finer things living in a townhouse had to offer. Most servants found themselves relegated to the attic, but Magdalena was no true servant.

All the neighbors knew of her parentage. Some scoffed at Olivia's treatment of a lowly Negress servant and would not suffer her being included in the joint dinners shared in the courtyard. Magdalena hosted a dinner inside for the maids and house girls of the other townhouses on those occasions.

Olivia would have to go around and meet the new neighbors. Since the war, many of the tenants had changed. She was not sure who still lived in the other houses. When she and William had lived there and her grandparents before that, this had been a relatively good address, but since the war, the city had shifted, and people in New Orleans no longer held the townhouses on Basin Street in high esteem. Taverns had replaced cafes and exclusive boutiques with more common shops. The neighborhood housed more of the mundane working-class people of the city than before the war.

This shift did not bother Olivia in the least. Knowing that few of the backwater gentry would be present on the streets here suited her just fine. She could live her life as she chose without rumors filtering back home, causing her parents grief.

Olivia threw her suitcases on the bed and draped the

loose dresses over a chair to be hung in her wardrobe later. Dust covered the vanity in a thin layer, giving the oak top a white, powdery finish. Tomorrow she and Magdalena would give the place a good cleaning and take stock of what they would need from the mercantile and the green-grocer. Two streets over, the open-air market where farmers and fishermen sold their goods was always a delight to wander.

"This place nothin' but dust and cobwebs." Magdalena came in and opened up the French doors leading out to the balcony over the street. "I thought Miss Marie paid someone to come in and keep this place clean in case the family popped in unexpectedly."

"I think she does, but Benjamin and his wife are getting up there in years." Olivia shook the dust from the lace curtains on the doors, creating a powdery storm in the room. "I think their son just comes around now and then to make sure people know the place is looked after and won't try to break in." She pulled the cotton cover off the bed and shook it out over the street. Olivia breathed in the fresh, salt-laden air of the nearby Gulf and smiled. Sea birds squawked in the sky above, and in the distance, she could see the masts of the tall ships in the harbor. For a moment, she wondered if any of those ships belonged to James Devaroe. She left the doors wide open to air out the stale room, though the threat of mosquitos still loomed here. If a few of the little buzzing beasts got in, she would deal with them later. For now, she wanted the fresh air and what was left of the daylight to put her things away.

"Did you open your doors, Magda?" Olivia asked about the French doors in her sister's room to the balcony over the courtyard.

"Yes, ma'am, Miss Livvy, ma'am, and I opened the ones downstairs too, ma'am if you was wonderin'."

Olivia rolled her eyes and laughed to herself at her sister as she pounded the dust from the pillows on the bed and shook out the doilies from the bedside tables. "Hello, Miss," someone called up to her from the street. "I'm Ben Benoit. Me and my folks look after this place. Are you with the Thibodeauxes?"

"Hello, Ben," Olivia called back to the tall young man with curly blonde hair and a sunburned face, "don't you recognize me? It's Olivia." She and Ben had played together as children. Three years older than her and a head taller, he had always won their games, but she could always find him when they played hide and seek. The Ben she looked down at now still had the bright blonde hair that gave away his hiding places, but now he towered much more than a head taller than Olivia, and the once skinny, lanky lad had grown into a broad-shouldered, muscle-bound man. "I'll be down in a minute," she called to him and threw the now dust-free doilies onto the bed as she rushed out of the room and down the stairs.

Olivia opened the front door and noted it needed a fresh coat of green paint. The light from the setting sun shone on the front of the townhouse, and she saw that the entire building could use some attention. The once butter-yellow paint had faded to a dull creamy color, and the paint on the tall green shutters appeared to be peeling, as well.

"Come in," Olivia offered, smiling. Upon a closer look at her childhood friend, she saw his shoulders were exceptionally broad, and Olivia wondered if he could even fit through the door.

The big, blonde man turned sideways and had to duck his head a little to get inside, but he came in and peered around the room as if to make certain everything still sat in its proper place.

"I work at the livery just down the block," he told her without meeting her eyes. "Mama has been ill for the last few months and hasn't been here to dust and sweep. I hope that's not a problem for you, ma'am."

"Don't you ma'am' me, Ben Benoit," she called to the man, grinning, "it was Livvy when we played tag in the courtyard, and it's Livvy now, too. How is your father?"

"Papa died last winter of influenza. I've been lookin' after things since then." He looked around and shuffled his feet nervously in her presence.

"I am so very sorry, Ben." She put a hand on his shoulder, and he flinched a little at her touch.

"And I was sorry to hear about your husband. I was a drummer for the infantry at Vicksburg. The Captain was a good soldier."

"You knew William?" Olivia looked at the man in a different light now. Not only had he participated on the battlefields, but he had known William.

"Yes, ma'—Livvy," he corrected with a shy grin. "He remembered me from here when I came with Papa to do work around the place, and he asked for me to be in his company. I think he thought he had to look out for me because of Papa bein' a Thibodeaux family retainer."

Olivia smiled, knowing that would have been exactly what William would have done. "If you work at the livery, could you take my horse, Blue, and my buggy down there and store it? I'll come down in the morning and make payment to the manager."

Ben puffed up a little, standing taller and squaring his broad shoulders. "I'm the manager of the livery and do the blacksmithing, as well. It's a dollar a week to keep and feed your horse, but keepin' your buggy won't cost nothin'."

"Wonderful." Olivia smiled and opened her bag. She

counted out ten dollars and handed it to him. "Here is ten weeks' worth, and I'll come in sometime this week with enough for six months." She walked to the stairs and called up, "Magda, do we have everything out of the buggy now?"

Magdalena came to the top of the stairs and looked down to see Ben standing there. "Is that Ben down there?" she asked and skipped down the stairs. "Good Lord, boy, what your Mammy been feedin' you?" she asked with a big smile.

"Shrimp and rice, mostly," he replied and wrapped his arms around Magdalena, who had also been their playmate as children.

"Well, she must be puttin' some extra special gri-gri in it to grow you up so big from that skinny little boy we chased around the streets with."

Ben smiled and put the money in his pocket. "I don't know what she puts in it, but I've surely been missin' her cookin' since she took to her bed."

"What wrong with Miss Evangeline?" Magda asked as she pulled on the handle for some water from the sink pump for a drink of water.

"She won't go to no doctor, but I think she's just grievin' herself to death over Papa. They were very close, you know," he told them with a sad stare out into the empty courtyard. "Did you see the fountain we put in?" They all walked to the doors and peered out into the courtyard, where an alabaster-white fountain trickled in the late afternoon glow. "Papa found it in a pile of rubbish after one of the big houses was bein' fixed up and thought it would look nice here."

Olivia admired the beautiful piece but felt saddened that the fire pit now no longer existed. The fountain had taken its place in the red-brick courtyard.

"The sound of that water is pretty and all," Magdalena said, "but it gonna have me on the pot all night long."

"Want to trade rooms with me and listen to street noise all night?" Olivia asked, laughing.

"Yes, and that noise is pretty bad now that the tavern has opened down the block," Ben told them with his brows furrowed. "You ladies shouldn't be out too late after dark in this neighborhood. That place draws a scurrilous bunch from the wharves. There's always fights and knifings goin' on there," he told them with his face grim.

"We'll keep that in mind." Olivia went into the small kitchen and looked around. "I'd offer you some coffee or tea, but we just got here and haven't got things organized yet."

"That's alright, Livvy. It's nice to see you and Magda again. I'll be goin' now and get your horse stabled and rubbed down. I imagine he needs it after that long trip in the rain."

"Thank you, Ben," Olivia said, smiling at the man's broad, muscular back as he walked toward the door. "I'll see you soon with the rest of Blue's stabling money."

"No hurry on that, Livvy. I know you're good for it, and I know where to find you." He laughed at her, turned, and ducked out the door, and headed to the alley.

"Now that boy turned into one fine hunk of man-flesh." Magdalena giggled and sipped her water. "I bet he's still sweet on you, too. He couldn't keep his eyes off your chest when you weren't lookin'. You want some water?" Magdalena pumped some more water into her glass and reached for another from the open cabinet. She handed the heavy green glass to Olivia, who took it and drank deeply.

"Thank you, sister, that would be nice. The water from

this well has always been so sweet and comes up nice and cool."

"Daddy say this house has a deep well down past the point of bein' salty from the Gulf or dirty from the river."

All four townhouses pumped from the same well, and Olivia could never remember it going dry, even in the driest and hottest of summers, though those were relatively few dry ones here in southern Louisiana.

"I hope all the storm shutters are still working," Olivia said as she shook the dust from the curtains over the French-doors to the courtyard and the one window on the street side of the parlor. That one was wide with multiple panes of heavy wavy glass. It took four panels of the airy lace fabric to cover it. Dust filled the room as she shook them out, and both she and Magdalena began sneezing and rubbing their eyes.

"Will you stop that," Magdalena said before emitting another loud sneeze. "We can take them all down and throw 'em in a washtub tomorrow."

Olivia relented, realizing the futility, and dropped down onto the blue velvet settee. The room began to darken as the sun fell behind the buildings across Basin Street and Magdalena began lighting lamps.

"We gonna need some oil for these lamps, and we better get the kind with the tansy oil in it to keep away these damned, pesky mosquitos."

Olivia went to the desk next to the little fireplace and rummaged in the drawer for some paper and an inkwell that was not dried up. When she finally found one and a sharpened quill, she set to work making a list.

"Look in the canisters and see what we need in the way of dry goods from the mercantile," she told Magdalena, who still rummaged around in the kitchen.

"Oh, sweet Jesus," Magdalena said with her nose wrinkled, "that tin of lard is rancid as Hell. The coffee tin is almost empty, and what is here is most probably stale. It looks like we got plenty of bags of tea, and it been sealed up good." She continued to look in canisters and bins in the small kitchen. "The flour and meal here are both full of weevils, so put them on your list. We gots plenty of sugar, but if you want to make some bread, we gonna need some fresh yeast. We should get some eggs, butter, bacon, ham from the market, and some fresh fruit. If they have some berries and peaches, we can make up some jams and such to put away for winter. It might be good to get some rice and dry peas too."

"If we're going to do preserves, we are going to need crocks with seals or some sealing wax."

"Your crank churn is here in the cabinet," Magda said, lifting the square glass jar with a crank on the top that turned little wooden paddles inside. "We can just get some cream and make our own butter. Freshly made is better than what's been sittin' for God only knows how long at the market."

Olivia agreed and crossed butter off her list, replacing it with cream. She also added a column for the bakery that listed croissants, baguettes, and pastries. Both she and Magdalena were excellent bakers, but why heat the house with baking when she could buy bread and pastries from one of the many excellent bakeries in the area?

"Is that cake plate with the glass lid still here?" Olivia asked as she scribbled.

"Yes, but the base has been chipped some. It will still stand, and the cover is fine. I guess thieves and looters don't care much for kitchen wares." Magdalena laughed. "Most all the basics seem to be here, but the good silver is all gone along with the tea service and trays. They were only pewter, but I guess they couldn't tell the difference if it was polished. I hope you weren't planning any fancy afternoon tea parties, Miss Livvy, ma'am. We still have the pretty porcelain, though," Magdalena teased as she came in and dropped onto the settee.

"I think I'll limit my entertaining to meeting the neighbors to see who is still here and who's gone."

"I hope that crabby old Purdue couple are gone. I never met such a rude, hateful couple in all my days. Their girl, Suzy, said the old man caned her and tried to bed with her regular-like."

"I doubt they're still here." Olivia finished her lists and joined her sister on the settee. "They were both old when we lived here, and that was seven years ago. Some old folks are just set in their ways, and they lived with slaves all their lives. It's hard for them to adjust. Shall we find a café and get some supper? There used to be one up the block and across the street."

"You think we should be goin' out in the dark? Ben said it weren't safe around here no more."

"You have your knife, and I have my pistol." Olivia smiled and patted her thigh. "I feel plenty safe."

"If you say so, Miss Livvy, ma'am. Let's go. I'm powerful hungry." Magdalena giggled as her sister slapped at her shoulder.

15

They left the townhouse with the light of dusk. The street lights along Basin Street had not been lit yet. They crossed the street to bypass the rowdy tavern, and Olivia saw the wrought-iron tables and chairs sitting in front of the café she remembered. They picked up their pace and arrived to find the place still open for business, with waiters lighting candles on the tables and around the overhanging balcony that protected their customers against the weather.

They took seats, and the men lighting the lamps kept giving them sideways glances without speaking to them. One of the men went inside, and soon another gentleman in a waistcoat and string tie came out. He headed straight for them, looking stern.

"Good evening, madam," he said to Olivia, "but I am afraid your girl can't sit out here. If you want to order something for her, she can go fetch it at the kitchen door and eat it standing out back."

"Sir, my family, and our retainers have been patron- izing this establishment for decades, and never have our servants been relegated to the back of the building like stray dogs begging for scraps. We were always allowed to eat here as long as we ate out here on the sidewalk tables."

"I am sorry, madam, but with the Black Codes instituted by the state since the war, persons of color are not allowed to eat at the same tables possibly occupied by white customers. Down closer to the waterfront, there are some nigger establishments where she would be welcome."

"Very well, sir, but could I order some food to take back home? We just got here to my townhouse and have not provisioned it as of yet. I thought the Republican administration disavowed all the Black Codes here in Louisiana."

"Most of my customers are Democrats and still abide by the old codes of the proper government, not these Republican Yankees," he sneered, looking at Magdalena. "I believe the cook can wrap something up for you to carry home. I would recommend the rice and peas with shrimp, a nice loaf of bread, and perhaps a chardonnay bottle. But your girl will have to stand in the street to wait. She can't sit at the table."

"Very well," Olivia said curtly. "But *my girl* will wait right here with me. She is not a dog; you can shoo away to the street."

The man went back into the building, and several people looked at them as they came up to the café and went inside rather than taking a table out in the fresh air with them.

"I'm sorry, sister," Olivia sighed as she watched coaches pass on the cobbled street. "I had no idea things had gotten so bad here in the city. I had read that the White League was trying to put Kellogg out of the office for his pro-Negro views, but I couldn't imagine it had gotten so bad."

"It's fine, Miss Livvy," Magdalena said, playing her part as the resigned servant of a Lady of Class. "Food always taste better at home where we can relax and enjoy it without all these highbrow folks givin' you dirty looks for sittin' out here with your house nigger."

"But this is ridiculous. When you were my property, it was fine for you to sit out here and eat with me, but now that you are free, you must eat at the back door like something dirty?"

"Don't you worry 'bout it none, Miss Livvy. Tomorrow we'll go to the market and get food to cook at home. I guarantee my cookin' be better than anything we be gettin' here or anyplace like it."

"I know that for certain," Olivia said as the man in the waistcoat came out with a short wooden crate containing a chaffing dish, a narrow loaf of bread wrapped in white paper, and a bottle of wine. He sat the box in front of Magdalena without looking at her.

"That will be three dollars, madam because I have to charge you for the dish."

"Of course you do," Olivia said with a huff and handed the man three dollar bills. The man stood there looking at her expectantly for a few minutes while Olivia and Magdalena left their seats.

"Very well, madam," he said with an indignant huff, "come back again soon."

"Not damned likely, and neither will any of the Thibodeuxes from Sweet Rewards or their friends if I have anything to say about it." Olivia joined Magdalena, already a good way up the sidewalk, leaving the man standing at the table open-mouthed.

"Stupid little man," Olivia spat. "Does he honestly think I'd come back to his shabby little café after being treated that way?"

"It the new way in Louisiana, Liv. All the white people are afraid of us niggers now. They think we gonna rise up against our old masters and kill 'em all or somethin'. They all a bunch of fools. This country ain't like the Islands where them niggers run crazy killin' and rapin' when they got free. People ain't like you, sister. They see black skin, and they think we like a bunch of pigs been set free in the field that's gonna run crazy rootin' up and destroyin' everything we see."

"That's just it, sister; you are darker than me but lighter skinned than most of the white folks out there with mixed Indian blood. You have almost as much white blood as I do. The same blood as I do, for God's sake. They should not see you as a black-skinned woman. From now on, when we're out in public, you walk by my side, not behind, and stop talking like a backwater cane-field nigger. You know proper diction, and I want you to use it all the time."

"Livvy, folks aren't ready for educated, well-spoken niggers. It will scare them."

"Let the foolish sons-of-bitches be scared. You are my sister, and these low-born fools will treat you as such. Tomorrow we are going shopping and getting you some clothes that befit the daughter of the Thibodeaux family. Take off that damned kerchief. From now on, you are not just Magdalena, my maid; you are Magdalena Thibodeaux, my very much loved sister."

"Oh, Livvy, you don't have to go doing something like that. If Daddy gets wind of it, he'll be here with blood in his eyes. He'll whip the both of us black and blue."

Olivia patted her thigh and smiled. "Just let the old bastard try."

"You may have gotten past the law for shootin' that ass Simon Montrose, but if you shoot Daddy, the law's gonna come down on you hard."

They were almost at their door when they heard salacious whistling and calls from men coming from the tavern.

"Come on back here, ladies," one of them called after them. "I got something here, especially for you." He saw them headed for the townhouse and whistled louder. "I didn't know new meat moved into the quad. Why don't you let me have a poke as a special new meat sample? If you both fuck and suck me nice, I'll bring you back plenty of customers."

They got to the door, and Olivia unlocked it as quickly as she could, and they both got inside with the man still calling to them with insidious propositions.

"I think our new neighbors may be very different sorts than lived here before," Magdalena said and laughed as she set the box of food on the table.

Olivia looked out the door to the courtyard. Through the open doors of the other townhouses' upstairs balconies, she saw men and women in various stages of dress engaged in several different sexual activities.

"Oh, my." Olivia laughed and pulled the curtains shut. "I can't imagine Mother knew this was going on here."

Magdalena looked thoughtful for a minute. "I never noticed anything when we were here last fall, but we were out most days and weren't out in the courtyard much at night because it was chilly."

"I wonder why Ben didn't mention it this afternoon."

"It's a bit of a delicate subject, and most men don't like to broach it with ladies, Livvy."

Olivia got two plates and two wine glasses from the cabinet before grabbing two forks and the wine corkscrew. Magdalena took the white porcelain chafing dish and the bread out of the box and set them on the table with the wine bottle. When she saw what her sister brought to the table, she went back into the kitchen and pulled a small black ladle from a hook on the wall by the stove.

When they took the top off the oval dish, the room became inundated with the savory shrimp dish's mouthwatering aroma. Steam curled toward the ceiling and filled the room with the smell of file gumbo, green peppers, onions, shrimp, and spices from the Islands.

Magdalena dipped the ladle in and scooped out a healthy portion of the rice, shrimp, and brown peas soaked in the savory sauce. She tore off a hunk of the warm, crusty bread and handed it to her sister. Olivia dipped out of the chafing dish as well and took the bread, tearing off a hunk for herself.

Olivia looked at her beautiful sister and smiled. Before tonight, Magdalena would never have dared serve herself before serving Olivia. Many times they had shared the same table, but Magdalena always deferred to her as her mistress.

"Magda, your hair is wavier than mine but not nearly as coarse as your mother's."

"I know. Mammy always said I had *good* hair." She ran one hand over her head to the bun wound tight at the back of her neck while she stabbed a shrimp from her plate with the other. "This stuff ain't bad."

"From now on, wear your hair the same way I do. I'll give you some pins, and we'll get you some proper bonnets with feathers and frills."

"When we go into those shops, you better introduce me as your cousin instead of your sister. It wouldn't be a lie. I am your cousin from the LaMonte side of the family. My daddy may be a Thibodeaux, but my granddaddy was a LaMonte from Biloxi. Some people around here might know that Armand Thibodeaux only has one daughter—at least only one white one." She laughed and took a drink of the wine Olivia had just poured her.

"Very well," Olivia gave a resigned sigh, "you are my cousin Magdalena LaMonte from the Greenbrier Plantation outside Biloxi, who has come to live with me here in the city in the Thibodeaux/LaMonte Family Townhouse which I inhabited with my husband William before he went off to war and was killed."

"That will suffice. Livvy, do you think I can pass for white? I mean, I do have my Mammy's full lips and round ass."

"The lips we'll rouge up, and these new bustled skirts will take care of your ass."

"I thought I done a good job on my dresses," Magdalena pouted.

"You did, sister, but it is time you had some store-bought clothes of the modern style and not things handed down from before the damned war. Skirts are slimmer now with ribbons and big bows to hide your round ass, and the sleeves are not worn nearly so full now."

They finished their dinner, cleaned up the dishes, drank the wine, and talked late into the night, listening to cackling laughter coming from the other townhouses.

"Your mother is going to be so excited to know we are living in a brothel." Magdalena laughed. "I'm going to bed now. Good night, Olivia Thibodeaux Montgomery almost Devaroe." She laughed more as she went up the stairs.

"Good night, Miss Magdalena Thibodeaux LaMonte." Olivia blew out the lamp and followed Magdalena up the stairs.

❧ 16 ❧

July thirty-first, eighteen seventy-four, in New Orleans dawned bright and clear. No one could imagine the devastation on its way. Olivia and Magdalena rose early and began stripping down the townhouse to its bare bones. All the curtains went into tubs of hot water to soak the years of dust out along with the bed linens. The windows got washed with rags soaked in vinegar, the wood polished with bee's wax and walnut oil, the floors swept and mopped, and the hearth and cookstove cleaned of their black ash.

In the afternoon, just after Magdalena took the curtains and bed linens off the line in the courtyard, the wind began to blow, and the first fat drops of rain fell. Thunder sounded out over the Gulf, and when Olivia went out onto the balcony, she saw jagged streaks of lightning over the masts of the tall ships in the harbor.

"I think this is going to be a big storm, Liv." Magdalena dropped Olivia's linens and curtains on her bed. "You think we should close the storm shutters?"

"I don't guess it can hurt." They went out onto the

balcony wrapped around the building from Olivia's bedroom overlooking the street, the alley, and ending at Magdalena's overlooking the courtyard. They began closing and latching the tall shutters. First, they closed up the window next to the doors in Olivia's room, then they walked around the corner and closed the shutters on Olivia's other window and the one on the south end of Magdalena's room. After struggling with the latch on Magdalena's window's shutters, they rounded the corner and closed up the final window to Magdalena's room. Their hair dripped, and their clothes hung in a sagging mess before they finished.

While there, they wrestled the shutters over the French doors to Magdalena's room and heard their names called from below. Olivia looked over the fancy iron railing around the balcony to see Ben Benoit, his curly blonde hair hanging straight in the drenching rain. "I'm getting the ground floor windows," he called up to them. "I'll get the ladder so I can close up your doors, Livvy. Now go inside and get dry." They could hardly hear the last through the pounding rain and the wind that had grown stronger by the minute.

Back inside, Olivia hurried to strip out of her wet things and wrap up in her soft cotton dressing gown. She waited for Ben to come to close up the storm shutters on her French doors, but he was taking his time. *Perhaps he's just hoping the rain will let up before climbing the ladder.* In the meantime, the wind blew green leaves that plastered themselves against the glass.

"I told you this was gonna be a bad blow," Magdalena came into the room, wrapping her dripping black curls in a towel. They jumped when a loud blast of thunder followed a flash of lightning that struck the balcony's metal railing across the street. "Let's get the Hell downstairs before we get a bolt of that shit between our eyes," Magdalena said as she grabbed Olivia's cold hand and tugged her toward the steep stairs.

The two sisters ran down the stairs and began lighting lamps and the small hearth in the darkened room. Almost an hour after coming down the stairs, they saw a soaked Ben Benoit carrying a ladder to prop against the balcony and climb up to Olivia's room. They heard the banging of the shutters as Ben shut and latched them tight against the advancing storm.

A light rapping on the door and a bedraggled Ben came in dripping water onto the newly mopped wood. They bundled him in towels and pulled him in front of the small, glowing fireplace. Olivia had started a fire to warm both women, who still shivered from their drenching.

Olivia used a towel to soak up the water on his head until his curls returned. "Why don't you take off that shirt," Olivia said, "so we can wring it out and dry it here at the fire."

With some reluctance, he finally began unbuttoning the wet cotton shirt, peeled it off his soaked torso, and handed it to her.

"I ain't takin' off my drawers," he blurted with his cheeks turning red, "so don't even ask."

"Then stand in front of the fire and let it dry them a little," Magdalena told him as she draped another towel over his broad, muscled shoulders, lingering there just a little longer than she needed to fix the towel in place. "You had better take off those boots so they can dry too," she ordered.

Ben did as she told him and removed his wet boots. He handed them to Magdalena, and she set them on the bricks in front of the fire to absorb the heat and dry. Ben rolled off his wet socks and laid them over the top of the boots. Magdalena used another towel to begin soaking up water from his pants by pressing a towel onto his legs and backside. She handed the towel to him to press on the front. He turned away from the women and proceeded to tamp the towel over his groin and the insides of his legs just below his crotch, which Magdalena had avoided in her attempt to soak the water from the fabric.

Olivia took his shirt, wrung out in the sink, and hung it from the mantel. She secured it by the wide collar with heavy marble statues of David and Venus.

"What took you so long with the ladder?" Olivia asked him and handed him a hot cup of coffee boiled from the stale beans in the canister but brewed well, nonetheless.

"I was helpin' the girls in the other townhouses close up the shutters on their places," he replied without giving any sign of embarrassment.

"About that." Olivia took a deep breath. "When did these townhouses become brothels, and why didn't somebody let us know?"

"After the war, Pierre Matisse, who owns that tavern down the way, bought up the other townhouses. I'm certain he tried to buy this one too, but your mother wouldn't part with it."

"Maybe she would have," Magdalena intoned from the settee, "if she knew what he meant to do with the others. Your parents should have let her know about it. Miss Marie would be disgraced to know prostitutes plied their trade around her family's lovely townhouse for all eyes to see." She stood indignantly and strode off to the kitchen to boil water for tea.

"I'm sorry, Livvy. I thought y'all already knew what was goin' on here. Your mother has been back here several times when she was in town." He turned again to face the fire, and Olivia saw tendrils of steam wafting from the backside of his pants.

"I'm certain she has no idea about what is going on here," Olivia snapped, "or she wouldn't have signed the place over to me to have as a residence in town." Olivia watched him pulling the legs of his pants away from his skin as the fire warmed them past being bearable.

"You two plan to stay here, then?" He turned back to face her with a nervous smile stretched across his boyishly handsome face. "That's wonderful."

Olivia saw him glancing at Magdalena in the kitchen. He grinned as he watched her work. She remembered Ben and Magdalena being especially close when they were children, sharing treats and toys. The fact that Magdalena's mother was a Negress never seemed to bother Ben. That was one thing Olivia had always liked about him. Other children in the quadrangle of townhouses would not play with Magda because of her skin color and her station as a servant's daughter. Still, Ben never treated her any differently than he did any of the other children. Once, he even got into a scuffle with one of the other boys for calling Magdalena 'a dirty little nigger.'

Lighting struck again nearby, and Olivia dropped her teacup when the loud crack of thunder followed. The cup was empty, and it landed on her lap, so it did no harm to her dressing gown.

"Shouldn't you be at home closing up the house for your mother against this storm?" Magdalena asked him as she brought in the teapot to refill Olivia's empty cup.

"We don't have the house anymore," he told them with a sad countenance. "After Papa died, Mama couldn't bear to live there any longer, so we sold it. She moved in with her sister, who has a big house in the District. I live over the office at the livery."

"I'm so sorry," Magda told him and offered to refill his empty cup with tea. When he wrinkled his nose in displeasure at the offered tea, she took his cup into the kitchen and refilled it with coffee. "And you've never married?" she asked when she returned with the cup of bitter, black coffee.

"No," Ben replied, staring at Magdalena with a raised eyebrow. "Magda, why aren't you talkin' normal like?"

Olivia laughed, and Magdalena replied, "You means, why ain't I talkin' likes a Southern Louisiana house nigger?"

Ben nodded his head uneasily but didn't speak, unsure of what was taking place with his friend. Olivia and Magdalena were both slapping at each other with hilarious laughter, and tears rolled down their cheeks. He stood in front of the fireplace, his face contorted in confusion.

"I'm sorry, Ben." Olivia hiccupped through another fit of laughter and wiped the tears from her cheeks. "You are aware that Magda is my sister?" Ben nodded, and Olivia continued, "Before we left Sweet Rewards, I found out that she is also my cousin."

Ben looked even more confused with a deep furrow in his brow above his nose, and Olivia went on to explain everything to him. She also told him about what happened at the café and her plan to take Magda out, not as her maid but as her cousin Magdalena LaMonte from Biloxi.

Ben appeared to chew on the idea for a few minutes, and the women waited in silence, sipping their tea. "It's not like it is a complete lie," Olivia added. "She *is* my cousin, and her grandfather *was* a LaMonte from the Greenbrier Plantation near Biloxi."

"And if you want to be exacting about it," Magdalena spoke up, "my ma... my mother's name is LaMonte because she was born a LaMonte house slave and given that name on her papers. She is Georgia LaMonte, and since she was never married to my father, my name should be the same as hers, LaMonte, though I think my papers would say Thibodeaux because we were Thibodeaux property by then."

"I think it's a grand idea," he finally said. "I've always thought Magda looked more white than black. The only thing holding her back was bein' a house servant to the Thibodeauxes." Ben walked around the settee and took Magdalena's latte-colored hand, and kissed it softly. "It is a pleasure making your acquaintance, Mademoiselle Magdalena LaMonte, from Biloxi."

She stood and curtsied low. "Why, thank you, sir. I am most certainly pleased to make your gracious acquaintance, sir," she said, and Olivia giggled, but Ben turned his eyes away. Olivia realized then that both of them wore just their dressing gowns. He had turned away because when Magdalena curtsied, a bit of her cleavage was exposed to his eyes.

Such a gentleman.

Olivia tugged on her sister's sleeve and whispered in her ear. Magdalena blushed and pulled her gown tighter over her firm cleavage.

"Magda, why don't we go upstairs and get dressed." They rose with a start when they heard a loud clattering outside in the courtyard. Ben was in the kitchen in a few strides, looking out the small window he'd left unshuttered.

"The wind is blowing the slate tiles off the roof," he told them and jumped when another crashed just outside the window. "This is more than just a regular summer storm." He walked back into the parlor and wrapped both women in his muscular bear arms. "This storm is a damned hurricane."

If you lived on the Gulf, you knew hurricane season

began in July. The thought of actually getting caught in one had never occurred to Olivia. "Do you think we are safe here?" she asked Ben.

"This is a sturdy building built of brick that the builders plastered over, and there are taller buildings all around it. You may lose some more tiles, but the windows are shuttered. I think you'll be fine here."

"We may starve to death, though," Magdalena quipped. "There ain't a bit of food in this house. We were supposed to go shopping today but got caught up in our cleaning before the storm started."

"I have food down at my place over the livery. I'll run down there later and bring some back. I'll need to check on the horses anyhow." Ben slipped back into his warm semi-dry shirt and buttoned it while Olivia and Magdalena rushed up the stairs to dress in something more than their flimsy dressing gowns.

Magdalena went to her room while Olivia went to hers. The storm shutters rattled over the windows and the doors, adding to Olivia's already riled nerves. She opened her wardrobe and pulled out a simple day dress, and then she pulled out two others and took them to her sister's room.

"Don't even think about putting on one of those old dresses, cousin," Olivia said and dropped the three dresses on Magdalena's bed. "My cousin from Biloxi will not be going around in old, worn things like those, not even in the house." Olivia rushed back to her room, buttoning her dress as she walked. She left her sister staring wide-eyed between her wardrobe and the fine dresses tossed across the bed.

When they came back down the stairs, Olivia motioned for Magdalena to sit in one of the chairs around the table and began brushing her thick, wavy hair. She brushed the front locks back and tied them with a ribbon, leaving the bulk to hang in glossy, raven waves down Magdalena's back.

"Now, Ben," Olivia said, pulling her sister, dressed in a lovely blue, brushed-cotton dress in the latest style, trimmed with lace and mother-of-pearl buttons, toward Ben. "Tell me this does not look like a perfectly sophisticated Southern charmer off a Biloxi plantation."

Speechless for a moment, Ben simply stood staring at Magdalena with an open mouth. "You're beautiful, Magda," he finally spit out before opening the door and rushing out into the wind and rain again.

"Oh, my." Olivia giggled. "I do believe you might have a suitor, Miss LaMonte."

"You think so?" Magdalena reached a hand up to feel the hair falling down in the back. A house servant never would be allowed to wear her hair down like that. Olivia watched with a smile as Magdalena turned her head to feel the hair swing free on her back. "I think this is the first time I've ever really felt free, Liv," she said as she ran a hand over her hair. "Working in the house at Sweet Rewards just felt like it did when I was a slave. Nothing changed for Mother and me. Daddy still bedded her and sent men to my room to couple with whenever he wanted to. But now I finally feel free." She swung her hair, and they laughed together in the parlor with the rain beating on the street and tiles crashing in the courtyard outside.

❧ 17 ❧

The storm raged around them for eighteen hours before it finally blew itself out, moving further inland and away from the city. Ben spent most of that time with Olivia and Magdalena. He brought back a feed sack laden with a bacon slab, some eggs, a loaf of crusty bread, and several apples.

They enjoyed a meal of bacon and French toast covered with apples cooked in sugar and cinnamon. Ben also had a couple of fried eggs, but Magdalena did not mind making them for him in the least. Olivia rolled her eyes at the two staring at one another like besotted school children while the slates from the roof kept clattering around them.

In the end, the storm claimed over a hundred lives, destroyed most of the wood-framed houses along the waterfront, and decimated most of the ships in the harbor. Many of the deaths were those of sailors on those ships. Boats docked upriver from the city on the Mississippi escaped damage, but those docked at the city harbor suffered.

The day after the storm, Ben went up on the roof to make an inspection. The storm had blown nearly a quarter of the slate tiles from the roof. He told them it was a miracle the roof had not leaked. When he checked it, he found the attic rooms dry and secure. They hadn't even lost a window up there.

"Olivia," Magdalena yelled up to her from the kitchen, "we need to get some food in this house. I can't survive on tea and toast much longer."

"Fry up the last of Ben's bacon," Olivia called back. "I don't think any of the businesses will be open today or the open-air market either." Olivia spent the morning rehanging the curtains over the windows, now streaming in bright sunlight since they had opened all the storm shutters. "We can go out tomorrow. I want to walk down to the docks anyway. Ben says it is a real mess down there with ships turned over in the water and roofs torn clean off the buildings."

"You have a morbid fascination with destruction, Livvy." Magdalena climbed the stairs with two cups of hot tea. "Why on earth would you want to see all that wreckage and misery?"

"Some of those ships probably belonged to James Devaroe, and it would do my heart good to see a little of his wreckage and misery."

"I can't fault you none there," Magdalena said with a weak grin, "but people died down there Livvy. Do you think they have all the bodies picked up yet?" Magdalena sat on the edge of the bed while Olivia dropped into a cushioned armchair and picked up her cup of tea from the side table.

"I should imagine, but I don't know about such things. Ben said men organized by the constable's office are searching the wreckage, and the fishermen are pulling the bodies of sailors out of the water. The fire brigades are keeping an eye out for fires in the destroyed homes. If a fire gets loose, the whole city could go up in flames."

"Where is Ben now?" Magdalena asked as she stood staring out the window and enjoying the warm sun on her skin. Olivia noticed a new glow on her sister's face but couldn't decide if it came from the newfound freedom Magdalena felt or the attention Ben paid to her. Olivia had walked in and caught them holding hands last night on the settee.

"I think he's out with the fire brigade or one of the search teams down by the waterfront," Olivia said and sipped her tea. "After checking the attic, he said he had some work to do at the livery. Then he was going to go check on his mother before going down to the waterfront to pitch in."

"He's a good man," Magdalena sighed and sat her empty teacup on the table. "Do you think there's a chance he might be…" She dropped into silence while she ran her fingers through her loose hair.

"I think there is every chance in the world, sister. I've seen the way he looks at you." Olivia stood and picked up both teacups. "The curtains are all done up here. I'm going to go down and hang the ones in the parlor now."

"I already hung the ones over the doors." Magdalena stood and followed Olivia down the steep, narrow stairs. "I didn't want those whores or their clients lookin' in our windows."

They jumped when a quick tapping sounded on one of the panes of glass in the French door. Olivia opened the door to see a pretty young woman in a smart pink day dress standing there with a basket on her arm.

"Hello, I'm Nell Perkins, and I live in the house across the courtyard," she said with a smile that showed dimples on her pretty face. "I know you just moved in and didn't figure you'd had a chance to get to the market yet, so I brought this by." Nell handed over the basket to Olivia. "It's not much, but with the storm and all, I didn't figure you'd be able to get to a market for another day or so. Sarah went out this morning and said all the stores had signs sayin' they'd be closed until further notice. Most are still shuttered up." She sighed. "Don't they think folks are gonna need supplies after a blow like that?"

Olivia took the basket and smelled peaches. The contents, covered with a white cloth, could not be seen, but the basket tugged at her arm with its weight. "Won't you come in?" Olivia opened the door wider to allow the young woman entry. She pushed it closed with her hip and took the basket to the kitchen, where Magdalena stood with a sour look on her face. "Won't you sit down and have tea with us, Nell? My cousin Magda and I were just having some." Olivia elbowed Magdalena, and she went out into the parlor where Nell sat in the plaid brocade wingback chair across from the settee near the fireplace.

Nell stood when Magdalena came into the room and offered her hand to Magdalena, who took it reluctantly. "Nell Perkins," she said, smiling as she grasped Magdalena's hand.

"Magdalena LaMonte," she replied with a curt smile. She took her hand back as quickly as she could and sat on the settee.

"Tea would be lovely, thank you," Nell said to Olivia, who still stood in the kitchen watching the exchange between the other two women. "There are some pastries in the basket if you don't have anything already."

"Lovely," Olivia said and busied herself putting plates, saucers, and the tea service on a tray. She took the towel off the basket and lifted out a pewter plate mounded with sticky, sweet pastries. Olivia added them to the tray and carried them to the low table in front of the settee. "I'm sorry, but we don't have any cream yet."

"Oh, that's no problem. In this heat, who does?" Nell laughed, and Olivia thought the young blonde woman quite lovely. Her blue eyes sparkled with genuine merriment when she laughed, and her lips were naturally pink without rouge.

Olivia poured the tea, and they each took a cup from the tray. The awkwardness of Olivia serving Magdalena showed, and she saw the hint of delight in her sister's eyes at their sudden role reversal. Grinning, she offered Magdalena the plate of pastries. "Something sweet for you, cousin?"

"It most certainly is." She giggled, took the plate, and lifted off a sticky bun before she handed the plate over to Nell.

"No, thank you, just tea for me. I've already had my fill this morning," Nell told them, and Magdalena handed the plate back to Olivia to replace on the tray. "This house has been empty for a long time. Did you just buy it, or did old Matisse finally get the folks who had it to sell and move you, two girls, in?"

Magdalena huffed at the insinuation they were prostitutes, and Olivia laid a hand on her arm to keep Magdalena from saying or doing something inappropriate. "I own this house," Olivia told her calmly. "It has been in my family for three generations now. Our grandfather, Gerard LaMonte, owned it originally and used it when the family was in the city from their home near Biloxi. When he died, it passed to my mother, Marie Thibodeaux." Olivia sipped her tea and could tell none of the names she mentioned had any meaning to the girl. "I lived here with my husband, William Montgomery until the war took him.

He went off to fight, and I went back home to stay with my parents. We refurbished it after the destruction wrought by the war and have only used it occasionally when in the city since then."

"And your husband?" Nell asked. "Did he make it through the war? Mine didn't."

"No, the Yankees killed William at Vicksburg. We buried him in the family plot behind my parents' home near St. Johns."

"I'm sorry," Nell said, sitting with the cup and saucer balanced on her knees. "I lost my husband at Bull Run. They told me he's buried there with many others."

"Too many lost," Magdalena chimed in with a bite of pastry in her mouth, "for no good reason that I can see."

"You don't think freeing the Negroes was a good reason to go to war?" Nell asked and picked up her cup.

"How many do you see walkin' around free now?" Magdalena snapped. "Most are still workin' on the same plantations for the same masters and still not getting wages enough to support a family. If the law catches them out on the street without papers, they can throw them in jail and rent them out as indentured servants for no wages at all. That's just legal slavery, in my opinion." Magdalena took a breath, and Olivia tried to motion her to calm down, but she persisted. "All those men and boys died fightin' a war that didn't amount to a pile of shit."

"I'm afraid I have to agree with you on that point, Magdalena," Nell said. "I know other political factors were leading to the war, but the emancipation of the Negroes was the main contributing factor, and they have not been freed at all as far as I can see. The Black Codes keep them from getting jobs or being allowed to gather together in one place. Our husbands died for no good reason at all. Governor Kellogg is doing a good job trying to get rid of the Codes in Louisiana and allowing the Negroes to vote and own property here, but the Democrats don't like it and block his way every chance they get."

"Where did you live before the war, Nell?" Olivia asked.

"We had a little farm outside Shreveport. Nothing big, just enough to keep us fed. Jason taught school at the boys' academy there, and I taught at the girls'."

"You were a school teacher?" Magdalena asked in surprise. "What are you doing down here doin'---" She did not finish her question, cheeks red with embarrassment.

"You mean, why am I a whore now?" Nell asked for her. "It's a long story, but after my husband died in the fighting, his brother moved in and took possession of our farm. As a woman, I couldn't claim ownership if my husband had male relatives who wanted the property." She held her teacup out to Olivia to have it refilled and took a long drink of the warm liquid.

"My brother-in-law told me that if I agreed to share his bed, he'd let me stay on in my own house and cook for him, clean for him, and fuck him," Nell told them with tears in her eyes. "I refused, and he gathered up my clothes and tossed them and me out the door. I picked everything up I could carry and went to the barn, where I turned out all the stock, lit a lantern, and set the place on fire. While he was screamin' and tryin' to put it out with buckets from the trough, I snuck around with my feed sack full of clothes and set the house on fire too. Then I lit out for the main road with nothin' but the clothes on my back, the shoes on my feet, and my paltry sack of belongings." She took another sip of tea and sat demurely in the chair.

"I wasn't going to let that lazy son-of-a-bitch live in my house and take over the farm Jason and I had worked so hard to build up. It wasn't much, but it kept us fed. We built the house and barn with our own hands." She rubbed her trembling hands on her skirt. "None of his kin, who all lived close by, even offered to help us any. My folks were gone by then, and my grandmother couldn't do much, but at least she came out and helped with the cooking while we built the place."

Olivia shared the girl's pain. Losing a husband to the war and then being left in the hands of male relatives who possessed their agendas brought them closer than Olivia could have ever imagined. Granted, Nell's circumstances were much more alarming than hers, but she still felt a kindred spirit in the thin, pretty girl. And judging from the admiration in Magdalena's eyes, she was warming to her as well.

"The only thing better you could have done," Magdalena said, reaching for another pastry, "would have been to burn the house with the son-of-a-bitch in it."

"I thought about that, but his father would have had me hunted down and hanged for it."

"And you had no other family to take you in?" Olivia asked.

"No, Granny was dead by then, and her house burned by the Yankees. I had nobody and nothing but the farm. The school had closed, or I could have roomed there, so I sold my wedding rings and found my way here to New Orleans. There was no work here, and on the streets, I met other women in similar circumstances. They brought me into the trade and showed me the ins and outs of working on the streets and in the cribs." Nell drained her cup and replaced it in the saucer on her knees. "I ended up here last year. The rent is reasonable, and Matisse, who runs us girls here, doesn't take a big cut of our earnings like some pimps in the city."

"How many of you are there here?" Magdalena asked.

"Six," she said, "two in each building. All of us are in the same circumstances. None of us wanted to be whores. The war put us here in Matisse's employ. He wanted your place too so that he could have the whole block, but your mother wouldn't sell." Nell set her cup and saucer back on the tea tray and stood. "I wouldn't be surprised to see him here, tryin' to get you to sell or lease the place to him." She walked to the door. "I need to get going now. Thank you for the tea and the pleasant conversation."

"Oh, no," Magdalena said as she smiled and stood to see Nelle out, "thank you for the basket. I was beginning to worry that we would starve before the stores opened again."

"Yes, thank you for the basket," Olivia said before closing the door. "Stop by anytime." They watched the young woman walk across the courtyard, dipping her hand playfully in the fountain like a child as she walked by.

"She's nice," Magdalena admitted, "for a whore."

"And just how many whores have you known, *cousin*?" Olivia giggled as she picked up the tea tray to carry back to the kitchen.

Three long days after the storm, most of the stores and other businesses in the city finally reopened, and things began to function as close to normal as could be expected. Bells tolled almost constantly to announce funerals over that time, and Olivia's heart ached every time she heard them.

"Get dressed, Magda," Olivia called from her room, "we are going out. I want to go to the bank, and we need to go to the mercantile and the market. Wear the green dress, you look lovely in it, and I have a bonnet that goes with it you can wear."

This would be their first adventure out introducing Magdalena as her cousin from Biloxi. After their tea with Nell, they had both breathed a sigh of relief that the girl had not doubted their relationship or that Magdalena was anything but another white plantation princess from Southern Mississippi.

Ben, who had visited later that afternoon, had assured them he had no doubts their ruse would work. "Magda, you are whiter than I am after I spend an afternoon in the sun fishing. If you keep yourself shaded, no one will ever remark on the color of your skin except to say it is as soft and sweet as one of these summer peaches." He bit into one of Nell's peaches, letting the sweet, sticky juice run down his chin. Olivia rolled her eyes as Magdalena blushed and batted her big green eyes at Ben from across the room.

Magdalena walked into Olivia's room wearing the mint-green dress with cream piping around the yoke, collar, and cuffs. She wore her hair down except for the front and sides, which she had brushed back and tied with a cream ribbon that matched the piping. Olivia pinned a green velvet French bonnet to her head, cocked a little to one side, and changed its feather to one that matched the ribbon in Magdalena's hair.

"You look stunning, Magda," Olivia gushed. "Here." She handed her a gold ring set with an oval piece of dark green jade. "I always wear this ring with that dress."

Magdalena slipped the ring onto her finger and stared at it for a minute. Then she gazed at her reflection in the mirror over Olivia's bureau. "Is that really me?" Magdalena gasped. "If my mam … mother could see me now, she'd whoop my behind for puttin' on airs, not to mention for puttin' on your nice clothes. Then Daddy would whoop me again for steppin' out of my proper place as Miss Livvy's house nigger."

"Oh, stop that kind of talk," Olivia shushed her. "You are my beloved cousin Magdalena LaMonte from Biloxi. I will hear no more talk about house niggers and the like from you." She picked up her drawstring bag with the leather bank book inside, grabbed Magdalena's gloved hand, and pulled her down the stairs and out onto the sidewalk into the gray, overcast morning. The women walked side-by-side on the wide sidewalk, their bags hanging from one wrist and their parasols on the other.

They passed the tavern that was blissfully quiet in the early morning hours and stopped in front of the livery. "I want to go in and say hello to Blue," Olivia said, "and I'm sure you'd like to go in and say hello to Ben." She winked and giggled as she stepped into the livery door that smelled a mixture of hay, horse dung, leather, and coal smoke from the smithy. They could hear the pinging of a metal hammer on the anvil and knew they would find Ben sweating over his forge in the back of the building.

Bent over his work, he did not notice the two women walk behind him toward the stalls where Ben housed the horses. Olivia found Blue, and he came to her happy to take the apple she offered him and the gentle pat on his muzzle as he chewed the fruit. In the stall next to Blue stood a sway-backed old mule, and Magdalena held out her apple to him. He walked up to her with guarded curiosity but gladly accepted the offered treat.

"Be careful of old Buck," Ben said, causing both women to jump, startled at his voice behind them. "He is old and has a bit of a mean streak. He bites and kicks if he doesn't get his way."

Magdalena smiled and petted the gray muzzle of the old mule as he chewed up the apple. "He's just been over-worked and underappreciated."

"That he has," Ben laughed, "and I think he recognizes a kindred soul."

"I beg your pardon." Olivia looked at him indignantly. "Magdalena has never been overworked or underappreciated, not by me, anyhow."

"Well, I don't know about that." Magdalena laughed, joined by Ben.

Olivia gave them both a mock pout and grabbed Magdalena's arm. "Come now, *cousin*, we must be off to buy you a new wardrobe, as you lost yours in a fire and all." Magdalena waved at Ben with a coy smile and a wink as Olivia pulled her back out onto the sidewalk.

"We have to find this bank first," Olivia told her, fishing out the bank book for the address. "Lafayette Bank, ninety-one Lafayette Street, I think that is this way." She pulled Magdalena along for several streets before giving in and stepping into a café to ask directions. Olivia was going in the right direction, but they still had several blocks to travel west and then a few south to get to the address.

When they found it, the Lafayette Bank left Olivia a little disappointed. The building was old and shabby, needing a new coat of paint. At one time, the brick structure may have been quite stately, but years of wear and neglect showed on the exterior. They made their way up crumbling brick stairs and into a quiet lobby. The chipped marble floor in need of a good polishing did nothing to bolster Olivia's confidence in the place.

At the counter, a skinny man in wire-rimmed spectacles stood slumped over a pile of papers.

"Excuse me, sir," Olivia said politely, "I would like to withdraw some funds from my account." She opened the little book and laid it on the counter.

He glanced up at her with rheumy eyes through his spectacles and then took the book to study. "You are not Mrs. Thibodeaux," he said flatly and held onto the book.

"No, I am her daughter, Olivia Thibodeaux Montgomery, and I believe my name is also on this account. That is what my mother told me when she gave me the account book. She said she and my grandfather, Gerard LaMonte, had been banking here for some time."

At the mention of her grandfather's name, the old man's eyes widened, and he stood a little straighter behind the counter. "Gerard LaMonte was a very good customer, and we opened this account in your and your lovely mother's names though it's not technically legal because Mr. Lamonte was such a good customer and requested it of us. We held the mortgage on his townhouse for some years, and your mother, Marie Thibodeaux, has been a faithful depositor. How is she, by the way? We have not seen her in quite some time."

"She is not well, I'm afraid," Olivia told him. "That is why she has passed the townhouse and this account on to me. My cousin, Magdalena," Olivia pulled her cousin forward, "and I have taken up residence in the townhouse now."

"Of course, of course," he muttered, and his eyes darted between the two women. "I can see Mr. LaMonte on both your faces. He was a handsome man, and you are both handsome young women. How much did you want to withdraw today, Mrs. Montgomery? Your mother has spoken of you often. I was sorry to hear of the loss of your husband."

"Thank you ever so very much," Olivia said sweetly to the old man. "I believe a hundred dollars will do for now. We need to buy provisions for the house and make some repairs due to the storm."

"Nothing major, I hope. I always liked that house. A very fine address indeed there on Basin Street in its day." He fumbled with the drawer below the counter in front of him.

"No, nothing major. We just have to replace a few roof tiles, and the place requires paint. I think we'll have it all done at once before it falls into too much further disrepair." Olivia could not help glancing around the inside of the old building in which she now stood.

"Yes, this old place needs a good bit of work, but the owners no longer feel keeping it up is worth the cost. They are talking about moving the whole operation to a more central location. I've been here for almost forty years. I work down here and live in an apartment upstairs. They tell me I'll be able to keep the apartment as a retirement benefit, but I won't be moving with the bank," he told them with sad, watery eyes.

"Forty years is a long time to devote to an employer," Magdalena said sweetly. "It's time for you to retire and sit on a dock in the sun with a fishing pole."

"I do love to fish," he replied and began peeling bills out of the drawer and laying them on the counter. "I hope you don't mind paper scrip. They don't let us handle gold here any longer."

"Paper will be fine." Olivia smiled.

He counted out the hundred dollars, took the bank book, and made the necessary notations. "I added in the accrued interest since the last time Mrs. Thibodeaux was in, and after your one-hundred-dollar withdrawal, you have a total of two thousand, seven hundred and seventy-five dollars and fifteen cents. Is there anything else I can do for you?"

"I don't believe so, but when will the bank be moving and where?" Olivia asked as she put the money and the bank book back into her bag.

"They are putting it in a building on Decatur Street near the Opera House, but with the storm, I don't know when the actual move will be. Some damage to the scaffolding will require rebuilding before the building's refurbishing can be completed. I will have more news the next time you visit," the old man told them as they walked away.

"*Au revoir, monsieur.*" They smiled and left the building.

"I had no idea Miss Marie had that kind of cash hidden away from Daddy," Magdalena whispered. "You are a rich woman, Livvy."

"I think most of it was left to her by Grandfather, and she's just added a little to it over the years as she could. There was more, but she told Daddy she sold the townhouse and took money out of the account so he'd think it was gone."

"Now I see where you got your sneaky side from." Magdalena laughed.

The rest of the afternoon, they spent in dress shops outfitting Magdalena in the wardrobe befitting a southern Louisiana lady of means. They went into shops and tried on dozens of dresses and suits. Never once were they questioned or given any trouble. They brushed shoulders with New Orleans white elite who would have swooned if they'd known a mulatto woman had just been trying on clothes in the shop. They both had to laugh after coming out of some of the shops run by snooty bigots.

"If the stupid bitches think the black rubs off," Olivia laughed, "all y'all would be white by now."

"And most of y'all would be black, 'cause we been washin' your lily-white asses since you slid out the womb."

At the mercantile, they purchased all the things on Olivia's list and a few other items. One of the things Olivia decided they needed was an icebox. They had one at Sweet Rewards, but her mother had never fitted the townhouse's kitchen with one. Olivia knew there was an icehouse in the city and spent thirty dollars for the insulated wooden cabinet that would hold a block of ice and keep their cream, butter, and eggs from spoiling in the New Orleans heat. She paid a little extra to have it all delivered, and the lady at the counter raised a suspicious eyebrow when Olivia gave her the address. She ignored her and continued to the open-air market that smelled of fresh-ground spices, fruit, and fish.

With the icebox purchase, they could also buy more

than a day's supply of shrimp or fish. Olivia haggled with the man for a while but finally talked him into selling her a block of ice for her new icebox along with two pounds of large shrimp, a large, skinned catfish, and two pounds of fresh crayfish. Magdalena made the best etouffee in Louisiana, and Olivia was dying for some. He, too, agreed, for a fee, to deliver their purchases.

They bought spices, rice, dried peas, onions, peppers, potatoes, yams, more peaches, blueberries, and apples. Olivia wanted to make some jams and apple butter to put up for the winter.

"Olivia, with the market here, we don't need to put up our preserves. There are vendors here who sell them."

"Magda, the money in the bank won't last forever, and I have no skills with which to make money. Unless you plan to join Nell and the other women in their trade to earn a living, we will have to be frugal. I spent the money on the icebox so that spoilage wouldn't plague us, but until we can figure out a way to make a little extra money, we can't be too free with our funds."

"I'm sorry, Livvy, you're right. I wasn't thinking." Magdalena, crestfallen, remained silent for the rest of their outing through the market and began picking up the packages as Olivia sat them down. Seeing her newly independent sister going back to her subservient habits saddened Olivia and made her feel guilty.

On the way out of the market, they passed a café, and Olivia led them in without regard to any looks from the proprietor. They took a seat at a corner table and dropped their packages on the floor.

"What may I get for you, ladies?" the waiter asked them.

"Tea and beignets, please," Olivia told him.

"Yes. Mademoiselle," he told her, bowed, and left.

"You see, Magda, we've made it through the day. You are now officially my dearest cousin, Magdalena LaMonte, here from Biloxi after losing your home and family in a fire."

"That might play, for now, Liv, but what happens when we run into someone who knows us? This town and this state ain't that big. We're going to run into somebody sometime who knows Olivia Thibodeaux and her nigger maid."

"Oh, hush." Olivia quieted her with a pat on the hand. "We were all over town today and didn't bump into a soul."

"Yes, but everybody is still cleaning up from the storm. What about the next time? Be just our luck, we run into one of them nigger-haters who'll have me lynched, and you burned out of your house."

The waiter brought them their tea and plates of beignets, dusted with powdered sugar. He left, and they dug into their pastries.

"We shouldn't tarry here long," Olivia said and stirred cream into her hot tea. "The deliveries should start arriving soon."

"Was this just another test to see if I could fit in?" Magdalena jabbed and smiled.

"I'm sorry, Magda. I suppose it was, but I needed to eat something too."

"Mrs. Montgomery?" They jerked their heads up to see an elderly woman leaning on a cane coming toward them. "It is you. My Lord, girl, I hadn't seen you since before the war when you left the townhouses. Mr. Mollier and I moved out two years ago when the neighborhood began to decline."

Now Olivia remembered the woman. She and her husband owned the townhouse where Nell now resided.

Olivia remembered her as a notorious busy-body who gossiped about everyone on the block. Her husband, a retired clerk from one of the shipping lines, never mixed with the others and seldom joined them in their festivities in the courtyard, preferring his solitude and books.

"And how is dear Mr. Mollier?" Olivia asked, and the woman took a seat with them without being invited.

"Oh, he is much the same," she huffed. "He still prefers his musty old books to good company or fresh air. I will tell him you asked after him. He will be pleased." She looked at Magdalena, giving her an appraising stare. "And who is this lovely young thing?" she finally asked.

"Mrs. Mollier, I'd like you to meet my cousin, Mademoiselle LaMonte, from Biloxi. She has moved into the townhouse with me since losing her home in a fire."

The old woman took Magdalena's hand in hers. "I am so very sorry to hear that, my dear. You are lucky to have such a loving cousin as Mrs. Montgomery to take you in. But dear," she turned her attention back to Olivia, "that neighborhood has become overrun with trash and degenerates. I cannot believe your family has kept the place. Your mother is such a gentle and aristocratic woman. I am surprised she didn't get shed of the place long ago. I heard the houses are now all filled with trashy women selling their bodies. How can respectable women like yourselves live amongst such squalor?"

"Really?" Olivia said in feigned surprise. "We just met the young woman living in your old house, and she is quite lovely. Didn't you think so, cousin?"

"Indeed, I did," Magdalena agreed. "She is a war widow who taught at the Academy for Young Ladies in Shreveport until it was closed during the war. She seemed quite refined and very well-spoken."

"Yes, a lovely woman who brought us a basket of

provisions after the storm," Olivia told her. "She saved our lives. We had only just arrived the day before and had not been able to get to the market for provisions. We had no food in the house, and all the markets were closed."

"Well," Mrs. Mollier sighed, "Mr. Mollier will be glad to know a decent woman is living in our home. Perhaps what I've heard about the Quad has been exaggerated. You know how some people live to carry tales," she said and gave a nervous laugh.

"Indeed," Magdalena huffed and raised an eyebrow at Olivia. "Shouldn't we be going, cousin? Aren't the things from the mercantile supposed to be delivered this afternoon?" She began gathering her bags from the floor around her chair and stood. "It was a pleasure to meet you, Mrs. Mollier, and please give your dear husband our best." She followed Olivia to the counter, waited for her to settle their bill, and went out onto the street.

"You see," Olivia laughed, "that old bat knew you for years as my maid and didn't even recognize you. This ruse is going to be a breeze."

❧ 19 ❧

For two days after their shopping excursion, Olivia and Magdalena busied themselves with putting the house in order. After much rearranging in the kitchen, the new icebox finally ended up not quite in the kitchen but against the stairway wall in the hall that led to the alley door where they kept the trash bins. That door stayed locked and seldom used due to the offensive odor in the alleyway.

Olivia stood peering at the oak-doored, insulated cabinet from the kitchen center with a finger resting at the corner of her mouth.

"Liv, if you think I am going to help you move that heavy damned icebox again, you be out of your ever-lovin' mind. I've broken my back from pushin' that thing around. It looks fine where it is, and it's close to the door so that we can dump the water out of the drip tray." Magdalena dropped into a chair with a heavy sigh.

"No, the spot is fine. I was just wondering if there was enough sun from the back door for a fern. I think a fern would look nice on top of it."

"You and your plants," Magdalena huffed. "No, ferns

need to be in direct light like in front of this big window. Begonias would be good, maybe, or violets. How about a sweet potato? They vine out nice and green and don't take much tendin' to at all."

I suppose you're right." Olivia went to the bin, picked out the scrawniest-looking sweet potato, and laid it on the counter. She found an old mug from the cabinet, filled it with water, put the orange root into it, and set it on the window sill above the sink.

"Shall we walk down to the waterfront?" Olivia asked.

"Whatever for?" Magdalena groaned.

"We need to make arrangements with the icehouse for deliveries, and the icehouse is down by the harbor," Olivia explained as she went to the stairs. "I'm going to wash and change."

Within the hour, they left the townhouse together in lightweight cotton suits, carrying their parasols to ward off the relentless summer sun. Magdalena had covered her face and hands with a cream Olivia purchased from the apothecary. The man had guaranteed it to keep the skin from darkening in the sun and even to lighten it some. She had taken it from her sister and promised to use it but told Olivia she doubted the packaging's claims. Magdalena told her sister it simply felt like lard mixed with some beeswax and coconut oil. It did soften her skin some, so she put it on before going out into the sun, as did Olivia to preserve her porcelain complexion.

As they'd heard, the devastation along the waterfront proved to be terrible. The sisters saw homes and warehouses without roofs or destroyed, and ships lay in the harbor on their sides or washed up onto the beaches with their masts shattered and their keels in the air. Olivia shivered when Magdalena pointed out a bloated corpse bobbing in the surf, as yet unclaimed by any of the boats patrolling the waters.

Funeral bells still tolled daily for the victims, and Olivia hoped this poor soul would soon be recovered and given a proper resting place. She turned her eyes away from the grisly mass in the water and continued along the board-walk following the seawall. A big warehouse with its pit lined with straw, sawdust, and Spanish moss stood where boats from the north brought down huge cakes of ice to be cut up and sold to southerners for their iceboxes and sweet tea.

The walkway bustled with city dwellers curious to observe the devastation, fishermen were hauling their catches in hand-pushed carts to the market, and families with children trying to find a pleasant spot on the beach to cool off in the blue waters of the Gulf. It wasn't surprising that neither woman saw the man until he was right in front of them.

I can't believe she's here. What am I going to say to her? She has to hate me after I ran out on her the way I did. What can I possibly say?

"Good afternoon, Mrs. Devaroe," he said and stopped Olivia with a big, tanned hand on her shoulder. "Or should I say, Mrs. Montgomery?" James Devaroe asked, giving them both a dark, questioning stare. "My banker told me Mrs. Olivia Montgomery had returned to the city from her parents' plantation, Sweet Rewards, and has resumed residence at the family townhouse along with her beautiful *cousin*, a Miss LaMonte from a plantation near Biloxi."

"Yes, Mr. Devaroe," Olivia said nervously as her eyes darted to those passing around them. "My cousin, Magdalena LaMonte, and I are now residing in the city. If you'd be so kind as to let us pass, we need to visit the icehouse." She tried to push past him, but he would not release her shoulder.

"Why don't you and your *cousin* come and join me over here for a coffee?" He pulled them toward a shabby waterfront café with boards nailed over windows and shutters hanging askew.

With reluctance, both women walked with Devaroe to the establishment and took seats on benches set around tables made from boards nailed atop barrels. The place stank of stale coffee and fish, but they sat on the benches and waited for Devaroe, dressed in a casual brown suit, string tie, and straw hat common to the Islands, to speak. A waiter in a dirty white shirt with sleeves rolled up above his elbows came out of the old brick building. "What can I get for you and your ladies today, Mr. Devaroe, sir?"

"We will all have lattes and a tray of beignets, Paul," Devaroe told the man, who bowed and went back into the building.

"So, wife, have you come down here to gloat over my losses?" he asked, gesturing out at the ruined ships in the harbor. "Thank God I had surety on everything, or this storm would have ruined me."

"I *am* sorry for your losses, James, but I am not your wife. Mother has seen to it that *Pere* Dominic has annulled the ridiculous marriage. You left plenty of witnesses, including the good Father, to your desertion of me on our wedding day. You mortified my parents with your behavior, James. I believe you can forget about any shipping contracts from Sweet Rewards in the future."

Devaroe set his eyes on Magdalena in her fine suit and sneered, "And just how mortified are they going to be when they find out you're trying to pass off your nigger sister as your *white* cousin from Biloxi?"

"Magda *is* my cousin through my grandfather from

Biloxi. Her mother and mine are sisters, and her skin is whiter than yours is at the moment," Olivia said and patted Devaroe's very tanned hand.

Paul brought out their coffees, the tray of pastries, and three small plates with dingy, frayed cloth napkins. "Will that be all, sir?" he asked Devaroe, completely ignoring the two women.

"*Oui*, Paul, *merci*." The man retreated into the building to leave them alone once again.

"My banker tells me your quad on Basin Street is nothing but a den of whores now. Is that true? Are my wife and her cousin taking up the oldest profession to make ends meet now? I don't know about your cousin here," he grinned rudely at Magdalena, "but with that tight little cunny and asshole, you could probably make a good living at it. I'd be more than happy to give you some referrals."

"You are insufferable, Mr. Devaroe," Olivia seethed and tried to stand. He grabbed her wrist and tugged her back down roughly.

"You haven't finished your coffee, Mrs. Montgomery." Devaroe had yanked her back down so hard that he pulled her glove from her hand. "I'm not done talking to you yet, Olivia," Devaroe scolded. "When I'm finished, and we've come to an understanding, then you and your lovely sister both may be on your way." He threw the white glove back into Olivia's startled face.

"What sort of understanding," Olivia asked, wary of the man's intent.

I can't believe I'd almost talked myself into thinking this pompous ass had feelings.

"I have plenty of whores I bed regularly here in the city, but you are my wife, and I truly do enjoy those two tight little holes of yours." He smiled and reached out to lay a finger on Olivia's pink mouth. "And I haven't had the opportunity to enjoy this one yet." Olivia snapped at the offending finger with her bared teeth. Devaroe pulled his hand away, laughing,

"You will agree that when I am in town, I will visit your bed whenever I please and use you as I see fit. For that, I will not reveal that you are trying to pass off this negress as a white woman. That, you know, is a grievous offense and could find you both suffering *charivari*. I don't think either of you would look good in tar and feathers," he said and laughed maniacally.

"You're an insufferable bastard, Mr. Devaroe. We should have left you to die by the side of the road like the animal that you are," Olivia hissed at him.

"Now, now, wife, don't give yourself the vapors." He patted her bare hand and lifted her wrist to inhale her orange-blossom-scented oil and shuddered with the memory of her in his arms.

Why can't I just tell her how I feel? She's not my mother. She won't slap me and call me a fool for telling her I love her. She's not Suzette Devaroe. Olivia won't laugh at me and send me away. Why can't I just trust her?

"I will present myself this evening, say around six," Devaroe curtly informed them. "Your cousin will have a supper prepared for us, and then we will adjourn to your boudoir where we will officially consummate our marriage vows." He took a final drink of his coffee and stood. "If I enjoy both the meal and the dessert," he said as he grinned down at Olivia and winked, "I will set up an account with my banker to accommodate your household funds every month. I would like to keep your favors mine exclusively." He walked away, laughing, and Olivia wanted to toss their empty cups at his bobbing head.

"I knew this was gonna blow up in our faces, Livvy," Magdalena muttered. "I think I saw some castor bean plants on our way down here. I'll fix his sorry ass a really fine supper with a few of those ground up in it."

"If anyone is going to poison that sorry bastard," Olivia blurted with angry tears stinging her eyes, "it's going to be me, but castor beans would be a good fix. We'll pluck some on the way home. Make sure you have your gloves on, though. I don't want you getting sick."

"Long as the shell of the bean stays on, you can't get sick from it," Magdalena reminded her. "We still goin' to the icehouse?"

"We may as well since we're already down here by the warehouses." Olivia rose and headed back to the board-walk. She thought for a minute to ask about the bill, but the man seemed to be well acquainted with Devaroe. He probably had a running tab with the shabby waterfront establishment.

They found the icehouse amongst the maze of ware-houses, and Olivia made arrangements for regular deliv-eries of ice blocks cut to size ascribed to their icebox. She paid the man for a month of deliveries in advance, and they walked back toward home.

At the hedge where the dark green, five-pronged, waxy leaves of the castor bush hung over onto the sidewalk, Magdalena bent and rummaged on the ground. She even-tually came up with a handful of the brown speckled beans of the castor bush. Ground into a powder or boiled, they made a deadly poison for which there was no antidote.

The foul-tasting oil pressed from the fresh beans was used as a medicine by some for stomach ailments, though Olivia thought some women used it as more of a punish-ment or a threat to their children than an actual healing oil.

"I remember your mother threatening us with that horrible stuff when we were children," Olivia laughed. "If you girls don't settle yourselves down and act like civilized young ladies, I'm gonna get out the castor oil," she mimicked Georgia, and they both laughed.

"Lord knows, I've had my share of it," Magdalena said and wrinkled her nose at the memory of the disgusting-tasting oil. She dropped the handful of dry beans into her jacket pocket, and they walked on.

In front of the livery, Ben swept the sidewalk with a worn straw broom. "Hello, ladies," he said with a broad, cheerful smile. "What have you been up to today?"

"Livvy had to make arrangements at the icehouse," Magdalena told him as Olivia passed by them to go in and say hello to Blue.

"Oh, for the new icebox? Having one of those must be nice." He sighed wistfully in the humid afternoon heat.

"Having cold milk is most definitely a treat, and not having to worry about the butter goin' rancid is nice too," Magdalena admitted. "We even have us some shrimp and crayfish in there. They stay as fresh as when they come out of the water."

"What you gonna do with all that?" Ben teased.

"Well, tonight I'm makin' up some gumbo and rice. I can bring some down if you'd like. Livvy is havin' company for dinner, and I'd just as soon not be around."

"Who's comin'?" he asked, noting her obvious irritation.

"Just a fella who's a friend of Livvy's father. We ran into him on the way down to the icehouse, and he just invited himself to dinner."

"That's very rude," Ben said, continuing to sweep the debris from in front of the livery blown up by the morning's winds.

"He is for certain a rude person, but Livvy thinks her father would want her to oblige the man."

"Is her father still lookin' for a husband for her?" Ben asked with a little laugh.

"Yes, it's one of the reasons we came back here to the city. Livvy was tired of all of Daddy's fancy parties to introduce her to new matrimonial candidates, and she hates it." Magdalena glanced toward the livery and saw Olivia coming out. "I'll see you tonight, Ben, with a big, hot bowl of gumbo and fresh biscuits."

"I'll be here." He smiled and waved at the two women as they walked away.

"What's that about gumbo and biscuits?" Olivia asked.

"It's what I'm makin' for you and your *husband*, and as I do not intend to have that bastard inflicted upon me, I'm taking my dinner to share with Ben," she replied, giddy with anticipation.

"Are you trying to win him over with your skills in the kitchen?" Olivia laughed.

"Maybe, but if you and your Mr. Devaroe are going to be making a night of it here, I may just try winning him over with my skills in the bedroom."

The thought of Devaroe in her bed both excited and annoyed Olivia. Anytime she thought of him inside her, she got all hot and tingly, but she did not want to think about what he might have in mind for her. She thought it would certainly be more pleasurable to him than to her. She still couldn't believe his harsh treatment of her and Magdalena.

Maybe he was just upset over his losses due to the storm, and he was taking it out on the first people who happened to cross his path. Father could be that way if he suffered business setbacks.

Olivia didn't want to dwell on James Devaroe for the moment and smiled at her grinning sister. "Magda LaMonte," she teased, "you're a shameless little tart."

"What is it they say about when in Rome, do as the

Romans do? We live in a quad of brothels. I'm just trying to fit in with our new neighbors." She laughed and slapped Olivia on the back as she unlocked the door to the townhouse.

"You start boiling the chicken, and I'll slice the onions, peppers, and okra for the gumbo," Olivia told her sister and slipped out of her jacket before going to the kitchen and removing things from the icebox. She handed Magdalena the chicken wrapped in brown butcher's paper and took out the crock of butter she would need to sauté the onions, peppers, and shrimp.

The remainder of the afternoon they spent in the kitchen. By the time the clock struck five, a large pot of gumbo simmered on the stove, and biscuits rested on the warming rack above the flat iron top. Olivia also sliced some peaches and whipped some sweetened cream, though that was not the dessert Devaroe had in mind, she was certain.

Magdalena spooned some of the gumbo into the chafing dish from the offensive café. She wrapped some biscuits in a napkin and scooped some of the peaches and cream into a chilled crock. All of this, she carefully stowed in a basket with a handle.

"I think I am going to be on my way, Livvy unless you want me to fix up the table for ya."

"No, you go on ahead, Magda. I can finish this on my own. You're not my maid any longer."

Magdalena picked up the basket, careful not to upset the chaffing dish with the gumbo, and walked toward the door. "If that man starts getting' mean with you, just go to the window and scream. We'll be able to hear ya and come runnin'."

"Thank you, Magda, but I think I can handle Mr. James Devaroe. You go on and have a good time." Olivia watched her sister leave and envied her. Magda and Ben would share the same sweet, tender love she and William had shared. All she had to look for from Devaroe was sated lust on both their parts. There could be no lasting relationship based only upon that.

❦ 20 ❦

Olivia set the table with china from the cabinet. It did not compare to the ornate Thibodeaux family set, but it was nice, and the deep-dished plates would be perfect for the rice and gumbo. She added the bread plates, flatware, napkins, and candlesticks. As this was an obligatory dinner with the man who called himself her husband and not a romantic dinner for two people who loved and wanted one another, Olivia omitted any flowers or other ornamentation. Her table was neat but made no illusions to romance.

When the knocker sounded, Olivia had just finished changing from her suit into her dressing gown over her best camisole and bloomers. She hoped all he wanted was dinner and sex. She wished she could be done with him soon.

The knocker sounded for a second time, and she went to the door and opened it. Devaroe, dressed in his more formal black waistcoat and top hat, stood there with roses in his hand. He stepped in, and Olivia shut the door.

"I dressed for dinner," he sneered, taking in her choice

of apparel. "You could have done me the courtesy of doing the same."

"Just having you in my home is courtesy enough in my way of thinking," Olivia retorted. "We made you dinner, and I dressed for your required dessert." She pointed at the table and then her choice of dress.

Devaroe looked around the townhouse, taking in the furnishings and the modest decoration in the place. "And where is your lovely *cousin?* I was hoping she might be joining us for dinner *and* dessert." Devaroe burst out laughing when he saw her blanch at the suggestion. He handed her the roses and walked around her to look into the kitchen.

"Magda went out for the evening." Olivia followed him into the kitchen with the flowers and an empty vase from the mantel. She pumped some water into the vase and arranged the roses before setting them atop the icebox.

Devaroe took them from the icebox and put them into the center of the table between the two candlesticks, which he then lit. He took a seat at the table and undid the buttons of his waistcoat. Olivia brought in a dish of gumbo over rice and placed it on the table. As she stood by the table, Devaroe slipped his hand inside her dressing gown and ran it down over her behind, sending shivers of both pleasure and foreboding through Olivia.

I refuse to enjoy this. If the ass wants to be crude and make this a transaction between a paid woman and her client, then so be it.

"That smells wonderful, wife, and this," he squeezed a butt cheek, "feels wonderful. Perhaps we should have dessert first." He brought his hand around to find the opening between the legs of her bloomers and slid his hand inside to explore the hot wetness there.

He pulled her closer until his cheek rested against her belly, and he pushed two fingers inside her, rotating them in a slow, steady motion that made her moan with both pleasure and uncertainty. Olivia did not want to admit that the man excited and pleasured her, but he did. Olivia wanted to pull away from him and retreat to the safety of the kitchen, but instead, she relaxed and leaned into him as he teased her throbbing cunny. He pulled his finger out of her, massaged the throbbing mound above the slit, and then pushed back into her again with more vigor. With his teeth, he tugged on the ribbon of her camisole until it came free, and he lifted his head from her belly to suck a throbbing nipple into his mouth.

Devaroe practiced at the art of pleasuring a woman, brushed his tongue over her hard nipple with the same motion as he touched her throbbing cunny. Within minutes, Olivia arched into his massaging fingers and pressed herself into his teasing mouth. Sweat dripped off her brow, and she gasped in wicked pleasure with her release. The hot burst of pleasure between her thighs exploded in delicious waves, and she wanted to collapse into his arms.

Devaroe pushed her away and gazed at her with a leering smile. "Now it's my turn, wife." He yanked Olivia down to her knees in front of him, unbuttoned his trousers, and released his erect cock in her face. He pushed her head down until her mouth hovered over the bulbous head. "Kiss it," he demanded as he pushed her mouth down to meet the oozing organ. "Kiss it and lick it clean. Then put it in your sweet little mouth and suck it dry."

Olivia tried to pull back in horror at what he wanted her to do, but he held fast to her head and pushed her head down until her lips met the organ, and she tasted the thick, sticky fluid on her mouth. She pursed her lips and kissed the purple bulb, then hesitantly pushed her tongue out to explore the throbbing head of his thick cock.

"Oh, yes," Devaroe moaned. "Lick it all around the head. Use that tongue, wife."

Olivia did as he instructed, not because she wanted to but because Devaroe gave her no choice, holding her head down on his cock. Then he pushed hard, and it was between her lips and in her mouth completely. He pushed until she gagged on the thick organ but allowed her to pull back a little.

"Open up and take as much as you can," he said breathlessly as he pushed Olivia's head back down onto the stiff organ with his hand twisted in her raven hair. He pushed and pulled. "And don't stop using that tongue. Keep licking my cock," he moaned and pushed and pulled her head up and down on his hot, bulging erection. He pumped his hips, pressed into her mouth, and moaned as she continued to flick her tongue around, teasing the spot just under the head that seemed to elicit the most groans when she played with it. "Oh, yes," he groaned, stiffened his body in the chair, and released his hot, bitter fluid into her mouth.

Olivia gagged as the fluid gushed into her mouth, and she tried to pull back. "Oh, no," Devaroe told her and continued to hold her head tight to his crotch. "I want you to swallow everything I give you. Every damned drop."

With Devaroe's hand gripping her head tight and pushing it into his crotch, Olivia had no choice but to swallow the foul mess that lay on her tongue like runny egg whites. With the realization that he was not going to release her until she did as he told her, Olivia closed her eyes tight, fought back the urge to gag, and swallowed the warm, bitter fluid.

When he felt her swallow, Devaroe relaxed his grip on Olivia's head, and she sat up. She wiped her mouth on her sleeve and tried to stand. Her neck ached from Devaroe's tight hold on it, and her knees hurt from pressing on the floorboards for so long. He helped her to her feet with a lascivious smile. "You see, wife, I knew that hole was going to pleasure me too. We shall do that before every meal, I think."

Olivia pulled away from him and stumbled into the kitchen, working the pain from her abused knees. She took the biscuits from the warming shelf and picked up the crock of butter. Then Olivia set them both on the counter and went to the sink for some water. She took a sip, washed it around her mouth, and spit it into the sink. It didn't do much to get the taste or feel of him out of her mouth, but it would have to do.

She took the biscuits and butter to the table where Devaroe sat, opening a bottle of wine. He must have chosen one from the rack near the table and found the corkscrew.

"Come now, wife. Let's enjoy this lovely meal together before we retire and enjoy one another for the night." He gave her a lascivious smile and filled their glasses with the dark red wine.

Olivia picked up her glass and drank deeply of the sweet, hearty vintage made from the wild grapes found in the local swamps. It was one of her favorites, and she had purchased several bottles at the market when she'd seen it.

"I don't know how you can abide this backwater swill," Devaroe spat. "We'll have to get some good French vintages if I'm going to be residing here on occasion."

"If you are going to be residing here, you are more than welcome to spend *your* money on whatever you like. I happen to enjoy the Clairvoux wines." She took another drink and set the glass down. The wine helped to refresh her appetite, and she spooned some of the rice and gumbo, thick with chicken and shrimp, onto her plate. Then she buttered a biscuit and laid it on her bread plate.

If I must share my meal with this bastard, I'm going to enjoy it.

Olivia stabbed a shrimp with her fork and stuffed it whole into her mouth. She chewed it and dabbed at the corners of her mouth to wipe at the escaping, spicy juices. The rice, savory with the gumbo sauce, filled her, and she enjoyed every bite.

Devaroe soaked up the sauce with his biscuit and popped it into his mouth, followed by a long drink of the wine.

"Your *cousin* is a fine cook," he sighed and laid his napkin over his empty plate.

"Magdalena didn't cook this," Olivia told him. "I did. She helped with some of the prep, but the recipe is mine, and I made the biscuits. There are peaches and whipped cream if you would care for some."

He looked at the remains of the savory meal and smiled. "Perhaps you will make a passable wife after all. You're a good fuck and a good cook, too? How did a pampered little plantation princess like you learn to do either of those?"

"I had good teachers." She watched him raise an eyebrow and smiled to herself. "Magdalena's mother taught us both to cook. She set us to kitchen chores when we were little and underfoot. As for the other, William was a good teacher. He showed me how to pleasure him while allowing me to experience my pleasure as well."

"You seemed to enjoy your pleasure earlier," he said with a chuckle deep in his throat.

"Yes, but it was the first time you've ever actually allowed my pleasure before pleasuring yourself." Olivia stood and began collecting the dirty plates. "Do you want some peaches?" she asked before carrying the pile of dishes into the kitchen.

"That would be nice, thank you, wife."

Why does he refuse to use my name?

Olivia took the bowl of cold, sliced peaches, and whipped cream from the icebox. Dipping her finger into the cold, fluffy cream and sticking it into her mouth to savor, she was certain the investment in the icebox had been well worth it. Olivia spooned peaches into shallow dessert dishes and topped them with the sweetened whipped cream.

At the table, she found a glass filled with white wine awaiting her. "The red is fine with the gumbo, but peaches and cream deserve a more delicate vintage." Devaroe lifted his glass and smiled over the vase of fragrant roses.

Olivia lifted hers in return and drank. She had to admit that his choice of the sweet, white dessert wine paired much better with the peaches and cream's delicate flavors. They sat quietly, enjoying the dessert, and Olivia looked at Devaroe intently. The man was a conundrum. One minute he was a brutal, foul-mouthed thug, and the next, a perfectly refined gentleman of class and taste. She watched him eat the peaches with their sweet cream, savoring his pleasure in the simple treat. She watched him lick the cream from his spoon like a little boy trying to get every last bit of the sweet delight.

He caught her smiling at him and smiled back. "Summer peaches have always been a favorite of mine. My mother's cook whipped cream and sugar together this way to put on top of them." He picked up his glass of wine and drained it. "How much do you anticipate your monthly expenses to be here, Olivia?" he asked, using her name for the first time that day. She liked the way it sounded coming from his lips.

"I can't imagine that food, ice, and household necessities will cost us more than ten dollars. I've already made arrangements with Ben to repaint the house, doors, and shutters. He is going to do that for thirty dollars, including the cost of the paint. He already replaced several roof tiles after the storm." Thinking of Ben reminded her about Blue, and she added, "And keeping my horse and buggy at the livery is four dollars a month."

"Very well, then." He let out a long sigh and pushed back in his chair. "I will have a household account set up for you at the bank and deposit fifty dollars a month into it for your expenses here. That should also cover any unforeseen repairs such as storm-damaged roof tiles."

Olivia was caught off guard for a moment by his generosity.

"Shall we retire to your boudoir now that I may have what is due me as your husband?"

With that, Olivia realized he was not generous at all. He was paying his whore for her services.

Devaroe followed Olivia up the stairs after she'd cleared the table and straightened the kitchen. He had taken that time to have a smoke in the courtyard. From the window over the sink, she had watched him stare up at the rooms of the neighboring townhouses in the quad. Olivia wondered if some of those women were the regulars he'd mentioned earlier in the day, with just the slightest pang of jealousy. She shook her head at the absurdity of it and finished her chores.

In her room, he opened the French doors and stepped out onto the balcony, bathed in the red glow of the setting sun. "This is a nice house, Olivia. I think I am going to be very happy here. It's a short walk to the harbor and my offices there." He came back in and swept her up into his arms. "And it houses a beautiful woman with a tight cunny, a very tight asshole, and a delicious mouth." He bent and kissed her as he pushed the dressing gown off her shoulders.

Olivia could not deny her attraction to this man and his crude desire to tell her those unseemly things. Once again, when their lips met, she got a lightning jolt that caused a tingling across her lips. She could not remember ever feeling that sensation with William.

Am I just imagining that? I know I felt it the first time, just like he did, but did I just imagine it this time?

Devaroe undid the tiny buttons on her camisole with ease and pushed it off her shoulders to flutter to the floor. She did the same with his silk shirt, though he had to undo the cuffs before she could get the garment off his muscular, tanned body. The last rays of the sun cast a brilliant glow over his rippling muscles of his arms, gleaming with a fine sheen of sweat. The long summer days meant longer hours of heat and humidity.

He pulled the ribbon on her bloomers loose, and they fell to puddle on the floor at her feet. She stepped out of them, and he pushed her down onto the bed. She watched him unbutton his trousers and release his erect penis. Olivia swore she could see the veins pulsing in the hard cock, just like the pulsing of the hard button throbbing between her legs. She slid her feet back, bringing her knees up and letting them fall open so he could see her the way she could see him.

"Wife, you entice like the whores in the other town-houses around you." He fell on her then, burying his face in the curve of her neck, biting and sucking hard. Olivia felt her nipples harden and rise against his hot skin. He felt them too and slid down to suck one into his mouth, nipping it with his teeth until she squealed. James brought a hand up to the other nipple and pinched it between thumb and forefinger. The attention to both nipples brought a gushing sensation of pleasure between her thighs, and she longed for him to be in her, but he denied her momentarily while he continued to pinch and suck her nipples.

He traced a finger down her taut belly through the hair above her womanhood and into her. "You are so wet, wife. Just wet enough, I'd bet." He sighed and slid into her so slow she could feel every inch of him stretching her as he wet his erection with her juices. "Oh, yes," he breathed in her ear, and she felt him pull out of her cunny and drop down to her other hole. He shoved into her and moaned with pleasure. "Wife, you have the tightest asshole in all of New Orleans." He pumped into her, and she winced in pain. The wince excited him, and he pushed farther into her, pumping faster and faster with his ballocks bouncing off her ass cheeks.

Olivia looked up at his face. With his dusky blue eyes closed, he smiled and breathed heavily through his aquiline nose. James grabbed her delicate, slim hips and pulled her closer to him as the power of his thrusting pushed her up in the bed and away from him. He opened his eyes and saw her studying his face.

"Shall I finish this in your tight cunny or your pretty pink mouth?" he asked without slowing. "Your cunny." He smiled. "It's too late to get it to your mouth." Without missing a stroke, Devaroe pulled out of her ass and shoved into her throbbing cunny.

Olivia massaged herself in readiness for his release and wrapped her legs around his waist. She pulled herself into his every thrust, luxuriating in the long, hard cock pummeling her to that peak of exquisite pleasure, which, when it came, brought a guttural explosion from her throat as the waves of pleasure pulsed through her groin and her heart pounded.

Her groan of pleasure brought on his release, and he wailed like a wild man, falling on her to nuzzle her ear. "Was that better for you?" he whispered and nibbled at the lobe of her ear. "I let you go first."

"Yes, thank you," Olivia sighed and wrapped her arms around his shoulders, her hands resting on his spine and scratching it in gentle circles with her nails.

"Um, that feels good," he moaned, "don't stop."

She didn't. They lay there together like that for a long time. Olivia watched the sky fade from red to pink, then a deep lavender until finally, stars twinkled in blackness.

"James." She breathed his name and again when he did not respond. "James, I need to use the privy." She pushed at him, and he rolled off her. She pulled herself up, threw her legs over the side of the bed, and stood. She felt his fluid running out of her and slicking the insides of her quivering thighs.

Olivia hurried to the privy closet in the dark and tripped on a pile of clothing. She recognized her dressing gown's feel and bent and picked it up to carry with her to the privy closet. Olivia dipped a washcloth in the water in the washbasin as she sat on the commode chair, first washing the sweat from her face and neck, then attending to the mess between her legs. Her eyes adjusted to the darkness, and when she brought the cloth away from her backside, she didn't see any dark splotches there. No blood this time. She threw the soiled cloth back into the bowl.

Olivia thought about lighting the lamp in the privy closet but did not want to attract mosquitos through the open doors. The damp night air felt nice, and she didn't want to close the doors if she didn't have to. If they didn't light a lamp, maybe the little bloodsuckers would stay outside. The other downside of having the doors open was the occasional whiff of refuse from the muck pits in the alley and the street. She tried to keep their hole coated with lime to manage the smell, but others in the neighborhood did not, and the stench of human waste ruined many a lovely evening on the balconies of Basin Street. The storm's heavy rains had flushed and cleaned the city's streets and alleys, sending the filth to drain into the Gulf and the nearby river.

Crawling back into her bed, Olivia pulled a light coverlet up over her body more to shield it from mosquitoes than for the need of warmth and snuggled in next to a softly snoring James Devaroe. Her feelings for this man perplexed her. Her body yearned for his attentions, but she also experienced revulsion at his crudeness and his delight in rough treatment. He was just so much like her father—perhaps too much.

Olivia refused to allow this man to treat her how her father had treated her mother for all their years together. Had her mother ever enjoyed the attentions of her father in the bedroom? Had they ever been in love? Marie had told her that she'd loved her husband, but Olivia could not fathom how that could have been true. Her parents' marriage, an arrangement between families, had never been a loving one, as far as Olivia could remember. Armand Thibodeaux regularly bedded with slaves and white-trash women of the bayou without regard to her mother's feelings. He kept whores in the city and possibly a mistress or two there also. Then there were his drunken rages and the beatings that followed. Olivia had sworn all her life that she would never be treated that way by a man.

But look at me now. I'm allowing myself to be treated like a common whore by a man with the same brutal proclivities as my father. What kind of fool am I?

She had been so very lucky to find her sweet William. He had been the sort of husband every young girl dreamed of having. He had been educated with gentle manners and put Olivia first in all things. The only real argument they ever had was when he had enlisted. Her fear of losing him had caused her to take on some of her father's mannerisms, and she'd stormed at William for being willing to leave her alone. At his wake, she'd stormed at him again, pounding on his casket with her fists and cursing the war, the Yankees, Jefferson Davis, and William. Georgia had had to dose her with a sleeping potion to calm her, and she had missed the actual burial mass.

Now she lay here in their bed with another man. Devaroe was the only other man to share her bed or her body besides William. He rolled and draped an arm over Olivia's body, pulling her close.

"Come here to me, wife," he whispered before drifting back into sleep.

Olivia snuggled into his body. He smelled of Bay Rum cologne and stale tobacco smoke. He smelled like a man, and Olivia had to admit that she'd missed having a man in her bed. His soft, even breathing lulled her to sleep.

His sucking on her breast woke her. The shadows cast by the building told her the sun had risen, but only just. "Good morning, wife," he whispered, noticing she had opened her eyes. He slid a hand down between her legs and went back to sucking and biting her nipple. His finger found that sensitive knot between her thighs and massaged it, causing her to moan and arch into his touch. Olivia felt his hardness against her thigh and reached over to caress it. He bit down on her nipple, causing her to yelp in pain.

Her reaction excited him, and he sucked and chewed harder. His hand between her thighs explored, and after inserting two fingers without a response, he tried three. She yelped, and he withdrew his hand. "Tell me you want my cock in you," he said as he positioned himself over her body. "Say it," he demanded and pinched her nipple hard.

"I want your cock in me," she said with some reservation.

"Say it as though you actually mean it, wife. I want you

to beg me for it, Olivia. Beg me to put it in all your pretty little holes."

Olivia conceded to his unusual foreplay and found herself in the throes of ecstasy twice. It amazed her, but the combination of the crude talk and his demanding actually excited *her.* Devaroe got up to visit the privy closet, and Olivia rolled on her side, opened the drawer of the bedside table, and rummaged through it. When he returned, she held out her hand to him.

"I have a gift for you." She offered her clenched hand.

"What, another?" He smiled and cupped his hands beneath hers. When Olivia dropped what she concealed, his eyes went wide. "I thought I had irretrievably lost at the bottom of that pond," he gasped, staring at the pearl ring. "How…?" He clenched the lovely pearl ring in his fist and held it to his chest with his eyes closed. Olivia watched his lips moving in a silent prayer of thanks. "I never thought to see this precious family token again in my lifetime. How did you retrieve it?"

Olivia smiled at his joy. "Jimbo, our groom at Sweet Rewards, spent nearly a whole Sunday diving to the bottom of the pond and running his hands through the muck until he found it, along with some silver coins and a fork." She laughed.

"I owe this Jimbo my undying gratitude." He opened his fist and stared at the ring resting on his palm. "And you, of course, wife." He took her hand and positioned the pearl ring to place on her finger when he noted William's ring already there. "I will not remove that," Devaroe told her, crestfallen. "It must mean more to you than this one ever could."

Twisting the tiny gold band on her finger, a wave of pain and grief overcame Olivia, and the sting of tears flooded her eyes.

He's right, of course. William's ring will always mean more. But then, why do I feel so upset that I've disappointed him? James Devaroe will never be able to take William's place in my heart— maybe in my bed, but never in my heart.

Devaroe collected his discarded clothing and dressed in haste. "I will trouble you no more today, Mrs. Montgomery. I will open the household account on Monday. You can retrieve the passbook from Henri at the bank any time after that." He stormed down the stairs, and Olivia heard the door slam as he left the townhouse. Voices on the street below her window and the door's reopening alerted her of Magdalena's return.

"Did that man hurt you again, Livvy?" her sister bellowed up to her. "If he did, the bastard be gettin' some of that special gumbo next time he visits."

Olivia wiped her eyes, wrapped herself in her dressing gown, and went down the stairs in her bare feet. "I am fine, Magda."

"Why are you cryin' then?" Magdalena grabbed Olivia by the chin, turning her head from left to right. "Did he slap you around again?"

"No, he didn't hit me." Olivia went into the kitchen to put water into the pot to boil some coffee. "I gave him his ring back."

"That should have made the bastard happy." She began taking dishes from her basket and returning them to the cabinets.

"It did. It made Mr. Devaroe very happy," Olivia sighed.

"So why are you cryin' like a baby?" she asked and stood her ground until Olivia answered her.

"He wanted to put it back on my finger, but…" Olivia held up her hand with William's ring.

"Oh." Magdalena picked up the basket and carried it

to the storage area's door beneath the stairs, where they kept it. "And did he want to put *his* wedding ring back on?"

Olivia wiped her eyes again and put a smile on her face. "He couldn't have if he'd wanted to. It's still in the drawer of my night table back at Sweet Rewards. How was your evening?"

Magdalena threw her head back, and a broad smile creased her face. "Olivia, our little Ben ain't so little no more."

"I know. He's as big as a house." Olivia saw the mischievous twinkle in her sister's eyes and giggled. "Oh," she said in understanding, "oh, my."

22

A few mornings after Devaroe's visit, Olivia woke to the aroma of frying bacon. The rich, hearty scent usually made Olivia's mouth water with anticipation. Still, that morning it sent her flying into the privy closet to bend over the commode chair and empty her stomach. She knelt over the seat for some time, trying to remember what they'd eaten the night before to bring on such violent heaving.

She finally stood, wiped her mouth and face with a cool cloth, and trudged down the stairs. "I think that gumbo went bad," she said and went to the sink for some water. Magdalena stared at Olivia's blanched face and smiled.

"When was your cycle due, Miss Livvy? That gumbo's been in that icebox since you cooked it, and I smelled it good before heatin' it up last night. I think that mornin' pukes is from something other than bad gumbo. You haven't washed a dirty clout since we left Sweet Rewards."

Thinking back on it, Olivia realized Magda was correct. Her last monthly cycle had been before the party at Sweet Rewards when she'd first met James Devaroe. That was over two months ago. She suddenly felt light-headed and dropped into one of the chairs at the round dining table. "Oh, my God."

"Daddy's going to be mighty happy with you, Liv. If you got a boy in that belly, he'd be shootin' off fireworks over the damned Bayou Tesche."

"Must I remind you, sister, that I don't have a husband any longer? Mother had the marriage annulled."

"So, when that riverboat man of yours comes back to town, drag him down to St. Louis and get married again. Ain't no big deal." Magdalena shrugged her shoulders and forked bacon out of the skillet. "How many eggs you want?"

The thought of runny eggs turned her stomach again, and she ran for the alley door to heave into the offal pit. The odor rising from there only brought on more, and she stood in the alley, braced on the wall, vomiting for almost twenty minutes before returning to the table and resting her head on her arms with a long moan. Magdalena brought her a wet cloth, and she wiped her mouth and face.

"No, weren't no bad gumbo." Magdalena laughed at her sister's obvious discomfort.

"Oh, hush, Magda. When was your last monthly? I haven't seen you washing any clouts, either."

"I started mine last night," she said with a relieved sigh. "No little Jimbos or cane-field niggers in me."

"Well, you better take precautions, or there will be little Bens."

"And what would be so terribly wrong with that?" Magdalena cracked eggs into the hot skillet.

"His mother knows your origins. Do you think she would stand for it?"

"That woman is at death's door," Magdalena said as she walked back into the kitchen to rinse out the cloth. "But Miss Evangeline always liked me. She never treated me any differently than she treated you."

"We were children then, not adults. Do you think she'd be pleased about the possibility of a Negro grandchild? You have a goodly amount of white blood, but any child of yours could still be born dark."

"I know, and I wouldn't do that to Ben," Magdalena sighed, and a tear ran down her cheek. "I almost think I was happier bein' a house nigger sometimes."

"Magda," Olivia took her sister's hand and held it to her lips, "there are plenty of men that have mixed blood in this city. You can find one, and it won't make any difference if a child is born dark-skinned with nappy hair."

Someone tapped on the glass of the front door, and they looked up to see Ben's smiling face at the window. Magdalena jumped up, wiped her eyes, and fled back into the kitchen. Olivia opened the door, and Ben came bounding through in his overalls, and a faded blue cotton shirt with the sleeves rolled up over his bulging biceps.

"Smells good in here. Is breakfast ready?"

"We have bacon, hard-fried eggs, biscuits, and coffee," Magdalena called from the kitchen. "Livvy, can you get the butter, cream, and jam out of the icebox while I dish this all up?"

Olivia went to the icebox and took out the cold items, hoping her stomach would not decide to burst forth again when she smelled the contents of the icebox. The spicy aroma of the leftover gumbo wafted up to her nose, along with that of the raw catfish, but thankfully, her stomach remained calm.

"Liv, I was wondering if you'd decided on the colors you want for the paint. I'd like to go down and get it mixed. We should have a few nice clear days, and I thought I'd get started." Ben took a seat at the table, and Magdalena brought in cups and the steaming coffee pot. She sat the hot pot on a pad and whipped around back into the kitchen without looking Ben in the face. Olivia watched his eyes, full of hurt, follow her as she sped away.

"I think I want to stay with the butter-yellow for the body of the house," Olivia told him as she poured their coffee, "but I want to change the doors and shutters from green to blue that matches the slate tiles on the roof."

"That's a good idea. It will give the place a fresh look. I've been scraping the shutters, and they were blue at one time. I peeled off a few layers and saw some blue." He leaned into Olivia. "Is Magda alright? Did I do something to upset her?" he whispered with a worried look on his broad face.

Olivia shook her head and turned to smile at her sister, who carried in plates filled with food for the three of them. "I think we'll keep the balcony rails black. What do you think, Magda?"

"They wouldn't look right anything but black. Maybe if we were painting the house blue, I'd say white for the railings, but with yellow, they have to be black."

"I agree," Ben said, digging into his eggs after buttering his biscuits and smearing them with jam.

Someone knocked on the French doors. One of them pushed open, and Nell popped in her pretty blonde head. "Good morning. I thought I saw Ben coming up the walk." She smiled at the big man, which earned her a withering glance from Magdalena. "He told me y'all were going to be repainting your place. I think I want to have mine done, too. What colors are you doing this one?" Olivia told her their choices, and Nell smiled. That sounds lovely, but I think I want to go with a pastel orange like the color of a conch shell with white shutters and ironwork. The slates on my roof are such a light gray, they look white, and I have all those pots of orange lilies."

"Doesn't your landlord have something to say about all that?" Magdalena asked the thin young woman dressed in her usual pink attire.

"That old skin-flint doesn't care what we do as long as we pay for it." Nell stepped completely into the room and shut the door. "Did I see James Devaroe here the other evening?" she asked Olivia.

"Yes, he's a friend of my father's. Do you know him well?" Olivia stabbed a bit of egg with enough force to scoot her plate on the table. She glanced up at Magdalena, who had a smirk on her face as she chewed.

"He's a business acquaintance," Nell told her with a nervous grin. "Ben, if you'll drop by later, we can work out the particulars. You might want to stop over at Sally's, too. I think she wants some painting done inside." Nell opened the door and slipped out as quickly as she'd come.

"Do the girls pay well for your services, Ben?" Magdalena teased him bitterly.

"Magda, I've been doin' little chores around here for some time now. As Nell said, that bastard who bought up the places don't want to spend a penny on them. If the girls want the places kept up, they have to pay for it, and then he wants their rent and a little extra, as well. If you know what I mean?" He blushed, and Olivia had to choke back a giggle.

"Oh, I know exactly what you mean, Ben Benoit," Magdalena snapped and dropped the coffee pot onto the table.

"The girls pay what I ask," he said, still blushing, "and I never ask for anything extra."

"That's good, Ben." Olivia smiled at him. "We understand."

"It's just that since Papa died, we need the extra money to pay for Mama's medicines. I give my aunt a little every month for her upkeep too."

"I'm sorry. Is your mama much worse?" Olivia asked, thinking about her own sick mother.

"My aunt says the doctors are not hopeful of a recovery. At least she's finally seeing a doctor now, though." He sighed as he filled his cup with coffee. "She suffered another apoplexy and cannot leave her bed. She's ready to join Papa, I think," he said sadly and drained his coffee cup. He stood, walked to Magdalena, and kissed her cheek before going out the French doors into the sunny courtyard where Nell stood with some of the other women.

"Damn that little blonde bitch and her pots of orange flowers," Magdalena growled and pulled her napkin from her lap to throw it onto her empty plate. "And don't you go laughin' at me, Olivia Thibodeaux. I saw the color drain from your lily-white cheeks when Miss Nell said Devaroe was a *business acquaintance*. Your ears were blowin' out steam like that coffee pot just off the stove."

Olivia stuck her tongue out at her sister and collected plates from the table. "We should walk down to the bank on Lafayette and see if Devaroe opened an account for us. I don't know about you, but I could use some fresh air."

"What fresh air?" Magdalena huffed.

They washed, dried, and put away the dishes before changing into respectable suits to wear, strolling out into the city. The thick, stagnant air in New Orleans sent most people who could afford it out to Grande Isle or into the cooler, less crowded bayous where the fears of cholera and yellow fever did not haunt them.

The miasma of stinking filth in the streets and the

byproducts of hundreds crowded together in close quarters did not make for pleasant summer living in the city. Olivia longed for the cooler months to come when the sun would shine and soft breezes would blow in off the Gulf without the fears of thunderous storms. On those days, she could leave her doors open without being plagued by flies and mosquitoes or sit in the courtyard and read. Those lazy days of fall and early winter were her favorites.

At the old bank building on Lafayette Street, the elderly banker told Olivia her husband, James Devaroe, had opened a household account for her to draw funds. Olivia withdrew thirty dollars to pay Ben for the painting and another fifty from her other account to have in her bag.

"I will change the name on this account from Montgomery," he told her with a smile, "to Devaroe. I did not realize you and Mr. Devaroe had wed until he informed me of it. Congratulations, James Devaroe, is a good customer of the bank. It is a shame about his losses in the storm. Though I'm happy to say, his surety company has already paid off his ships' outstanding loans, however. We are happy to be able to write new ones for the rebuilding of his fleet."

Olivia smiled at the old man for his compliments and left the building.

"Well," Magdalena said with a giggle, "Mrs. Devaroe, how long before you start receiving visitors? I am sure all the fine ladies of New Orleans will want to come by and offer their heartfelt congratulations on your nuptials with the fine Mr. James Devaroe."

"Oh, hush, Magda." Olivia grimaced as her belly began to roil once more. She took a deep breath and continued toward the townhouse, where Ben busied himself with scraping paint from the window sills, doors, and shutters to prepare for the new paint. "When we get home, I am going to make some lemonade. We still have some lemons, don't we?"

"There's a whole bag full in the pantry. Lemonade sounds good. I'll be glad when this summer is over and done. It's been a frightful hot one so far." Magdalena waved up at Ben with a coy smile before going into the house.

Olivia went upstairs, opened the doors, and stepped out onto the balcony where Ben sweated over his labors. She opened her bag, took out thirty dollars, and handed the bills to the big blond man. "Here's the money for the painting, Ben."

"Thank you, Olivia. Most won't pay until I've finished the job." He pocketed the money and went back to his scraping. "Is everything alright with Magda? She was real quiet this morning."

"It's nothing you did, Ben. It's just some female concerns." Olivia smiled and went back into her room.

"Is she with child?" Ben asked, startling her.

"No, she's not pregnant. We were just discussing what she might do if that should happen."

"I'd marry her, Olivia. I love Magda. I always have." Ben wiped the sweat from his forehead with a paint-stained kerchief.

"I know that Ben and she feels the same," Olivia assured him, "but there are other things to think about there. Even though you are very fair-skinned, any child she might conceive with you could be born dark like her mother and grandmother. Just because you are both fair-complected does not guarantee a fair-skinned child. She does not want to cause you any embarrassment. There is also the worry that if people found Magdalena to be colored and passing herself off as white, she could be whipped or worse. *Charivari* can be very nasty and even deadly. She might just get a public whipping, but a mob of angry people might even lynch her for it."

"I've been thinkin' on that, and I think we just might move out to St. Martinsville. I hear folks out there don't hold with that nonsense. We could live there as man and wife without worry."

"We were thinking of your mother, Ben. What would she say about you marrying a Negress?" Olivia watched his face cloud, thinking of his ailing mother.

"Mama has always known how I feel about Magda. We have discussed it, and she told me to follow my heart. Life is too short to live by other people's rules about who can love who. She has always loved Magda the same as she loves you."

"Are you going to ask Magda to marry then?" Joy for her sister flooded her heart. Olivia studied Ben, and pride swelled in her breast for the brave young man who was willing to buck the system for the woman he loved and move away to a place he didn't know so he could be with her. She could see why William wanted to look after him during the war.

"Her birthday is next month. I'm going to ask her then." Ben smiled and went back to the balcony and his work.

🌿 23 🌿

Bouts of morning sickness continued to plague Olivia for the next few weeks, and she worried that she was losing weight because of it.

"Look at this," she complained to Magdalena one morning when the dress she chose hung on her loosely, "I look like a scarecrow in a bean patch."

"I wouldn't worry none about that. In a few months, you're going to look like you *ate* the bean patch." Magdalena laughed as she poured Olivia some tea to have with her dry biscuit, the only thing she could generally tolerate in the mornings.

Though Olivia had not had a monthly, she had begun to wonder if this was pregnancy or some summer malady like malaria or yellow fever.

"You got no fever, Livvy," Magdalena grimaced when Olivia brought up these alternatives. "What you got is a baby in your belly. It's been almost three months. It'll be passin' pretty soon. When is that riverboat man husband of yours 's'pose to be back in town?"

"It's been over a month," Olivia sighed. "I suspect he'll

be back down here any time." For the past two weeks, Olivia had run through her mind, over and over again, how she was going to tell James Devaroe she carried his child. A letter from her mother had arrived the week after the morning heaves' onset, confirming their marriage annulment.

What if he no longer wants to have me as his wife? What if the lure of Sweet Rewards is no longer enough to tempt him? What if my continuing to wear William's ring was too much of an insult to him? All these things plagued Olivia at night in her bed, chasing sleep away.

The weak scrawl of her mother's once beautiful flowery handwriting also worried her. In her letter, Marie Thibodeaux assured her daughter that she was well and overseeing the household as usual, though Olivia seriously doubted it.

"Magda, I'm going to go up and take a nap. I didn't sleep well last night with the heat."

"*Mais oui, Cherie,*" Magdalena said and cleared away the teacup and saucer from the table, "go and rest. I am heating water for the wash. Just toss your dirty things down the stairs."

Olivia trudged up the stairs, each foot heavier with every step. Fatigued in the stifling heat that hung like a damp blanket over them, she scooped up her dirty laundry from its basket and pitched it down the stairs. Olivia stood for a few moments in front of the open doors hoping to catch even a little breeze, but there was none. She crumpled onto the bed, using her toes to pull her slippers off by the heels. Pulling her knees up into a fetal position, Olivia drifted off into fitful sleep.

In the maze of chaotic dreams, Devaroe argued with her. He accused her of lying about her child's paternity, claiming it must be the child of Simon Montrose and not his at all. He yelled at her, and then he spoke softly, lovingly even. Then, the sting of his slaps on her face made her cry out in pain and humiliation. She saw his beautiful ring on her finger again, and then in her dream, he pulled it from her finger, yelling at her and slapping her again. Tears ran from her eyes.

Olivia woke with someone shaking her by the shoulders. She opened her eyes to see James Devaroe bending over her. He pulled her close and held her to him. "Olivia, my darling, Magdalena told me the wonderful news. We are going to have a child?" He wrapped his big arms around her and hugged her tight.

"Did she tell you everything?" Olivia asked, pushing back from him to look into his eyes. "Did she tell you the priest annulled the marriage?"

"Yes, yes, but that's of no consequence. We can go to see the priest at St. Louis Neuf Cathedral this very afternoon. You are my wife, Olivia." He lifted her hand. In place of William's gold band, she now beheld the pearl ring with its two little yellow diamonds. He must have exchanged them while she slept and dreamed.

"Come now." He pulled her up from the bed. "Dress in something pretty, and we shall go see the priest and make this completely official." He looked over his shoulder to Magdalena. "You as well, *cousin*. You know she will want to have her family there as a witness."

The lavender silk Josephine dress remained at Sweet Rewards, so Olivia opted for a red satin gown she'd worn for last Christmas's festivities. The sleeves were long, but the red with her raven hair shone exquisitely. The bodice shimmered with glass beads of red and gold, the high collar and cuffs were trimmed with red French lace dusted with gold along its scalloped edges.

Magdalena emerged in her green suit that set off the

green of her eyes, and Olivia handed her the jade ring. "Ben is coming too," she told them as she slipped the ring onto her right hand. "He just ran down to his apartment to change." The broad-shouldered blond had been working on the shutters outside Magdalena's room when the impromptu wedding was announced and invited himself to come along with Magdalena.

Olivia bent in to whisper to Devaroe, who frowned at the delay. "I think he's going to propose."

Devaroe screwed up his face in dismay. "You can't be serious. Does he know she's a Negress?"

"Of course he knows," Olivia said, grimacing, and led him out into the courtyard where they could speak more freely. "We all grew up together here. He's been in love with Magda since we were children."

"I don't know that I can condone this," he said with a shake of his dark head. "It's against the law and, I believe, against God."

"And the great James Devaroe has never done anything against the law," Olivia demanded and gestured toward the other townhouses that housed the prostitutes, "or against God? Anyhow, Governor Kellogg has changed all those old laws against inter-racial marriage here in Louisiana."

"But we could be disgraced if it ever became known that we participated in this fraud."

"For God's sake, James, you pirated vessels on the high seas and probably committed murder. You own a business. Tell me you've never committed fraud. How many of those old tubs sunk there in the harbor were insured for more than they were worth?" Olivia stormed with a scowl on her pale face.

"Very well, wife." He cleared his throat and attempted to sound gruff. "You are a shrewd negotiator. I will keep this confidence for you." He kissed her forehead and patted her belly. "I do not want to see you lynched by a mob of Democrats with our son in there." They walked back inside hand-in-hand.

Olivia smiled as they sat on the settee together, awaiting Ben's arrival. Abruptly Devaroe stood and moved toward the stairs. "I need to use your privy closet," he said and bounded up the stairs, passing Magdalena on her way down.

"Where is he goin' in such an all-fired hurry?" she asked, straightening her jacket he'd pulled on his way past her on the narrow stairs.

"Privy," Olivia answered. "I think he might be nervous."

Magdalena answered the door when Ben tapped, and she squealed when he pulled her out to join him on the sidewalk. Devaroe came back down the stairs and was about to push the door closed when they heard a loud, shrill scream from outside.

"Yes, yes, yes," they heard Magdalena shrieking.

"I guess he did it," Devaroe said, but he was not smiling.

"James, if you're not comfortable with this, we can do it another time, or not at all." Olivia sighed. "I don't think I want to be married to a man who has such leanings toward the White League."

"I am not White League," he protested, "but I am a Democrat, and the whole idea of a good white man marrying a Negress rubs me the wrong way."

"Look at her, James; she's whiter than you are."

"It's not the shade of her skin, wife. It's her blood. You cannot deny her blood is Negro, and any child they may have will be Negro because of the blood, and I can't countenance it."

Olivia looked at him in shock. Without hesitating, she

pulled his ring from her finger and handed it to him on her way back up to her room. "Get out of my house, James Devaroe, and don't you ever come back."

She heard him following but continued up. "Here," he said coldly. Olivia turned, and he held out William's band to her. "I was going to give this to Ben to use. I didn't think you'd mind." He dropped the ring on the stair at her feet, turned, and left. She heard the door slam and came close to following after him but did not. She bent, picked up the ring, and held it in her hand tightly as hot tears coursed down her cheeks.

Magdalena and Ben came into the townhouse together, grinning. "Where is *your* man going, Olivia?" Magdalena asked. "I thought we were going to the church."

Olivia wiped tears from her face with her red sleeve and came back down the stairs. "There will be no wedding between that man and me today or any other."

"What the hell happened now? He was pleased as could be when I told him about the baby. What did you do to change his mind?" Magdalena demanded.

"He didn't think it was his. Did he?" Olivia asked, remembering snippets of harsh words from her dreams.

"Did he say that to you? I told him he was ridiculous even thinking such a fool thing."

"It's of no consequence now, Magda," Olivia told her sister and went to Ben. "I'm happy for the two of you, though. You should go to the church." She reached up with the pretense of an innocent kiss of congratulations on his cheek but whispered in his ear and slipped the gold band into his hand.

"Off with you now, go to the church and make this official." Olivia hugged her sister tightly. This would mean losing Magdalena for good. Since childhood, they had been together, only separated while Olivia attended finishing school in New Orleans in her early teens before meeting William and marrying late in her fifteenth year. Then Magdalena had come to live with them here. Now she would marry and move in with Ben. Her sister, her companion, her friend would be gone from her side.

Feeling light-headed at the thought, Olivia sat. She leaned back on the settee and waved goodbye to Magdalena and Ben as they went out the door, both wearing broad smiles. In her heart, she wished them well but found herself overwhelmed with grief and loss. Suddenly a fluttering in her midsection caught her by surprise.

Is it gas or something I ate? The fluttering came again, and she put a hand over her lower abdomen, realizing with a start that it must be the babe rolling around in there. *He's telling me to think about him. He's here. He won't be leaving me, not for a good long time.* Tears filled her eyes. *I have more than just myself to think of now.* Olivia clutched at her abdomen, and the light fluttering occurred again.

"Very well, child," Olivia cooed. "I will begin thinking of your needs over my own." She stood again and went to the kitchen, where she poured a glass of milk from the icebox. Olivia drank it down, rinsed the glass, and went up to her room, where she changed out of the red dress and into a comfortable, cooler day dress.

Out on the sidewalk, she looked up at the townhouse's façade, scraped by Ben of loose and flaking paint. In her mind's eye, Olivia saw it with the warm butter-yellow paint and slate-blue shutters and doors soon to come.

But will this be a good place to raise a child? Olivia could hear the raucous laughter of drunken men from the tavern down the block and a carriage splashed stinking filth onto her skirt as it passed. The laughter of whores drifted down from the balcony of the townhouse next door. *No, this is no place to raise a child. Should I return to Sweet Rewards then? It is a place where a child can run and play without the filth of sewers, drunks, and whores at least.*

Olivia felt the flutter in her belly once again and reached for it protectively. *Very well, child, we will return to Sweet Rewards. Perhaps your Grandmama will want to live long enough to hold you in her arms.* She shook the muck from her skirt and returned inside.

❧ 24 ❧

"What do you mean you're going home?" Magdalena demanded as she stood watching Olivia pack her cases. "I thought you wanted to get away from that damned place for good."

"I did, Magda," Olivia said and raised her hand to her abdomen, "but I have another to consider now." She rested a hand over her belly protectively. "Can I raise a child in a house surrounded by nothing but filth, drunks, and whores? At Sweet Rewards, he will have room to run and play, at least. And possibly, with a grandchild to look forward to, Mother will hang onto life a little longer. I want to be able to put a grandchild into her arms before she passes from this world." Olivia's voice choked with a sob, and she allowed the tears that had been welling in her eyes to fall. "Daddy will be pleased."

"And if it's not a boy," Magdalena said with a frown, "what will he go and do if that child in your belly comes out a girl?"

Olivia had considered that. If the child were a boy, she knew her father would embrace it with joy, but she did not know what his reaction would be if it were a girl. He might send them both back to New Orleans, his disgraced daughter, and her bastard child. With no husband to explain the existence of the child, Olivia would be a burden. He would not be able to procure her a husband of genteel birth. Olivia imagined he would name one of her cousins his heir and be done with her and her bastard girl-child. A boy, he would legitimize with his condoning their betrothal premarriage sex, but Olivia did not think he would do the same for a girl.

It was a chance she would have to take. If she bore a girl and her father denied her, she would have no choice but to return to the townhouse. Perhaps she could sell the place to the other houses' owner and find something in a better part of town. If it were not for the hope of allowing her mother the joy of a grandchild, Olivia would do just that now and stay in the city.

"I have a plan if that happens," Olivia said and told her sister about the idea of selling the townhouse and relocating to a better part of the city. "I still want you and Ben to move in here, though. It's going to be months before we have to face that." Olivia folded the last of her things into the case and closed it. "You're gonna have to sit on this one, too," she laughed, "so I can buckle it."

"This is most certainly better than Ben's room over the livery," Magdalena said as she moved to sit on the bulging case. "If me and Ben have a babe, we couldn't stay up there. It hardly has enough room for the two of us as it is. I can have Ben make some inquiries about selling to that Matisse fella. Ben knows him and can negotiate a good price when the time comes. We are talkin' on movin' out to St. Martinsville anyhow."

"That's a good idea, but don't get ahead of things. If I have a boy, I'll be staying at Sweet Rewards. If it's a girl,

I'll get word to you, and then he can begin negotiations for the sale. I'll be in childbed for a while after the birth before I can travel anyhow."

"What about that riverboat man of yours?" Magdalena asked as they carried bags down the stairs to where Ben waited to pack them into her buggy. "What do you want me to say if he comes round askin' after you and the babe?"

"I seriously doubt James Devaroe will be coming back around looking for me." Olivia had gone to her bank and found that Devaroe had closed the household account he'd opened for her. "He does not care about anything for his child or me. You can tell him whatever you like. He won't have the gall to show his face at Sweet Rewards after running out on me the way he did. Daddy, if he gets his heir, would pepper his ass with lead. The other we'll deal with when we must."

"Be careful, Liv." Magdalena hugged her in the predawn glow. "People in this city are goin' damned crazy now. Ben said he heard the White League is gatherin' troops out on Iberville Road to march in and throw Governor Kellogg out of the office and put that Democrat nigger-hater into the State House in his place. You take the long way round to get out of town to avoid that lot."

"I'm not worried, Magda. Kellogg has his Black Militia to guard him and the city. President Grant isn't going to let the Democrats and their White League take Louisiana."

The dawn was just breaking in the East as Olivia set Blue on the road north out of New Orleans and toward Sweet Rewards. She had no idea what her reception would be when she got there, but Olivia knew she needed to do this for the child growing inside her. Getting out of the city now would be a good thing with the political tensions mounting between the Republican Governor Kellogg and the Democrats who wanted to put their own man in office who would stop the freedoms being allowed Negroes by Kellogg's administration. The Democrats blamed the last Republican governor for giving the Negroes the vote and signing them up as Republicans to get Kellogg into office in the first place. They claimed their man was the rightful governor because they didn't recognize the Negro votes.

She passed through a few roadblocks on her way out of the city, but things went smoothly once she was well north of town. The last of the summer heat made an appearance, and Olivia began to sweat under the jacket of her traveling suit by early afternoon. The days had begun to shorten, but she was determined to make it to Sweet Rewards that night. Ben had mounted a lamp on the buggy so she could light it and travel after sunset if she must. Olivia remembered the theft of their goods at the King's Inn on their way to New Orleans and did not intend to have a reoccurrence by stopping there.

She came very close to pulling into the horrible place for a bite of food when she and Blue came to it, but she thought better of it as she saw the sun was beginning to dip lower on the horizon. Instead, she snapped the reins and set Blue at a faster pace. Olivia had only been away for a short of three months but had almost forgotten how wonderful the air smelled outside the city. She breathed deeply and enjoyed the sight of the leaves beginning to change colors on the oaks, maples, and sweetgums. Deer crossed her path a few times, and the chirping of birds in the hedges reminded her that she was back in the swamps.

A few miles past the inn, a group of men stopped her progress with barrels blocking the road. Olivia pulled Blue to a halt and waited for a man in a tattered waistcoat and straw hat, who barked orders as if he were the leader of this motley assortment, to walk up to the buggy.

"What you doin' out here on the road so late, Miss?" he asked and eyed the cases stacked in the back with interest.

"I am on my way home to Sweet Rewards," she told him bluntly.

He eyed her closely then and took hold of Blue's bridle. "You that daughter of Armand Thibodeaux's who killed Simon Montrose and his daddy?" he asked as he walked closer to the buggy, running a hand along Blue's sweaty flank.

"I did not kill Simon's father," Olivia answered, irritated by the man's impertinence. "Mr. Montrose died of an unfortunate heart attack at my wedding."

"But you admit to killing Simon?" he asked with a sneer. "You killed him because you're a nigger-lover is what we heared." He tilted his head toward the others manning the barricades. Then he had his hands on her, pulling her down from the buggy onto the red gravel of the road.

"Get your hands off me, sir," Olivia demanded and jerked loose from his grasp while the others looked on, twittering with laughter. She could smell liquor on the man's breath and suspected the whole group had spent the day passing around a jug or two.

"You gonna let that bitch by, Mason?" one of the others said, laughing. "Why don't we make her pay a toll to pass?" Olivia heard them hooting their ideas about what the toll should be and shivered. "I say we make her show us her bosoms and let us all have a little taste of those sugar-sweet things."

Olivia heard them all laughing uproariously as the leader, Mason, grabbed her again and ripped open her jacket and blouse. "I think that's a good idea." He laughed and reached around to pinch her tender nipples with both hands. "Line up, fellas, for a taste of our *sweet reward* here."

They rushed around and over the barrels to get to Olivia and her exposed breasts. She squirmed to get out of Mason's grasp, but he held tight. Soon her breasts were being assaulted by the group. First one, then another sucked into his mouth a nipple of one breast and then the other while pinching the one he did not have in his mouth.

From behind her, Mason loosed his grasp and lifted her skirt. Olivia tried to kick at him as he tore her bloomers off and threw them over her head to his cheering cohorts. She had felt his erection through her clothing and now feared what his intentions for her were.

"We gonna get a taste of that too, Mason?" one of them called. "Just bend her over one of these barrels, and we can use her mouth too. No sense lettin' it all go to waste." Olivia felt them begin dragging her toward the barricade, hooting and laughing. She screamed and struggled, kicking at the closest men.

"Let me go, you ignorant, filthy swamp trash," Olivia yelled and bit into the ear of one of the attackers, drawing blood and a scream of pain.

"Son-of-a-bitch," he yelled. "The bitch just bit my ear off." He backhanded her, and Olivia saw bright pinpoints of light before her eyes. "That's what you do to a mare that bites," he said angrily and hit her again. Olivia sagged with the blow.

From behind, there came the loud blast from a firearm, and she was dropped to the ground as the men let her go to turn and see who'd fired the shot.

"Gentlemen, that's no way to treat a lady," Olivia heard a male voice saying as she fell to her knees in the rough gravel. Though she was addled and dazed with shock, pain, and embarrassment, Olivia thought she recognized the voice of James Devaroe. Another blast from his gun sent the offending men scurrying for the hedges. "Wait a minute," he yelled to them, "move these barrels so we can pass."

"Aw, come on, friend," one of them whined. "We'll let you have a taste too. What's this pampered little cunny to you? We can all have a little of that sweet plantation-bred stuff."

Olivia heard another shot and the splintering of wood in the hedgerow. "The pampered little cunny just happens to be my wife, sir," she heard Devaroe say before she fell in a relieved faint to the gravel roadway.

She woke with her head resting on Devaroe's shoulder as they bounced along in the buggy down the road in the waning daylight. He pulled Blue to a halt when she lifted her head.

"I think we're probably clear of them now," he told her and got out of the buggy to light the lantern. "What in hell's name put the idea in your fool head to travel on the day the whole state was about to erupt into warfare?" he scolded her. "If I hadn't stopped by the townhouse to make certain you were alright and heard from Ben that you'd taken off for Sweet Rewards, God only knows what that lot would have done with you. I'm certain using your body for their pleasure would have been the least of it." He climbed back into the buggy and handed her the torn remnants of her jacket and blouse. "Do you honestly think they'd have left the daughter of Armand Thibodeaux alive to run home telling tales?"

With the realization of the situation, from which she'd just been rescued, Olivia broke down sobbing bitterly and clutching at the abdomen that housed her child. He left her that way for a while before finally wrapping an arm around her shoulders once more and pulling her close.

"Hush now, wife. You are safe, and I will see you safely home to your parents." That statement sent her into even more bitter sobbing. He stopped the buggy again. "Olivia, quiet yourself now. This caterwauling cannot be good for the child."

"What?" She sobbed. "What do you care about this child? You left us without support or care."

"I left you because you told me to go," he said sternly. "As for the support," he continued, urging Blue on once again along the dark track, "my banker insisted you had plenty in your private account to more than care for you and the child's needs for the time being."

"And it was fine with you that your child would be born in that part of town, surrounded by filth, drunks, and whores?"

"You are the one who chose the accommodations, wife. Not I."

"I am no longer your wife."

"As I told you before, when you first accepted my ring and accepted me into your bed as your betrothed, you became my wife in the eyes of God and the Church of Rome. I need no papers signed by magistrates or priests to claim you as a wife or this child as my legitimate heir."

"And if the child is only a girl and not a male heir?" She sobbed again. "Will you be like my father and treat her as a second-best prize?"

"I am not your father, Olivia. I will cherish a daughter just as I cherish her mother."

Olivia had no words to return and sat beside him quietly for the next two hours until they turned into the wide, tree-lined lane leading up to the mansion house of Sweet Rewards.

"Magdalena told me your mother is ill," he said as they neared the darkened house. "I'm sure she'll be happy to see you and hear our happy news."

"I am hoping it will give her a reason to hang on a little

longer," Olivia said softly. "I want to put a grandchild into her arms before she passes."

"That would be a fine thing," he agreed and pulled the buggy to a halt before the wide porch with its tall white columns. "I see the light within," he told her and jumped down to bound up the stairs and knock on the door with its brass knocker.

❧ 25 ❧

"You are what?" asked Marie Thibodeaux of her daughter after being awakened by the noise in the foyer that brought her from her bed.

"I'm pregnant, Mother. I suspect the babe will come sometime in March if my approximations are correct, and I conceived on our betrothal night."

"Is that why you came back here? I wanted you to get away from here and have a good life in the city. I thought that was what you wanted as well, *Cherie.*"

"It was, Mother," Olivia said to her pale mother and laid a hand on her abdomen. "But I have another to think of now. I could not raise my child there. The neighborhood is not as it once was."

"So Georgia tells me. Magdalena has written. I had no idea things had changed so desperately."

"Yes, and with the political unrest, I thought it would be prudent to come back here now."

Marie touched the bruises on her daughter's face and frowned. "Perhaps not as prudent as you thought, *Nez pas?*"

"Perhaps not." She laughed weakly. "If it hadn't been for James..." Olivia closed her eyes and shuddered.

"Yes, we owe him for so very much." She smiled and patted her daughter's hand. "Your father is going to be so very pleased with this happy news."

"What happy news?" Armand Thibodeaux huffed as he came into the parlor, followed by James. "That this fool girl decided to come home for a visit when the State of Louisiana is about to declare war upon itself?"

"No, Armand." Marie silenced him with a smile. "The happy news is that you are going to be a grandfather."

"What?" he asked with his eyes wide and his brow furrowed in surprise.

"Yes, Father," Olivia said, looking past her father to Devaroe. "I am with child. I wanted to get out of the city *before* it exploded."

"And almost got yourself defiled and killed by Jerome Mason and his ridiculous crew of White Leaguers," her father growled. "I'll see that fool bastard and his lot hung for it."

"I'm fine, Father. There is no sense in muddying the waters when you know for a fact that all these fools out here will side with him. They are all afraid the Republicans are giving the Negroes too much power and that they'll have their throats slit in the middle of the night by their former slaves. Just let it go. James had them running with their tails tucked like whipped pups as it was."

Armand turned and slapped James Devaroe on the back with a broad smile on his scarred face. "Yes, it sounds like he certainly did, but I can still make life very hard for Mason and his pack of pups. We own a goodly portion of the banking company's shares, holding the mortgages on all their pitiful little farms. It will be a cold day in Hell before any of them get another extension of credit, and I will personally be presenting the eviction notices when any of them misses a payment." He gave Devaroe a sly smile. "Some of those properties border Sweet Rewards. If I buy up the paper on their loans, we can extend our holdings here some."

"My wife has a little money, Armand." Devaroe smiled. "Why don't you let her buy it up and serve the evictions?"

"Where would Olivia have gotten that kind of money?" Armand demanded. Olivia frowned at her unborn child's father and glanced toward her mother with a slight shake of her head.

"Where else would she get it? I gave it to her as a wedding gift," Devaroe said.

"Of course you did," Armand said, slapping him on his back again.

"Cherie," Marie said with a relieved sigh, "I must get back to my bed." She rose, and Olivia noted how weak her mother was. Armand put a supporting arm around his wife's waist, and Olivia was surprised to see what looked like an actual loving concern in her father's eyes.

Olivia took her husband's hand and led him to the stairs. "Are you ready to retire, husband?" she asked and squeezed his hand.

"Are you inviting me to join you in your chamber?" he asked her seriously as he followed. Halfway up the stairs, he stopped her. "Olivia, I will respect your wishes. If you do not want to continue with this marriage, I will not force the issue." He reached a hand to touch her belly. "But this is my child, and I will love and care for it as I promise to love and care for you."

Olivia laid a hand over his. "You have never uttered the word love to me before, James." She continued up the stairs. "I lust for you, that I do not deny, James, but I can't honestly say that I love you. Not like the love I had for

William. I can't promise you that I ever will, but I will do my very best to be a good wife to you and a good mother to your children."

"Children?" he said quizzically.

Olivia smiled up into his face. "When Georgia examined me after we arrived and listened to my womb to make certain the attack had not injured the child…" She took a deep breath before continuing. "She is fairly certain she heard two heartbeats with her glass and says my womb is larger than it would normally be at this stage of pregnancy. She is certain I am carrying twins."

"Twins?" he gasped. "Twins!" James Devaroe swept her up in his arms and crushed her to him, kissing her passionately. "Yes, wife, I love you. I love you all." He beamed and pressed his hands to her belly. Together Mr. and Mrs. James Eduard Devaroe retired to their chamber on the second floor of the mansion house of Sweet Rewards to enjoy their joyous news and enjoy one another.

Dear reader,

We hope you enjoyed reading *Sweet Rewards*. Please take a moment to leave a review, even if it's a short one. Your opinion is important to us.

Discover more books by Lori Beasley Bradley at
   https://www.nextchapter.pub/authors/lori-beasley-bradley

Want to know when one of our books is free or discounted? Join the newsletter at
   http://eepurl.com/bqqB3H

Best regards,

Lori Beasley Bradley and the Next Chapter Team

ACKNOWLEDGMENTS

I'd like to thank Adam Sterling for pushing me to write a romance. I set in the Historic South where I'm more comfortable, but here it is. I know it's not the 'Classic Romance,' but I attempted to keep the story in tune with the times. Racial bias in the post-war deep south was rampant, and women had no rights, and women of color had even fewer. I wanted to write a story about two sisters separated by race but who loved one another despite it. Forgive me for the use of the 'N' word, but there wasn't much political correctness in the Jim Crow South, and I wanted the story to be true to the time.

Thank you to my critique group at HobNob's in Phoenix, The Central Phoenix Writers' Workshop. You guys have taught me so much!

Thanks to Wikipedia for all the historic fact-checking. I'd be lost without you.

Lightning Source UK Ltd.
Milton Keynes UK
UKHW022001030521
383075UK00003B/508

THE [...]
GUID[...]
LEARNING
MARTIAL ARTS

CAROL ANNE STRANGE

JANUS PUBLISHING COMPANY
London, England

First published by Castle of Dreams Books in 1997 as
'Starting Out in Martial Arts' by Carol Anne Strange

This edition first published in Great Britain 1998
by Janus Publishing Company Limited,
Edinburgh House, 19 Nassau Street,
London W1N 7RE

www.januspublishing.co.uk

Cover Illustration of Mark Strange © Ellen Fincher
Other Photo Illustrations © Paul Banister

**A CIP catalogue record for this book
is available from the British Library.**

ISBN 1 85756 384 0

Phototypeset in 11.5 on 15 Sabon and Frutiger
by Keyboard Services, Luton, Beds

Cover design Creative Line

Printed and bound in Great Britain by
Antony Rowe Ltd, Chippenham, Wiltshire

CONTENTS

CONTENTS

ACKNOWLEDGMENTS

Many thanks to all those who have provided quotes, information or practical assistance in the production of this book. Special thanks to my brother Mark Strange for providing technical advice, to my SG for guidance, to my family and friends (especially my children Jason and Stephanie) for their interest and understanding and to my partner Paul Banister for his love, support and encouragement.

DEDICATION

For my brother, Sifu Mark Strange – A tribute to his dedication and martial spirit – and to those who made the way difficult and, in so doing, gave us the strength to achieve our goals. Thank you!

PREFACE

Martial arts is one of the fastest growing participation sports and leisure activities in the world today and appeals to men, women and children of all ages, abilities and from all backgrounds. Ask around friends and work colleagues and you are bound to come across a practitioner of Karate or Judo, TaekwonDo or Kung Fu, Tai Chi or Aikido.

Despite the attraction, martial arts is not the easiest of activities to engage in and many take up the practice completely unprepared. As a result, many students drop out before they have grasped any real understanding of the art.

This book is aimed at the beginner and novice martial artist. However, that does not mean that more experienced students won't find the book useful. Written in a concise and easy to understand way, appealing to all practitioners regardless of style, there is advice on choosing a martial art, how to prepare for gradings and tournaments, how to progress, and learn new skills right up to black belt standard. There is also information on safety and fitness to ensure you get the most from your training. In short, The Essential Guide to Learning Martial Arts is a handy reference guide which will help you survive the course of learning.

The book is structured so that you may choose the parts

most relevant to your needs. If you want to compete, you will find Chapter 6 of interest together with Chapters 3 and 5 which deal with fitness and safety. Throughout the book, you will also find quotes and anecdotes provided by a variety of established martial artists. These come under the heading 'Voice of Experience' and aim to give encouragement, advice and inspiration.

Whatever the reason for learning, whether for self-defence, to enhance fitness and health, to compete or to study an ancient art, these pages will prove indispensable.

I have based The Essential Guide to Learning Martial Arts on my own experiences of study and practical training alongside my brother, Sifu Mark Strange, who is an established professional martial arts instructor and tournament champion of Chinese forms and kickboxing. In 1992, Mark was the youngest martial arts teacher in the UK to set up his own full-time training Academy. It was here where I became Clubs Manager and fitness consultant and worked with many students and instructors of all ages and from many different styles, all who were in pursuit of mastering martial arts. This book is therefore based on sound practical experience and knowledge through being fortunate to work with these martial arts practitioners.

Today, I write books, run a Holistic Health Network and am a Natural Health Therapist but still practise Tai Chi and continue to be available to provide consultations at Leyland Martial Arts Academy. As for my brother Mark, he has gained great recognition for his skills and ability. He has studied in China with the Shaolin monks and has trained with renowned masters in Hong Kong and Foshan. He is one of the few full-time dedicated professionals, now with his sights set on promoting martial arts through film and television.

This book is for all martial arts practitioners whatever standard of proficiency they wish to obtain. I would be happy to hear from anyone who has found this book useful and would be happy to take more quotes for a future second edition. Letters should be addressed to me c/o my publisher.

CHAPTER ONE

GETTING STARTED

Martial arts cultivates discipline and respect

'The tree that brushes the heavens grew from the tiniest sprout.
The most elegant pagoda, nine stories high, rose from a small pile of earth.
The journey of a thousand miles began with but a single step.'

Lao Tzu

WHY I WANT TO LEARN MARTIAL ARTS

The world of martial arts is an enthralling place for the beginner. Some find themselves intrigued by the very essence of dynamism, the ancient teachings for self-preservation passed down through generations and the mystics of the Orient which amazes even the most sceptical. But for many, the reasons for taking up a martial art are far less complex. Indeed, there is something special about learning an art which originated out of the mystical East but most of today's practitioners study martial arts for more practical, down to earth purposes. These include:

SELF-DEFENCE

One of the main draws to martial arts is that it is a means of learning how to defend oneself. Sadly, we live in an age where violent, aggressive crime is prevalent and learning self-defence, even if you never have call to use it, will instil a sense of self-confidence so that you can go about your day-to-day life quite normally. Self-defence classes are widespread and attract just as many men as women. Children who are timid or victims of bullying often find classes helpful in building self-esteem.

SELF-PRESERVATION

Some people have mistaken beliefs about martial arts and think that the combat element actually insights aggressiveness. In reality, good martial arts practice is all about self-preservation and what students effectively learn is not about how to hurt somebody but about how to protect oneself. And protecting oneself may not necessarily mean defence in combat. Many martial arts students practise to improve and maintain health and fitness and this is deemed another fundamental part of self-preservation. If through practice you gain essential vitality and a sense of well-being then you are in effect preserving the quality of life.

SPORT

Another reason for taking up martial arts is the sporting element. Kick-boxing, point-sparring and kata (forms/patterns) display, all award trophies for the best just like any other sport. Fuelled perhaps by the 'Karate Kid' films, the attraction to compete for the champion spot has increased enormously in the past decade and to meet the demand, more tournaments are being organised to cater for all styles of martial arts. In Great Britain, Europe, America and the Far East, competitions are constantly taking place throughout the year and fresh martial arts talent is being discovered. There is certainly plenty of scope for the martial arts competitor on a National level and many of the larger Association clubs hold selections for international tournaments thus providing the opportunity to travel and pit your skills against the world's best.

RELAXATION AND HEALTH

If competing does not appeal and you prefer a more leisurely pace then martial arts can offer this too. There are many classes available which concentrate on 'soft' martial arts and these mostly derive from the Chinese systems. Tai Chi Chuan is a martial art but is elegant and genteel in comparison with the likes of karate and kung fu. The movements are almost dance-like, slow, graceful and leisurely, and if you need to relax and banish stress, recuperate after an illness or wish to simply maintain mobility and health, then this martial art is perfect for your needs.

SOCIAL

Of course, many people join a martial arts class without any discernible reason except, perhaps, as a way of making new friends or just taking up a new hobby and, surprisingly these same people often go on to gaining their Black Belt grade.

HOW MARTIAL ARTS CAN BENEFIT YOU

Before you continue reading, analyse why you want to take up a martial art. Is it to learn self-defence, to get fit, to improve confidence, to compete or to learn a new activity? Have you been inspired by your favourite martial arts action movie star? Perhaps it's a combination of these things which has sparked your interest. By assessing your motives for learning, you can quite readily set yourself achievement goals for the future. If, however, your motives for learning are born out of a negative situation; for example, wanting to take revenge, to bully or to be aggressive, then don't even think of trying to learn as your reasons will not be tolerated.

Whether you wish to live like a humble Buddhist monk and take in the entire philosophy of martial arts or simply just fancy sporting a Black Belt round your hips as a symbol that you have completed the tests, the way of martial arts will no doubt prove a very personal challenge. Experienced by people from all walks of life, most arrive in a class with reason and ambition but not all manage to survive the course. As you read on, you will find practical advice to guide you on your chosen journey. But first, let us find out what inspired other martial artists to take up the activity:

QUOTES ON TAKING UP A MARTIAL ART

'A friend talked me into going with him to try out a new martial arts class. I wasn't really interested but after attending several lessons, I became hooked. It's been three years now and I've trained almost every single week. That's more than 150 lessons and I'm still going strong. Ironically, my friend packed it in after a month!'

Kung fu student.

'I got made redundant and my life fell to pieces. I desperately needed a challenge in life, something to regain my self-confidence and esteem. Karate has certainly helped. It has given me something to channel my energies into and I feel much more positive about the future.'

Karate student.

'After being the subject of bullying for almost a year, my son was at an all time low. I'd heard that learning martial arts would give him more confidence and help him to defend himself. In just a few months, he became a different boy altogether. He doesn't get picked on any more and he's far happier in school.'

Parent of martial arts student.

'I find the study of martial arts to be quite fascinating. Some people think it's all about fighting and being aggressive but this couldn't be further from reality. The real benefits are to health and well-being. For me, martial arts is about self-preservation and I would never use my skills to harm anyone.'

Ju-jitsu student.

'Martial arts is more comprehensive than most sports I know. There's more learning options. I've been practising Chinese martial arts for several years and I'm still developing new skills. It really is an education.'

Kung fu instructor.

'I used to have bad asthma attacks and wasn't in good health. After hearing about the benefits of Tai chi I found a class several miles away and decided to join. These days, I feel more healthy and although I still have asthma, my attacks aren't as severe.'

Tai chi practitioner.

'Martial arts keeps me fit. The exercises are more challenging than anything I know. Both body and mind gets a thorough work-out and I feel great after a class.'

Kick-boxing student.

These quotes are typical of people from all walks of life and that is one appeal which attracts so many to take up the activity because, no matter what your colour, sex, race, religion or social status, you can enrol into a club and stand equal with all the rest!

FINDING THE RIGHT MARTIAL ART

Once you have decided that you want to learn martial arts

the question is which style would you like to study? You may find only a few classes to choose from in your area or perhaps you aren't too particular about what you take up but it does help to know something about the style and whether or not it is suitable for your needs.

There are basically three traditional origins of the most recognised martial arts. These include China (which is widely accepted as the birthplace of martial arts), Japan and Korea. From these origins come a multitude of styles and systems ranging from the popular Tae kwon do to the lesser known art of Pa-Kua. It would be near impossible to list every single martial arts system in this book and indeed, there are books already available devoted to cataloguing styles from around the world.

In China alone, although you have renowned arts which generally come under the term Kung fu, there are literally hundreds of established styles and many others constantly being developed. Kung fu is a term to describe a multitude of Chinese martial arts; so many that it would be impractical to learn them all in one lifetime!

Apart from the traditional based, established martial arts, the 1980s gave rise to the development of 'freestyle martial arts' which has been born out of the West to accommodate modern trends. Freestyle is deemed as being a more flexible approach to learning with emphasis on sport and rapid advancement and tends to be a popular choice for those who wish to compete.

Of course, with so many different styles of martial arts, today's student has plenty of learning options. The final choice, however, will depend on the individual. All styles have something to offer but if you are keen to find a martial art to suit you then be prepared to travel.

Many beginners will settle for the community martial arts club just out of convenience. In a town, where there is often more choice of classes, you may be initially attracted to the martial art which has received the most media attention, perhaps highlighting tournament or grading success. Whichever martial art you choose just remember that it is one of many and if after a while you discover it is not what you expected then you can always try something different.

DIFFERENCES BETWEEN TRADITIONAL AND MODERN CLASSES

As you may have already gathered, there is more to martial arts than kicking and punching thin air. Apart from the wide choice of styles, a new student has also to consider whether they prefer the traditional or modern approach to learning.

TRADITIONAL

Traditional martial arts stem from their original roots and students usually follow a syllabus of training which has been passed down through generations. Quite often, associated skills are taught such as healing, philosophy, meditation and history so that the student gains a complete approach to the martial arts. Learning a traditional system may demand more self-discipline, time, effort and attention to detail but the rewards are often far reaching. Students are usually expected to observe a strict code of conduct and endorse traditional martial arts values to work closely to the original teachings as passed down in the Far East.

MODERN

A club which is more interested in sport martial arts with emphasis on competing and winning trophies is considered to be 'modern'. Many freestyle and kick-boxing clubs fall under this banner. Modern martial arts is quickly evolving and tends to appeal to those who enjoy competition and rapid development of skills. Such kick-boxing type clubs are springing up everywhere in the West and many of their instructors have little or no background in traditional martial arts but may have gained some reputation in the sport. The modern club does not necessarily offer the same comprehensive and in-depth knowledge and skills as the traditional run club but if you are only interested in sport martial arts, then this may be what you are looking for.

There are some instructors who teach both traditional and modern martial arts and this seems to be a successful combination. Apart from having far much more to offer, students gain an all-round appreciation of the martial arts. So, if you are looking to experience the different elements, perhaps wanting to test your skills in the tournament arena while leaning the ancient values of the art, then look for a club which offers both a traditional and modern approach to learning.

QUOTES ON TRADITIONAL AND MODERN MARTIAL ARTS

'My Sifu (instructor) teaches traditional kung fu as well as modern kick-boxing so we get the best of both worlds. I wouldn't consider joining a sports martial arts club because I believe there is more to this than trying to win trophies.'

Kung fu student.

'I chose a traditional martial art because the emphasis is on learning the art for health and self-preservation. There are tournaments to compete in but there is never any pressure to participate.'

Karate student.

'I joined a kick-boxing club because I enjoy competitive sport. There are tournaments all year round and lessons are geared towards improving competition skills and fitness in order to compete well. I like a challenge!'

Kick-boxing student.

'I used to train at a modern club. All the lessons focused on tournament style semi-contact sparring and after a year of this, I got bored of the routine. The instructor was a successful competitor himself but he didn't know enough about martial arts. I decided it wasn't for me and found a more suitable club.'

Tae kwon do student.

CHOOSING YOUR CLUB

Finding a suitable martial arts club which offers qualified and professional instruction while providing a good environment in which to learn isn't necessarily an easy task. If you want to make the right choice, every effort must be made to find a club which will teach you fairly and look after your needs.

Quite often there is an abundance of clubs in town and city locations affording plenty of choice, and even in rural areas, you may come across a class busy practising in the village hall. Whatever options are open to you, don't ever settle for the one round the corner just because it's convenient and easy to get to and costs less than the rest. Do some essential prior research about the club, establish facts about its history, reputation and suitability to ensure you are making the right choice. It might be that you have to travel an extra mile to find the right club but in the long term, it will save you time, money and effort.

On the whole, with rising standards, most of today's clubs are run well with a qualified, experienced instructor standing at the helm. But even in this day and age, you are still likely to discover the existence of a sham operation and this isn't always obvious to the beginner. These 'cowboy' clubs are run by inexperienced instructors who are more concerned with financial gain than teaching the art or they may have fallen out with another club and decide to set up in direct opposition without any experience to do so. Further investigations may reveal that these instructors have no authentic martial arts background, no real skill or qualifications and often wear an illegitimate Black Belt. This type of club should be avoided at all costs.

Unlike other sports, there is little control and very few regulations governing the setting up of a martial arts club, especially in the UK, at this present moment in time. This is largely because there are so many different styles and lead Associations that it is difficult to keep a check on the practice of every single one and near impossible to set official standards which would apply to all. As a guide, reputable clubs should belong to a leading Association of which there are several covering all major arts.

The beginner should be aware that as it stands now, almost anyone can sport a Black Belt and produce a false certificate and call themselves a martial arts expert. The unsuspecting public do not know for sure whether that instructor has actually earned his qualification or bought it. It is common place to hear of students suddenly jumping from ungraded or low graded to Black Belt status as if they have time warped ahead of everyone else. The beginner can easily become a victim to such a sham and waste valuable time and money in the process, so it is vital to be aware and know what you are looking for when choosing a martial arts club.

MAKING CHECKS

Consider the following:

* First, you should go and check out the club you wish to join. The instructor should be approachable and will readily answer your questions. It should be possible to watch a class in progress and see what is being taught.

* The instructor should be knowledgeable and fully conversant with the martial art. He should demonstrate effectively and possess qualities which make him easily identifiable.

* The instructor should set an example and have a reasonable physique appropriate to the art being taught, gained through training.

* He should also have an exemplary attitude and be skilful in his approach with a strong rapport with the rest of the students. This 'experience' should be evident.

* Ask to see certificates of qualification and find out about the instructor's background. How many years has he trained, where did he study and who were his teachers?

* Check whether there is an approved student's licence and insurance scheme in operation. Is the club recognised as a member of any governing body? Is the instructor insured with professional indemnity cover?

Although it may sound like an interrogation, asking these questions is important. As a potential student, you have the right to know. Many teachers of martial arts have a personal portfolio carrying information, photographs, certificates and evidence which documents their careers and training to date. This will give you proof of their experience and time spent engaged in the practice of martial arts and is usually a reliable indicator.

Apart from past experience, you can judge a good instructor by his current approach to his position of responsibility. He should be constantly developing and improving his own skills and knowledge. He should attend regular courses to advance in his own practice and may also have his own teachers or master who he will go to for further experience. He may also be knowledgeable, or be engaged in other spheres of study such as exercise application, anatomy, first aid, coaching skills or other aspects of the art like healing or philosophy. The mark of a good instructor is one who is prepared to carry on learning after gaining his black belt!

Once you have performed a thorough check on the instructor's professional status, a final thought should be to the club itself. Consider the following:

* Does the club have a friendly, positive atmosphere?

* Is the venue suitable to train in?

* Are the other students enjoying their training?

* Would you like to be training with them?

These points, although minor considerations, will make all the difference to you.

Choosing a good instructor and the right club will certainly influence the way you learn and develop, not only in martial arts but also in other areas of your life too. There are many instructors with all the right credentials who will take every effort to help you achieve and progress.

CHECK LIST

Consider these points when choosing a club:

* Is the instructor suitably qualified?
There are no set exams to become a martial arts instructor but a good teacher should have certificates detailing his grades up to Black Belt standard together with other documentation. On average, a martial arts instructor should have a minimum of between 4–5 years of martial arts experience. This varies between martial arts styles. Ideally, the instructor should have gained other qualifications in first aid, fitness and coaching. He should also have professional indemnity insurance organised through his Association.

* Does the club provide an insurance/licence scheme?
All practising martial arts students should have access to insurance cover arranged through their club. Ideally, it should be endorsed by a governing body/Association to provide personal accident/liability member to member insurance.

* Have you chosen a reputable club?
It is usual for a recognised martial arts club to belong to a National Association or governing body. This will afford

extra protection for the student as any complaints can be taken to a higher authority and investigated. It isn't in the interests of any reputable Associations to accept the membership of clubs who have a poor reputation or lack of qualification/experience as this will place the Association's good name in jeopardy.

* Does the Club have a good atmosphere?
The instructor should be approachable and students should be friendly and appear to be enjoying what they are learning. A certain amount of discipline and strictness within a class is considered quite normal and is encouraged.

* Does the Club have standards?
Good moral standards are indicative of a reputable club and there should be a code of conduct in operation. A martial arts club should not encourage violent practices or promote a bad image. Students should not engender ill feelings or use the art in a negative, potentially damaging way.

DEMONSTRATING CORRECT ETIQUETTE

How you behave as a martial arts student is extremely important. Every club has rules or a code of conduct which should clearly define standards which all students should observe, follow and strictly adhere to.

As we live in a society which is quick to pre-judge, martial arts is an activity which is vulnerable to adverse comment. Because it is primarily a fighting art, people look upon it as being an aggressive, dangerous sport. In reality, martial arts is an activity far removed from this negative evaluation and most of its participants are quiet, peace loving people!

Of course, in any sphere of life, you will always get the sad, rotten few who spoil it for the rest. Martial arts is no exception and there will be a minority who abuse the code of conduct and have no etiquette or moral feeling whatsoever. This obviously does not help in the promotion of martial arts practice.

Correct etiquette and code of conduct originates from traditional martial arts practice. When you join a decent club, you will be introduced to these standards in the course of your training. Rules may vary from club-to-club and entirely rests upon the attitude of the instructor. Basic common sense instructions designed to protect you and others in training should be in operation. For example, keeping finger and toe nails short and removing jewellery as a precaution to prevent injury or not talking in class are all common regulations. Code of conduct or martial etiquette however, sets guidelines on how to behave in order to respect the importance of discipline and martial spirit. Examples here may include bowing to your instructor and fellow students, showing respect, not engaging in any ill feeling between rival clubs or only ever using the art in self-defence and so on.

Club rules are often made available or displayed. It is vital that you get to know them and abide by them at all times. Show that you are keen to set an example. If the club doesn't have any rules displayed, then ask the instructor for guidelines. Don't ever take anything for granted.

Correct etiquette should basically create a positive image, not just for the club and martial art but also for yourself. It's all about 'doing it right and to the best of your ability'. Of course, the instructor should set a precedent and reflect proper morals and martial arts spirit as an example to his students both in and out of the training hall. Such an instructor is an excellent role model for young children.

Apart from adhering to the rules and demonstrating acceptable behaviour, maintaining correct etiquette is also about having respect for fellow students whatever style of martial arts they practice. Alas, many students fail at this point and lose so much valuable time engaged in pointless rivalry and petty disputes with other practitioners. Politics within the martial arts has destroyed so much excellence and spoils one's appreciation of the art itself. It will prove more productive to get on with training and stay clear of any conflicts or negative situations.

With the right attitude, expressed at all levels from master down to student, it becomes easier to appreciate martial arts practice in a way that will prove highly rewarding.

STANDARD CODE OF CONDUCT

Whatever martial art you engage in, whether strictly traditional or totally modern, make every effort to follow this code to help raise and maintain standards in the martial arts.

1. Only use your skills in self-defence, self-preservation and the protection of others.
2. Respect your fellow martial arts practitioners, regardless of style.
3. Do not engender ill feeling or engage in petty rivalry with other clubs.
4. Be disciplined in your training and appreciation of martial arts.
5. Uphold martial arts spirit.
6. Set a good example to promote martial arts practise.
7. Abide by the rules of the Club and Association.

COMMON SENSE RULES

1. Keep finger and toe nails short.
2. Do not wear jewellery.
3. Wear appropriate equipment (club suit, padding for contact sport practice.)
4. Refrain from talking or eating in class. Listen carefully to instructions.
5. Keep active throughout the class to keep muscles warm.
6. Arrive to class on time.
7. If you need advice, ask the instructor.

PLANNING FUNDAMENTAL GOALS

After officially enrolling into a martial arts club, it may help to set yourself a few attainable goals. With those first lessons, students often find they have an overwhelming urge to push ahead before they are physically ready to. This is a common mistake and one which deserves full marks for eagerness but rushing ahead simply does not help you in the long term.

The general mentality in the West is 'wanting it all here and now!' Too few people actually sit back and consider that it takes time and effort to learn. And, to really master martial arts, you need a fair degree of patience and the wisdom to accept that it's not going to happen overnight.

Setting manageable goals, apart from inspiring development, will help you to slow the pace. Rather than trying to digest too much knowledge at the beginning, it will give you chance to perfect the fundamentals. Once you enter the training room, leave behind all the rush and bustle of modern life and tell yourself that you are going to learn at a gentle, relaxed pace. Let the instructor guide you but also learn to rely on your own instincts. Ultimately, you will know when you are ready to progress.

Some students may quite confidently aim towards passing their first grading while others may concern themselves with perfecting a single technique or drill. It does not really matter how long it takes to get to the next stage. What does matter is that you learn, understand and work to the best of your ability.

The Way Forward...

BASIC GOALS

* Learn and then perfect what you have learnt before progressing on to the next subject.

* Do not overwork yourself for compete with other students in an attempt to get ahead. It just does not work in the long run.

* Take your time! Do not rush. Better to progress slow and get it right!

* Only advance when you are ready to. If you have a problem or don't understand a certain element then ask the instructor for advice.

* Have patience and learn to control your enthusiasm. Extra time and effort will ensure long term success.

ADVICE FROM PRACTITIONERS ON GOAL-SETTING

'In the early days, I couldn't tell my left foot from my right and I felt really slow and awkward compared to everyone else. No one seemed to mind if I got in a muddle or fell over my own two feet. I guess everyone had been in the same situation when they started out. I found that it helped to set goals to get me moving forward. These were quite simple in the beginning like being able to balance on one leg or memorising a technique until I knew it backwards. Goal-setting proved an excellent way of getting from one stage to another and it has certainly worked for me. I have just gained my first Dan Black Belt!'

Karate instructor.

'Goal-setting has been especially important to me. I have dyslexia and often do things the wrong way round. Progress has been slow but I have passed two gradings and I feel as though I've come along way.'

Kung fu student.

'I find that by setting goals, I can really focus on the techniques I am learning. It helps to place every-thing into perspective. Once I have perfected a technique to the best of my ability, I can move on to the next goal.'

Aikido student.

'As an instructor, I often see the impatience of many new beginners. They try to rush ahead, eager to get their first belt and give no consideration to the practice and understanding of the techniques they've been taught. I try to get students to set goals and will not let them move on to the next level until I am satisfied that they know the techniques and are able to perform them competently'

Kung fu instructor.

FIRST DAY NERVES

The day has finally arrived for your first martial arts lesson. You may be feeling apprehensive and wondering how you will manage. You may worry about making mistakes or looking foolish in front of everyone else. Your stomach may churn at the very thought of starting something new. On the other hand, it is possible that you are feeling confident and looking forward to the new experience.

Everyone reacts differently to a new situation but it is quite normal and even expected to have first day nerves. Many established martial arts practitioners have vivid recollections of their first lessons and can even recall exactly how they felt. It is almost like starting school.

For some, the first lesson is a traumatic experience. The environment is foreign, the people are strangers, the instructor seems strict and uncompromising and the exercises look difficult. Halfway through you may ask yourself whatever possessed you to take up the activity! And then, as you near the end of the lesson you realise that you have actually enjoyed the experience and can't wait for the next session.

After a few more lessons, the environment loses its strangeness and becomes more familiar to you. You discover that your fellow students are quite human and the instructor is really a nice guy and the exercises do get easier with practise.

To overcome first day nerves, think positively about your first lesson. Apart from learning valuable skills, you should enjoy the activity and be looking forward to taking part. Try to relax. Although it's normal to be a bit nervous, you don't want to feel tense. Above all, don't expect too much of yourself. You may worry if you have difficulty in understanding instructions or can't manage some of the exercises or techniques but don't be disheartened as results will come.

TACKLING FIRST DAY NERVES

* Think positively!

* Try to relax and enjoy what you are doing.

* Arrive early and talk with the other students.

* Take each step one at a time. Don't worry if you have problems remembering, or find techniques difficult. It will get easier.

* If you make a mistake, it's not the end of the world. Just compose yourself and try again.

* Keep an open mind.

Although club practice varies, most instructors will allocate a more established student to a new beginner and this often proves beneficial. This student will help guide you through those first lessons until you are settled into the routine. Alternatively, you may be placed in a new starter group which is overseen by a senior grade student.

It may take several lessons before you start to feel comfortable with the activity so do not become too hasty in deciding whether you like it or not. You can't really judge off one lesson. Take your time so that you will fully appreciate those initial experiences which could one day make you a master of the art!

Before we move on, here is one student's humorous account of his first ever lesson in the martial arts.

'Waking up one Saturday morning, the nerves in my stomach riddled like a bait box full of maggots. Why? Because today I was to experience my first afternoon of kung fu. All sorts of thoughts flooded my brain. "Will I make a fool of myself?" "Will I get home in one piece?" It wasn't the end of the month, but I washed my feet anyway. Must create a good impression if nothing else.

'I arrived at the leisure centre. "Kung fu, luv," I said going through the turn style. Must admit, it felt good just saying it. Turning down the corridor, there they all were, flicking out their legs, confident but worst of all, staring. I disappeared to the changing room, hoping perhaps that the door would get stuck and jam me in for the duration but no such luck. I had to go in and face it. Fortunately, the welcome was amazing and the nerves began to crawl away.

' "Line up!" called the instructor. I ran to the back of the room – well, didn't you on your first day? "Left palm, right fist and bow!" he said. There goes my first mistake. Must learn my left from right or right from left – I'm getting confused – just do my best, I thought. "Run round the room", was the next command. A piece of cake ... until the press-ups, sit-ups, leg raises, jumping up and down and heaven knows what you'd call the rest.

'Next, he spoke in some foreign tongue. "Um-bay-yawn sheep-paw-soup" or something like that. It sounded more like a chinese menu but who was I to argue. I then went on to learn some basic kicks and started to absorb the art. This is fun. I'm actually enjoying myself. At the end of the lesson, I felt really good and approached the changing room kicking the door open using a new kick I had learnt. I crippled my toes, smiled and thought this is a day I'll never forget!'

Mark R. Smith, Kung fu student

QUESTIONS AND ANSWERS

Q. I'm in my early twenties and would like to take up martial arts. There are two clubs in my area for Karate and Aikido. Could I join both?

A. It might prove more fruitful if you choose one club to begin with until you find out the routine and how demanding it is. Later on, when you are feeling more competent, you could try out the other martial art and, if you enjoy it, see if you can fit the extra activity into your schedule.

Q. Most martial arts seem so energetic. Surely you need to be fit before you join a class?

A. New beginners build up their fitness gradually and most good instructors will encourage this. It takes time and effort to achieve a well-conditioned physique and this will arise through consistent training (read Chapter 3 on How to Get Fit).

Q. I'm a pensioner interested in keeping active and in good health. I have heard that Tai chi is ideal. How can practice help me?

A. Tai chi is slow and gentle and can be taken up by anyone regardless of age. Practice is reputed to improve general health and well-being while increasing overall mobility. It is said to help people who are recovering after illness or injury but it is mainly practised to promote and maintain vitality. It is often referred to as 'meditation in movement' as it encourages mental and spiritual calm.

CHECKLIST

Starting out in martial arts is a commitment that requires planning. To recap, the key areas to consider are:

* Reasons for practising martial arts – what are they?

* Finding the right martial arts – do you have choices?

* Joining a suitable club – have you made the recommended checks?

* Rules and etiquette – do you understand what is being asked of you? Are rules clear?

* Planning goals – what do you wish to achieve?

* Surviving the early days of practice – are you prepared?

ACTION

1. List five ways martial arts could improve your lifestyle.
2. Consider how much time you can devote to the practice.
3. Plan out your goals for making progress.

MARTIAL ARTS STYLES

...Listing just some of the better known styles.

CHINA	JAPAN	KOREA
KUNG FU	KARATE	TAEKWONDO
Wushu	Bushido	Hapkido
Tai chi Chuan	Kenjutsu	Tang Soo Do
Wing Chun	Jiu-Jitsu	
Shaolin	Judo	
Pa-Kua	Kendo	
Hsing i	Aikido	
Praying mantis	Goju Ryu	
Jeet Kune Do	Wado Ryu	
Hung Gar	Iaido	
Choy Lee Fut	Shorinji Kempo	
White Crane	Shotokan	
Chi Kung	Kyo Kushinkai	
Chinese boxing	Shukokai	
Snake & Crane	Shotokai	
Monkey boxing	Kyudo	
Tiger Kung fu	Sumo	
Chinese weaponry		

OTHER

Asia: Thai boxing, kali
West: Freestyle, La Savate (French kicking art)
       Eclectic systems (mixture of different styles and
       methods.)

CHAPTER TWO

THE LEARNING PROCESS

© Paul Banister

Practising technique builds firm foundations

'The Master said, "Learning without thought is labour lost; thought without learning is perilous."'

Confucius

GETTING INTO ROUTINE

Initially, your interest for participating in 'something new' will carry you along in those first few weeks of study but once the buzz of excitement disappears, you will be left with the bricks and mortar which will build your foundations. This is the time when many students question their actions and ask 'Is this what I really want to do?'

When the novelty wears off and you realise that there is hard work ahead, your feelings may waiver. You will probably think how much easier it looked when you watched the other students in action. In reality, to become the best you can be takes a considerable amount of time, effort and commitment but it does not mean to say you can't enjoy the experiences of learning along the way.

Casting doubts aside, you must move yourself along quickly by settling into a routine. Regular attendance coupled with consistent training will help you feel part of the club and will instil a sense of belonging. Getting to know your fellow students a little better will do no harm and may help you to feel more at ease with the training. Of course, there will be times when you think you've had enough, perhaps after encountering a difficult test such as a new technique or exercise which you can't get to grips with but a little perseverance and will-power should keep you on track.

As soon as you enrol, get involved with the club to build your interest. Participate fully and record your achievements, however minor, from week to week. Charting your progress in this manner is particularly useful in identifying areas of strengths and weaknesses and will also help you maintain a good training regime.

Ask any Black Belt about how they managed to survive the course of practice and you are bound to hear the words hard work and dedication mentioned. As with any sport or activity which is practised to high levels, you need these crucial elements to succeed. Even if your main aim is to enjoy yourself, the learning process offers a challenge and most martial arts prove to be greatly inspiring. The sooner you get yourself into a routine which feels comfortable, the more likely you are to stay on with the club. The feeling is rather like a shoe that fits right and which you will wear to the very last!

VOICE OF EXPERIENCE

'I remember my first few weeks as a beginner quite clearly. Because it was so new, I found it novel and absorbing. I couldn't wait for the next class such was the initial burst of enthusiasm. But, once you get into routine, you realise there's hard work ahead. There's a lot of repetition in order to improve skills and it takes a fair amount of perseverance to keep going. However, it's all part of the course.'

Judo student.

'The early days were quite a test for me. I had taken a couple of gradings and then ended up having a few weeks off recovering from a really bad dose of flu. Once I was fit again, I found it difficult to pick up where I left off and I kept finding excuses for not bothering to return. Luckily, I came to my senses and realised that I was only cheating myself by missing classes. I made a determined effort to go back. I'm glad I reached this decision as I'm now working towards my Black Belt.'

Kung fu student.

BASICS COME FIRST

The old adage 'Learn to walk before you can run' certainly applies to martial arts. You can't expect to be performing advanced kicking techniques or drills until you first master the basics of the art.

With most martial styles, basics are very similar. A punch is a punch and a kick is a kick, with slight variations in how they are delivered. Whatever your style, you can be sure that you will need to practise basics until you are completely competent. This often requires constant repetition and often 'boring' routine drills which involves pacing up and down the training hall week after week perfecting techniques and application.

The problem most beginners have, and this especially applies to the younger generation, is that they are lacking in patience. When the instructor tells you to go away and practise, it's probably because you need to! Many beginners run through a technique a few times and then believe they know what they have learnt. After these sparse attempts, they'll probably be able to remember the technique and be able to demonstrate it in a fashion when asked. But, unless they have digested the basics to perfection, how can they understand what they are performing? And, indeed, how can they be expected to learn the next steps?

Many beginners have made the mistake of rushing through their martial arts practice, eager to attain their grades and many amateur instructors have allowed students to swim through the nets so to speak without fully realising the implications. The dilemma is that if you haven't practised your basics to a competent level then this will become more and more evident as you get closer to achieving your Black Belt. If you have built your foundations on rocky ground, it won't take much to knock down the structure of your experience. As one sage once so aptly said, 'If you build your house on a precipice, do not expect your walls to remain intact. Cracks will form and no amount of mortar will hold your house together!'

Whatever martial art you are studying, take one step at a time and do not move forward until you are happy with the knowledge you have acquired. Question anything which you do not fully understand. Some skills may require a degree of physical dexterity to perform at higher levels. For example, a kicking technique may require good flexibility and strength in the lower body to be totally effective and these qualities will not appear overnight. If, however, you concentrate on perfecting the technique of the kick, you will gain strength and flexibility as you advance in your training. The secret is aiming to get the technique right and understanding what you are doing from the very start. This will enable you to build on solid ground.

CHECK LIST

1. Ask if you don't understand.
   It doesn't matter how many times the instructor has to explain it to you. Never be afraid of asking for help and guidance.
2. Practise again and again.
   Pacing up and down the room might sound monotonous but it does have a purpose. Each time you practise, you are getting better. Remind yourself this each time you repeat drills.
3. Don't advance too soon.
   You can either be a poor Black Belt or a skilful Black Belt. The choice is yours but if you want to excel, you have to work hard. Part of the learning process involves having the patience to digest a technique or skill and although it may take longer, you will benefit by it in the end.

THE STUDENT AND INSTRUCTOR RELATIONSHIP

How you get on with your instructor will have some bearing upon your future in martial arts. There may be times when you think highly of your mentor, proclaiming him to be the best of the best as he guides you through the complexities of study and then other times when you hate every fibre of his being for putting you through a punishing training session, but at the end of the day, this love-hate relationship is one that has to work in order that you benefit from your participation.

Traditionally, in the far East, martial arts teachers and revered Masters were regarded so highly that students feared them. A single look from the eyes of the teacher could send his students a quiver, such was their authority and it took little to command discipline and respect. But then was a time when students had to earn the right to learn martial arts by doing humble chores for the Master's family, and this tradition is still maintained in some parts of Japan and China.

Today, martial arts has been greatly westernised and the instructor has to work harder to gain the respect, discipline and attention of his students without driving them away. Apart from being a father figure, he must also be a disciplinarian to strike the right balance so that students learn the correct ways. In effect, this is a two-way deal, based on mutual understanding and respect. The relationship needs to be carefully nurtured by both parties in order to gain results.

As a new student, you may feel awkward with your instructor, unsure of his temperament. You may feel that he snubs you or seems largely disinterested by your presence. More often than not, he is giving you time and space to acclimatise so that you can decide upon whether you are enjoying the training.

Apart from being approachable, a good instructor needs to be able to communicate easily with his students. He will give encouragement where it is needed and will take great steps to work hard at his role so that students develop. He should have an even temper (although some instructors are prone to occasional outbursts) and a pleasant approach and will strive to make learning an enjoyable experience.

But, there will also be times when the instructor stands solid like a wall of steel, giving firm commands to put you through your paces. He may set an example of you or pull you up for something you have done wrong but this is all part and parcel of the learning process to prepare you for the hard work to come and you must try and take it all in your stride. At the end of the day, the instructor is working to get the best out of you.

You will find that most instructors maintain a slight distance from their students and avoid becoming over familiar. Just like schoolteachers, they have to strike the right balance to preserve correct conduct. This degree of authority can evaporate if the relationship becomes too friendly. The instructor must also set a good example by exemplifying correct moral code and behaviour both in and out of the training venue.

Ideally, you should feel comfortable with your instructor. Although he might shout and make you work hard at times, in general, he should be good-natured and approachable. After all, he is only human!

Does your instructor meet up to requirements? Check these guidelines:
A good instructor is . . .
Approachable and easy to communicate with.
Able to command respect and gain discipline in an acceptable way.
Good-natured and keen to set standards.
Stern but fair in his approach when needed.
Knowledgeable and skilful; works hard to get results.

Avoid at all costs the instructor who:
Tries to command respect by using bully tactics.
Threatens students physically.
Makes training totally unbearable.
Is constantly bad-tempered and ignorant.
Lacks self-control and moral standards.

As a student, it is ultimately up to you what you are prepared to put up with. Some people find they are better motivated by an instructor who is bad-tempered and constantly shouting at his class but, on the whole, the best results come from an instructor who takes the balanced approach. Students thrive in a positive training environment where encouragement is plentiful and where students and instructor work together in harmony.

VOICE OF EXPERIENCE

'I remember the first club I joined. The instructor, although skilful, was more often than not bad tempered and even quite violent at times. You were never quite sure what he would do next. If you placed a foot wrong, he'd knock you off your feet. If your guard was down, he'd hit you in the face. Perhaps it made you learn more quickly but everyone feared him. It made you dread going to lessons. A lot of people, including myself, left the club in the end because of his unpredictable attitude and the way he manipulated the class through physical force. As a teacher today, I have learnt from these early experiences and strive to develop a good working relationship with my students.'

Kick-boxing instructor.

'Right from the start, our instructor has been very fair. Apart from being a skilful Sensei, he is looked upon as a father figure. He's great with the kids and always gives encouragement to get the best from his students. At the same time, he can also be quite strict. When he shouts, the whole class is silenced!'

Karate student.

'The first time I saw the instructor, I almost turned for the exit. He looked so mean and bad-tempered. I soon realised, however, that appearances are deceptive. He's actually the most pleasant guy I've ever come across. I learnt a valuable lesson not to prejudge.'

Kung fu student.

TIPS FOR GAINING YOUR INSTRUCTOR'S RESPECT

1. Train hard at every opportunity. Concentrate on performing quality exercise and technique. Show the instructor that you are willing to go that extra mile.
2. Turn up promptly for class and warm up quietly.
3. Ask questions when appropriate and show your interest and enthusiasm by listening carefully.
4. Maintain a good moral attitude and follow club rules. Respect your fellow students and demonstrate self-control and discipline.
5. Respect your instructor. He is the one who has accepted you as his student and in so doing is working to enrich your life with knowledge and experience.
6. Keep out of bother in and out of the club. Do not boast about your skills as trouble will surely follow.

MAKING PROGRESS

New students often find it takes several weeks to settle in with their training and perhaps even longer before any real progress is made. But, with a good instructor and the right approach to learning martial arts, results should be apparent after approximately six weeks into training. This doesn't mean you'll be performing jumping, spinning kicks or executing a complicated kata. This would be wishful thinking. But small results will come as you improve on your basics and although you may regard it as insignificant, this small progress is actually building your foundations in preparation for learning the more complex disciplines of your art.

How you progress as a student largely depends on the commitment you place into learning. The more time and effort you put in, the more you should expect to gain. It's certainly a case of being down to the individual and how you prioritise your study. If martial arts takes second place to another hobby or sport then progress may be slower than someone who can devote more time to practice. On average, to become reasonably skilful, it is said that two lessons a week is usually sufficient. If you wish to compete and are aiming to become a champion then, the more training you can fit in the better your chances will be.

Your progress is also dependent on the quality of instruction you receive. If the instructor is lacking in skills or is difficult to understand or communicate with, then you may not achieve the anticipated results, or at least not in the allocated timescale. At all times in martial arts training, a student should be moving a step closer towards reaching his goals, whether it be moving closer to taking a grading or winning a competition or gaining self-improvement. The instructor has a duty to try and enhance a student's ability and if you feel that this is not happening then talk with your instructor in an effort to resolve the problem or failing that, try another club.

Of course, in the end, it is really down to how much progress is made. How many classes are you able to attend? How much attention do you give to learning and practice? Do you study with commitment or waste time chatting or standing idle? Do you listen and heed instructions? Do you make an effort to progress? Answer these questions honestly and then assess how you wish to continue.

The important thing to remember in the learning of martial arts is that practice should be non-competitive. You study at your own pace and even if your progress is slower than the rest of the class, the fact that you are making progress is the most important factor. If, however, you are keen to get ahead, then try to team up with an enthusiastic training partner so that you can work together.

VOICE OF EXPERIENCE

'Listen, watch and practise if you want to get somewhere. The emphasis lies on the practise and you will need to do plenty if you want to be good at your chosen discipline.'

Tae kwon do practitioner.

'Don't let anyone hold you back! If you want to progress, stick with those who train hard. Even if you are a beginner, you can differentiate between those who want to learn and the ones who are just messing about.'

Kung fu student

'Never stand about idle. Class time is short and you should use every second to practise if you want to improve your skills.'

Karate student.

'Practise at home whenever possible. Every hour spent in training will lead to a higher level of proficiency.'

Tai chi practitioner.

PROGRESS CHECK LOG

Make a note of the skills acquired in each training session by keeping a Progress Check Log. After six sessions, review your progress and detail any action required for improvement.

VOICE OF EXPERIENCE

The learning process is a lengthy, time-consuming journey and when students first take up martial arts, progress seems slow but with consistent training, the mind and body gradually transforms to take on board new skills and disciplines as these two students have found.

'A friend asked me if I wanted to study martial arts

for self-defence purposes and, game for anything, we found a club at a local village hall which taught Chinese martial arts. I remember my first lesson quite vividly. The instructor was so agile and experienced; he certainly left a lasting impression on me because I couldn't get enough of training after that initial session. It took a while, but once I got into it, movement became less awkward and my skill began to improve. Several years down the line, I feel fit, in much better shape, more confident and have gained a sense of achievement. Apart from regular training, I have entered competitions, taken part in displays and martial arts events for charity and feel a real sense of worth which can only be experienced by taking part. I have learnt so much and would recommend martial arts to anyone who wants to improve themselves. My advice to beginners would be to train hard and stick at it. Progress is slow at first until your body and mind grows accustomed but results will come.'

Paul Banister, Chinese martial arts student

'I started martial arts as a means of keeping fit and to learn to defend myself should it ever become necessary. I have thoroughly enjoyed my training for the last 3 years, made some good friends and met many interesting people. It gives me great satisfaction that I can now do something which I previously regarded as being impossible for me to achieve. I enjoy gradings particularly because of the thrill of knowing that I am completely prepared and focused for the task. It's a bit like a competition. You prepare and then perform to the best of your ability with no compromise. Although it's difficult to fit training into normal work and family life, it is worth persevering. As well as hard training, good rest is vital! Train hard when you feel good, take it easy when you don't. You can only progress at your own pace. Martial arts requires commitment but if you are patient, you can achieve your goal.'

Colin Wait, Chinese martial arts student

GRADING PREPARATION

The grading system, where one is tested on a series of skills in order to gain a coloured belt/sash, is an idea which quickly flourished in the West, seen as an incentive to encourage reward-hungry students to give active participation. Although styles differ, generally the belt system starts from white and continues on to Black, and in many ways acts as a symbol of status in the martial arts world.

Traditionally, there were no gradings for coloured belts in the Far East. The old Masters tested their students in more practical ways and usually without any reward except, of course, for the attainment of skill and knowledge. The only belt to be worn was the one which held up the practitioner's trousers! It is said that the belt became old and grubby as the practitioner gained experience thus possibly explaining the reasons for the progressive darkening of belts in the later grading systems.

Some of the martial arts practised do not follow any coloured belt grading system. Instead, some arrange tests which award certificates of achievement or competence. And, even in the clubs which run grading schemes, not every student decides that they want to grade. Many take the option not to bother, preferring to learn the art itself without the pomp and ceremony.

For those who do decide to grade, preparation is important. Regardless of the style of martial arts, the approach is usually the same for all. Students learn the skills required for the grading, then practise and perfect what they have attained. More often than not, as grading day draws near, students begin to feel apprehensive and a little nervous.

A martial arts grading is basically like any other exam; the better prepared you are, the better the result will be. Constant practise and revision of techniques and applications will enable you to feel comfortable with the disciplines and that is where the perpetual pacing up and down the training hall comes in to its own. But, you need to do more than just memorise an application and go through the motions. Do you understand the technique? What is it applied for? To know what you are doing needs total comprehension which is why you should listen carefully to the instructor and always ask questions about anything you are not sure about.

Be familiar with the grading rules and regulations. You should have a club syllabus or grading information at hand which clearly explains expected etiquette for the grading. If this isn't available, ask the instructor for guidelines. Apart from the technical aspects of the grading, you need to know if your grading mark will be influenced by other factors such as appearance (wearing the correct uniform) or etiquette (bowing where appropriate). Don't leave yourself in the dark. If the information hasn't been made available, ask! You have a right to know.

In the final training sessions leading up to your grading, whether this is the first or eighth, go through the syllabus to make sure you are familiar with and understand every aspect of the grading requirements. Some instructors hold mock gradings close to the event as a preparatory test and this can prove extremely useful, to check you are at ease with it all, as well as giving you a taste of what is to come. Now is the time to make final checks on technical applications. Are you in the correct stance? Is your arm in the right position in the block? Have you remembered the correct terminology? Work with a senior student if at all possible for extra guidance but always get your instructor to look over what you have learnt.

Learn to practise with conviction. Demonstrate clearly and show that you know what you are doing. Perform the techniques with the relevant speed and power so that your effort is distinctly visible. Not only should you aim to pass your grading but you should aim to pass with merit. Consider these points in those final training sessions so that you are fully prepared.

It doesn't matter whether you are a beginner taking the

first test or about to be graded for your Black Belt, you must give the same attention to each level in order to be ready. The examiner is generally an unrelenting soul and will not easily take exception. He will know, above all others, whether or not you have prepared and will judge you according to what he sees.

GRADING DAY

After weeks or even months of preparation, your grading day has finally arrived. No one would blame you for feeling a trifle nervous; it is, after all, an important event and the only thought on your mind should be that of passing your exam.

Everyone responds differently to being tested. It doesn't matter whether this happens to be your first or last grading, if it is in your blood to feel nervous or on edge then that's the way it will be. Some people panic or start to feel ill. Some get so worked up that they are unable to perform, while others remain calmly unruffled by the impending experience.

Feeling nervous or apprehensive is quite normal and some believe that by carrying this state of emotion, achievement can be much greater. If anything, it is good because it will make you sharper and more aware and these are qualities which can help you pass. If, however, you are very nervous and believe it will affect your performance, you need to calm down and focus your thoughts.

Tips for Combating Nerves

1. Try to relax and remain calm before the event by quietly meditating. A gentle walk might help you gather your thoughts in order that you feel at ease.
2. Keep your mind busy. Try not to think too much about the grading.
3. Think positive and tell yourself that you are going to do well. If you've practised hard, you have no reason to do otherwise.
4. Warm-up with some gentle stretching before the event to relieve tension from the muscles.
5. Visualise passing your grading and then make it become reality.

If you are extremely nervous to the point of panic or feel unable to cope with the pressure of the test, then see your instructor for advice and direction. Some clubs will consider organising a private or more relaxed grading to make you feel at ease. By knowing how nervous you are, the instructor/examiner can, in certain circumstances, make allowances.

How gradings are organised, is down to the individual club or Association. Some are grand affairs with a table of examiners and even a room bursting full of spectators while others are more informal and are held by the instructor at the usual training centre. If this is your first grading, it helps to know a little of what to expect so that you can mentally prepare for the test. If you are concerned, ask the instructor to give you an idea then you will be ready for every eventuality.

Pre-Grading Tips

1. Arrive at the grading venue early to register and quietly warm-up.
2. Make sure you have the appropriate uniform and documents (licence/insurance booklet).
3. Once warmed up, practise quietly.
4. If your grading involves partner work, go through the applications with someone else quite early in training.
5. Focus on what you are doing but, at the same time, try to remain relaxed.

If you have any last-minute worries, talk to a senior student. Many instructors do not like to be asked questions on the day for the simple reason that they expect you to be knowledgeable about what you are grading for. Asking an instructor to run through a technique or explain a movement does not inspire confidence at this stage in the proceedings.

While you are waiting to grade, keep warmed up by practising and running through your applications or doing a few exercises to liven you up. Keep cool, calm and collected as best you can through quiet meditation. Carry this mood with you as you enter the grading room.

Whether you are facing one examiner or ten, you will probably be feeling apprehensive. Tell yourself that it's just like a training session and that the examiner is on your side, willing you to do well.

What Happens if I get something Wrong?

If you are aware that you've made a wrong move, ask if you may repeat the application. Most styles give some room for slight error. Give yourself a second to re-compose and then start again.

How Do I Greet the Examiner?

Use the expected club etiquette to greet the examiner. This may simply comprise of a bow. Perform without expression to show that you are focused and concentrating your efforts into the test.

Where Do I Look when facing the Grading Panel?

Most students feel comfortable looking straight ahead, eyes focused on a point above the examiner's head.

What Happens if I Fail?

To fail a grading is not a disaster nor does it signal the end of your participation in the martial arts. If it happens to you, first accept it and then ask yourself why you failed. Rather than sulk or give up, make an effort to analyse the result and aim to rectify any problems in order to perform a retake. Do not let it deter you from reaching your goals. Use the experience wisely and learn from it.

If you fail a grading, more often than not, you know why it happened. Perhaps you had not prepared thoroughly or maybe you made too many mistakes. Occasionally, the reason isn't obvious. If this is the case, speak with the examiner immediately after the grading and ask for an explanation as to why you failed. It is possible that an error has been made; it does happen, so contest a result if you are not happy with it.

Failure often results when students try to grade before they are fully ready and prepared. Most failures take place in the middle to advanced levels. These days, many instructors will not put forward a student for grading until they know they are completely ready for the test. This ensures a higher pass rate which is good for the club and the instructor.

Anyone who fails a grading should be entitled to a re-test. Everyone deserves a second chance. Normally, a re-test is free of charge although if you fail for a second time, then it is probable that you will have to pay to take a third re-test on a later occasion.

How Do You Cope With Failure Among Other Students?

You will find most of your fellow students to be understanding, sympathetic and, above all, willing to help you shape up for the re-test. There's no reason to feel embarrassed or ashamed by the result. Make an effort to take it all in your stride and gain encouragement from the thought that you will be perfect a second time around and will have gained from the experience.

Gradings are an important time in your martial arts development so treat them with respect and careful consideration. Plenty of practise, sound learning and positive groundwork will provide every opportunity for getting the desired result.

Even though gradings may become more difficult as you progress, with intricate applications and extra syllabus to remember, every step will bring you closer to the achievement of your Black Belt grade and once you get there, you will know that it has been worth every endeavour.

VOICE OF EXPERIENCE

Looking back, most students will have certain recollections of their grading experiences giving rise to either a grimace or laughter at the mere thought. You may have endured a nightmare grading where everything went wrong or encountered a rare occasion where everything went right. Whatever the outcome, take it all in your stride as these martial artists have done:

'Gradings have always been a nerve-wrecking experience for me although I would not let my own students know it. I think I would sooner take a driving test! Everyone reacts differently to a situation like this. Some people do not seem to show any nerves at all!'

Karate instructor.

'The early gradings were quite easy and then became progressively more difficult. I actually failed once by underestimating one of the higher grade exams. I just had not prepared well enough. It didn't do me any harm though; I believe I actually learnt a valuable lesson and it made me train harder.'

Kung fu instructor.

'I am a Grading Examiner and for my contribution, I wish to remain anonymous to safeguard any embarrassment to any of the students I have graded over the years for I have pretty much seen it all! Life on the grading table is certainly an eye opener into human nature; you get to witness all kinds of behaviour and situations which present themselves when the individual is under pressure. Great gradings are most memorable when a talented student performs to excellent standard. These are few and far between but a joy to behold! Also memorable are those disasters, whether on a small or large scale, which may totally consume a student to a point of him being inconsolable or create some fit of laughter which, when starts, is not easy to stop. How I have felt for those students who have failed or made embarrassing mistakes and crippled themselves with remorse. Is it really worth such emotion? Many moments stand out in my career as a Grading examiner; perhaps too many to mention but there are a few which deserve saving for prosperity. Like the one where two young students, who were no more than the age of seven, proudly walked into the grading room with suits five sizes too big, trousers on the wrong way round and noses running uncontrollably. I can still picture them now, getting tangled up in their suits, almost falling over as they performed their techniques as they tried to control their runny noses with the sleeves of their gi. And, to the overenthusiastic young man who failed to notice his trousers slipping as he executed his kata. Somehow, the teddy bear blazoned boxer shorts did not go with the occasion. Fortunately, he managed to see the funny side of it. Not like another young man who was inconsolable purely because he had forgotten part of a kicking sequence. He was so angry with himself that he walked out of the grading room, punching himself like a man possessed. Goodness knows what the pensioners thought as they met for bingo in the next room! These gems are just a few that come to mind; there are many more, of course, which I cannot mention for fear of retribution but it gives the student an insight as to what the examiner sees. To my mind, the secret to a successful grading is to relax and treat the experience as you would with any training session. Don't give too much importance to the way you feel about the occasion otherwise you will make yourself more fretful. And, if you do experience a minor disaster, do not dwell upon it. In a few years time, you will look back and laugh!'

Martial arts instructor/examiner.

COMMON QUESTIONS ANSWERED

Q. Week after week, we just seem to be running through basic techniques. I'm getting really bored doing the same moves constantly but the instructor maintains we need the practise. Is this really necessary?

A. If the instructor says you need the practise then that's the way it is. An experienced instructor will have an eye for these things and also the knowledge to avoid progressing before the basics are mastered. It might seem laborious but the repetition will prove invaluable and the techniques will eventually become like second nature. If you are most unhappy and certain that you have grasped the rudiments fully then by all means speak with your instructor and let him know your feelings.

Q. What is the purpose of having a grading?

A. Not all styles conduct gradings but they are popular and provide a way of assessing progress. From the instructor's viewpoint, a grading will highlight how much the student has developed and will also reveal areas which need working on. As for the student, a grading is something to aim to. It involves learning and performing a series of skills to the desired level of competence. Passing a grading is considered a major achievement in the sport and is most rewarding.

Q. How do I know if I'm ready to grade?

A. If you feel comfortable with the acquired techniques and skills and know the syllabus instinctively then you should be ready to enter a grading. Above all, you should feel confident and capable of performing well. If you harbour any doubts or feel unsure about what you are doing then you're obviously not ready. Talk to your instructor and keep practising until you feel ready to grade.

CHAPTER THREE

SURVIVAL OF THE FITTEST

© Paul Banister

The key to all-round fitness is hard work and self-belief

'Strength by itself is not equal to knowledge and knowledge is not equal to training; but combine knowledge with training and one will get strength.'

Anonymous Sage

Fitness in the martial arts is a prime requisite if you wish to practise at a good standard but, more importantly, fitness is essential if you aim to be healthy for life. Everyone should make time to include exercise into their daily rituals.

For some years, I have worked on the principal of there being five main components for good health which must be combined to achieve a state of total fitness. These include: exercise for cardiovascular health, exercise for muscular strength and power, exercise for mobility, balanced nutrition for energy and body maintenance and lifestyle considerations for overall well-being and vitality.

In this chapter, we take a look at the benefits of each component and how they can be successfully combined for optimum results. In doing so, we shall also examine the close relationship between body, mind and spirit and determine how this delicate balance can be enhanced and maintained throughout martial arts study and life itself.

ESSENTIAL CARDIOVASCULAR FITNESS

Cardiovascular fitness, using aerobic training techniques to work the body is, primarily, the most important of exercise components. It is considered vital for maintaining health and well-being and, from a sporting viewpoint, is deemed essential in gaining stamina and lean body mass.

Despite its importance, aerobic work is often neglected in martial arts training. Most classes are structured to give a warm-up period followed by a selection of exercises followed by the teaching of the art; there isn't normally sufficient time to fit in a thorough cardiovascular work-out. This is something you should include in your own time on a regular basis.

So, what type of exercise must be performed to achieve cardiovascular fitness? Well, quite simply, it is any activity which raises the heart rate adequately between 65% and 85% of its maximum rate. Ideally, such activity would need to be sustained for approximately 20 minutes to prove effective although some fitness professionals now believe that only 10 minutes per day is enough to maintain the qualities of cardiovascular fitness. Personally, I find a 20 minute aerobic session much more rewarding and beneficial if you are only able to commit 3/4 exercise sessions per week.

Aerobic exercise includes:

Fast paced walking
Jogging
Swimming
Skipping
Cycling/rowing
Dance

Aerobics/Step Aerobics
Sparring/bag work/shadow boxing

As you can see from the list, the choice is varied and you can try any of these exercises for aerobic benefits but remember to work at the correct pace, without interruption, beyond the 10 minute target.

UNDERSTANDING THE BENEFITS

Aerobic exercise utilises oxygen and involves the major muscle groups such as the legs. Short bursts of activity are not effective. Exercises such as press-ups and sit-ups are considered to be anaerobic (where oxygen is not required). Therefore, don't expect toning exercises such as these to be efficient in burning excess fat tissue. Only aerobic activity will do this.

The first, early signs of improvement with habitual aerobic training is that your stamina (the ability to endure an activity for longer periods without becoming easily tired or breathless) will increase. You may feel more energetic. More obvious signs may reveal a shift in body mass. Aerobic training, performed correctly, will burn fat reserves when combined with a sensible diet and muscle toning exercises and you will notice improved muscle definition and a leaner body shape.

Other benefits include healthier internal functioning. The heart and lungs will work more efficiently while the circulatory system will ensure the transportation of oxygen and essential nutrients and the removal of waste products which, in turn, will lead to a finely tuned body that is capable of responding effectively to exercise demands thus improving overall performance.

To understand the principals of the aerobic metabolism, let us take a look at the body's energy systems:

Systems 1 & 2 ... the ATP-PC (Adenosine Triphosphate Phosphocreatine) and the lactic acid systems are ANAEROBIC. They do not require oxygen to produce energy.

System 3 is AEROBIC and requires oxygen to combine with the breakdown of nutrients for re-bonding the ATP to provide enough energy for endurance activities.

The aerobic system can produce ATP for hours and comes into effect when the length of activity exceeds three minutes.

The physical response to aerobic activity is quite profound and only after four weeks of consistent exercise, can you expect some physical adaptations. After three months, the changes produce what is commonly known as 'The Training Effect'. The body will have developed into a highly efficient working system, achieving optimum levels of fitness and performance. The actual results of the Training Effect include:

A stronger, more efficient cardiovascular system.
Quicker recovery after exercise.
Heart beating slower at rest

Delivery of greater amounts of nutrient rich blood to the muscles.

The body's greater utilisation of oxygen (relying less on the lactic acid system).

Increased stores of chemical energy ATP

Establishment of more capillaries to cope with increased blood flow.

The ratio of fat to muscle shifts as more calories are spent.

The physique will take on a leaner appearance.

An aerobically fit person can also enjoy a sense of greater well-being. With aerobic activity, there is a release of endorphins producing a 'natural high' and it is thought that this can also help to keep stress and psychological problems at bay. So, if you feel 'down in the dumps', try aerobic activity to give you a lift!

Once you have achieved the Training Effect, you need to maintain regular exercise so as not to lose the benefits of cardiovascular fitness which can quickly depreciate when exercise is stopped. Bearing this in mind, include aerobic activity into your programme at least every two days. If you have a busy lifestyle, look at ways where you can increase cardiovascular fitness. For example, using stairs instead of lifts, walking or cycling to work instead of driving or taking a brisk walk in your lunch break.

ESSENTIAL WARM-UP AND COOL-DOWN

The warm-up and cool-down period is perhaps one of the

most essential and most overlooked components in an exercise programme. Essential because it helps to prevent injury and overlooked because many people forget or ignore its importance before and after exercise.

Whatever the weather or environmental conditions and no matter how experienced you are, the warm-up and cool-down (pre and post exercise) phases should be included into your regime. Approximately 10 minutes of gentle stretching, gentle jogging on the spot and loosening up will prepare your body for more intense exercise in the warm-up stage. The routines will gradually help your body acclimatise to exercise as well as preventing much of the post exercise stiffness which often occurs in the muscles. Do not neglect this vital routine!

WORKING AT THE RIGHT PACE

How can you be sure that you are training at a pace which is adequate for cardiovascular improvements? Well, as a guide, there are signs to look out for which should provide you with a fairly accurate indication:

A. Your breathing rate should increase although you should not be breathless nor gasping for air. Experts say that you should be able to hold a comfortable conversation while engaged in aerobic exercise.

B. Your body should perspire and feel warm.

C. Your pulse rate should increase to between 65% and

85% of the maximum. To find your 'training heart rate', minus your age from 220 then multiply by 65% and 85% to find the two figures which will provide your training pulse.

At no time should you feel ill, faint or in any pain. If you are unfit or just starting out in the martial arts, consult your doctor for a health check preferably before you start any exercise.

INCREASING AEROBIC INTENSITY

After approximately 8–12 weeks of regular training, you may feel ready to increase the intensity of exercise to encourage extra improvements. There are ways to do this. You can alter your training routine by extending the aerobic session or including an extra aerobic work-out into your programme. Depending on the type of activity you do, you can alter the exercise to increase the intensity. For example, jogging followed by bursts of sprinting or jogging combined with uphill and downhill running, will tax the muscles in different ways. In indoor aerobic work-outs, you can utilise equipment such as hand weights or skipping rope. For the martial arts kick-boxing competitor, shadow boxing, focus mitt and bag work will provide aerobic benefits if performed consistently. This will also improve technique, speed and co-ordination, proving beneficial in more ways than one.

THE BENEFITS OF CROSS TRAINING

Before we move on to muscle work, I must mention the remarkable benefits of cross training, which can help the individual to achieve peak fitness.

Cross training is basically about participating in a variety of exercise activities and/or different sports to establish all round ability. It is said that the different physical and mental demands from cross training will ensure total body conditioning making it ideal for fitness enthusiasts and competitors alike.

Training in a variety of activities conditions more muscles than any one sport can. Although most martial arts are generally quite comprehensive in what they can offer to keeping fit, combining practice with an activity such as swimming, cycling or circuit training will increase the benefits further and encourage improved performance.

Cross training is ideal for people who are already relatively fit but looking for extra physical gains. If you have reached a plateau in your fitness and don't seem to be achieving the desired results, then introducing a different activity in to your exercise regimen will provide a fresh challenge.

Another benefit of cross training is that a carefully planned programme of activity can help reduce the occurrence of over-use injuries and repeated stress on specific body parts. For example, a martial art which causes participants stress at the joints might benefit from including a weekly swim into their routine. Swimming is a perfect activity to consider if your joints are fragile or subject to injury.

MUSCLE STRENGTH AND POWER

On the whole, martial arts does not require the participant to have bulging biceps or a superhuman physique but it does help to be toned up and have a degree of strength and power in the muscles in order to withstand the disciplines of your art in form and movement.

Many of the energetic martial styles accommodate muscle work into their class routine. More often than not, the routine comprises of press-ups, sit-ups and other general toning exercises which target the main muscle groups. Alas, it isn't always possible to vary the session or work on specific body parts at any length. This is often owing to lack of class time. Thus, it is wise to include extra muscle work into your exercise schedule to achieve these extra gains wherever possible.

Before we consider muscle in more detail, I wish to stress that there is no short, safe, natural way to gaining a Herculean physique (that's if you should want one!). It takes a good diet, plenty of hard work and a degree of time to create a muscular body. Forget artificial muscle enhancing products. They spell trouble and may well put you on a course for self-destruction.

Most people are content to achieve a well toned physique and for martial arts training, this is sufficient. It is pointless becoming too muscle-bound as this will restrict movement. Decide upon the body shape you would like to attain. Take a close look at yourself and identify any weak areas. Through self-examination, you can begin to plan an exercise routine to meet your needs.

WHAT IS MUSCLE?

Looking inside a muscle, you will discover bundles of muscle fibres packed within cylinder shaped fasciculus. These fibres can extend several inches and this is where movement begins through a process called contraction. Within the environment of the cell are tiny protein threads of actin and myosin. With regular, consistent exercise performed over a period of time, the muscle is stimulated and grows larger to meet increased demands.

When the brain commands movement, muscles start to contract. During exercise, we can experience four basic types of contraction:

Concentric: the muscle shortens as it develops tension. e.g. Curling a barbell, performing a sit-up

Isometric: The muscle develops tension without changing length e.g. holding out arms, locking out a side kick etc. (This training provides greatest strength at the joint angle.)

Eccentric: The muscle lengthens as it develops tension. e.g. Downhill running.

Isokinetic: Uses specific equipment to work muscles at constant speed.

MUSCLE Vs FAT

Muscle is denser than fat tissue and with regular training, although you will look trimmer, it is possible that you will gain in weight. Unless you are aware of this, it can be quite disconcerting to discover that you have put on extra pounds! As a rule, do not judge your fitness and body composition by the use of a pair of scales as it is usually a poor indicator. With aerobic exercise, fat is burned and used for energy and as fat stores decline, muscle becomes more visible. With a programme of muscle work, whether general callisthenics or weight training, muscle will develop and grow thus causing a shift in body composition. Muscle and fat are two different types of tissue and one cannot turn in to the other but if muscles are not exercised, they will eventually shrink.

MOVEMENT

When it comes to movement, muscles generally work in pairs and consideration must be given to the opposing muscles in an exercise programme to avoid any imbalance or weakness. For example, apart from working the biceps in the front of the arms, you should also consider exercises for the triceps (back of the arms).

In martial arts, especially in the kicking styles, the sheer variety of techniques tends to engage all the muscles in the lower body and you can be reasonably sure of gaining all round muscle conditioning. For the ardent martial arts practitioner or competitor, a work-out which targets the muscles should be performed at least three times a week after a thorough warm-up. Anything less will not produce the desired results. For the greatest rewards and overall conditioning, it is considered best to vary the muscle work-out.

Try not to target the same muscles day after day because they will not have time to recover and develop. If you are already quite strong and in good shape and find basic callisthenics (such as press-ups and sit-ups) relatively easy, then try some weight training for extra gains.

BEGINNERS

If you are a new student or unaccustomed to exercise and would like to gain muscle tone and strength, then you may find that the class exercises are enough to contemplate in the early weeks. You can, however, add extra muscle work sessions or combine it with your aerobic work-out, as in circuit training, for extra benefits. Just 20–30 minutes of exercises working on all the main muscles or targeting specific areas (such as the upper body in one session, the lower body in another) will prove productive.

Some people are able to devote an extra couple of hours per week, on top of their martial arts training, to engage in a thorough muscle work-out at the gym. This is fine if you have got the time and resources to do so. However, if time is limited, you can still achieve admirable results by performing quality exercise.

Once you are in shape and reasonably satisfied with your physique and your ability to perform the exercise, then it is possible to reduce the time spent in training by concentrating on specific exercises to maintain fitness. You can do this by increasing the load on the muscles by using extra weight or body resistance or by carrying out a more difficult exercise variation. Also, consideration should be given to the smaller muscles, such as those in the hands and wrists. The object at this stage should be to eliminate any weaknesses or muscle imbalances.

As muscle strength and power improves, you can intensify some of the exercises or increase the number of repetitions and sets to gain absolute strength and endurance. To avoid reaching a plateau stage, vary the exercise technique, repetition and load. It is essential that the body remains challenged and that you are kept motivated by the activity in order to achieve those extra gains. Fortunately, martial arts offers so much exercise diversity, it is near impossible to become jaded or stale.

EXERCISE TECHNIQUE

Slow, controlled exercise technique is considered best for muscle gain and definition while fast repetitions will produce dynamic strength. Prolonged repetitions of muscle work will encourage endurance. As a rule, it is best to vary the exercise technique regularly in order to gain the full range of benefits.

Exercises must be performed correctly for results. Ask your instructor for practical advice.

GUIDELINES:

1. Always warm-up thoroughly before muscle work.

2. Begin by working the major muscle groups (legs and arms).
3. Rest in-between sets of exercises. Time to recuperate is essential.
4. Do not push yourself beyond your current capabilities.
5. Check with the instructor that you are performing correct exercise technique.
6. If you feel pain, stop and tell the instructor. Pain is an indication that something is wrong.
7. Vary your exercise programme regularly and keep a record of the muscles worked.
8. Do not exhaust yourself. You should exercise to a point of mild fatigue.
9. Do not compete with others while exercising as this can result in injury and a lengthy lay-off from training.
10. Learn to listen to your body. Take your time. As exercise becomes easier, modify your training so that your muscles react to the increase in load or change of stimulus.

If you suspect or know of any muscle or joint problems, consult your doctor prior to exercise. Some joint conditions are the result of weak muscles so exercise might provide a remedy. Your doctor will be able to advise.

FLEXIBILITY TRAINING

The third component of physical fitness is flexibility and this is required in order to maintain mobility and a free range of movement. In martial arts training, a fair degree of flexibility is needed to execute technique and reach maximum potential.

Stretching and mobility exercises are considered, by most, to be an enjoyable and relaxing part of fitness training. Whereas aerobic and muscle work quickly tires the body by placing muscles under tension, flexibility training elongates the muscles, releasing tightness and removing stress from the body.

Most martial arts incorporates some flexibility training into the class programme. Stretching is essential to encourage the ability to flow with freedom of movement through the disciplines of the activity. Without a certain level of flexibility, action becomes restricted, muscles tighten, joints become stiff and the body becomes more susceptible to injury and even conditions such as arthritis.

Ideally, basic stretching and loosening of joints and muscles should be performed on a daily basis. This can be carried out at any time of day whenever you feel like it. You can stretch in the car, sitting down at work or even while watching TV and there's no time limit or set routine to follow.

If you are embarking on a programme of developmental stretching, to improve or reach maximum range of movement, then you will need to consider a warm-up and cool-down period to prepare your muscles and joints. Research suggests that advanced stretching is far easier when the body is warmed up. Some people prefer to work on flexibility after an aerobics/muscle work-out. This is highly effective and, of course, helps the muscles relax after a hard training session. Others choose to focus on a specific period of developmental flexibility after a thorough body warm-up.

Begin your routine with easier stretch positions before progressing on to more demanding exercises. Again, listen to your body and learn to accept current limitations. At the end of the session, ensure you cool-down with lighter stretches, joint mobility and gentle massage around the joints and along the muscles. This helps to remove post exercise waste such as lactic acid.

GENERAL GUIDELINES FOR DEVELOPMENTAL STRETCHING

There are various types of stretching programme which you can undertake to achieve improved flexibility. Whichever you decide to follow, apply the following guidelines:

1. Warm-up thoroughly.
2. Begin with easy stretches, targeting one area at a time.
3. Do not bounce to try and achieve the desired flexibility. This can severely injure muscles and joints.
4. Once in a stretch position, hold for approximately 30 seconds to achieve benefits.
5. Do not push beyond your current limits.
6. If there is any pain, release the stretch. The exercise should only be mildly uncomfortable.
7. Cool-down after developmental stretching. Massage around joints and along muscles.
8. Stretch regularly to maintain flexibility.

To safely achieve maximum flexibility gains, it is advisable to follow guidelines. A little knowledge combined with self-control will help prevent injury. In developmental stretching, care should be exercised. A torn muscle, especially in the groin area, can take literally months to heal, so be warned!

Gradually, as you hold a stretch position, you will feel the muscles relax. At this stage, you can push the stretch just a little bit further. If you are a beginner or have restricted flexibility, do not bounce in and out of stretch positions. Ballistic stretching, as it is known, is an extreme, rapid movement which can damage unconditioned muscles and cause an array of joint and tendon problems. Many beginners make the mistake of bouncing and jolting through a stretch not realising the effects and I have seen many people, over the course of my own training, with severe and painful joint damage.

The length of time a development stretch is held often depends upon the individual's muscular response but, as a guide, 30 seconds is often sufficient. If you are comfortable in the stretch, you can push a little further and hold for a slightly longer duration.

DYNAMIC STRETCHING

Flexibility training for maximum gains requires regular practise and, above all, patience. It takes time to see results and it won't do any good trying to force positions in an effort to achieve the coveted side or box splits. The object is to reduce tension in the muscles and improve the total range of movement. It should not be stressful.

Extreme positions, such as the splits, should only be attempted after a good warm-up. There has been a lot of research into the logic of dynamic stretching, which involves moving part of your body and gradually increasing reach, speed of movement or both (eg. front, side, back leg swings). Dynamic stretching combines relaxation of extended muscles with contraction of moving muscles and is said to greatly improve the elasticity of muscles and ligaments as a controlled movement. Performed on a daily basis, research suggests that hyper-mobility can be gained within as little as 12 weeks, providing that the individual is receptive and is being consistent with training.

Combined with other stretching techniques, such as Isometric Stretching, which involves tensing and relaxing muscles while in the stretch position, and Static Stretching, which is simply relaxing through the stretch position, Dynamic Stretching has proved to bring about excellent results.

TAKE YOUR TIME

The object must be to train safely so as to avoid injury although, it is quite common to suffer slight muscle tears in the beginning. Repeated injury, however, may lead to a loss in flexibility and severe muscle and joint weakness.

Muscles are protected by a stretch reflex, a receptor mechanism known as the Golgi Tendon organ. It is located at the end of muscle tendons and fibres and serves as a monitor to sense pain. If the contraction is too strong, a message is sent to the central nervous system to encourage the muscle to relax. If you force the stretch by fighting against your body, you will end up doing more harm than good so go easy and take your time.

JOINT FACTORS

Flexibility isn't just about stretching the muscles, it also concerns mobility in the joints. This is the area where two or more bones meet allowing movement to take place. Each joint has its own characteristic range and type of movement and the range of motion about a joint can vary considerably from one person to another.

A typical synovial joint, such as the knee, is made up of a joint capsule, ligaments, cartilage, synovial fluid, a membrane, bursae and fat pads. It is an intricate structure requiring care in order to maintain joint health and stability for movement.

The ligaments hold the joint in place and are vital to maintaining stability. If ligaments become torn or ruptured, the joint becomes insecure. This may cause dislocation or excessive joint instability and weakness. Ankles and knees are common sites for ligament damage. It is essential that you take care of your joints by taking the following steps:

1. Keep mobile.
2. Warm-up effectively prior to exercise.
3. Combine flexibility with strength training to maintain a balanced programme.

Once ligaments are damaged, they can take up to nine months to repair if indeed they manage to heal at all. Many ligament injuries require micro-surgery to put right.

AGE CONSIDERATIONS

Any exercise programme should give full consideration to the age of the participant. The young and old are especially vulnerable and prone to injury and care should be taken by the participant and by anyone devising a programme, namely the instructor, to ensure the delivery of safe exercise.

When it comes to flexibility, attention must be given to avoid haphazard movement. In the young, growing muscle and bone is prone to injury and damage which can hinder growth and cause problems in later life.

As one matures, anatomical and physiological changes may make it more difficult to achieve optimum flexibility. There is often greater calcification around the joints thus restricting mobility. Degenerative conditions such as osteo-arthritis may be present, muscles may have shortened or atrophied, the spinal column may have lost its elasticity and compression tolerance and these factors will restrict development in older people. Despite this rather grim outlook, it is possible to improve the situation with regular stretching and mobility exercises. In fact, it isn't impossible to achieve hyper-mobility, such as the splits, and with a consistent, safe programme of flexibility, all manner of degenerative conditions can be improved.

Gains in flexibility may vary from day to day. Factors such as muscle warmth (environmental conditions), previous activity (muscle fatigue) and stress (mental or physical) can affect your flexibility levels, so bear this in mind.

Apart from the physical gains of being supple and having the flexibility to perform high kicks and withstand the stresses of stance and movement in martial arts, stretching is also extremely beneficial to health and well-being. It is deeply relaxing and encourages the development of body awareness and comes highly recommended.

EXERCISE SCHEDULE

(Suitable for beginners to advanced).

Duration	Exercise
10 mins	Warm-up: light stretches, joint mobility, jogging on the spot.
20–30 mins	Cardiovascular Work (Aerobics) Consistent jogging, pace-walking, swimming, cycling, step aerobics, shadow boxing, dance etc.
20 mins	Muscle Work: Variety of exercises to target upper, middle and lower body. Press-ups, sit-ups, squats, side leg raises etc.

10–20 mins   Flexibility:
Dynamic stretching (controlled leg raises/arm swings), followed by isometric and static stretching.

5–10 mins   Cool-Down:
Light stretching & joint mobility. Massage around joints and along muscles to help remove post-exercise waste.

GOOD NUTRITION

Fitness without good nutrition is like a sports car without fuel. You cannot expect the body to perform efficiently on a poor quality diet which is why balanced consumption of food and fluid is essential for everyday health and well-being.

In general, most people pay little attention to their nutritional requirements. They feel that if they exercise regularly, then that will be enough to maintain health. In reality, exercise and nutrition go hand in hand and if you want to achieve a reasonable level of vitality and fitness, you need to acknowledge your dietary needs. Good nutrition is also integral in enhancing sports performance, so if you compete, it is wise to check your diet to ensure you are consuming the best nutrients and fluid for optimum energy production and physical functioning.

A basic knowledge of nutrition will serve the purpose of educating ourselves to eat the right types of food and so in this section, we shall cover the fundamentals of healthy nutrition.

CARBOHYDRATES . . . ENERGY PROVIDERS

An active person's diet should be rich in unrefined, high carbohydrate foods to provide the most efficient energy source. You will find carbohydrates in abundance in all natural foods such as wholegrains, fruit and vegetables.

These foodstuffs break down and are stored in the body as glycogen to form the energy needed for movement. This reserve of glycogen will make all the difference to stamina and performance and so a daily diet high in natural carbohydrates is essential in maintaining these stores.

Natural carbohydrates are lower in calories, are free of cholesterol and low in fat. They also contain fibre and a rich supply of vitamins and minerals. Foods such as pasta, rice, potatoes, bananas, apples, cereals etc. should be included into your diet and because they contain low or no fat, they are excellent choices for weight-watchers.

Experts in sports nutrition generally recommend a diet high in natural carbohydrates to competitors, as the body performs more effectively with increased energy levels.

PROTEIN . . . FOR BODY MAINTENANCE

Research suggests that eating too much protein especially of the animal variety, can do more harm than good. Protein is necessary for growth, repair and maintenance of tissues and muscle and for the functioning of enzymes, hormones and antibodies but we do not require vast amounts of protein or protein supplements to build muscle and strength. Only hard work and a well-balanced, high carbohydrate diet will stimulate safe muscle growth.

Protein requirements may be increased slightly to meet demands of extra activity, especially when working to build muscle but it has been proven that muscle will grow even on a low protein vegetarian diet! So, don't waste your money on huge cuts of meat and masses of protein supplements. Excess protein is either excreted from the body, stored as fat or when carbohydrate stores are in short supply, it is simply converted into glucose for energy. On reflection, it's like lighting a fire with ten pound notes!

Research has also shown that the consumption of too much protein places pressure on the kidneys, can cause gout and mineral deficiency as well as dehydration problems. There can also be problems connected with high fat and cholesterol levels.

We should endeavour to include a reasonable amount of protein in our daily diet. Nutritionists advise upon eating plant protein opposed to the animal variety. To gain a complete protein from a plant source which contains all the essential amino acids, combine grains with legumes, rice with peas etc. If, however, you do eat meat, trim off all the fat or try poultry or fish rather than red meat.

FAT ... JUST A LITTLE FOR HEALTH MAINTENANCE

As fat can be easily manufactured from carbohydrates, we shouldn't have to worry about getting enough. If anything, our main concern should be limiting consumption as saturated fats, which are found in animal products, can clog up our arteries and increase our body weight causing a threat to long term health.

We only require about 3% of fats from our total calorie intake to maintain health. In general, we all eat far too much fat rich foods and conditions such as heart disease and cancer are thought to be caused by poor, high fat diets.

Keep a check on your daily fat consumption. Try to avoid sugar rich foods such as biscuits, chocolate, crisps and cakes, convenience foods and food which is fried. Check the contents on food labels to see just how much fat you are eating. You will probably be shocked by the amount. Choose low fat alternatives and try to have 'no-fat days' on a regular weekly basis. Apart from the benefits to health, a low fat diet will help to eliminate fat stores in the body when combined with exercise.

VITAMINS AND MINERALS ... HEALTH ENHANCERS

Vitamins and minerals, also known as micro-nutrients, enhance health and are necessary for the chemical reactions that affect growth, function and metabolism. All vitamins and minerals are equally important and can be readily found in a well-balanced diet.

If your diet is haphazard or you are recovering from illness or injury, you may benefit from taking a vitamin supplement to avoid any deficiency. For the active person, there is often an increased need for Vitamin B complex and Vitamin C. A multi-vitamin and mineral will ensure you get what you need.

There is no conclusive evidence to suggest that taking vitamins will improve sports performance but it will ensure you maintain a good state of health. If you do take supplements, be careful to stick to the recommended dose. Vitamins A, D, E and K are toxic if taken in excess!

There are many other supplements available. To aid mobility and maintain geneal health, cod liver oil capsules of foods/supplements containing Essential Fatty Acids (EFAs) such as fish rich in Omega 3 (sardines, mackerel, salmon) or Omega 6 which is found in vegetable oils (safflower, soybean, sesame seed) are recommended for all practitioners.

FLUID INTAKE

Fluid is vital to the body and if you are physically active, you should drink plenty to replace the fluid lost in perspiration during exercise. Don't wait until you are thirsty before taking a drink. By this time, you may already be feeling the effects of dehydration which will certainly affect your performance and the way you feel. Even a 3% loss of fluid can cause deterioration of performance and so it is important that you have access to drinks before, during and after vigorous training, especially in hot weather. It can take 24 hours to rehydrate the body so always drink plenty of water or fruit juices to maintain body fluids.

PRE-EVENT NUTRITION

How many times have you entered a tournament or performed at an event and felt below par? Possibly many times. Have you ever considered your diet in the build-up to an event?

Many competitors are so wrapped up in their training for a tournament that they often forget to put in the fuel which will provide them with the energy they need. Remember the sports car at the beginning of this section? Well, not only must you consider fuelling the body but you must also contemplate the quality of that fuel in order to perform at optimum levels.

Leading up to an event which requires endurance, research suggests that we can triple our storage of glycogen in the muscles by a technique called carbohydrate loading. Quite simply, this involves eating an increased amount of natural carbohydrates in the days before an event to literally stockpile on energy supplies. This might mean taking an extra helping or adding just a little bit more to your plate or taking extra carbohydrate snacks between meals. Good sources include pasta, rice, vegetables, cereal and fruit.

The pre-event meal should be consumed at least 3–4 hours beforehand and should be light and low in fat and protein which are notoriously slow to digest. Protein also contributes towards dehydration by removing fluid from the muscle tissue during metabolic processes. Eat adequate natural carbohydrates to ensure good blood sugar levels and to stave off hunger and weakness during the event. Some believe that you can perform much better on an empty stomach as eating close to training/competing can drastically affect performance by interfering with blood sugar levels, causing early fatigue. Avoid everything except fluids in the hour before activity.

Do not eat an enormous meal on the day of an event in the hope that it will give you extra energy. Your fuel will derive from the carbohydrates stored several days prior and a meal on event day will only serve to ward off hunger pangs and weakness.

THE RESULTS OF GOOD NUTRITION

The effects of good nutrition on general health and performance are noticeably profound. It can make all the difference to how you bear up in training or competition. Energy levels and reserves increase, making it possible to work to a higher standard for longer durations. Apart from increased strength, you can expect a significant advancement in mental awareness, giving you sharpened reactions. And, because good nutrition keeps you healthy with a boost to the immune system, there is less chance of falling ill and losing valuable training time.

Of course, no one is perfect and we all, at some time or

another, succumb to the temptation of forbidden foods but allow for the occasional treat. It won't do any harm providing that your diet is sensible at all other times.

LIFESTYLE ... THE WISDOM FOR LIVING

To achieve a state of total fitness, we must look beyond the benefits of exercise and good nutrition and consider lifestyle as a whole. How we live bears great significance on our health and well-being and one of the gains of practising martial arts is that it helps us to look within and consider the holistic approach to living.

In today's complex, often highly stressful world, it is difficult to achieve a sense of well-being. We are constantly fighting against time and often one's own conscience, facing one conflict after another in the battle for survival. We are simply too busy or too indifferent to consider the effects of our folly and realisation only comes when the damage has been done.

Trying to balance the proverbial scales of life in order to achieve health and well-being requires a certain amount of discipline but this does not need to be too difficult for the martial arts practitioner. To understand the elements of living a balanced life, we should look to the East for inspiration and consider the Taoism philosophy, symbolised by the black and white 'yin and yang', popularly associated with the Chinese martial arts.

Briefly interpreted, yin and yang represents opposites coming together, reaching a point where one cannot exist without the other. It follows the principals that everything in the universe has an opposite such as day and night, male and female, hot and cold, black and white, sun and moon, good and bad etc, co-existing in harmony.

If we were to put this philosophy into action, learning to calmly accept the negative aspects of life as easily as the positive and avoiding the extremes and excesses of actions in order to maintain a balance, we would then have the perfect recipe for a peaceful, stress-free life. On the whole, most of us strive hard for this reality and come close to achieving a fairly balanced lifestyle.

Too much or too little of whatever we do or whatever affects us will create problems in the long term. Consider the effects of excessive eating, alcohol or cigarette smoking or not enough exercise or too little sleep or rest and think about how this would affect your long term health. Also consider external factors such as working in a heavily polluted environment, staying in the sun too long or being subjected to prolonged levels of stress. Excesses of anything in life will have an adverse effect and rock the delicate balance of our existence and this can apply to the individual or as a whole.

To create a stable lifestyle, thus increasing our chances of living well and to an old age, we need to analyse and check the factors which affect us. Examine your way of life in fine detail. Scrutinise everything to disclose any excesses and then make a plan to show how you are going to change the situation. Making changes isn't always easy, so take it one day at a time. Create gradual adaptations to your routine.

For example, if you live in a highly stressful environment, perhaps through working long hours or have conflicts or worries about money, family or anything which makes you on edge, then look at ways of countering the stress.

IDEAS TO COMBAT STRESS:

Treat yourself to a little self-indulgence.
Take time to relax and have a break from routine.
Listen to music.
Go for a walk.
Have a warm bath or massage.
Take up a relaxing hobby.

The aim is to give yourself a break from the stressful situations which can cause all manner of harm if left unchecked.

If you smoke or drink alcohol regularly, try to cut down to the minimum. If you smoke or drink to gain confidence or control nerves, look at other, more natural ways to achieve these effects. Alternative therapies are very good for this.

NATURAL RELAXATION

To counter the destructive forces of stress, you should aim to include adequate amounts of relaxation into your lifestyle plan. Time to relax is vital, especially if you lead a busy life and will ensure you keep mentally refreshed and physically well.

For the martial arts practitioner, a regular session of meditation will prove highly beneficial. Spending just 10 minutes a day, sitting or lying in a relaxed position with mind focused on breathing or relaxation of muscles, will help you cope better with the daily demands. Choose a peaceful time to meditate when you won't be disturbed. Don't leave it too late in the evening when you are tired as chances are you will fall asleep. You need to be fully awake and alert in an effort to adopt a passive state of mind. Some people just try to empty their head of thought while others envisage tranquil scenes, like a waterfall, trees or some distant paradise.

Tai chi, most commonly thought of as meditation in movement, is effectively a Chinese martial art now mainly practised for its health and relaxation gains. For practitioners engaged in explosive martial arts, Tai chi will make a pleasant and much needed contrast and should actually complement training.

There are a variety of Tai chi styles to choose from. The most popular is the Yang system which emphasizes health promotion rather than combat. Yang is characterised by its easy, graceful and leisurely style and is perhaps the most practised system of Tai chi in the Western world.

From Tai chi, an effective exercise system called Qigong is enjoying great popularity. Qigong which basically means 'cultivation of energy' is made up of a series of exercises, most of which can be performed in limited space, to enhance health and well-being. Some practitioners say that Tai chi and Qigong are one and the same but there are some subtle differences in the way they are practised. To find out more, check out a variety of classes in your area and choose one which you feel comfortable with. For the full benefits, it is essential you learn Tai chi from an experienced teacher.

Suitable for all ages and abilities, Tai chi is a gentle exercise system attracting many senior citizens who find the graceful movements easier to practise. It is highly salubrious to health and like meditation, will help to combat stress. Despite the slow, controlled movements, Tai chi is still demanding enough to tax the muscles and is quite an efficient, low impact work-out. Practitioners often report feeling re-energised after regular training.

Other methods of inducing relaxation and beating stress for an improved lifestyle include complementary therapies such as aromatherapy, reflexology, acupuncture and massage. Find a qualified practitioner to administer complementary therapies for the safest, most effective results. Treatments will also help with healing, correction of chi (energy) flow and is ideal if you have any sports injuries or muscle aches and strains.

COMBINE THE FIVE WAYS

Learning to integrate healthy practices into your daily lifestyle will help towards preventing illness, disease and degenerative problems which can shorten life span or impair the quality of life if left unchecked. By combining all five ways to total fitness: cardiovascular exercise, muscle work, flexibility, good nutrition and healthy lifestyle considerations, you will have the recipe for leading a long and active life. For the martial arts practitioner, being aware of these ways and putting them into action will provide you with a better understanding towards mastering the art.

VOICE OF EXPERIENCE

'It is up to each and everyone of us how we wish to live. No one can make us healthier or improve our lives unless we are prepared to make the effort to change our ways. We all have a choice to make ourselves the best we can be, whatever our backgrounds. We are more in control of our own destiny than most would care to imagine!'
Sifu Mark Strange, Chinese martial arts practitioner.

COMMON QUESTIONS ANSWERED

Q. On average, how long does it take to gain a good level of total fitness?

A. If you train consistently, engaging all five mentioned components, then results will become evident in as little as four weeks. More obvious improvement can be gained in 12 weeks. It largely depends on the individual and factors such as previous health and fitness, metabolism, age, body composition, mental attitude and the amount of time and quality effort dedicated to becoming fit and healthy.

Q. How can I get the splits? I'm reasonably supple but it seems to be taking such a long time.

A. To achieve advanced flexibility, you need to follow a specific programme of training comprising of developmental stretching. There are several books dedicated to the theory and practice of attaining hyper-mobility which cover the technicalities of achieving the front and box splits. Dynamic stretching combined with isometric and static stretching are considered the best methods for quicker results. Be prepared to work at it but above all, have patience and self-control. You need to be consistent in your training.

Q. Although I attend two karate classes a week, I easily become out of breath when walking or running. What am I doing wrong?

A. You could attend a class every single night but if there is no specific cardiovascular/aerobic conditioning, you will not reach peak fitness. To increase stamina, you need to maintain a regular and consistent programme of aerobic exercise. Read through the cardiovascular section at the beginning of this chapter and choose an activity which you can work on at your convenience. The activity must be performed to a level which will comfortably raise your heart and breathing rate.

Q. I haven't time for a meal before training so I usually eat a few chocolate snacks on the way to the gym. However, during the lesson, I feel weak and quite sick. How can I avoid this?

A. Chocolate snacks may provide a quick burst of energy but it soon diminishes and you are invariably left feeling weak, nauseous, drained of energy and light-headed. For training, especially if it is energetic, you need to be eating natural carbohydrates wherever possible in regular, well-balanced meals in order to maintain high energy levels. If you haven't got time for a meal before training (and ideally you should have 1–2 hours space between eating and training) then opt for natural carbohydrate snacks, such as fruit. Try to include a late afternoon snack, comprising of wholemeal sandwiches, fruit, nuts etc. to stave off hunger. But do try to make time to consider your diet. Food is fuel for the muscles and without quality food, your body will grind to a halt.

Q. Although I've been training for years, I still experience a lot of stiffness in my muscles a day or so after training. Quite often, there is a good deal of soreness. What can I do to avoid this?

A. Some people are prone to post-exercise aches more than others but there's some guidelines which you can follow to avoid it:

Make sure you warm up and cool-down effectively. Pay particular attention to the cool-down section after training and spend some time gently stretching and massaging along the muscles.

Try a warm bath with lavender oil or herbal relaxing oil to soothe muscles and joints after training.

Drink plenty of fruit juice or water to replace lost fluids and flush out waste products.

If after taking this action, you are still suffering muscle aches and pains then take a look at your training schedule. Are you pushing too hard beyond your current capabilities? Are you forcing stretch positions and causing muscle strain and tears? Is the programme of exercise too taxing? Consider these aspects and speak with your instructor about the problem.

Q. Is it true that muscle power and skill improves when muscles are warm?

A. Yes! research has shown that warmer muscles function more effectively than cold ones which is why the warm-up period is essential for development. It is said that force production increases 10–15% for every 1 degree rise in Celsius within muscle temperature. The results being that nerve impulse time is quicker so benefiting speed.

CHAPTER FOUR

THE WAY FORWARD

© Paul Banister

Progress and achievement comes with dedication

'Keep your mind busy to accomplish things; keep your mind open to understand things.'

Tut-Tut

IMPROVING SKILLS AND TECHNIQUE

Building skill in the martial arts takes time and effort and this is a fact which many students overlook in their eagerness to get through the grading system. Even if you have memorised all the moves and techniques from just a handful of lessons, it is still highly unlikely that you will have become adept enough to perform these skills effectively.

Throughout the martial arts world, despite the variety of styles available, one can easily distinguish between who has spent time on practice against who has not. Experience is visible in the way the practitioner moves and how he performs the art. The skill is such that it is clearly evident even to the lay-person.

The expertise gained through practice, accumulated in time, becomes like second nature to the martial artist. Techniques such as blocks, hand and footwork, defence combinations and the like can be performed instinctively without prior thought. To reach this level is to attain mastery of the art but to tune in your senses and create this degree of superiority requires a dedicated approach to training.

Level of skill varies between one person and the next and is largely dependent upon extrinsic factors such as regularity of training, the ability of the instructor to teach you effectively and the study environment. All these have an effect on how you attain skill in the long term, however, the decision to learn and make the effort to become skilful is one which rests with you alone.

If your aim is to become highly proficient in martial arts, whether the end goal is for self-satisfaction, to be the best in competition or to become a martial arts instructor, then the only way forward is to learn and train consistently. You need a thirst for knowledge. There is no easy way to achieve a greater level of skill. You can't cut corners because, in the end, you will only be cheating yourself.

It is not uncommon to hear of beginners jumping to an advanced level in their rush to reach the pinnacle of their martial art. True enough, stories exist about low grades awarding themselves a high grade or even paying for their Black Belt to by-pass the system. As wrong as this is, it does still happen although with the introduction of tighter controls by governing bodies, Black Belt impersonators are becoming a thing of the past. In any case, students who foolishly by-pass the system and years of training are, in the end, only fooling themselves and a charlatan will eventually be caught out.

To become an accomplished martial artist, it is essential that you are receptive to learning. It is not enough to mimic your instructor's actions; you must understand why he acts. You must use all your senses to determine the way forward, to gain comprehension of every single technique and know why it is administered.

Your ultimate aim should be to become the best and that means setting a realistic goal which you can work to. Skill can be nurtured. It is, if you like, an essential ingredient which needs to be shaped over a period of time to improve its potential. The essence of skill is not dissimilar to a vintage bottle of wine!

ACTION FOR IMPROVING SKILL AND TECHNIQUE

1. Practise at every opportunity.
2. Do not be content to simply copy actions without thought. Instead analyse what you learn and understand why and how the technique can be effectively used.
3. Accept that your instructor is not your only teacher. You can learn from fellow students, assimilate information from books, use your eyes and ears to find out more and you can even learn from the animals around you! Movement and action is a universal language.
4. Have patience in your learning. There is no rush and it should not be treated like a competition. Give yourself time to understand what you are learning.
5. Do not advance until you have perfected technique to the best of your current ability.
6. Be constantly revising what you learn until it becomes second nature.

VOICE OF EXPERIENCE

'As a school teacher, I realise that all people, children and adults alike, have mental skills that need training. I am highly impressed by the way in which these skills are improved through the teaching of martial arts. I am talking about the skills of concentration, of concentration of an ever-increasing time span, memory skills, co-ordination of parts of the body and of mind and body. It includes a greater sense of self-esteem, self-discipline, patience and the ability to work as an individual, group member or even group leader. It teaches self-respect. Many of these skills are needed for pre-reading, pre-number and pre-learning. They are taught to us in schools but we forget how to use them. These kung fu and Tai chi lessons I have experienced are helping me not only to use them but also to improve on them. This is part of a "hidden curriculum" much of which is inherent in the rules of behaviour instilled in the students.

Sometimes, we take for granted the time and effort put into the guidance and support we get from our instructors. This guidance results in students helping each other and sometimes putting their own needs to one side. From training, I have gained both mentally and physically. Also, and this is very important, I have made many new friends of

all ages and both sexes. I am grateful for the excellent teaching I have found in the martial arts.'
Evelyn Haworth, Chinese martial arts student.

PRACTISE VARIABILITY

Varying technique or routine is a good way of maintaining interest in the learning process. It prevents the onset of boredom while helping to maintain motivation and is considered highly beneficial. Varied practice leads to adaptability.

More complex skills may be broken down into smaller, more manageable parts and practised in sections rather than the whole together. This is particularly advisable when practising forms/kata. If you perform a limited range of variations of technique, then you will attain quality in repetition.

ACQUIRING THE MOST OUT OF PRACTICE

1. Set yourself attainable goals. These must be realistic and based upon your understanding and level of ability.
2. Mentally rehearse specific skills using imagery. This helps to improve memory.
3. A short period of intense effort with attention to detail is considered more effective in the attainment of skill.
4. Focus your attention on learning and concentrate.
5. Listen carefully and analyse any feedback your instructor, coach or fellow student gives you.

DEDICATION AND DETERMINATION

To master the martial arts, or achieve a reasonable amount of skill in any discipline, one must take a determined and dedicated approach to guarantee results. But, what does it mean to possess these qualities and how can one attain them?

Well, fundamentally, determination and dedication are intrinsic elements. In simpler terms, they are qualities which come from within us and are part of our character and fabric. Having these attributes can shape development in the martial arts and will influence the level of study intensity. Everyone has these qualities at their disposal but not everyone has the will-power or tenacity to call upon these resources when needed.

In martial arts training, dedication is considered to be an important element in acquiring a high level of skill. To be dedicated is to devote one's time and energy to a special purpose while determination involves firmness of purpose. Combined, these two powerful attributes will carry you forward in your endeavours and will undoubtedly keep you going even through the hardest of times.

Of course, not everyone finds it easy to tap into these often latent strengths. Much depends upon your characteristics and the individual ability to control one's actions and impulses but these qualities can be shaped by taking positive steps:

1. Visualise what you want to achieve. If you want to become a Black Belt expert or a tournament champion, visualise it in your mind. Building a positive image gives you something to work for and helps you to clearly focus your ambitions more clearly.
2. Decide what you want and go for it. Make a decision and keep to it. If you are unnerved about setting yourself a mammoth task, worried that you might not complete it, then set easier, more realistic targets. Don't look too far ahead if this is the case. Instead, plan a month at a time and aim for smaller goals.
3. Don't ask for what is really beyond your reach. Do not set yourself impossible goals. If you are a beginner, don't expect to be performing advanced techniques in the early days. Aim within your current capabilities.
4. Don't give up too easily. We've all had a day which has made us want to throw in the towel and give up completely. This might come after a particularly difficult training session or after losing in a tournament. Yes, it is easy to give up but what would you be left with? If you ever find yourself in this position, contemplating an early retirement from the activity, then consider the long term and what you will be losing out on.

VOICE OF EXPERIENCE

'One can take a determined stance and apply it to aspects of training without being dedicated to the whole. One can be dedicated to martial arts practice and yet not show any signs of being determined. If, however, you were to combine determination with dedication, you would have a great strength at your disposal. Only few in the martial arts possess both qualities.'

Martial arts instructor.

'I believe that martial arts training shapes us and reveals our hidden strengths over the course of time. I did not realise how determined I could be until I started martial arts.'

Ju-jitsu student.

'When it comes to dedication, there are several degrees of enthusiasm ranging from being slightly devoted to having absolute commitment. We can not all give the same dedication to martial arts as the Shaolin monks but should offer what we can and accept it as being a valid commitment. After all, we practise to please and benefit ourselves and not to the tune of others.'

Kung fu student.

NURTURING POSITIVE MENTAL ATTITUDE

There is one essential attribute which can make all the difference between success and failure. It is, once again, an intrinsic quality which when applied correctly can shape one's destiny, be it in the martial arts or in any sphere of life. This crucial force is 'positive mental attitude', or PMA, and it is the most talked about component in the world of sport.

Having PMA will help one reach the pinnacle of success. It is a vital characteristic which can give the individual the edge over one's contemporaries. This inner strength will enable you to ride over obstacles as if they are non-existent and give the courage and confidence to succeed, whatever the challenge.

PMA has been well documented in recent years. Coaches from all sports readily agree the benefits of having a positive mind to enhance performance. The sportsmen of our time have all learnt how to tap into their positivity in order to achieve results. But, PMA can be utilised throughout life and applied to all manner of situations whether it is to pass an exam, learn a new hobby or even when tackling a dangerous or challenging predicament.

In the martial arts, PMA will help you achieve your goals whether it is to become the best martial artist you can be or the champion of champions. It will act as a deciding force, to some degree, and provide you with the vitality of mind needed to determine positive results. It can ultimately give you the advantage over your fellow practitioners and is a particularly useful quality to possess if you compete to a high level.

PMA is all about self-belief and calls upon qualities such as courage, self-confidence, discipline, ambition and single-mindedness to make it effective. It can be trained in the same way you work your muscles to build strength.

In the Far East, martial arts masters regard physical training alone as being incomplete. The mental training is considered just as important as the physical and is positively encouraged through meditation and specific exercises. In the

West, many practitioners lack the required mental powers. They concentrate on building strong bodies while neglecting to build a strong mind and this is perceived as a weakness.

A student can nurture PMA by focusing his mind in an assertive and constructive way. By beginning this training early, you will gain mental vitality as you progress through your grades and it will certainly point towards more positive results.

GUIDELINES FOR GAINING PMA

1. Believe in yourself whole-heartedly.
2. Have confidence in your abilities.
3. Discard negative thoughts.
4. Do not give up. Always make an effort.
5. Congratulate yourself for every achievement, however inconsequential.
6. Be disciplined in your training.

During training, take a positive stance even on the most difficult of tasks. If you inwardly tell yourself that 'it's impossible', it will become just that! So, be affirmative. Tell yourself, 'I can do it!' Clear away any negative thoughts.

You can apply this philosophy to any aspect of your life. At first, in your training, you might use PMA to achieve the best out of physical exercise or you may call upon it to help you perform a complex technique. There are so many situations which you can apply a positive mental attitude to.

It is important to feel good about yourself. Having confidence will encourage the development of PMA. Look for ways in your training where you can put it to the test and focus on improving your positivity through all aspects of your life.

VOICE OF EXPERIENCE

'Positive mental attitude is the stuff which turns dreams into reality. It is a form of conscious energy, if you will; a state of mind which creates a heightened sense of awareness. It is very difficult to explain the "hows" and "whys" of it but you just know, without doubt, when it's there. PMA is generated through training and, to me, seems to appear when I am at my peak of physical fitness. It's like a buzz; a very real energy which carries you along in waves and makes you feel on form. In competition, if you have PMA at your disposal, greater achievements will result. I feel sharper, quicker and far more confident in my abilities. Without it, I tend to lose the edge over my competitors and feel awkward or out of touch. I believe PMA is a state which one can nurture and even control, to some extent, at a higher level. It's all about believing in yourself and having the determination to work hard for your goals.'

Sifu Mark Strange

LEARNING WITH AN OPEN MIND

To embody the spirit of the martial arts, one must maintain an open mind. It is a special ability which many find formidable because it requires sitting back and being receptive to all ideas without being too quick to judge. We say it is a special quality because a great number of students and instructors lose their way through closing their minds and not accepting the importance of being enlightened.

In martial arts, an open mind is seen as the proverbial key to the door. It enables the student to be responsive to knowledge and creates opportunities which may otherwise have been lost. It is also encouraged so that all practitioners, regardless of style, can work together in harmony rather than wasting time and effort bickering and condemning each other. Generally, all styles of martial arts have their purpose and only the most enlightened of practitioners will realise this.

In a more practical and worthwhile sense, maintaining an open mind encourages student development. It makes you look at life more objectively and will help you attain a better understanding of the world around you.

GUIDELINES FOR MAINTAINING AN OPEN MIND

1. Do not be too easily dismissive in your learning of martial arts. Carefully evaluate knowledge and do not pre-judge.

2. When seeing a new technique or experimenting with another style of martial art, sample it out thoroughly for yourself before assessing its worth and remember what isn't useful to you might be quite valuable to somebody else.
3. Think before you act! As one wise sage once said, 'disaster often spills out of the mouth.' It's far better to ponder quietly before speaking or acting upon anything which is new or different.
4. Believe that all things are possible. The world is full of surprises and mysteries.
5. Do not speak against what you don't know.

Throughout the martial arts, especially in the West, many students possess a closed mind and it is an attitude which can severely hamper development and understanding. Indeed, we have perhaps all been guilty at some time or another of undue criticism or disbelief. How many times, for example, have you picked on another martial art without appropriate reason? How many times have you knocked another student or dismissed a training technique without really thinking? How many times have you been without faith or scoffed at something you haven't fully understood? No doubt plenty of times because it is an attitude which seems to prevail throughout the Western world.

I can bring to mind one example of a young, martial arts student who was forever making fun out of another martial arts style. He spent all his time passing negative remarks at their techniques until one day, he met up against one of their students in competition and was beaten a humiliating 10–0. He certainly learnt a lesson from that experience.

But having an open mind isn't just about attitude and morality within the martial arts and how you think and act among fellow practitioners; it's also about how you cultivate what you learn. Each Master of martial arts will have his own ideas, his own techniques and his own ways for living. These may differ from what you believe or practise but it doesn't mean to say that their way is wrong or useless. To become enlightened, one must first learn to question what we learn and to accept the variables. It doesn't necessarily matter if you don't understand what is placed before you; what is important is that you take it in and learn from it and remain open in your assessment.

We only have to look at the mysteries and complexities of life to realise that there is more on heaven and earth; much more than we can ever perceive. So by keeping open to ideas, we are able to expand in our practice of martial arts and by accepting the ways of others we are able to seek enlighten-ment.

VOICE OF EXPERIENCE

'Rather than developing an open mind, many prac-titioners become closed and unable to see further than their own horizons. They become restricted by the confines of their own knowledge and fail to listen to the wisdom of others. They begin to see their own way as the only way. If only they would open their minds, their knowledge would become greater.'

Karate instructor.

'My teacher once told me that the key to knowledge lay in the ability to be open-minded. He likened the open mind to a doorway which entered a room full of treasures. While the doorway remained open, the treasure was accessible but if the door was to close, one would never stumble across it. He said that because so many martial artists have closed minds, many never find real wisdom.'

Kung fu student.

'Because so many practitioners engage in petty rivalry, they miss out on what is important. Through ignorance or indifference, they fail to see what is significant and as a result, lose time and waste effort.'

Kick-boxing student.

PRACTISE, PRACTISE AND MORE PRACTISE

The route to becoming a skilful martial arts practitioner is often a long and difficult road. It requires constant practise to acquire and perfect technique and knowledge.

Not everyone finds study easy, especially if it means repeating boring drills, constantly going over and over the same routines. Ask any instructor how many times he has paced up and down a room in training or how many times he has executed a punch or a kick and he will probably look heavenwards for the answer. In China, stone floors have permanent recesses in them to mark the dedicated footwork of students training throughout the years. Their effort has worn away the stone as water would erode a riverside banking.

Practise is what makes us good at what we do. The more we practise, the better we become but everyone is different and the amount of time you need to devote to training in martial arts basically depends on the following:

1. What you wish to achieve from learning.
2. How receptive you are to learning.
3. How efficient your memory is.
4. How in shape you are in relation to the martial art being taught.

If you are learning just as a spare time hobby or for fun then your approach to study may be relatively relaxed. On the other hand, if martial arts is your main activity and figures highly in your life, then you will probably devote more time and energy into your training.

When you are starting out in martial arts, it's difficult to know how you are going to get on but your enthusiasm will carry you along and like a sponge, your mind will soak up knowledge. As you progress, study becomes more complex and your memory will be taxed to the limit. You may have to devote extra time to study.

One question a beginner most commonly asks is 'how many lessons will it take to become good at martial arts'. It's like asking how long is a piece of string! It's difficult to assess or put any figure on it seeing that everyone is different. You can't really tell just by looking at someone how they will progress. I have known people to plod on quite happily with one lesson a week and go on to gaining their Black Belt. I have also seen students who take three or more classes a week but still find it difficult to develop. It really does depend on the individual and how receptive the student is to learning and processing what they have been taught to acquire a proficient level of skill. If you are taking one lesson a week and are quite happy with the results then that is fine and you should carry on as you are doing. If, however, you feel you are falling behind or are anxious that you are not learning as quick as you would like, then speak with your instructor about how you are bearing up. He may suggest you attend an extra class or engage in more training at home.

PRACTISE OUTSIDE THE CLASS ENVIRONMENT

Many students practise their martial arts skills at home in-between lessons as a way of remembering techniques and perfecting what has been learnt. If you are able to train from home and feel comfortable with it, then this is advisable and will not do any harm. You can practise anywhere and at any time, even if it's simply going through part of a technique or just running through the motions.

I remember one particular practitioner whose training was

a way of life. He would train in the kitchen, running through a sequence while waiting for the kettle to boil; he would practise balance and focus if in a shopping queue or while waiting for a bus; if he had friends round, he would sit on the floor improving his stretch positions and if he had to go on an errand, he would use the opportunity to work his fitness. He never let a moment slip by and his dedication finally blessed him with many talents and achievements.

Practising at home alone does require discipline and motivation. Some find it too difficult and become easily distracted. Arrange a time to train which suits you, away from family, away from the distractions of television and at a time when you feel enthused. If you still find it hard work, invite a fellow student to practise with you.

TIPS FOR TRAINING ALONE

1. Choose a time of day when you are feeling energetic and at your best.
2. Do not let yourself become side-tracked.
3. Set out a training routine and make the effort to stick to it.
4. Train hard but do not overwork yourself nor practise techniques which you are not physically ready for.
5. Vary the routine regularly to avoid boredom setting in.

TRAINING WITH A PARTNER

If you are finding martial arts training too intense or are unable to understand some of the elements of study then consider practising with a partner. This can prove to be a winning motivational exercise, especially if you work with a partner who shares the same enthusiasm. Partner training can prove extremely productive for practitioners at all levels, whatever the style of martial arts. It helps with the assimilation of information and encourages speedier development. You can practise and perfect certain techniques which requires contact with another person, such as throws, sensitivity training, kick-boxing, traditional free-fighting, blocking sequences and the like and, as well as working together trying out technical applications, you can also pick up on faults, encourage each other and discuss any training difficulties.

TIPS FOR TRAINING WITH A PARTNER

1. Choose a partner who shares your enthusiasm for martial arts.
2. Concentrate on quality training time. Don't get carried away with chatting.
3. Set a routine which is appropriate to your level.
4. Train with someone who is of a similar grade/experience.
5. Encourage one another and be constructive with any comments.
6. Consider safety in training and stick to the rules.

TRAINING FOR VERSATILITY OR SPECIALISATION?

In the course of learning martial arts, the opportunity may arise where you can either branch off and specialise in a certain discipline of the art or practise all areas to gain a general, all round knowledge of the subject.

For example, some practitioners become experts in weaponry or even one particular type of weapon, such as the Staff or Bo, while others may become highly experienced in the application of traditional syllabus, able to perform technical wizardry. Some choose to stick with the modern approach and become champion kick-boxing competitors while only a few manage to become renowned as 'good-all-rounders', able to perform well in all aspects of their particular martial art.

Whether you eventually choose to specialise and become an expert in your chosen subject or try to become versatile with a wider knowledge of your art, the way you progress will depend upon the commitment you put in. Many martial artists discover in the course of study that they are more adept at a certain aspect of training and this usually leads to the practitioner opting to specialise.

As you progress, you will get a feel for what path you wish to follow. Whether you want to specialise or prefer to be versatile, the rules for reaching your goals are still the same. Give commitment and time and your efforts will be realised.

VOICE OF EXPERIENCE

'The practice of martial arts is both a science and an art. It is the art of using one's natural weapons for combat and the science of body movement. Both combine to bring perfection of technique. This perfection, however, cannot come to you over-night or by just attending a few classes. You must be willing to give a lot of your time to train each technique, making each training drill realistic so that it becomes simple enough to use. If you train on technique which is simple and direct, allowing it to be part of your mental make-up as well as your physical make-up, you will find that your sensi-tivity and awareness will also be improved. This will benefit you so that you can recognise the build-up to a fight or situation before it escalates to the full thing. It is not just martial arts that can bring you inspiration or help in your training, so keep your mind open to new ideas and experiences that will aid you. This may come in the form of a book (helping you to think or see things from a new angle) or from some other physical activity (dancing/aerobics to help with mobility, timing and relaxation). Remem-ber, if it can improve what you do, go out and do it!'

Thomas Carruthers, Jeet Kune Do
I.M.A. instructor, GLASGOW

COMMON QUESTIONS ANSWERED

Q. I train regularly and consider myself to be conscientious but find that my fellow students are far more skilful. What am I doing wrong?

A. Everyone progresses at their own pace and as long as you are making progress then there is nothing to worry about. It's easy to compare our skills with that of our fellow students but rather than moan about how much better they are, it would prove more conducive to analyse why they appear to be more advanced. Take a more constructive approach and have patience in your own training.

Q. I am considering getting together with one of the students to do some extra training outside the class in the hope that it will benefit us both. Is this a good idea? Also what kind of skills should we work on?

A. If you are equally matched in terms of size and capability and share a similar enthusiasm for the martial arts then there's no reason why such a partnership should not benefit you both. Any extra training you do besides attending a class is a considerable bonus and will help you in the development of skill. The kind of training you do depends on your situation but it is often best to keep it varied so that you both maintain an interest. Work on areas of weakness and encourage one another throughout and be constructive so that you learn from the extra study.

Q. I've always considered myself to have an open mind and

I love to learn but when it comes to having positive mental attitude, I fail miserably. This is a huge downfall for me. Is there anything I can do to improve my outlook?

A. Yes, of course there is and your first lesson is to believe that you can change the situation and develop PMA. It is a state of mind which can be trained. It partly derives through the attainment of skill in martial arts but it can be summoned through specific mental training. Believing in yourself, having confidence and self-discipline are all qualities which shape PMA. In your training, learn to strengthen your resolve with positive statements. Instead of thinking, 'I'll never do that', try 'I'll give it a go!' or 'I'll keep going until I succeed'. Think positive all of the time, even outside of training, and in time you will notice a definite change for the better.

CHAPTER FIVE

SAFETY ISSUES

© Paul Banister

Being aware will sharpen your senses

'To go a little too far is as bad as not going far
   enough.'

Confucius

Safety in the martial arts is an issue which is receiving far
more attention these days, and rightly so. Instructors and
coaches from all sports are having to take more care and
extra precautions to safeguard students' health and well-
being throughout participation. Fundamentally, instructors
are becoming more safety conscious because they care about
their students welfare but also because of having a reputation
to uphold. With the constant threat of law suits and legal
battles for compensation resulting from sporting injuries,
instructors need to be prudent. This rule also applies to
students who are also at risk of being sued if they injure a
fellow student or member of the public. Apart from taking
care, all martial arts practitioners should have adequate
insurance cover as a back-up in-case of any unforeseen
incident and this is most advisable considering martial arts is
renowned as being a high risk sport. So, make sure you have
insurance!

On a more practical level, you can prevent injury to
yourself and others by being safety conscious and sensible in
your practice. Simple requirements such as wearing correct
equipment (head-guards, groin guards, padding for kick-
boxing or contact work) to ensuring that you warm-up

effectively to minimise the risk of injury, all counts towards overall well-being. Yes, it might take extra time, effort and commitment to follow safety measures but it will be worth it if it protects the health of yourself and others.

This chapter is dedicated to safety issues and I would urge all practitioners to read through this section carefully. It might not be the most interesting aspect of your training nor will it reveal any secrets for mastering martial arts but it will serve to achieve one very important goal and that is to make sure you survive the course of training intact and without serious injury.

INJURY PREVENTION

Martial arts is, without doubt, generally considered to be a high risk sport where contact is involved but even in lone practise, injuries can occur often as a result of poor concentration or indifference to the safety procedures.

In the relatively few years I have been involved in martial arts, I have seen how easy it is to attain an injury. Most of them are fortunately superficial, such as bruising or grazing, but just as many are potentially serious such as head concussions and ligament injury.

Students who are keen to advance often ignore personal safety by pushing too hard in their work-outs, forgetting to warm-up effectively, ignoring the use of safety equipment and through exercising poor technique. This is when most injuries occur. It is commonly muscle and joints which are affected, muscle strains and tears, over-use syndrome injuries or, more seriously, ligament damage affecting joint areas. As for martial arts which involves contact, there is certainly an increased risk. Injuries can range from soft tissue bruising to concussion.

To use a well-worn cliché, prevention is better than cure. How often do we hear this mentioned? More to the point, how often do we heed these words? It sounds relatively straightforward but when it comes to the crunch, preventative measures are overlooked. New beginners often fall victim to injury as much as the enthusiastic practitioners in their rush to get ahead. Competitive students, who enter tournaments on a regular basis, are also more injury prone. Perhaps you identify yourself as being at risk?

PRACTITIONERS WHO ARE PRONE TO INJURY

1. NEW BEGINNERS
   Injury occurs through lack of initial knowledge or in the rush of enthusiasm. Most try too hard at the start and then ignore the warning signs.
2. THE ENTHUSIASTIC MARTIAL ARTIST
   This person often trains too hard and never knows when to stop. He is usually ambitious and will go beyond the pain barrier and even work through injury. This commonly leads towards burn-out (over-training).
3. THE COMPETITOR
   Despite being a reasonable performer, this practitioner always seems to come up against a rougher, tougher

opponent and sometimes the contact is too heavy and technique requires polishing.

4. THE LAZY TRAINER

    Takes too many short cuts and shirks hard training. Injury results through lack of attention to warm-up or through training hard after periods of inactivity such as standing around in class.

HOW INJURIES OCCUR

Personal Factors:

1. Failure to warm-up effectively.
2. Failure to wear correct protective equipment.
3. Failure to listen to instructions.
4. Training too hard beyond current capabilities.
5. Ignoring pain and/or symptoms of impending injury.
6. Ignoring club rules and safety procedures.
7. Messing about while training.
8. Not taking care when engaged in partner/team work.
9. Taking short cuts in training.
10. Training when ill or before full recovery from illness.

External Factors ... The instructor

1. Incorrect teaching techniques.
2. Poor instructor-to-student communication.
3. Lack of knowledge in safe exercise.
4. Does not emphasise safety procedures.

5. Class size too large (There should be no more than 30 students per instructor).
6. Lack of understanding in safety procedures.
7. Lack of order and discipline within the class.
8. Poor class organisation.
9. Instructor sets no example.
10. Pushing students beyond their current level.

External Factors ... The Venue

1. Poor floor conditions (e.g. uneven, cracked tiles, wet areas, dirty etc.)
2. Venue too small for number of participants.
3. Poor lighting.
4. Poor ventilation.
5. Dangerous protrusions on the walls or on the floor area.
6. Lack of suitable equipment (mats for sparring, judo etc.)
7. Exercise equipment damaged and not suitable for use.

External Factors ... Other Practitioners

1. Competitor using too much force against you.
2. Poor standard competitor whose lack of expertise results in the delivery of poor technique (kicks to groin, excessive contact etc.)
3. Class training partner poorly matched (either not the same standard or because of size/weight difference).
4. Other students inflicting injury through their own lack of care and attention.

As you will clearly see from this list, there are an array of factors which can affect your well-being in the martial arts but just about all injuries are preventable. Many occur simply through lack of attention to detail or failure to identify risks.

TAKING PREVENTATIVE MEASURES

Whether you are a beginner or an advanced martial arts student, you are the one who is ultimately in control of your own body and actions. Although the instructor can teach and guide you through your training, he cannot physically feel your pain or discomfort and won't always be aware of your individual response to exercise during the class training so you must use your own initiative and take care to avoid injury.

Know when to stop. If you are in pain, feel intense discomfort, feel ill or are greatly fatigued while training, then you must stop and let the instructor know. Do not try to battle on. Pain is one of the body's symptoms to point out that something is wrong and, if you ignore it, you could end up worse off. Many students foolishly push too far, ignoring pain and fatigue and, as a result, their bodies are placed under great strain.

Many beginners are at risk of injury purely because of their lack of experience, their rush to get ahead and often because they are not fit enough for the level of exercise taking place. A good instructor will gently guide the beginner through those early weeks without major mishap. There is a lot you can do yourself by trying to exercise patience and care whilst you train. Your fitness, whether aerobic, strength or flexibility, will improve with time and gradual effort, and as it improves, you will be able to advance in your abilities. In a way, your development in martial arts is like that of the apple tree. You cannot expect it to bear fruit until it has emerged from the soil. It takes time to grow and any damage to the root will only hamper that growth!

A correct warm-up is very important to reduce the risk of injury and this applies to all practitioners. This is a period of mental and physical preparation and cannot be over-emphasised. The warm-up gently stretches the muscles, increasing the heat in the tendons, ligaments and joints in readiness for activity. The warm-up is especially needed prior to vigorous training and should be related to the activity and the individual's capabilities. At the end of the exercise session, a cool-down will help the body recover. Stretching and light massage strokes will help stimulate the body to remove excess fluid from the tissues which accumulates after exercise stops. If left, this fluid may cause muscle soreness and cramps so pay particular attention to the cool-down.

Where appropriate, use the correct safety equipment. For contact work, say in kick-boxing, you should take all the necessary precautions to protect yourself and fellow students from harm. Apart from hands and feet pads, it is most imperative to wear a head-guard. Although this won't necessarily stop you from getting concussed if you receive a heavy blow, it will nonetheless provide a good degree of protection and prevent the possibility of serious head injury. Of course, it is up to the instructor to ensure that contact in training is kept to a minimum. Other equipment includes groin guards, which are available for male and female practitioners and are highly advisable to safeguard against low kicks from inexperienced students; chest guards for ladies, mouth guards, shin and elbow pads and even full body armour is available for specific training.

Abiding by the rules of the club is also considered a measure for preventing injury. Most clubs advise students to keep toe and finger nails short to avoid cutting or scratching your fellow practitioner. It is also advisable to remove jewellery. Loop earrings are a danger. If they get caught up, it can cause a nasty ear lobe tear. Rings and watches can also be a hindrance and should be removed while training.

Other rules, such as 'do not fool around in training' or 'refrain from standing about talking' are fairly common sense. Fooling about can cause injury to yourself or others. It only takes one wrong impulsive move to fall or cause harm. Standing about talking means that your body is cooling down thus is more at risk of injury, such as muscle strains or sprains when activity suddenly resumes. So, take heed of your club rules. They are there to protect your interests!

GUIDELINES

1. Always warm-up before exercise.
2. Do not exercise beyond your current abilities.
3. If you feel pain, stop and tell the instructor.

4. Do not train if you feel ill or are recovering from illness or injury.
5. Listen to your instructor and follow club safety rules.
6. Take care when working with other practitioners.
7. Wear correct safety equipment where appropriate.
8. Keep finger and toe nails trimmed and remove jewellery when engaged in partner work.
9. Cool-down with light stretches and soothing massage strokes at the end of training.
10. Do not take your body for granted!

INJURY TREATMENT

Despite the best will in the world to keep injury free, chances are you might become a victim purely through bad luck and you will want to know the best way to treat any damage so that you can return to activity as quickly as possible.

As we know, some systems of martial arts carry more risk than others. Kick-boxing and the energetic styles such as Wushu or Tae kwon do fall into the high risk category. Injuries often result through contact, such as a blow to the body or soft tissue. Styles which include Judo, Aikido and Ju-jitsu see injuries which are synonymous with throws, locks and grappling. The activity which poses the least risk is the genteel Tai chi.

Of course, we are well aware of the dangers of martial arts when we enrol and we know the preventative measures we must take in an effort to avoid injury but sometimes, an accident will happen regardless of the care taken and it pays to know what treatment to administer to ensure a speedy and effective recovery.

Injury commonly strikes:

1. Soft tissue ... muscles, ligaments, tendons, skin.
2. Bones and joints.

More rarely and potentially life threatening are injuries to the organs ... brain, spinal cord, lungs, heart and abdominal contents.

CAUSES OF INJURY IN THE MARTIAL ARTS

1. Contact/Direct Force: such as a blow to the body using too forceful a punch or kick or injury sustained through a bad breakfall.
2. Over-use/Indirect Force: caused by too much stress on the body or strain through repetitive activity.
3. Environmental Factors: includes inappropriate or incorrect use of equipment or facility.

FIRST AID BASICS

There are already plenty of specialist books available dedicated to first aid techniques and procedure so I'm not going to go into great detail except to mention basics which every practitioner should endeavour to know. It is advisable that all instructors attend an approved First Aid course.

R.I.C.E. TREATMENT

Soft tissue injuries are quite common in the martial arts and immediate 'on-the-spot' treatment can help to speed recovery. R.I.C.E. treatment, an acronym which stands for Rest, Ice, Compression and Elevation, should be applied to any injury affecting tissue of the muscles, tendons or ligaments to protect the area from more extensive damage and reduce the painful symptoms.

REST ... means not to return to training until the injury has had sufficient time to heal.

ICE ... means the application of an ice pack on the injured part (over a bandage covering) for 5–15 minutes to reduce bleeding in the tissue.

COMPRESSION ... refers to bandaging the affected area.

ELEVATION ... means raising the injured area to remove the pressure or stress placed upon the injury.

After some 24–72 hours have elapsed, movement and light massage may commence and exercises can be increased gradually to encourage complete healing. This should only start after pain and swelling has subsided.

FIRST AID EMERGENCIES

Having some knowledge and experience of first aid will prepare you for the rarer, more serious injuries which do occur, especially if you participate in a high risk sport. A serious injury requires emergency first aid and one must act quickly but calmly to ensure the injured person receives treatment. If you are qualified in first aid, then you can render the appropriate assistance but if you have no experience, then you must make the injured person comfortable until medical treatment arrives.

First aid emergencies include head injuries, broken bones, damage to internal organs through direct force or contact. If in any doubt, call an ambulance.

TYPES OF INJURY AND ACTION TO TAKE

Soft Tissue:

BLISTERS ... May occur when using new equipment as a result of friction. Cover the blister or if necessary, puncture the blister with a sterile needle and then tape up.

ABRASIONS/MAT BURNS ... Clean thoroughly with running water or sterile water/tissue. A dressing can be used while training but these types of injury tend to heal if left open.

CUTS ... Stop the bleeding by direct pressure over the cut and clean the area under running water. Cover the cut with suitable dressing. If the cut is deep or does not stop bleeding, then seek immediate medical attention.

BRUISES ... Occur through knocks and bumps and causes bleeding within the tissues. If severe, apply R.I.C.E.

PULLED MUSCLE ... Can occur through lack of warm-up or when body is tired. Commonly affects muscles such as the hamstrings, triceps. Apply R.I.C.E.

TORN MUSCLE ... This involves a larger number of muscle fibres which tear through force such as pushing too hard in training. This results in painful swelling and restricted movement. Apply R.I.C.E. and seek medical attention if severe.

TENDONITIS ... is considered to be an over-use injury and often affects areas such as the groin, wrist, Achilles or elbow. Tendon rupture, however, is more severe and can occur under direct force. Apply R.I.C.E. and seek medical attention immediately in the case of a suspected rupture.

LIGAMENT INJURY ... In martial arts, the most commonly injured ligaments are those of the ankle and knee joints. A torn ligament can occur when a joint is twisted or forced beyond its normal range of motion. A sprained joint involves a few torn fibres while rupture or part rupture is more severe, causing joint instability. Apply R.I.C.E. and seek immediate medical attention for assessment of the injury.

EMERGENCY INJURIES

Bones and Joints.

Fractures and joint dislocations are less common but do still happen. Apart from being in considerable pain, symptoms affecting the injured person may include rapid swelling and disfiguration of the injured site. Call an ambulance to transfer to casualty and make the person comfortable until help arrives.

ORGAN INJURIES

Head Concussion

Concussion is potentially serious and is a result of a blow to the head resulting from direct force, such as a punch, kick, or a fall. Everyone who has suspected concussion should seek medical attention straight away. Whether the person has been knocked unconscious or not, great care should be taken after a head injury.

Symptoms to look out for include disorientation, loss of memory or awareness regarding the events of the injury, headaches, disturbance of vision, nausea or anything unusual. If you find yourself having to deal with a victim of concussion, take the following action:

1. Do not leave the person alone.
2. Do not permit him to continue training.
3. Assess the situation and obtain medical advice. Seek urgent attention if the victim seems to deteriorate or feels ill.

4. Don't allow the victim to drink alcohol, drive or operate machinery.
5. Make sure he is accompanied with a trip to casualty.

If you have had concussion, it is important not to engage in any further contact sport activity until your doctor gives you the go ahead. On average, it is recommended that you avoid combat sport for 4–6 weeks. If a further concussion injury is sustained within 3 months of the initial injury then contact sport must be stopped for a further 3 months. Anyone who sustains 3 concussions or knock-outs in a year should rest for 12 months and give serious consideration to retiring from the activity which caused it.

OTHER INJURIES

More serious injury is thankfully rare. Smaller injuries, ranging from groin strain to dislocated fingers are far more common. Here we list just some of the injuries which you may come up against in the course of your training.

SPECIFIC INJURIES CAUSED BY CONTACT:

Type: Broken nose.
Symptoms: Pain, deformity, swelling, bleeding.
Cause: Usually a direct blow.
Action: Ask the person to sit up and breathe through his mouth. Gently pinch the nostrils together to stem bleeding. Take to casualty to assess damage.

Type: Broken/dislocated tooth.
Symptoms: Partial dislocation of tooth from gum or knocked out tooth. Bleeding.
Cause: A blow to the mouth.
Action: Seek immediate dental treatment. Save teeth, especially if root is still attached.

Type: Eye injury.
Symptoms: Swelling, redness, bruising, sight affected.
Cause: Blow to the eye or foreign body in the eye.
Action: Apply cool sterile eye patch or covering and seek medical attention.

Type: Winding injury.
Symptoms: Difficulty in breathing, gasping for breath.
Cause: A blow to the pit of the stomach or chest.
Action: Loosen any tight clothing and allow person to recover own breath. Encourage him to be calm and breathe normally. Seek medical attention.

Type: Broken or bruised ribs.
Symptoms: Pain which is worse when taking a deep breath. Some swelling/bruising.
Cause: Direct blow or crushing of chest.
Action: Apply an ice pack and encourage the injured person to relax and sit in a comfortable position. Seek medical attention especially if breathing is affected.

Type: Concussion.

Symptoms: Disorientation, memory loss, headaches, nausea, vision difficulties, cold, clammy skin, confusion.

Cause: Blow to the head.

Action: Keep calm. Record person's symptoms and responses. Refer to hospital immediately. A concussion victim should be accompanied at all times until medical attention is received.

SPECIFIC INJURIES CAUSED WHILE TRAINING

Type:Groin Strain.

Symptoms: Pain, inflammation.

Cause: Over-use, poor technique or forced movement.

Action: Apply R.I.C.E. treatment and follow up with ample rest to aid recovery. Physio treatment may prove successful.

Type: Muscle Tear.

Symptoms: Immediate pain on injury, swelling.

Cause: A blow to the muscle or through vigorous training.

Action: Apply R.I.C.E. treatment for 48 hours. Early bruising will signal a speedier recovery. After 48 hours and when pain has subsided, gentle stretching is recommended.

Type: Sprained ankle.

Symptoms: Joint instability, swelling, pain.

Cause: Turning over at the ankle, forcing ligament to stretch, tear or rupture completely.

Action: Apply R.I.C.E. and seek medical attention to assess the damage. Do not attempt to walk or bear weight on the joint. A severe ligament injury can be very slow to heal.

Type: Heat stroke/exhaustion or dehydration.
Symptoms: Burning hot skin, nausea, headaches, thirst, collapse and absence of sweat (if severe).
Cause: Vigorous training and failure to replace fluids.
Action: Encourage person to drink (fruit juice, fluids containing sugar and salt to replace body fluids), keep person cool (fanning with towel, damp cloth). Heat stroke can prove fatal so seek medical attention.

Type: Dislocated fingers.
Symptoms: Pain, swelling, deformity.
Cause: Common in contact sport martial arts. Fingers or thumb being forced back.
Action: If dislocated finger cannot be pulled back by a first-aider immediately after injury, seek medical advice. Apply R.I.C.E. treatment and strapping.

POST-INJURY CARE AND REHABILITATION

If in your martial arts training you have never been afflicted by a bad knock, a twist, a pull, a tear or a sprain, then you have indeed been truly blessed with considerable good fortune. On the other hand, if you have experienced an injury, you will know how long it takes to gain full recovery.

Some 80% of sports injuries affect the soft tissues and amount to being the most common injuries sustained in martial arts practice. And, injuries, however slight, require care and attention to ensure a speedy and complete recovery. Most of us have the know-how to administer some initial treatment; a bandage here, a plaster there, but fail miserably in making provision for post-injury rehabilitation.

Post-injury treatment is a crucial factor in aiding full recovery in the shortest possible time. Treatment may include massage, physiotherapy, heat treatment, complementary therapies (such as acupuncture, aromatherapy etc) and specific exercises to stimulate repair and encourage a full gain in strength and mobility. This care, or rehabilitation, should be provided until the injury has completely healed and there is a return to full fitness.

Apart from the physical benefits of post-injury treatment, self-help provides a psychological boost and enables us to build positivity. Quite often, an injury can knock confidence and make us feel low. This frequently happens to active competitors whose injury forces them to rest or retire for a period of time. Rehabilitation is a good time to think inwardly, reassess goals and become focused on returning to peak fitness, and should be looked upon with positivity.

HOW POST-INJURY CARE AIDS RECOVERY

Treatment works in a variety of ways.

1. Heat and massage techniques increase circulation of nutrient rich blood to the afflicted area which will aid the healing process of repair and regrowth. An improved circulation also helps in the removal of waste products, which can accumulate at the site of the injury and also prevent the build-up of calcification.

2. Manipulation and physiotherapy works in correcting and easing stresses, pressures and problems within the muscles and joints.
3. Complementary therapies such as herb compresses, aroma-therapy oils, acupuncture etc calls upon the powers of natural healing and restores the body in an unobtrusive way.
4. Specific exercises such as gentle stretching and mobility work to increase blood flow and ease muscles and joints back into activity as well as strengthening weak areas.

Treatments can be combined to complement each other especially if the injury is severe enough to warrant it. Your doctor may be able to refer you to a physio on the NHS but it's highly likely that you will have to pay for complementary therapy.

Knowing when to start the treatment often poses some confusion. It basically depends upon the extent of the injury and individual circumstances. Rather than give a definite timescale, it is better to recognise the signs which tell you that your body is ready for recovery. Your doctor or coach may be able to provide more specific guidelines relating to any injury you sustain.

After an initial soft-tissue injury, you may have initiated the R.I.C.E. treatment (Rest, Ice, Compression & Elevation) to help minimise and reduce further damage. This is the first step to post-injury care. In the case of any injury, resting of the afflicted area is vital to avoid making the problem worse.

The second stage of Post-injury care can take place anywhere between 12–72 hours after injury, depending on the nature and severity of the damage. As a rule, massage and movement should only take place once pain and swelling has subsided. Providing that the injury has been rested and saved from further aggravation, post-injury care can commence fairly quickly.

In the case of broken bones, this presents a different matter. Obviously, you have to wait for plaster to be removed before any real rehabilitation can take place. As for sprains, where there is ligament damage, this may take a considerable amount of time to heal and this type of injury is generally thought to be more problematic than a break. It can take up to 9 months for a ligament injury to heal and if completely torn, resulting in joint instability, then you may have to turn to surgery.

Injuries to the head and internal organs are, again, a separate matter and require your doctor's advice. Such injuries may mean a lengthy lay-off or even retirement from the contact sport.

RETURN TO TRAINING

With any injury, good communication between your instructor, coach or physician is extremely important in the period leading up to a return to training. You will have to start off with a gradual programme of exercise which takes full account of any limitations in the early stages so that you do not irritate or weaken the previously injured site.

If you have been out of action for several weeks, your fitness levels will be down so do not expect to be on form straight away. You will need to rebuild your strength slowly. Many students find that private lessons or instruction in a non-competitive environment is preferable in those early stages while you are regaining your fitness. The instructor can work with you, providing an evaluation of your progress with the view of returning to normal training.

It takes time for your body to acclimatise after injury. Recovery can be slow and will also be hindered if care isn't taken to start off at a gentle pace when exercise is re-introduced. Any sudden or rapid movement may exacerbate the site of a soft-tissue injury. Many practitioners make the mistake of returning to class training too soon or even pushing themselves too hard and this usually proves counter-productive.

Self-awareness is the key to making a full recovery after injury. I am sure we have all been guilty of ignoring pain of an injury and continued training totally oblivious to the damage being caused. What we should be doing is exercising a little patience and accept that we need to rest and treat the problem rather then making it worse.

REHABILITATION GUIDELINES

1. Always seek individual advice relating to your injury before undertaking rehabilitation treatment.
2. Wait for pain and swelling to reduce before starting movement and massage techniques.

3. Be patient in the rehabilitation stage. A gradual return to fitness will avoid stressing the injured site.
4. On return to training, if any pain or swelling affects the injured site then stop and seek medical advice.

VOICE OF EXPERIENCE

'I sprained my ankle while out jogging. My foot turned over the kerb of a pavement and I heard a sharp click which was followed by immediate pain and swelling. I thought, at first, that I had broken a bone but the doctor confirmed a partially torn ligament and strapped it up and advised me to rest it completely. He said that it would take time to heal as ligaments are notoriously slow to repair.

'It turned out that I was off work for over a week but even when I returned, I was hobbling about and using crutches to take the weight off. After a month or so, it started to improve but the ankle felt very unstable and there was still swelling. By this time, I was missing training and was frustrated because everyone else was preparing for their grading and I was unable to do anything. Eventually, I sought further advice and began to have treatment to encourage the healing process. I had massage and physio care and was given a series of rehabilitation exercises to strengthen the muscles in my lower leg and improve the mobility and stability of my ankle. Recovery speeded up and after three months, I was back to training. Apparently, I was quite lucky that the sprain healed so quickly! It can take up to a year in some cases. I'm still aware that I have an ankle weakness so I do take more care in training and make sure I always warm-up and cool-down thoroughly. It's made me much more knowledgeable to how treatment can help after injury.'

Martial arts student.

TAKING RESPONSIBILITY ... THE INSTRUCTOR'S ROLE

If you are a martial arts instructor or coach, it is your responsibility to ensure that all your practitioners are in safe hands in order to prevent injury from occurring. You must do your utmost to protect their interests by reducing (if not eradicating) hazards and by taking every step to provide a secure training environment.

The instructor's role requires a certain amount of dedication and commitment towards a student's well-being. It isn't easy to give so much in time and effort but is nonetheless expected and might even safeguard you against liability if legal proceedings should ever arise. But, perhaps more importantly, no instructor wants to see any of his students seriously injured.

LEGAL RESPONSIBILITIES

Recent years have seen a rise in legal proceedings related to sport and all instructors and coaches need to be *au fait* with their responsibilities, and exercise greater diligence in the way they run their clubs. This is an area which should not be ignored or taken for granted. The fact that you haven't been sued doesn't mean you won't be in the future!

The legal system is, as we all know, extremely complicated. As an instructor, great care must be taken in how you teach and run your club. Every detail must be considered, even the way you word one of your leaflets or the method you use to teach a technique, and accurate records should be kept to demonstrate that you take your position seriously.

A liability case can arise at any time from the most inconsequential of incidents e.g. not emphasising the use of safety equipment, not displaying warning signs where appropriate, teaching without a sufficient warm-up or teaching out-dated techniques. These are just examples arising to possibilities of liability cases where injury has resulted.

Any lack of reasonable or foreseeable care can land you in trouble so, as a responsible instructor, give careful thought to the legal implications. Seek professional advice from a solicitor on the legalities of teaching sport and make sure you have full insurance.

MEASURES TO PROTECT THE INSTRUCTOR AND HIS PARTICIPANTS

The instructor should implement good practice at all times and examine every aspect of the teaching role. He should consider taking the following measures to safeguard his students in training and to protect his own interests and reputation.

ADEQUATE INSURANCE

The instructor should hold professional indemnity and public liability insurance and also provide insurance cover for students through a recognised Association. This can be arranged through your Association's Governing Body.

SCREENING OF STUDENTS

All students should complete an application form on enrolment to provide information about their health and wellbeing which the instructor must keep in confidence. The form should highlight any health complications (such as asthma) and any medication which is being taken so that the instructor is fully aware of the student's position. If there is doubt whether the student can undertake training, he should be referred to his doctor to seek advice and approval before participation. The form should also contain an up-to-date contact number or address in case of an emergency.

PROVISION OF WARNING SIGNS AND LITERATURE CONTAINING RULES AND HEALTH CONSIDERATIONS

All students should be made aware of the club rules and safety regulations. These should be repeated regularly or whenever appropriate to maintain standards. Students should be reminded of the risks involved in the sport and the action they should take in training to prevent accidents.

Consider aspects such as regulations relating to jewellery, clothing, equipment, footwear and the general use of the facility. Highlight any known hazards so that students are aware. If possible, provide carefully written copy of rules and safety considerations.

HAVE FIRST AID KNOWLEDGE AND KNOW EMERGENCY PROCEDURE

All instructors should have experience of first aid treatment and procedures. They should know what to do in an emergency situation and be aware of the action to be taken and where the nearest hospital casualty department is.

ENSURE SUITABILITY OF TRAINING VENUE

The club's training venue should be suitable for the activity. Consider the floor surface, lighting, ventilation and facilities. Make regular checks of equipment and the facility. Ensure that there is no overcrowding in classes.

INSTRUCTION OF CORRECT TECHNIQUE

It is essential that students are taught correctly following Governing Body guidelines. There should be an adequate warm-up and cool-down period, approved exercises and techniques which are appropriate to the student's standard. An instructor should use only a reasonable amount of force in demonstrating or working with a student which is suitable to the student's current level of ability.

MONITORING STUDENTS

The instructor must keep an eye on each student to make sure they are not being overworked or placed under too much pressure during training. Students should be partnered with someone of equal size and ability wherever possible.

PARENTAL CONSENT

All students under the age of 18 require parent's consent before undertaking martial arts training and a signature to validate this is required on their membership or licence form.

ACCIDENT REPORTS

Accidents must be recorded accurately in the Accident Book and witnesses should be highlighted.

SPECIAL CONSIDERATIONS

Promoting safe martial arts practice not only rests upon the instructor but is a matter for all practitioners to contemplate. It is the responsibility of each individual to engage in safe training but quite often external pressures influence us to take risks and this is a time when we become the most prone to injury.

Whatever your age or level of experience, it is certainly beneficial to be aware of your actions in training and to know about the hazards and potential threats. We have already looked at the causes of injury and examined preventative measures in the space allowed but there are other circumstances which require special consideration and necessitate a mention.

CHILDREN AND MARTIAL ARTS

Young students, despite their beguiling appearance of being robust and full of energy, are often more vulnerable to injury than mature adults and care should be taken in the way in which training is approached. As each child is different, with widely varying degrees of mental and physical make-up, providing a safe training environment to cater for each individual child is one which presents great difficulties for the instructor.

With the physical demands which most martial arts impose, it is often best for young students to train separately from the adults if at all possible. From the instructors point of view, this enables him to structure a class accordingly and avoid the high-level training methods used by adults. The young student would benefit from such a training environment learning skills and participating in exercises which are relevant to their age and capabilities.

Care must be taken in training at all levels. The growing bones and muscles are highly susceptible to damage and over-training and excessive demands could cause permanent defects or problems which could develop later in life. Practising safe exercises should be emphasised right from the start and it is down to the instructor to get the message across but parents can also do their bit to encourage their child to listen to instructors and also look for signs of over-training.

SYMPTOMS OF OVER-TRAINING IN A CHILD

1. Listlessness and lack of enthusiasm.
2. Tiredness and disturbance in sleep.
3. Moodiness ... child is often tearful.
4. Frequent injuries.
5. Possible weight loss.
6. Nausea and stomach upsets.

If a problem is suspected, then it is often good practice for the parents to liaise with the instructor and, above all, seek medical advice to rule out any underlying cause.

THE OLDER STUDENT

Martial arts has always been regarded as a sport for all; an activity which can be enjoyed by people of all ages. For a student of maturing years, some considerations should be given to the type of training methods undertaken. An instructor should not expect an older person to be able to maintain the same intensity of exercise as a young student in their twenties. Let it be said, however, that some people in the fifties are much fitter than some of today's youngsters so it really depends upon the individual.

A maturing person, previously inactive, may have lost elasticity in their muscles. Their joints may be stiff and their fitness levels low but carefully planned exercise in martial arts can bring about marked improvement. The emphasis must be on the words 'gradual' and 'gentle'. Pushing too hard can cause injury or illness and serves no purpose. An understanding should be met between student and instructor and, of course, a mature student should check with their doctor to make sure they are fit enough to participate.

STUDENTS WITH SPECIAL NEEDS

With improved access to knowledge and facilities, many classes are now able to cater for the disabled or students who have varying degrees of health problems ranging from asthma to diabetes. Providing the student informs the instructor of their condition and acts sensibly by carrying any required medication and ensuring safe practice, then complications or incidents are rare and the student can enjoy full and active participation.

Special considerations call for open communication and a degree of understanding between the instructor and student. Depending upon the condition, training methods may have to be adapted and this is a factor which needs discussion from the outset.

VOICE OF EXPERIENCE

Having a health problem needn't be a hindrance to participating in martial arts. The following practitioner has diabetes and here is how he copes. Please bear in mind, however, that what works for one person might not be suitable for another, so if you do have any condition which warrants concern, discuss it with your doctor.

'In order to train, I have to make sure my sugar level is high enough. This can be achieved by having my insulin and eating sugar rich foods (chocolate). At the same time, I have to be careful that sugar levels don't get too high as this can be equally dangerous. It's important that I drink plenty as high sugar levels results in extreme thirst and this can be exacerbated further by sweating through training.

'You have to be aware of how the exercise – especially unaccustomed exercise – can affect sugar levels. If I start to feel dizzy or out of sorts then I

take a break and have a sugar laden drink or chocolate bar. If I feel unwell, I simply don't train as it's
hard enough to assess your sugar levels without the
effects of illness on top.

'After training, I make sure my sugars are balanced
before I go to bed. This is very important otherwise
you could wake up confused and short of sugar or at
worst, not wake up at all! Following the previous
night's exercise, I have to be aware that my sugar
level could be unusually low so again I must be prepared for this.

'Providing you are sensible and know how to
manage the diabetes, then there's no reason why
you can't practise martial arts as good as the next
person. Over the period of years I have trained, I've
actually found that I need less insulin, have less
stress and have far more energy to cope with life!'

Martial arts practitioner

*IF YOU ARE CONCERNED ABOUT YOUR HEALTH AND
FITNESS OR HAVE AN INJURY, SEE YOUR DOCTOR
FOR ADVICE*

COMMON QUESTIONS ANSWERED

Q. Since starting martial arts just a few weeks ago, I've
noticed a burning pain on my inner thigh. It twinges
when I do certain exercises and doesn't seem to be
getting better. What is it?

A. It sounds like a muscle strain but it is best to check with your doctor to confirm the nature and extent of the injury. Strains are relatively common and often arise through over-stretching, pushing too hard in training or through failure to warm-up properly. The best thing to do is rest the afflicted area and avoid any exercise which exacerbates the injury. Once the pain has gone, massage the area to encourage the healing process and undertake light, controlled stretching to ease the muscle back into action.

Q. In the time I've been training, I've had quite a few minor injuries ranging from torn muscles to slight sprains. I've heard that repeated injury can make muscles shorter. Is this true?

A. Generally, when soft tissue injuries heal, fibres tend to knit together quite tightly and this often results in a slight loss in elasticity. A correct rehabilitation programme which comprises of specific flexibility exercises will counteract this problem to some degree. Calcification deposits, especially around the joints, can also be a complication affecting mobility. Massage in the recovery period can help eradicate the problem. If you are injury prone, take a closer look at the preventative measures described at the beginning of this chapter.

Q. I've had burning pain along the length of my legs below the knee and the doctor has said I have shin splints. What is this and how has it been caused?

A. Shin splints is quite a generalised term for pain in the shin, which might also cause swelling or inflammation.

The pain might emanate from the muscle or the bone and the injury is looked upon as a common 'over-use' problem. This is usually caused by overloading the muscles, tendons and ligaments through high impact training (jumping on hard surfaces, jogging on roads etc) causing anything from a slight stress fracture to irritation of the muscle on the bone. More often than not, pain comes on while exercising and it can feel quite severe. Treatment of shin splints is to rest the area and look at changing your exercise routine to avoid any root causes. Once pain and inflammation has subsided, a massage oil might help as will specific exercises to improve circulation, strength and suppleness.

CHAPTER SIX

TOURNAMENT PREPARATION

© Paul Banister

Remain focused and you will succeed

'The true hero hardens his nature and controls his mind.'

Tut-Tut

THE DECISION TO COMPETE

As your skills improve, you may become drawn by the lure of the tournament scene. You may simply wish to compete for your club at a local level as a chance to test your growing skills or you may harbour more magnificent visions of becoming one of the country's greatest champions. Although many practitioners remain content to leave trophy hunting to those hungry enough to take up the test, there are those who dream of collecting shelves full of silver-wear (or more commonly plastic!) as they enter tournament after tournament.

This chapter is dedicated to the practitioner who has decided to take up the sport of competitive martial arts. It is also aimed at the more seasoned contestant who wishes to improve his chances of success. But what you will read over the next few pages isn't any secret formula. There are no short cuts to winning. Instead, I have given purely practical advice providing tactics which have worked for other successful champions. It's up to you whether you adhere to them.

You may have come into the martial arts for the opportunity to compete or it may be a desire which has grown on you in the course of training. Perhaps you have watched a fellow student or your instructor perform in tournament and been inspired to take part. On the whole, we all have a competitive streak within us and for some, this quality remains dormant until something sparks off an interest. It could simply be through spectating at an event, the thought of winning, the hunger of wanting a champion title to your name or merely because it looks good fun that the initial flame starts to burn and suddenly you are alight with the desire to compete. It really can be that instantaneous.

Of course, making the decision to become a competitor takes more than daydreams. Serious contemplation is required to put plans into motion and this necessitates a 'feet firmly on the ground', common sense approach to make it real. You need to ask yourself why you want to compete and assess whether or not it is something you will enjoy doing. It's no good participating just because your friend or instructor wants you to. At the end of the day, it is you who will be out there on the mats, testing your skills and making the effort.

As far as tournaments go, martial arts has competitions to suit everyone. Apart from traditional based club and Association events which may specialise in a certain style of martial art, the most popular tournaments are those which cater for all styles. These 'open' or 'freestyle' events are held regularly throughout the UK and also attract the masses in Europe and the USA. As well as the acclaimed fight events, many tournaments cater for the traditionalist with categories for forms (Kuen/kata or Patterns) and performers can display their skills with or without the use of weaponry.

Whatever style of martial art you practise and whatever style of tournament you decide to enter, the way in which you prepare for competition is very much the same and requires a certain amount of dedication and forward planning to ensure your efforts don't go to waste.

Once you have made the decision to compete, you must ready yourself to enter a new phase in your martial arts training. It is one which requires even greater discipline. You will have to step up a gear and keep stepping up until you reach your peak in mental and physical conditioning. You may need to explore new ways of thinking and accommodate different training methods to sharpen your skills. For many, this is an exciting albeit difficult time as you build yourself up towards an event.

Of course, some people just compete for fun and for the spirit of martial arts. Many smaller tournaments, run by club instructors, are considered more friendlier events and provide a taste to the sport martial arts scene.

HAVE YOU GOT WHAT IT TAKES?

To compete at a higher level, you need the following qualities to work towards tournament success.

1. MARTIAL ARTS SKILL
   You need a reasonable amount of skill to enter an event. This skill must be on a par with the other competitors, especially in a fight category to ensure safe participation and provide a good chance of winning.

2. A WINNING ATTITUDE

The right attitude will make all the difference between success and failure. If you are not too confident about your chances then it is pointless entering an event unless you are entering just for fun. You need to go in and give it everything you have got!

3. P.M.A.

A positive mental attitude will give you the edge over your opponent. It is the essential ingredient which you will need to improve your chances.

4. SELF-CONTROL

You should have an inner calm to compete successfully. Sometimes, decisions go against you. If you allow this to spoil your equilibrium, then you will lose the event. Remain in control of your emotions throughout.

5. OBJECTIVITY

Win or lose, you need to be objective and not let the final outcome of a tournament affect your goals for the future.

6. DETERMINATION

You need to stay hungry for the win. It is difficult to remain focused if you have had a run of defeats but you need to call upon all your resources of mind to be determined in your approach.

7. POSSESS SPORTSMANSHIP

Feelings may run high when the pressure is on but you

should not let this affect your sportsmanship. Aim to go on the mats with spirit and the right attitude and demonstrate enough discipline to gain instant respect.

Many of these competitive qualities are developed over time but it is a good idea to start as you mean to continue. It is quite acceptable to build renown as a 'mean performer' in terms of physical skill but no one wants to compete with an aggressive bully or someone who has no respect for his fellow opponent.

Everyone has within them the potential to become a successful competitor. For many, it is the taking part that counts and winning is merely a bonus. Others dedicate themselves to the task of winning, often striving beyond reason and unable to settle for anything less than first place. Well, as they say, it takes all kinds and some people prove to be more competitive than others. But, whatever category you fall into – if any at all – try not to lose sight of your goals. Keep on the right track, give your best, be positive and determined but, most of all, enjoy yourself! Win or lose, you must gain something positive from the experience to make it all worthwhile!

VOICE OF EXPERIENCE

Martial arts practitioners compete for all kinds of reasons. Some are driven by the thought of success while others take a more leisurely approach. Here's what the following competitors had to say:

'When I started to learn martial arts, it was never my intention to become a competitor but that all changed when I went to support some fellow students at an open tournament. I got a real buzz out of it and wanted to be out there on the mats fighting for my club. The desire was so strong that I commenced training with the aim of competing within three months. I worked pretty hard and the training was tough but I did get to compete. I got knocked out of the first round and didn't even score a point but the atmosphere was electric. I have since won a few events and am still as keen as ever.'

Karate student.

'I've always had a strong, competitive nature. Even as an infant, playing marbles in the school play-ground, I was determined to win. It doesn't take much to motivate me. It doesn't even matter if there's a trophy at the end of it because I enjoy competing purely for the sake of the challenge. I believe our competitive nature is part of our instinct for survival. It is a quality which we all possess.'

Kung fu student.

'If I go to a tournament, I just have to compete. It's unbearable if I'm injured or unable to take part because the drive is so bad that you just want to be out there giving it your best.'

Kickboxing competitor.

'As a martial artist of limited talent, I enjoy competing just for the fun of getting out there. Winning isn't what motivates me. Quite often, I lose before I even step out on to the mats but I always make sure I give 100% and have a good time in the process. I find people who take it all too seriously quite amusing. It's hard to imagine why they are taking part if they can't get any enjoyment from it.'

Freestyle martial arts competitor.

PHYSICAL PREPARATION

In order to compete, you need to be fit to take part. Your success depends on it. If you want to be a champion and beat the best, you must first become the best you can be. This requires dedication to training and a firm resolve.

Your body is the vehicle which can gain you a tournament title. Every fibre of your being must be honed in preparation to acquire total physical readiness. Muscles need training to cope with the demands of movement; not only must they exude strength but also speed and dexterity to ensure perfect deliverance of technique in performance.

Whether you are entering a fight event or performing a traditional kata, physical preparation must be considered during the weeks leading up to the event. If you want to make your mark then you shouldn't leave anything to chance.

Providing you are already reasonably fit and this assumes that you have been practising martial arts for an acceptable period of time and are fully conversant with the techniques, then training to peak fitness and skill should commence about six weeks prior to the tournament. This will provide adequate time to fine tune your body in all the relevant areas.

Whatever event you intend to enter, you will need stamina, strength, suppleness and speed sharpened to perfection. Your training programme must cater for each aspect. Your success not only depends on your fitness preparation but also on your martial arts skill and you should aim to practise on your specific ability in readiness for the category you are taking part in. For example, if you are a Japanese stylist wishing to perform a kata in the forms event then constant and regular application of kata, stances and all movement pertaining to this area needs to be worked on. If you are entering a semi-contact fight event, then regular sparring with various partners needs to be worked together with focus pad training, shadow boxing and speed-ball work. This is vital in the build-up to a tournament and is just as important as your physical fitness and health.

Let us look at the areas of physical preparation in more detail and consider the training methods which will promote results.

STAMINA WORK

Stamina derives from aerobic conditioning and is a very important quality of fitness. Without adequate levels of stamina, we would tire quickly, become out of breath and weaken considerably as energy levels fall. As a competitor, you can't afford to lose a tournament just because you are out of condition so it is essential to include plenty of 'road-work' in your pre-event preparation.

Most competitors find jogging interspersed with short burst of sprinting and explosive work will build their stamina to an excellent level. For fighting events, skipping and con-tinuous shadow-boxing, keeping on your toes, are methods which you can combine. Research suggests that you should build stamina with exercises that are relevant to the sport like the ones aforementioned. Aerobic activity such as cycling would not provide the same results, performed alone, so be careful in your choice of activity.

STRENGTH TRAINING

Muscles need to be kept in good shape and be fit for the task they will be used for. In forms display, your muscles must be able to comfortably withstand stance and movement. They must appear firm and strong.

Again, initiate specific training. For example, work on holding stances (like horse stance or kiba-dachi) for forms display. For fight events, build strong legs by holding out kicks and working on the kick-bag. Combine specific train-ing with other general strength exercises whether they are simple callisthenics or weight training for the best, all-round results. Work on a manageable programme. Pushing too hard, beyond your current capabilities, will only cause injury and weaken you before the event.

MAINTAINING SUPPLENESS

Apart from having strength, you must also maintain a good degree of suppleness in the muscles and mobility around the joints to perform at your best.

Maintain your programme of flexibility training, combining dynamic stretching with static, passive stretching in order that you cope with the demands of movement. Remember, a good degree of suppleness combined with strength will enable you to deliver a variety of techniques, allow you to move fluently and, in a fight event, will give you that extra 'reach' in order to score those points.

TRAINING SPECIFICS FOR FIGHT EVENTS
WORKING SPEED

Speed is of the essence in a semi-contact point-sparring event. It is a vital component. Not only do you need speed to score against your opponent, you also need it in response to your opponent's advance with quick and effective blocking and defensive manoeuvres.

In a competitive situation, being quicker will determine the outcome of the bout and so specific training to sharpen speed response is recommended in the pre-event build-up. If you are a seasoned practitioner with plenty of experience you should already have a good degree of speed developed through regular training but it is wise to concentrate on this area for maximum results.

There are various ways of working speed but let's just first focus on the essentials and consider the fundamentals of reaction and movement. The ability to react to a stimulus, such as blocking a punch or delivering a kick depends upon both physiological and psychological factors. The way to develop speed of response is to train diligently so that movement becomes second nature.

Speed can be cultivated by working on particular drills and exercises. There are many possibilities. Focus pad work is excellent for producing quicker reaction time. Exercise fast combinations and have the focus pad holder move round to make the drill more difficult. Set exercises, comprising of combinations of techniques, is another method. Running on the spot with 30 seconds of sprint work every few minutes is an effective activity.

WORKING TIME AND DISTANCING

The elements of correct timing and distancing mostly come with regular application although, in the pre-event training, it is wise to include drills which focus on this area. If possible, train with various partners so that you get a feel for competing against different levels. If you can exercise good timing and distancing before trying to score against your opponent, you can also exercise economy of movement and actually save yourself energy while out there.

Focus pad work can, again, help to develop these qualities. Have the focus pad holder move away from you, come in close to you and move round you so that you can get the feel of space and its limitations on the matted area. Consider the techniques which you can use when your opponent is too close or too far away.

WORKING DELIVERY OF TECHNIQUE

How you deliver your techniques on your opponent will have some influence on the final score. If you have been to a tournament and watched some of the action, you may have been confused by the outcome of some of the events. Perhaps it seemed as though one opponent had scored more points when in actual fact, the referee saw differently. Unless technique is delivered correctly, the referee will not score it and it's as simple as that.

So, what is good delivery? Well, it is simply a technique which strikes the opponent clean. It must not be too heavy or too light or too sloppy. It must be a recognised technique, following the rules of the event. Application of delivery can take place on the focus pads or kick-bag and, of course, in sparring.

TECHNICAL EXPERTISE

Working a variety of hand and leg techniques will ensure versatility. Try to train all areas so that you never get stuck with one technique. If you keep throwing reverse punches in at your opponent, he will soon get wise to this move so aim for variety to keep the element of surprise. Obviously, technical expertise comes purely with experience.

PRE-EVENT TRAINING PROGRAMME FOR THE FIGHT COMPETITOR

The following training programme is designed for the fit competitor and is taken over a six week period, prior to the tournament. The plan can be followed on a daily basis (with at least one day's rest in the week) or every other day or whenever it is convenient, but the serious competitor should train a minimum of four days out of seven to gain noticeable results.

The muscle strengthening exercises can be varied to suit your ability and needs. The programme can be divided so that you work lower body one day and upper body the next. Tailor the programme to suit you. Stamina, flexibility and specific training can take place daily without ill effect but it is advisable to have a rest day.

Always start with a warm-up and finish with a cool-down.

WEEKS 1 & 2

Warm-up and dynamic stretching	} 10–15 minutes
Aerobic: Jogging on the spot/ skipping, bag work, jogging and sprint work.	} 20–25 minutes
Training Specifics: Hand and leg combinations, defence & counter drills. Focus work. One-to-one sparring	} 20–30 minutes

Strength: Abdominal work (crunch
sit-ups, twists etc.) Press-ups, squats   } 15 minutes
to your own ability.

Stretch: Repeat dynamic stretching and   } 15 minutes
general all-round passive stretching.

Cool-Down: stretch & massage   } 5–10 minutes

WEEKS 3 & 4

Warm-up and Dynamic Stretch   } 10–15 minutes

Aerobic for stamina ... runs
combined with sprints, skipping, up   } 30 minutes
and downhill running, shadow-boxing.

Training Specifics: Partner work,
sparring drills, focus work-speed
techniques, hand and leg combinations,   } 30 minutes
one-to-one sparring (2 minute bouts).

Strength: repeat week 1 & 2 but add   } 15 minutes
extra sets and vary intensity.

Stretch: Dynamic stretching and   } 15 minutes
passive stretch exercises.

Cool-down   } 5–10 minutes

WEEKS 5 & 6

Warm-up and Dynamic Stretching   } 10–15 minutes

Aerobic for stamina: run combined with
sprinting. Skipping, up and downhill   } 30 minutes
running, bag work. Increase intensity.

Training Specifics: Focus work (moving)
for speed, distancing, timing and   } 30 minutes
technique.
Various Fighting drills. One-to-one
sparring (several 2–3 minute bouts non-stop)
Strength: Repeat previous weeks but add } 15 minutes
extra repetitions.
Stretch: Dynamic and passive   } 15 minutes
Cool Down   } 5–10 minutes

This programme may be followed by 'forms competitors' but exchange training specifics to forms/kata routines.

GENERAL GUIDELINES FOR PRE-EVENT TRAINING

1. Wherever possible work on mats to get a feel for the surface you will compete on.
2. Wear good jogging trainers for road-work to protect feet and joints. Do not run with ankle weights on.
3. Pace yourself in the pre-event training. Gradually intensify the exercises.
4. Consider safe practice (read chapter on Safe Practices) to avoid mishap.
5. Ask a fellow student, someone you can trust, to coach you in the weeks leading up to the event.
6. Do not overwork yourself. Tired muscles are more prone to injury.
7. Do not train the two days prior to an event. This is a time to relax.

TIMING PEAK PERFORMANCE

To be on form for a tournament, you need to be at your peak. Reaching this higher state of being isn't something you can switch on at will; it needs to be worked for with meticulous effort and precision timing.

As a guide, professionals believe that 6 weeks is ample time for the reasonably fit martial arts performer to hone his skills and mentally and physically prepare for the challenge. Anything less and you won't be ready; Anything more and you'll peak too soon. It's rather like baking a cake and making sure it stays in the oven for the right amount of time. Of course, the six week rule isn't set in stone and you may discover that you respond differently to training. In time, and with experience, you will find what works best for you.

We all know what it feels like to be off form. It might be identified as a general feeling of unease or being off balance. It's as if a vital ingredient is missing. Attaining peak fitness, however, is totally different. It inspires confidence and is seen as the accumulation of mental and physical skill, sharpened through training.

Of course, you can not maintain peak performance all of the time and from both a psychological and physiological viewpoint, it would be wrong and even dangerous to even try. After an event, you need to wind down several gears to give yourself time and space to recover. In retrospect, consider the mountain climber who struggles and toils his way upwards to reach the pinnacle. Once there, he is at the highest point and cannot go any further. He may spend a moment to marvel at the view from the top of the mountain but to stay there would prove unbearable. The environment is too unstable and extreme to survive. Accepting this, the climber makes his descent and will spend time recovering from the experience, recouping his energy before embarking on another challenge.

If you relate this encounter to your own training, you will see the sense of it. You have to aim to maintain a balance. To reach the highs, you must also experience the lows. These off-form periods are a time for reflection, repair, rest and renewal. They are crucial to your overall development.

PEAK PERFORMANCE FACTORS

1. Time your pre-event training.
2. Increase training gradually and at a rate you can cope with.
3. Consider your nutrition and fluid intake.
4. Work specific training related to the event.

With careful preparation, the competitor can expect to be on form and ready for the tournament. However, the actual result of the event will finally rest upon extrinsic factors such as luck and the referees decision. But, whether you win or lose, there is no greater feeling than knowing you have performed well and to the best of your ability and for many, this provides equal satisfaction to winning.

MENTAL PREPARATION

The potential champion should not only have good technique, skills and fitness but also the winning attitude, acquired through positive mental preparation. This is the essential ingredient which will strengthen your arsenal.

It is crucial to train and compete with the right attitude and state of mind. Activities such as Tai chi, meditation, stretching, relaxation and even hypnosis, will help prepare your mental and spiritual being. Combined with your physical training, these activities will help you to develop inner calm, inner strength, focus and mental awareness; qualities which are paramount to success.

As you physically train for peak performance, you must also concentrate on the powers of the mind. It should be a time of introspection and of self-examination as you focus your mind for the event. This is often referred to as having 'tunnel vision'; the competitor sees only one goal ahead of him and that is to win. All other matters seem to fade into insignificance.

In the build-up to the event, you should combine your physical training with mental preparation. Goal-setting is a useful tool during this stage and by setting yourself attainable targets, you will start to shape your winning attitude. From the very first pre-event training session, you must start thinking positive. Look ahead and see your goal. Visualise it as if it has already happened. Exuding this kind of positivity will strengthen your spirit and resolve. You only have to take Arnold Schwarzenegger as a prime example. Here is a man whose confidence and PMA is such that it has brought him universal success. You only have to look at his body-building days. Who else would call up their family to say 'I've won!' the day before the competition?

Of course, to be confident, you must believe in yourself. It is a quality often underestimated or worse, seen by others as conceit or egotism. Providing it is controlled and does not come across as arrogance, it will work wonders for you. After all, if you do not have self-belief, who else will have faith in you?

Throughout your training, work hard and with conviction. The mental powers, harnessed through correct training, are not paradoxical. They are real, just like the energy circulating through your body and can be called upon to give you the edge over your competitor whenever it is needed.

HOW TO HARNESS MENTAL POSITIVITY

1. Nurture the will to win.
2. Establish positive thinking.
3. Put in concentrated effort.
4. Let adrenaline work for you, giving that extra spark of energy.
5. Learn to become focused.
6. Relax!
7. Believe in yourself.
8. Free your mind of worry and clutter.

Through honing mental powers, you can establish a state of total awareness where everything around you seems sharp and clear. Practitioners of meditation often find they become more focused and report feeling a deep sense of calm despite any turmoil around them. This inner calm is a precious quality. If you can achieve it, hold on to it!

As your training continues, you will become focused. Not just in the technical sense but spiritually too. It will provide you with extra sensory perceptiveness to a degree whereby you can anticipate your opponent's next move before he even flinches!

You will begin to feel instinctive and more in control. This state of being can only arrive if you are relaxed and free of negative thoughts.

When you are out there on the mats, remember:

1. Don't be affected by your opponent or referee. Take only positive feedback.
2. Whether spectators are shouting for or against you, let it work for you or allow the noise to fade away into the distance.
3. Don't panic if you are down in points. Speed is of the essence. You CAN regain those points.
4. Don't think too much about what you are doing or want to do. Let technique flow naturally.
5. Be calm and relaxed. You are in control of the situation.
6. Discipline yourself and, most of all, express dignity and respect in your actions.
7. Smile! It'll make you feel more relaxed.

PRE-EVENT CONSIDERATIONS
IN THE FINAL DAYS BEFORE THE TOURNAMENT

In the days leading up to a tournament, it is essential that you try to remain free of doubt, injury and fatigue. It is perfectly normal to feel apprehensive and the mere thought of the task ahead may set the 'butterflies' a flutter in your stomach. Let this work for you! Remain positive. Try to keep your mind and spirit together, working in harmony regardless of any outside influences in the world around you.

Take time to relax. Meditate or engage in some Tai chi. Do not train in the two days before the event and avoid any heavy muscle work otherwise you will be stiff and aching on the day.

In that final week before the tournament, you should be feeling in good shape and seeing the benefits of your pre-event training programme. Maintain a positive atmosphere. Get together with fellow students and seek their encouragement and support. Look forward to the competition with optimism.

NUTRITION

Throughout your pre-tournament preparation, consideration should be given to your nutritional intake. After all, this is the fuel which feeds the 'fighting machine'. In the days before the event, step up on your carbohydrates so that your muscles have a good store of energy to call upon. Be careful what you eat and don't neglect your diet in these crucial pre-event days. Be sure to drink plenty of fluids (mineral water, fruit juices) to replace lost fluids and keep the body rehydrated.

On the day of the event, eat a hearty breakfast. Cereals, toast, fruit, scrambled eggs etc. will help to keep hunger at bay and set you off to a good start. Take food with you. Plenty of snacks such as fruit and sandwiches, will keep you going although remember that your body's energy will derive from the previous day's intake.

Often, the tournament day can be a long and drawn out affair. Waiting for your turn to compete is a time of anxiety and one where you will burn a great deal of nervous energy, so have plenty of food and natural drinks at hand to keep you topped-up.

VOICE OF EXPERIENCE

'To many, the word tournament conjures up excitement, thrill, the thought of becoming a champion, the glory and being able to return to your club with a trophy. All students, at some time or another, dream of some form of success. The excitement of being the best of the best is a reward in itself and is a measure of standard which can be shown off to family and friends. Tournaments, however, are only a small part of what is known as the art. They should not be viewed as being the only aspect of training but the development of oneself through experiences you are unlikely to find anywhere else. Many styles now distinguish the difference between a sports person and a true martial artist, instilling to the student from the onset of training the clear difference between the two. Briefly, a sports person is someone who trains for a medal, trophy or title whereas a martial artist trains through the success and failure not giving into their ego nor giving up. Students have often asked me how they can win a medal and what they should do to better themselves. My reply is always the same. We are all individuals who have something to give each other and in turn offer the martial arts. Sometimes our failures as we see them have a far greater influence on our lives than the changes that follow any form of success. Hence, a martial artist must learn to develop the qualities to deal with their success and failure. In doing so, they will develop through experience and gain respect a long the way. In preparation, train regularly whatever the outcome of previous events. Everyone who enters a tournament will leave the event a slightly different person than when they arrived, learning from their experiences and, in turn, developing themselves as a martial artist. And, as an individual, you will have won something far greater than any medal and that is understanding of yourself.'

Mr Ian H. Clode, 4th Dan
A.I.M.A.A. UK Regional Director

GOOD SPORTSMANSHIP

Throughout the years, martial arts tournaments have regularly been criticised. Every issue from competitor's conduct to the tournament's organisation has been condemned and sometimes not without undue cause. Alas, there are many poorly run tournaments whose organisers are more concerned about the cash takings on the door than the welfare of the competitors. Some are run by non-practising martial artists who do not have the level of understanding required to consider the competitor's plight and the effort he has taken to compete at their event. Such tournaments are often poorly organised, lacking in qualified officials. Other events are run by people who have little respect or consideration for the traditional martial artist. There may be bias towards one style, indifference to the spirit of the event or lack of sportsmanship. Fortunately, there are a number of good tournaments which set a precedent and are run in such a way that is fair to the hard-working competitor who has already lost blood, sweat and tears just in the pre-event training! These tournaments do exist but are sadly few and far between.

Many images of a martial arts tournament are often distorted. Films such as the 'Karate Kid' sees the bad guy using dirty tactics to disable the good guy. 'Best of the Best' and 'Bloodsport' both convey images of the bad guy character, competing without respect for the opponent. Rules and conduct are totally disregarded. Martial arts is a combat sport and a highly competitive one. Many have been known to come off the streets, with little or no real martial arts experience, just to have a go on the mats. There's no technique, no respect, no sportsmanship or traditional values and the fight turns into a street brawl. Others, who have trained in the martial arts, perhaps specialising in kickboxing, just possess the wrong attitude. They train to win at all costs, whether or not they hurt their opponent or break the rules. Sometimes, the organisation is just totally corrupt. Favouritism, bias decisions and all the negative aspects of poor sportsmanship are rife, leaving the good competitor feeling disillusioned and cheated. As wrong as this is, you may come across it in your own experiences as a competitor. Until greater steps are taken to eradicate the problems, little can be done except perhaps to boycott those that are poorly run. Whatever happens, strive to maintain good sportsmanship yourself and display all the positive qualities expected of you. Rise above any negativity.

If your opponent is a 'nasty piece of work', just keep your cool. A true martial artist will learn the way to deal with situations such as these without emotion and without ill effect. Even if your opponent is the worst possible competitor, stand before him, keep calm and dignified and meet the negativity with a positive response.

GOOD SPORTSMANSHIP

1. Accept the outcome of the event regardless of the result.
2. Respect the referee, officials and your fellow opponent.
3. If you wish to question a decision, do so in a polite and controlled manner.

4. Keep to the rules of the event.
5. Use good technique.

YOUR FIRST TOURNAMENT

After weeks of training, you wake up to find it's tournament day. It's not just any event but your very first competition and so you are understandably nervous and have mixed feelings about the outcome. You may be sorely tempted to roll over, sleep in and tell your friends you got up late, but this will not appease your conscience. As soon as you wake, get yourself up and ready. Do some light stretching, take a shower, look forward to a good breakfast and think positive throughout the routine. Remember, this is your day, the one you have trained hard for and you are going to step out there and give your best.

Because of the location of many tournaments, some competitors find they have a reasonably long journey ahead of them and need to set off early in the morning. Travelling isn't the greatest of pre-event routines but something which may have to be endured unless you can afford to travel down the day before. Always try to find someone else to drive you there to avoid the stress. You can then use this time to rest.

When you arrive at the venue, check yourself in. If you are fighting, you may have to be weighed. Mostly you will be asked to register by completing an entry card. Your event may not be for some hours but ask an official so that you have an idea as to when you will need to change and warm-up. The waiting time is, for many, the worst of it all so make sure you take a book, magazine or something to keep yourself occupied. Chat with friends, watch the tournament unfold. Remain cool and collected. If you feel the adrenaline pumping hard, nurture it. Let it build up slowly. If tension is mounting and you are starting to feel very nervous or uncomfortable, then get together with fellow competitors and do some stretching or meditation.

Although you may not feel like eating, it is advisable to have snacks and you should drink before thirst takes a hold. Nearer the time, get changed and start to warm-up so that your body is prepared. Try to keep loose and ready for action. Remain focused. See yourself winning. All thoughts must be positive ones. If you're feeling too nervous and out-of-sorts, then ask your fellow student, coach or supporter to stay with you. Everyone reacts differently in these final moments. Some prefer to be alone, some need the crowd cheering them on, others seem to play it so cool and handle their first event with such authority. Whatever way you react, keep the positivity up and try to enjoy the experience of being out there on the mats.

ENDURING THE WAIT

1. Take a book, magazine, newspaper with you to keep your mind occupied or chat with friends.
2. A 'walkman' is a popular relaxation aid. What better than your favourite music or motivational tape to put you in a winning frame of mind.

3. Watch the event. Encourage fellow team mates. Even follow the opposition for a while.
4. Engage in light stretching to keep loose.
5. Eat snacks to keep energy up and drink frequently to maintain body fluids.

Don't be too concerned about it being your first competition. Be confident and calm as you enter the area. Chances are that unless it is announced, no one will know whether this is your first or tenth event. Think back to all your preparation. Imagine you are back at your club, going through the routines you know so well. Forget the crowd. Many competitors find that the audience fade into the background as a blare once the event begins. Just focus on performing well.

If you are entering forms/kata, all eyes are on you alone and, perhaps, this is just as much pressure, if not more, than actually fighting an opponent. Before you begin, whether it's a forms display or a fight event, take a moment to compose yourself. Feel the adrenaline rush but allow it to sweep over you like energy feeding every fibre. Don't let it consume you to the point of oblivion. Take control of it. Ultimately, the way you perform depends upon you alone.

In time, competing will grow more familiar and you may find yourself growing a little more confident. This is a time when you will start to excel yourself. Work positively towards this goal and you will have every chance of gaining results.

POST-MORTEM (OR POST-TOURNAMENT ANALYSIS)

How you handle success and failure depends a great deal on the 'post-tournament analysis' and how you interpret the findings. This analysis, or assessment of your performance is often referred to by professional coaches as the 'post-mortem' and is a useful tool for finding any weaknesses in your skill.

Win or lose, many competitors leave the tournament day either on an emotional high or low, paying little attention to the overall performance and strategy displayed. Much may be gained by going over your event in fine detail. A video recording of the performance is even better to enable you to analyse your actions frame-by-frame. If you have a coach or fellow student supporter/trainer, it helps to go over the event to discuss every point from technique to strategy. Look for mistakes or weak areas. If you have lost, you might prefer to forget about it but this exercise, though painful, will provide information which may help you succeed in the future.

The best time for constructive analysis is a couple of days after the event when you have had chance to relax and settle back into normality. Even after a winning result, it still makes sense to examine the outcome and look at ways where you can improve further.

AND TO THE FUTURE

To become an overnight champion is extremely rare. It takes time and effort to hone skills and once you have entered the tournament scene, it takes further time and training to find your strengths so to speak. Try to be patient. And, if you should ever find that you are losing the way, then remember this: 'There is more to life than winning or losing. How much blood, sweat and tears lost for a piece of metal and a moment of triumph or defeat? Think not about the trophy, the score or the final result. Forget the highs and lows of emotion. Instead, look within your soul and know that the experience itself is what counts.'

COMMON QUESTIONS ANSWERED

Q. Why is there such a long wait at tournaments? Quite often, we have to register for 9am and then have to hang around for several hours before the event begins. It can prove extremely draining, especially under the glare of leisure centre lighting. Any suggestions on how to cope?

A. Waiting time at tournaments is quite common and is one of those irritating problems which organisers seem unable to solve. If the tournament allows 'entry on the day', and is well attended, it takes up time sifting through entries and sorting out the categories. Occasionally, there are more competitors per event than anticipated and this can place extra demands on the officials resulting in delays. The most successful tournaments which maintain good time keeping tend to be the few who only take entries in advance. This enables the organisers to be better prepared to some degree.

As for coping with the long wait (and in one incident, I knew a competitor who had registered at 9am and only got to fight 10 hours later!!!) it is best to arrive at the tournament fully prepared, with food, drinks, something to keep you occupied. Some competitors have a shower at the leisure centre to freshen up and this is a good idea. If you have a long wait, try to get some fresh air. Go outside for a while, away from the artificial lighting found in many tournament venues. Be careful you don't miss your event – I have seen this happen too!

Q. Why do I feel drained when I compete? I go on to the mats and find my muscles are weak and sluggish.

A. There could be a variety of reasons for the way you feel but the answer may point to your diet on the day. Weakness can attack you quickly if you haven't replenished lost energy. Make sure you eat throughout the day and replace lost fluids. Many competitors starve themselves through worry but this often proves counter-productive. Also, take a look at your pre-tournament training. If you feel off form, then you may not have reached your peak performance time.

Q. I've never really felt at home with contact sports so I would like to compete in the kata events. I have two katas which I believe are good enough to perform in competition but what do the judges look for?

A. The judges will score on a variety of points. These include technical skill, power, firmness of stance, fluency of movement, focus and, of course, the form must look good and be performed to the highest standard.

Q. I've entered several semi-contact tournaments and have been amazed by the level of contact allowed in some. What is the normal contact allowed?

A. Semi-contact should only 'touch' your opponent. The contact should not be enough to cause injury. This, however, is easier said. In reality, the amount of contact varies from one practitioner to another and is dependent upon what the referee is prepared to put up with. If the contact is too hard, the referee must give a warning and this will lead to disqualification if it continues to be excessive.

CHAPTER SEVEN

MAKE OR BREAK

© Paul Banister

Be positive and you will achieve your goals

'All things come from somewhere but you cannot see
their root; all things appear from somewhere, but
you cannot see the door.'

Chuang Tzu

THE WILL TO CARRY ON

There may come a time when you will ask yourself 'Do
I want to continue with learning martial arts?'. It may
arise through a period of self-doubt, before a high level
grading, after a tournament defeat or simply at a low point
in your training. Feelings change and sometimes our perspective on life alters. It doesn't necessarily figure that
what we start out in the learning of martial arts has to be
finished. It's common to reach a point where you feel you
have done enough or cannot see yourself progressing any
further. Occasionally, there is disillusionment or discontent
and it's simply time to move on but 'make or break' time
needs careful contemplation if you want to make the right
decision.

Statistically, it was once reported not so many years ago
that only one in every two thousand would make it to black
belt status. Today, the drop-out rate still remains high. Most
believe this is a Western 'problem' caused by a lack of self-
discipline and the 'I want it all yesterday' attitude. It takes
considerable time and effort to become a Black Belt expert

and many people are just not prepared to give the dedication or commitment.

The drop-out rate tends to be highest among the middle to high grades. Students leave for all kinds of reasons and it is often due to a personal change in circumstance such as a new job, pressure of exams, moving house or getting married but there are many students who slip away quietly, without any apparent reason. They seem to lose interest and may show signs of indifference as they train through their last sessions. Higher grade students often leave in this fashion. Perhaps they feel it best to go without a word, not wanting to upset their instructor or cause a fuss. Personally, I always find it sad when a high level student drops out after applying so much effort and energy into training. Whatever their reason for leaving, it is a shame to get so far and then give up.

If you find that you have reached a stage where you could 'walk-away from martial arts and never look back' then you need to analyse why you feel this way. If there is a problem and you know what it is then chances are it can be resolved quickly and easily allowing you to continue on your martial arts journey. It may be a problem which the instructor can advise on. Perhaps you aren't happy with your progress to date or feel that you are having difficulties in learning the techniques of your style. If the reason for your detachment is concerned with practice, then the sooner you speak with your instructor, the better.

As any Black Belt or Master will tell you, the road to achieving expertise and a degree of kudos is long and often punishing. That is part of the test. 'To ascend the mountain, one must first experience the depths of the valley', echoes the words of an ancient sage. In simple terms, one cannot expect to reach the position of mastery until they have encountered a physical and mental struggle. There are no short cuts to gaining skill, knowledge and understanding otherwise we would all be masters of the art.

COMMON REASONS FOR DROP OUT

On asking former students why they dropped out of martial arts, the following reasons were among the most common.

1. Disillusionment with one's own development and progress.
2. Loss of interest/boredom with training routine.
3. Change in personal circumstances.
4. Disheartened by martial arts politics and rivalry.
5. Dissatisfied with instructor.
6. Problems with fellow students.
7. Unable to cope with the demands of training.

Sometimes, dropping out is unavoidable but for many, the prospect of continuing on the path of study is possible and mostly only requires a change in attitude or approach or a push in the right direction in order to gain fresh momentum.

Having the will to carry on with your training, especially if you have encountered problems, is a challenge in itself. Some would say that it is a battle against one's own conscience. A good deal of contemplation is necessary before any firm decision is made and should not be taken lightly. After all, you may have already placed considerable effort into your development in the attainment of martial art skills, not forgetting to mention the cost of training and all that spent energy.

So, if you have reached a low point and are considering whether or not to drop out, think carefully. Don't just walk away from it all. Talk with your instructor or fellow students. If there is a chance that your flame for learning can be rekindled, then take the initiative.

VOICE OF EXPERIENCE

Many students find themselves facing a 'make or break' decision. The following people who I spoke to managed to resolve problems in order that they could continue.

'I reached a point in my training where I just couldn't see the point of carrying on. The negative feelings churned within me for weeks and I became more and more disillusioned. What I should have done was confront the problem head on. Eventually, I talked with the instructor. We came to the conclusion that I had reached that "testing time" where most students question their reasons for participating. Apparently, everyone goes through it at one stage or another. The instructor advised me to accept it as part of the test and step over the obstacle by changing tactics. So, I altered the way I trained and set myself new goals. It seemed to do the trick. I'm now on my way to gaining my 1st Dan, an achievement which might have been impossible if I had not confronted those earlier problems.'

Karate practitioner.

'Giving up had never crossed my mind until my purple belt grading. I just couldn't get to grips with it all. It was a very low period for me and I had also had a run of losses in tournament which certainly did not help matters. I considered having a break for a month but knew that I probably wouldn't get round to returning. Deep down, I wanted to carry on but felt so useless. I also wondered if I was worthy of the belt grade. I spoke to Sensei and he reassured me that it was just a rough patch and that everyone learns at a different pace. He told me that I was worthy of my grade, otherwise I wouldn't have been awarded it. He showed his belief in me. Just a few words of encouragement and support was all that I needed to carry on!'

Karate student.

'I'd had a poor introduction to martial arts. I joined a kick-boxing club run by an instructor who professed to be an expert. As it happened, he was a bit of a conman and this became evident as I found out more. I felt cheated and it made me wary but fortunately, I found another club. The instructor was a professional and, what a contrast! I'm glad I made the decision to carry on.'

Kick-boxing student.

ASSESSING PROBLEMS

Tests of spirit come to us throughout our development in life and we simply have to deal with them one way or another. In martial arts, the make or break point may be our first major test of spirit whereby we are faced with one of two choices; to give up or carry on.

We have already looked at the most common reasons for dropping out but let us now assess these in more detail and consider the alternatives.

Disillusionment:

Disillusionment stems from negativity. It may be that you are disappointed with your progress. Perhaps you haven't gained the skills you expected or maybe your fellow students are racing ahead and you are feeling left behind.

Action:

Talk with your instructor. Make an appointment, if necessary, to see him at a quiet time where you are able to talk in private. He should be able to support you and look at ways to improve your development. Remember, martial arts practice caters for every individual and progress rates vary from student to student. It doesn't matter how long it takes to attain the desired skill; what does matter is that you learn and understand without pressure. If you are feeling disillusioned, your instructor may be able to put your mind at ease or suggest ways to tackle how you feel.

Lost Interest:

Some students genuinely lose interest in the martial arts and give up to take on another sporting activity or hobby. This is quite common among children who are often persuaded to take up martial arts by their parents. Older students might try out several lessons before realising that it's not for them.

Action:

If you have genuinely lost interest and this is the only reason for dropping out then so be it. It will not prove productive carrying on if you have no interest or do not enjoy the activity.

Bored with Training:

Occasionally, students just simply become bored with the training routine. Some instructors do not change the training schedule enough to maintain interest. Students need variety and constant learning stimulation in order to progress.

Action:

Speak with your instructor if you are bored. It might just prompt him to look at the class structure and consider new training methods and activities. A good coach will listen.

Change in Personal Circumstances:

Many people leave because of a change in their personal circumstances e.g. new job, marriage, children, moving house etc.

Action:

Consider if there are any alternatives which will enable you to continue training. If you are moving out of town, perhaps there is another club you could join. If you get married or have children, see if it is possible to revise your training schedule so that you can manage a lesson a week. There is always a way if you really want to carry on.

Disheartened by Martial Arts Politics:

I have witnessed countless people leave the martial arts because of politics and petty rivalry. Some are only too pleased to say goodbye to it all, just happy to start afresh away from the demands. Sadly, politics in the martial arts seems to be a problem wherever you go. It is one of those unsavoury aspects of practice which has the awful affect of wearing people down. It is an extremely destructive element and many are wise to ostracise themselves from the political wranglings which frequently take place.

Action:

Do not get involved with martial arts politics and do not

engage in any disputes or petty antagonisms with other students or clubs. It is not worth the heartache and detracts from the real reasons for practising martial arts. Concentrate on your own development. Sometimes, it makes sense to just quietly get on with it.

Dissatisfaction with Instructor:

Some students leave because they are unhappy with their instructor. Perhaps he's a bit of a bully or maybe he's just not what you expected. It may be that you just don't get on with him or feel there is a lack of communication or understanding.

Action:

If you are unable to resolve any problems or grievances about your instructor then rather than give up completely, it may prove more beneficial to look for a new club or find another instructor.

Problems with Fellow Students:

The way you are treated by fellow students may influence your commitment to the club. Not everyone gets on with each other but there should be a good working harmony between club members. This isn't always the case. Some students have left because they are unable to cope with their counterparts.

Action:

Ignore any bickerings, be amicable and just continue with

your training. Consider it as being part of the challenge of learning. If you are being bullied or pushed around, then have a quiet word with the instructor. If the situation really becomes impossible and no one seems willing to do anything about it, then change clubs.

Unable to Cope with Training:

Martial arts has never confessed to be easy. To develop skills, you need determination combined with effort and a certain type of attitude to carry you over the rough patches. Occasionally, a student will feel unable to cope with the demands of training and may consider giving up.

Action:

If training is too difficult then discuss this with the instructor. Analyse why you are finding it too demanding. Are there particular aspects which you find more taxing? Are other students having problems? Most people feel that they need their own time and space to progress.

A CHANGE IN DIRECTION?

There may come a time when the way ahead looks uncertain. You may want to continue on your journey but are finding too many obstacles on your path, making it difficult to carry on or near impassable. It's plausible that you may need to consider taking another route.

In martial arts, you can find this alternative route by trying out a different style. It's not uncommon for students to move around, especially if they haven't found their niche and it is far better to do this than give up entirely.

A change in direction often works wonders, especially if you are feeling jaded. For many, the transition to a new martial art is often a successful one provided you have carried out a little initial research. To start with, ask yourself why you want to try a new martial art? Is it because you've found your current club to be unsuitable, the class routine too easy or too difficult or that you do not feel comfortable with the style? Assess your reasons before trying out another club.

I have witnessed students who have made a favourable change of direction to another style of martial arts and it is apparent that the move has proved to be the right one. Some have transferred to a slower, more genteel art such as Yang Tai chi after finding kung fu far too energetic for their needs or from one Japanese art to another. I have also seen students leave to travel around the 'martial arts globe' to gain experience of different styles before returning back to their original choice, older and often a lot more wiser.

Making a change isn't without some sacrifice. You may have to give up your belt and start again from scratch. This is usually so if you are joining another style of martial art because of the difference in syllabus but starting again isn't necessarily a bad thing. Basics are often very similar between styles and although technique may vary, you will still have the fundamentals from your previous experience. Armed with this, your advancement should be quick proving that experience really does count.

VOICE OF EXPERIENCE

'I had started out learning kick-boxing and was a keen competitor but after several years, I decided to call it a day. I needed a change. A friend of mine did Aikido and asked if I'd like to give it a try. I turned up, got stuck in and thoroughly enjoyed it and I haven't looked back since!'

Aikido student.

'Age and joint problems were the factors which caused me to change direction. I had taken up kung fu fairly late in life and had always found it a struggle. I just hadn't got the energy or strength and it became increasingly difficult to maintain the pace. I took up Tai chi and even after one lesson, I knew it was right. It felt comfortable and did not stress my joints, making it more suitable for my requirements.'

Tai chi practitioner.

'I had to leave my martial arts club because I moved out of the area. It was a great shame because I was really happy with my training there. I've found a class at the leisure centre but I don't feel it's the right one for me. I might try one out of town. It's further to travel but will be worth it if the training is suitable.'

Judo student.

For some practitioners, it is just a matter of finding the right style of martial arts. You may go to one club for several years before deciding that it's not what you wanted. There are more opportunities to learn martial arts today and even some of the obscure styles and many of the original Chinese systems are finding their place in Western society.

VOICE OF EXPERIENCE

'I first became interested in martial arts in 1979, inspired by books and films about Bruce Lee and Jackie Chan. The following year, I visited my Uncle in New Zealand. He is a Maori, ex-wrestling coach and Gojo Ryu martial arts practitioner. We spent a lot of time talking and on my return to Barnsley in South Yorkshire, I visited various clubs before set-tling for Lau Gar. I stayed with this style for six years until politics drove me out.

During the miners strike of 1984, I made contact with Sifu Derek Frearson for a long weekend sem-inar in Leicester. It really opened my eyes. Coming into a traditional Association was the best thing that could have happened. I placed all my effort into learning with a view to becoming a teacher and opening a club. I didn't want to fight. I just wanted to pass on all the wonderful things I had learnt. I finally took my Black Sash in December 1991, eleven years after starting training! What a feeling after so much effort, blood and sweat. It's wonderful when you have achieved something really worthwhile.

Master Lee Kam Wing came over to the UK in 1991 and I'm currently studying Seven Stars Mantis with the Association. Master Lee Kam Wing is a real gentleman and greatly respected. For me, it is the start on another long road. When I began, I wondered "where do I go now?" Many years on, and I'm still going, still learning. The road goes ever on. You stand at the beginning of a long, hard road and only the dream in your heart will keep you going.

Anyone who is wondering whether or not to start some kind of training, then my advice is don't settle for second best. Look and find what you want from martial arts and go for it! You only get out what you put in so enjoy it!'

A. S. Norman
Barnsley Praying Mantis Kung Fu.

BETTER TO TRAVEL THAN ARRIVE

An ancient master once said 'Martial arts is a never-ending journey' – and how true this statement. Even if you lived several times over, you would still not accumulate all the knowledge and expertise passed down through the centuries. Martial arts is constantly evolving and changing shape. For some, it forever remains an enigma and this factor alone is the inspiration which keeps thousands of practitioners focused in their learning with the hope that one day they will reach a state of enlightenment.

The concept of martial arts being a never-ending journey is one which either excites or intimidates many students. For Westerners, the prospect of studying for a lifetime can be a nightmare thought. Most prefer a short period of study with some award at the end of it to mark their achievement but this merely provides an introduction; their journey ended before they have reached the first milestone. But, there are many who realise the benefits of long-term training. They are the ones who are said to prefer to 'travel than arrive', continuing their study and appreciation of martial arts year after year without end.

If you are having a period of doubt and find it difficult, near impossible, to look upon martial arts as a lifetime pursuit, then break your learning periods down into smaller 'adventures'. Forget about destinations, the attainment of awards, belts, certificates, because these are superfluous to your needs. Instead, look at the journey, step by step, and the experiences you will gain a long the way. It is likened to walking around the world without even moving!

As you journey on through the martial arts, you will gain knowledge and skills along the way. On your travels, you will find changes in terrain and environment, occasionally, the going will be tough and you will meet obstacles which you need to stride over. There will be twists and turnings all the way but you will move forward, advancing with each step. Eventually, you may have gained enough information and qualities to guide others on this journey and this will bring new experiences to further enrich your life.

REMAINING FOCUSED

In theory, to practise martial arts one must have some conscious or unconscious reason for doing so. Usually, we can all attribute some kind of logic as to why we subject ourselves to training but what motivates us and keeps our minds focused so that we can maintain the momentum of continual learning? Indeed, what influencing factors are involved in keeping us motivated throughout?

Well, if you reach a plateau or a phase in your training when you are torn between giving up or staying on, often the best thing to do is sit back and look at why you took up martial arts in the first place. Remind yourself of those original goals. Have you fulfilled what you set out to do?

The make or break stage is one which deserves time to work through to make sure you take the right decision. If you give up without thinking, it usually proves difficult to return to training if you suddenly realise that you want to carry on. And, of course the longer it is left, the harder it becomes. If you can work your feelings out before you make any decisions then all's the better.

Remaining focused throughout your training isn't easy. People forget why they are there practising martial arts; They lose sight of their goals. To be focused, you must remind yourself of the reasons for learning, emphasising all the benefits of practice. Above all, you must be happy with what you are doing and should be gaining in your development, otherwise it becomes pointless.

Pointers for Remaining Focused:

1. Get the most out of your training.
2. Remind yourself of the reasons why you took up martial arts.
3. Look ahead with optimism and consider what you will gain through training.

OUTSIDE INFLUENCES

I once came across an advert in a newspaper placed by some religious group which claimed that 'martial arts is evil and is the work of the devil'! Being a glutton for constructive debate, I made further enquiries and received a booklet which went out to denounce martial arts practices, saying that involvement would open one up to the 'dark forces' and all such nonsense. It proved to be so narrow-minded and ill-informed that I wrote back to the group in order to put them straight on a few points. I never received a reply, more the pity, as I was keen to hear how they would answer my letter but the story is just an example of how external influences can have an effect on the practice and enjoyment of martial arts.

There will always be people who have strong, negative views about the arts of the Far East because they have no real knowledge or understanding of them. They will mouth all kinds of claims stating that martial arts is violent, encourages aggressive behaviour, has no real use or significance, simply because they do not know.

Despite the huge numbers of practising martial artists, there will always be some negativity. It is only natural and is, perhaps, the law of nature. If you come across it, don't take anything to heart. Enter into an interesting debate certainly if you wish but don't let it annoy you. Narrow-mindedness is like a disease in itself and is difficult to cure. Often, it is best to just walk away from any undue criticism.

Even friends and family can prove wearing at times. How often have you heard some sarcastic remark or been referred to as 'the Karate Kid' or 'Grasshopper'? More than once, no doubt. Perhaps many remarks are said in jest but it can become a little monotonous when you have been practising for years and have to contend with hearing the same old wisecracks.

As difficult as it may be, ignore the jibes and negative comments that you hear from the outside. They are just the wasted energies of the ignorant and deserve no attention. Sometimes, it's best to laugh them off!

VOICE OF EXPERIENCE

Many students learn to rise above the negative outside influences with a degree of wisdom. After all, how can people judge against what they haven't experienced for themselves? The following student realises that studying martial arts is a conscious decision to better oneself and that it doesn't really matter what other people think providing that it doesn't bother you!

'My fascination for the martial arts began, as with many people, with the inimitable Bruce Lee. As a youngster, I watched his films in awe and developed a deep respect and interest in what he could do. My only regret was that it took me another six years to join a club and start. I quickly discovered that the only thing the movies do not show is the amount of training and discipline that is involved if you mean to become good at your chosen art.

In my case, I have been training for only three years, as I write, but it has become part of my lifestyle and I will never be able to give it up. It has provided me with self-discipline, confidence, good health and fitness.

Some people ask me why I do it; why I subject myself to the pain of training but they have never tried it, so they don't understand that it's more than pain. It is a state of mind, a desire to improve myself. To me, that is what any martial arts is about. As soon as you step into any training hall, you have made a conscious decision to improve your life. A lot of people argue over which style or system is best but I believe that each system has its own merits. How can people make a judgement on something before trying it? Whatever style or system

an individual chooses, it is down to he or she to make their art work for them. After all, you have to want to become better before you can get better.'
Ste Gandy, Chinese martial arts practitioner.

IT IS YOUR DECISION!

Whether you continue to study martial arts or prefer to bow out, it is down to you in the end. No one should influence your decision. Try to think without clutter and find out what martial arts practice really means to you. Consider all the alternatives and the way ahead and when you've made your decision, be happy with it.

Making martial arts work for you requires strength of conviction. At whatever level of practice, you need a positive state of mind to continue developing and gaining new skills and expertise. If you decide to carry on with training (and hopefully you will find the encouragement and support to do so through this book) then make today a new start and look ahead with optimism as you work towards greater achievements.

COMMON QUESTIONS ANSWERED

Q. After three years of practice, I seem to have lost all motivation for carrying on. I've been under a lot of stress and missed some training through illness. Now, I'm wondering whether I should continue. What should I do?

A. Illness and stress affects us in many ways and often makes us feel negative and even confused about future direction. If you have only just got over the illness, do not make any decision about your martial arts training yet as it may be one you live to regret at a later date. Instead, concentrate on making a full recovery. Do things which make you happy and alive. Build up your Positive Mental Attitude. If after gaining all this positivity you still have doubts then speak with your instructor and try to get to the root of the problem.

Q. I've been in martial arts for years and I've come to a stage where I feel I've had enough. The politics and arguments within my club have caused much resentment among people I know and it hasn't helped to create a good training atmosphere. I've seen friends break-up, heated arguments, rivalry and all manner of negative vibes and it's taken away all the enjoyment. Is there any hope it can be resolved?

A. There comes a time when you just have to switch off to all the noise around you to protect your own sanity and this is one of those times. Get back to grass roots if you can and learn to enjoy the basic practice. If you are able, move away from all the political influence. Can you change Association? Will it be a case of changing clubs? You really need to get into a positive atmosphere and leave all the nonsense behind. Remember, it is martial arts what matters the most. Try to find another way of remaining active in practice without these complications.

Q. I want to change martial arts styles but will I retain my grade?

A. You will retain the experience but as far as grade is concerned, it is usually a case of starting from scratch when learning a new style. Consider it as being a new challenge but one strengthened by your previous expertise!

Q. I don't consider myself to be very good at the martial art I engage in even though I've been studying it for three years. Everyone else seems to have advanced but I still struggle with basic techniques. Is it worth me carrying on?

A. Ultimately, only you can answer this question! Ask yourself why you started martial arts? Was it for self-defence, to improve confidence, to learn new skills, to get fit or to make friends? Now ask yourself if you still enjoy what you do. From your answers, you will reach a conclusion. If you find that you still enjoy training, have made many new friends and look forward to participating despite not feeling as though you have progressed at the same rate as your fellow students, then there is still cause to stick with it. Sometimes, physical skill can be placed second in order of importance if study of the art makes you feel mentally well and in good spirits. You don't have to be perfect to continue on your martial arts journey. Providing you enjoy taking part, let this be your motive for carrying on.

Q. Since getting married earlier this year, I don't seem to have the time to give a commitment to training. I used to participate in three classes a week and then train at home besides. Now I'm lucky if I get chance to train once a week. Any suggestions?

A. You need to manage your time more constructively. A change in personal circumstances nearly always results in a change of lifestyle. Getting married is bound to put extra pressure on your time with all the new commitments of home and family life but it doesn't necessarily mean that your training has to suffer. It's simply a case of adapting your routine and reaching a compromise with your partner to work out the best times for martial arts. Even one session a week is better than none and if you can make time at home, perhaps an early morning work-out to maintain your fitness and run through techniques, then you will continue to progress.

CHAPTER EIGHT

BLACK BELT

© Paul Banister

The experienced martial artist continues to perfect skill and technique

'The spontaneous gifts of heaven are of high value but the strengths of perseverance gains the prize.'

Anonymous Sage

THE ULTIMATE ACHIEVEMENT

Throughout the martial arts, the Black Belt is considered to be the most important prize of all. It is a status symbol indicating years of hard work and a high level of expertise. For many, it is the ultimate achievement and with it comes a whole new set of responsibilities and visions.

The Black Belt is indeed a special kind of person. He has reached an understanding through the study of martial arts which sets him aside from anybody else. But, in a crowd, you would probably not be able to recognise him from the next man. As you will come to realise, the Black Belt practitioner comes in all shapes, sizes and ages and his skill may only become evident in the class environment or at an event.

As you progress ever nearer to the role of Black Belt, you will no doubt feel a little apprehensive as to what the future will hold. You may worry about the depth of your expertise and may even wonder if you are worthy of taking the grade. Misgivings at this stage are understandable; after all, it's a huge step forward and one which will take you into the unknown. But, if you've committed the time and effort and know every inch of your particular style then you should be ready to take the test.

Not all styles of martial arts conduct gradings but when it comes to the Black Belt title, it would seem to be a recognised and accepted symbol of mastery and experience throughout the world. And even if a practitioner does not wear a belt of any description, one has only to look at his performance and the execution of martial arts skill to realise his standard. A martial arts master can see a Black Belt in his first movement, in the way he is focused and in the way he breathes and carries himself. For some in the East, the belt is still regarded simply as an accessory for holding up one's trousers!

Black Belt expertise varies from style to style. Technicalities obviously differ so a Karate Black Belt would be a complete contrast to a Judo Black Belt and totally different to a Tae kwon do Black Belt. You will even come across vast differences in the standard and deliverance of technical experience within the same style and this is usually because of the variation in teaching. No two masters teach the same way even if they both practise the same style of martial arts. Despite this, all Black Belts are an authority on their chosen way and will have knowledge and skill synonymous with their system of martial art.

There is no correct way of by-passing the system of working towards Black Belt. Any attempt often falls foul in the long term. Yes, people still 'buy' their Black Belt or are hastily awarded them by a few greedy, impatient superiors but their lack of practical and theoretical knowledge is clearly evident even to the uninitiated. In the end, a Black Belt who has cheated his way to the prize has only let himself down. There is no substitute for hard training and study if you want to achieve with honour.

On average, it takes anything between three to six years of regular, consistent training to reach Black Belt level. Again, this depends upon the style and the individual's commitment. The build-up towards taking the ultimate grading is usually a slow one to allow time for study and full comprehension. This period is one where students can get back to revising basics by going over earlier syllabus and perfecting techniques and application. It is an important time and one which should be used to full advantage.

When you reach the Black Belt level, you will find that you are only one of a small number to attain this accolade at that given time. Martial arts just doesn't churn out scores of Black Belt practitioners (or not as a rule). So few make it to this stage so you will be in a very privileged position.

The ultimate achievement should be celebrated. For many, it is like passing a university degree. The experience will certainly shape your life to the point of influencing your future so treat it with the respect it deserves.

VOICE OF EXPERIENCE

'You never ever forget your Black Belt grading. It is the decisive test. And, once you've passed, the feeling of elation stays with you for some time. I suppose it's like passing your driving test. It's a wonderful sensation. However, once you settle down, you suddenly feel out there on your own. It's pretty daunting until you get into the swing of things.'

Karate instructor.

'Working through the grades, you look ahead and think, "I'll never get there; it'll take forever." But, with effort and determination, the time comes when your Black Belt grading looms over you and then you look back and think how quickly the time has flown.'

Tae kwon do instructor.

'Many people think that getting their Black Belt is the end of the road when really, it's just the beginning.'

Kick-boxing practitioner.

'The Black Belt is a sign of status in the martial arts. It should be safeguarded and treated with respect but I have seen those who abuse it. They let the authority and power go to their heads and often come unstuck in the end.'

Kung fu instructor.

THE ROLE OF THE BLACK BELT

In the run-up towards taking your Black Belt grading, it is wise to consider your forthcoming role in more detail. From the very moment your status becomes official, you enter a new phase in your martial arts development and will be looked upon as being an authority in your chosen field.

The Black Belt, if he chooses, may go on to teach martial arts and this seems to be the most increasingly popular route. Even if you do not find yourself consciously wanting to teach, many lower grades will come to you for guidance and you may find yourself instructing even if it is unintentionally. Some care not to teach and continue on their journey to gain more knowledge, skill and understanding. And then there are those who celebrate their success, wallowing in the glory of gaining the ultimate award before giving up entirely. For them, it is the end of the road; perhaps they have achieved what they set out to do and are happy to hang up their gi and frame their Black Belt certificate for posterity. It is hoped that on reaching this particular milestone, that you will find the courage and determination to continue your journey in the martial arts because there is still so much to learn.

Whatever direction you decide to take, you should present yourself well and act in a manner befitting of your status. In a sense, you are a role model in the public eye. Countless students will look up to you as an example and may well emulate your actions and even your behaviour. Take a wrong move and you can imagine the 'domino' effect this will have along the line.

The sensible Black Belt is a reserved character who knows it is futile to brag about his own prowess in public or behave in a way which is detrimental to the practice of martial arts. He will take care to protect his image and reputation. The fact that you are a Black Belt may place you in difficult situations. It is not uncommon to be challenged or threatened for, as we all know, there are people who are foolish enough to try. How you react to these situations may have a major effect on your future and all that can be said here is to take care and avoid trouble wherever possible. It just isn't worth it. It is often best to walk away or talk your way out of a challenging situation, regardless of how capable you think you are at defending yourself. As Bruce Lee once said, 'it is the art of fighting without fighting' and the way in which I interpret this is to fight (and not always in the practical sense) using wisdom and common sense. Obviously, if you're out on the streets or in a pub professing to be the best then don't be surprised if you get set upon. Such wild boasts simply ask for trouble.

As a Black Belt, you owe it to your club, to your instructors and to the art itself to act in a way which is appropriate. Humility is a quality which every good Black Belt should acquire and will certainly keep you on track.

THE BLACK BELT'S ROLE

1. To set an example.
2. To achieve excellence in the practise of their martial art.
3. To teach others.
4. To exemplify good moral standards.
5. To continue learning.
6. To pave the way for others to follow.

The Martial Arts Black Belt should:

1. Be an authority on his chosen style of martial art.
2. Be able to perform syllabus to a high level.
3. Be adept with technicalities from basics to advanced.
4. Be understanding of the art.
5. Be humble and accepting.
6. Be eager to learn more for self-improvement.

Each martial arts style will have its own set of standards and will explain what is expected of you at this level. Follow every aspect with care and you will gain respect for your actions.

VOICE OF EXPERIENCE

For some practitioners, the role of Black Belt opens up a world of opportunity and can influence your way of life.

'I originally started martial arts for self-defence purposes but as I progressed further and after gaining my 1st Dan, I wanted to explore the art in more detail. Martial arts has not only taught me to defend myself but has helped me develop in many areas to become a very successful coach and, where junior members are concerned, a father figure. Being a coach is very demanding but is worthwhile. All my children practise and martial arts has made me a lot of friends and allowed me to travel to places where I could never dream of being. Personally, I have found respect and confidence through practice and the success I have gained has given me a sense of achievement and knowledge which I can pass on to my family and members. Martial arts has certainly become a way of life for me and my family. The learning never stops. It's also a great scene to be part of.'

Ismail Saleh, 3rd Degree Chief Instructor
Cobra Kai International Academy.

BLACK BELT GRADING PASS GUIDE

As the day approaches for your Black Belt grading, nerves will no doubt begin to set in. Some find themselves thinking back to their first day of training, recalling events thought to be long forgotten. This regression can, in some ways, help towards preparing for the grading. It is an opportunity to go through the basics which are the fundamentals of everything you have learnt. Here lies the strength of your current level of experience and skill.

You have got this far. You may think that passing should be elementary. Not so! This will probably be the toughest grading you ever take. The examiners want to see perfection in everything you have studied. Standards will be high; after all, you are tomorrow's instructor.

Preparing for the ultimate grading requires slightly more care and attention than any other. Considering that most

Black Belt gradings go on for a considerable length of time, you want to be sure you pass. You should train up for the event in the same manner as you would for a tournament. Physically and mentally, you need to be at your best. At this level of practice, you will know when you are ready and, indeed, will have the foresight to prepare yourself accordingly. Look upon your previous gradings as a trial run.

Try to perceive, wherever possible, what will be expected of you on the day. The key to a good grading, apart from the display of practical ability and know-how, is good organisation. If everything runs smoothly and to plan, you will feel more confident and positive in your approach. Talk with others who have recently passed their Black Belt grading. Get a feel of the occasion. Visit the grading venue if you can to familiarise yourself with the atmosphere.

On the day of the grading, organise yourself as you would for any other. Get to the venue early to register and warm-up. Quietly practise. Meditate to relax. Despite the anticipated nerves and apprehension, keep everything in perspective remembering that you are in control of the situation.

As soon as your grading begins, focus yourself. To the onlooker, you will appear calm, with eyes still and appearing devoid of emotion as you focus on the tasks ahead. Concentrate on keeping your body relaxed so that energy may flow through you without hindrance. Too much tension may cause you to be off-balance. Ideally, you should look at ease but, in the same breath, you must be quick to react.

Being focused throughout your grading will not be too

difficult. Most people find that the level of concentration required prevents them from thinking about anything else and despite this often being a long grading, (in some cases as much as one hour in length), the sheer pressure will keep you on your toes. One of the worst scenarios is when you have to start thinking about the next move in a sequence. The consequences of this can often be disastrous causing one to forget or confuse the next part. There is nothing more annoying when your mind suddenly goes blank. The secret is don't think! Movement in technique or sequences should come instinctively at this level without any mental prompting.

Not even the most dedicated practitioners are infallible though and mistakes can happen. If you are aware that you have made a mistake then ask if you may repeat the sequence or technique. Remember to keep your cool.

Normally, only a small number of people take their Black Belt at any one time. A group of eight is usually the maximum (unless there are several examiners) but do not be surprised if you are on your own. A grading such as this requires close scrutiny. The examiners need to be content that you are totally acquainted with the syllabus and are able to function to a high level. They will not be as lenient in their scoring at this level so be prepared for a tough assessment.

People do fail their Black Belt grading often for the simplest of reasons. For example, omitting a technique or even forgetting to use the correct etiquette. If this happens to you then put it down to experience and make sure you book yourself in for the next available retake. Whatever happens, don't fall victim to procrastination.

PASS GUIDE

1. Do not enter the grading until you are fully prepared for the event.
2. Prepare yourself mentally and physically as you would for a tournament.
3. Keep yourself relaxed but focused.
4. Be familiar with the expected rules and regulations.
5. Demonstrate correct etiquette.
6. If you make a mistake, try to correct it in a way which is acceptable to the examiner (e.g. stop, bow, apologise and ask if you may repeat the sequence.)
7. Look smart and wear correct attire.

VOICE OF EXPERIENCE

On asking established Black Belts what went through their minds during their Black belt grading, answers were varied:

'I remember the run up to the grading very well. I had never been so nervous in my entire life! As for the grading itself, although it took almost an hour, I can't recall much of what I did or what I was thinking. It's all a blare!'

Kung fu Black Belt.

'The concentration was so precise on what I was doing that I can't remember anything but going through the motions of what I had learnt in all the previous years. If there had been a fire bell, I doubt that I would have registered it as I was so focused.'

Karate Black Belt.

'All the time, I was hoping that I had got it right. There was enormous pressure on me to perform at my best and I wouldn't have wanted to give anything less. It's such a relief when it's over!'

Kick-boxing Black Belt.

BECOMING AN INSTRUCTOR

If you are keen to become a teacher of martial arts, it is advisable to gain as much experience as possible. Many clubs encourage higher grades to try teaching by giving them the opportunity to assist the instructor with young students or groups of beginners. This is excellent practice, giving valuable exposure to the instructor's role.

As you will discover, the instructor requires a diverse range of qualities in order to teach effectively and with success. These qualities, or skills, need to be developed gradually and what better time to begin developing the role than when you are still a student yourself! Because you are still learning the syllabus, you will be in touch with the demands of being a student and will be able to relate to the experience with greater detail.

Teaching requires great patience and understanding. If you spend time each week, showing beginners basic techniques (such as how to form a fist) and enjoy sharing your knowledge, then chances are you will be suited to the teaching role. If you get no pleasure from it and find it boring repeating yourself lesson after lesson then perhaps it's just not for you.

Most instructors are keen for higher grades to share their experience. Apart from encouraging good martial arts spirit, the higher grade student can actually learn from instructing lower grades. This works by keeping you on your toes, making sure that you remember your early syllabus, testing your technical applications as you demonstrate the art and maintaining a mental alertness. It is without doubt an excellent practice and often results in gaining more experienced higher grades and better Black Belts. If the signs are there revealing that you will make a good teacher, your own instructor will provide encouragement and support.

Even before you reach Black Belt, you will probably have a good idea as to whether or not you would like to become an instructor. For those who do, the sooner you tell your club, the more opportunities will come your way. Actual teaching experience can be gained within your club on reaching the desired standard (usually from brown belt) and as your expertise increases, you will be called upon to take on greater responsibilities. So what begun as taking a small, beginners group through their paces might lead you to taking the entire class.

Once you have passed your Black Belt grading, you are in a position to start teaching. You could set up your own club or, if you are part of a large Association, you may well be designated a class or area to teach in. If you have gained teaching experience in the run up to taking your Black Belt then all's well and good but what happens if you haven't had any practise? Well, with tighter controls, there is a need to receive relevant training for the teaching role. Some Associations/clubs organise Instructor Training courses which you should attend while others integrate training into the Black Belt syllabus. Whatever system is used, you must gain the necessary knowledge and expertise before you start teaching.

If you have made the decision to become an Instructor, ask your club or Association how you would go about gaining a recognised qualification. Becoming a teacher isn't a career you can develop over night. Knowing the martial art and being a talented practitioner just isn't enough. To become a good teacher, you need the special qualities needed to communicate with students of all ages and abilities and this is an art in itself!

VOICE OF EXPERIENCE

Many Black Belts go on to share what they have learnt by teaching others but it is a commitment which requires a great deal of thought.

'I enjoy teaching others; it gives me immense satisfaction to share what I have gained and to see the progression of all those students who I have helped. Now that I'm a higher grade, my instructor is giving me more opportunity to assist in the lessons and I have greater responsibilities. The experience will stand me in good stead for when I become an instructor.'

Kung fu Brown Belt.

'Unfortunately, I do not have much patience and find it hard enough to learn myself without having the responsibility of trying to teach others. Somehow, I don't think I'll make instructor material but I will continue training after I've gained my Black Belt.'

Kick-boxing student.

'The Black Belt is the icing on the cake. It's a real achievement. Some think that's all there is to it when reaching this level but really it's only the start. There's still so much to learn and that is what motivates me to carry on.'

Martial arts Black Belt.

'I'm a 3rd Dan Black belt. It's several years since I took my 1st Dan and I'm still learning and developing new skills. It just goes to show that martial arts continues to have something to offer beyond Black Belt.'

Karate 3rd Dan Black Belt.

'When I got to Black Belt, I almost gave in thinking that I had reached my goal. My instructor put me in the right direction though and showed me that there was still much to learn.'

Tae kwon do Black Belt.

LOOKING TO THE FUTURE

On finally being awarded your Black Belt, uncertainty may follow the elation. You could even feel deflated as you look ahead and wonder about the future. After all, when you started out, your only goal was to get the coveted Black Belt prize so what happens now that you've achieved it?

Well, you may have already made the decision to teach and have plans to set up your own club. If this is the case then you will no doubt be busy organising yourself for this important role but teaching martial arts is not the only direction for the newly appointed Black Belt. You can continue with advanced study, working through degree/dan grades, experiencing other styles all in an effort to attain mastery of the art. This may yet be several years ahead of you but shows that achieving your Black Belt isn't necessarily the end of the road. For many who decide to continue with their study, it proves to be the start of a new and perhaps more challenging journey in search of greater enlightenment.

It is difficult to understand those who make a conscious decision to stop learning once they have attained their Black Belt. Perhaps for them, it is the end of an ambition achieved but it seems such a pity that so many suddenly decide to stop. The Black Belt is, after all, only the accomplishment of one part. There are still many more parts waiting to be attained.

Of course to maintain Black Belt standard, you need to maintain your training and keep up your study of the art. Someone who took their Black Belt several years ago and then stopped practising can not truly be recognised in the same light. Technique soon becomes weak through lack of training. Knowledge can be lost or forgotten. The body grows stiff and slow. To be a Black Belt, you must strive to maintain your standard throughout so it makes sense to continue your training.

Some Black Belts choose to learn a new style of martial art to add to their repertoire of skills. This means starting a fresh and presents a wonderful challenge for the dedicated practitioner and one which can bestow inordinate gains in knowledge and expertise but it is not a test to be taken lightly. It will demand effort and a good memory to take in so much information while trying to retain the skills already acquired but many practitioners have managed to gain their Black Belt in different styles with great success.

Some Black Belts concentrate on competition and keep up their skills on the tournament mats. Chasing a title maintains the incentive year after year. A few move into the area of coaching or officiating in the martial arts sports arena and find this sufficiently challenging.

As soon as you are awarded your Black Belt, know what your next move will be. Do not sit idle or give yourself a few months off as chances are you won't return to training. Plan out your next goal and how you wish to develop and be positive in your approach.

BLACK BELT OPPORTUNITIES

* *To Teach:*
  Become a class instructor for your Association.
  Run your own clubs.
  Run self-defence classes in the Community.
  Take up coaching.

* *To Continue with Study:*
  Learning advanced techniques.
  To find new teachers to learn other skills.
  To visit the Far East for study.
  To master the art.

* *To Compete:*
  To compete locally and Nationally.
  If good enough, represent country in International events.

* *To Officiate:*
  Use experience to train as a referee.
  Become an Association Committee member.

VOICE OF EXPERIENCE

Running your own club as a newly qualified Black Belt isn't to be taken lightly. Paul and Barbara Chadwick, karate practitioners for over 26 years and much respected both in and out of the martial arts fraternity, are keen to see all Black Belt instructors take their teaching role seriously.

'Consider this scenario. You've just got your Black Belt. You're young, fit, strong and dead keen. The Black Belt Blues haven't set in yet. Sensei comes up to you and asks if you will open a club in the community centre just round the corner from you. What a temptation. Your own club, students. You'll be your own boss. You can teach twice a week and still train at the honbu. But will a small acorn soon become a ruddy great oak?

How will you run the club? Will you have a committee? How will you organise the finances? Will you do it purely for love or money? You'll need to answer these questions from the word go and your personal circumstances will usually determine the outcome.

Most teachers in the martial arts are extremely diligent. They care about their students and it shows. But some do take advantage and some earn high amounts for quite mediocre performance. Just because you've come away from the training session sweating buckets doesn't mean it was a good one. And the size of fee asked for by an instructor doesn't necessarily relate directly to the worth of said instructor.

Whatever way a club is run, the students are the ones who matter. And they have little to compare with since most stay in the same club or organisation throughout their careers. At all times they deserve the very best on offer. Unfortunately, for

the martial arts however, they don't always get it.'
Sensei Paul and Barbara Chadwick

Here are the views of another martial arts couple keen to promote good teaching practice:

'We would like to comment on an encouraging trend of recent times. Karate and martial arts in general have attempted to "get their house in order", so to speak, in relation to the standards and calibre of instructors and clubs using their banner. The NVQ training schedules are a definite step in the right direction in ensuring that people who are teaching children as well as adults are doing so with the correct methods and ideology necessary to ensure those practices are not abused and misrepresented. We all have examples to cite concerning martial artists (students and instructors) who have displayed attitudes and behaviour which has horrified those of us who have a genuine admiration and concern for the mental ideals as well as the physical attributes extolled by the "true" martial artists. There are too many people out there who assume that because we participate in a martial art we must therefore be thugs and mental ingrates who spend our weekends fighting outside football grounds and nightclubs. This myth may be dispelled with the respectability of an officially supported training qualification such as the NVQ. As well as *improving the public's perception of our crafts, we believe these qualifications will improve the quality of training for those who employ it, improving both safety and quality of instruction. As martial artists of over 25 years experience, we have seen the effects science has had on our training practices and we admit that the changes have been much for the better.'*

Steve and Debra Baldwin
Standish Karate Club instructors.

COMMON QUESTIONS ANSWERED

Q. Is the standard for Black Belt the same throughout the martial arts?

A. Standards vary and depend upon the demands of the style's syllabus. In some martial arts, it is quite feasible to gain your Black Belt in 3 years but it does not mean you will be at the same level of proficiency as those who have learnt a system which takes 5 years to reach Black Belt. The level of expertise naturally varies and is also dependent upon the effort put in.

Q. Why does it take so long to reach Black Belt standard?

A. Even if you could learn and memorise all the syllabus in a week, you would still need years of study to perfect skill and technique before your Black Belt could be awarded. You can't study for a degree overnight and nor can you expect to be proficient at martial arts without committing time and effort. It is a deliberately slow process to enable the student to practise at a higher level.

Q. I'm an ageing Black Belt-to-be and I'm concerned that I might not be good and able enough to take the grading. Although I know and understand my syllabus, I'm not as agile as the others and find many aspects of training extremely difficult. Any suggestions? I sometimes wonder if its worth me carrying on?

A. If you know and understand the syllabus and are able to practise at a fairly competent level then there's no reason why you shouldn't enter the grading and be as equal as the rest. The emphasis lies in being the best you can be and not comparing yourself with everyone else.

CHAPTER NINE

NEVER-ENDING JOURNEY

© Paul Banister

Balance your training with calm meditation to enhance mind, body and spirit.

'He who wishes to know the road through the mountains must ask those who have already trodden it.'

Anonymous Sage

LIFE AFTER BLACK BELT

The way of martial art is forever moving forward. Through the centuries, masters have passed their skills and knowledge down through generations and over time, the arts have been shaped and improved for the benefit of practitioners today. As martial artists, we are in effect just passing through life and when we are gone, martial arts will still remain beating like an eternal pulse through time.

It seems strange to think that the movements we engage in as we practise the rudiments of our art are the same as those performed by the ancients in centuries gone by. Even stranger is the thought that what we practise today will eventually influence the lives of those yet to be born!

Martial arts goes on and on. And, we too must continue. There is life after Black Belt status. Many do not see this automatically and often end up straying from the path through lack of motivation. Whereas with hindsight, the Black Belt can focus upon new goals and see his way towards mastering the art.

The Black Belt instructor can often find himself in a

quandary. He may go on for years, teaching the art, without actually advancing a great deal on his own personal level. Most instructors are so wrapped up in the teaching role that they forget the need for continuation of their own learning.

Whatever style you practise, the Black Belt is considered to be universally accepted. Once achieved, one may continue to study for dan/degree grades leading to the highest order which is generally regarded as Grandmaster. This can take many years to achieve and obviously requires patience and tenacity.

The martial arts Black Belt must advance and move onwards, maintaining motivation by setting new goals and remaining focused throughout. As one wise sage once said, 'We are all students for a lifetime. The day we stop learning is the day we cease to exist.'

Remain focused:
On achieving your Black Belt, set yourself goals for the future.
Look ahead to your next dan/degree grade and set a mental date as to when you will reach your next target.
Consider adding to your skills by learning other martial arts.
Try learning associated skills such as healing or philosophy.
Do not sit back – this is only the beginning!
Keep up your training to be worthy of your Black Belt achievement.

QUEST FOR KNOWLEDGE

From the moment you take up your first martial arts lesson, a commitment has been made. It is the start of a quest for knowledge; one which will take you on a journey of experiences as you search for new skills and qualities which will lead to personal and perhaps spiritual advancement.

There is a lot of secrecy attached to the practise of martial arts at such an advanced level and much is shrouded in mystery. Far Eastern masters guard their secrets with zeal and are extremely particular as to whom should carry the 'family' knowledge. Some devout practitioners take their wisdom to the grave!

For some practitioners, the quest begins with a pilgrimage to the birthplace of their martial art. Many advanced students find a trip to the Far East a truly inspirational encounter and even more so if there is chance to work with the masters there. Some feel immediately at home – others decide to stay on. If you are lucky and have shown great effort, a master may take you 'under his wing'. This privilege is only for the few.

Of course, you do not have to travel all the way to the Far East to gain mastery of the art. Much may be learnt in your own environment through the accumulation of skill, effort and time. At this standard, you need to maintain an open mind. Many Black Belts find themselves experimenting with other styles to increase their knowledge and appreciation of martial arts as a whole and this practice comes recommended.

There is much to be gained from seeking out other instructors and learning new skills.

The quest for knowledge however should not stop at learning physical combat. The way of martial arts embodies elements of healing, philosophy, history and skills for survival; qualities adhered by every true martial arts master.

THE WAY AHEAD

It is hoped that this book has helped you in your study of martial arts. Whether you are a complete beginner or an established practitioner, the fact remains that the way ahead is likened to a long journey and one where guidance from those who have been there will help you to reach your goals. With this in mind, I would like to conclude the book with a variety of quotes from fellow martial arts practitioners as guidance, inspiration or advice to keep you on your own very special journey.

REFLECTIONS...

'Born from the need to defend oneself influenced by Buddhist and Taoist thought, the Chinese martial arts offer a unique way to improve one's quality of life. The practice not only allows the practitioner to gain self-defence skills but creates a positive mental approach to one's daily life. Through constant practise and hardship, one will build a determination to succeed against all the odds. This determination can best be seen in China by viewing the old masters. Through war, famine, persecution and political up-heaval, they have continued to train often in secret. These oldsters can be seen in parks and open spaces all over China doing their early morning exercises. Like an iceberg with only the tip showing, these exercises go much deeper than their physical actions. With the main body buried under the surface, daily training transcends the purely physical and becomes a way of life.'

Sifu Derek Frearson,
British Taijiquan and Shaolin Wushu Assoc.
Seven Stars Mantis UK instructor.

'I was always interested in the martial arts and my opportunity to learn Kyokushinkai Karate came when the bandleader of a music group that I played in offered me the chance to study with his instructor. This was back in the winter of 1973. I can tell you now that although I trained very hard, I was absolutely useless. I could not co-ordinate two successive moves during Kumite.

'The club trained at a greyhound stadium and on one particular night, I decided to have a nice large steak and chips for my dinner before venturing out to catch the bus. When I reached the bus stop, I found one of the green belts waiting there. We got chatting and decided to nip into the pub just behind us for a little warmth and a couple of pints of refreshment. We finally got to the club on time and quickly changed for the work-out. This was in the form of a thirty minute rigorous display of stretches, toe touching, jumping, windmills, walks and finally a knees up to the chest routine. At the end of this, we all stood to attention as the master walked into the ring. We all bowed and the master shouted at us "Ki Ya" to which everyone responded with a guttery "Ish" and then I threw up everywhere!'

Peter Seaman, Wirral.

'I worked as a door steward for a good few years and experienced quite a number of fights. Word got round that I taught Bruce Lee's art of Jeet Kune Do and a fellow steward, himself a 2nd Dan martial artist, invited me down to the basement to show me some of his stuff and in return, I would demonstrate some Jeet Kune Do. In his tight suit, white shirt and bow tie, he proceeded to jump into the air, spinning, kicking, grunting and sweating. This went on for quite some time; about five minutes of "classical mess" as Bruce Lee used to say. When he had finished with his flying kicks, he sat down pouring with sweat and looking exhausted. I was supposed to be impressed but I had seen it all before. Now it was my turn. I asked him to stand so I would have a target. I moved forward and told him we would be using only two techniques. He looked at me surprised.

Then, I fired a finger jab and a side kick, turned and walked away without a bead of sweat, demonstrating all that is required is economy of motion and simplicity.'

> *Thomas Carruthers, Jeet Kune Do I.M.A.*
> *Glasgow.*

WHY I STARTED MARTIAL ARTS?

'I remember the bend coming up fast – way too fast – and then I think I remember bouncing over the hedge like a stone skimming across a pond. I half remember the Z1000 crashing down on me. Then, the world gets kind of blank. Two and a half years of swinging on crutches, I had leg muscles of a sparrow and a posture that Quasimodo would have been proud of. I needed to get fit, I wanted my muscles to stand out like knots in thread and wanted to relax. So, I ambled along one Monday night to a martial arts class. Come Tuesday morning, I was in agony. Every muscle I had was aching and my pinned joints felt like they were going to explode. Still, by the following week, I'd partially recovered and so I went back again, and again.

'So, how has martial arts helped me? Well, I'm fitter than I was, my posture's improved and I'm slightly more flexible than an iron bar! But there's more to training than improving fitness ... much more. There's the friendly atmosphere of watching fellow sufferers – er – students train and helping you to improve. There's the inner calm that comes from the physical training – and a special thanks must go to Sifu Mark Strange who helped me to keep my sanity following the sudden death of my daughter, Emma.

'I think I've already gained a lot from martial arts, both physically and mentally. Sure, I'd like to achieve the splits, kick higher than a pygmy's kneecap and, most of all, stop blocking kicks with my head! In time, I hope to achieve this. Okay, I train the hardest I can but I don't think I'll ever kick my way out of a paper bag – each kick aggravates my knee and ankle joints, but I'll carry on. Let's face it, there's no better way to get yourself fit and happy.'

Christopher Gaskell,
L.M.A.A. Chinese martial arts student.

'I decided to learn martial arts after a terrible incident where I was attacked. I did not want to be in a situation like that again and joined a karate club to learn how to defend myself. Despite also having a disability which I've had from birth, I've found that the practice has helped me a great deal. I would like to express my gratitude to all those who have helped me and to say to any disabled people out there that you can do anything you put your mind to.'

Brandon 'The Ninja' Fuller.

'I began martial arts to keep myself fit and also to occupy spare time. Everybody needs something in their lives besides work. I have gained and hope to continue to gain great satisfaction from passing my knowledge of martial arts on to my students world-wide. There is no greater fulfilment of one's commitment to martial arts which for me spans over thirty years.'

George Maughan,
Universal Golden Eagle Kenpo Karate, Ireland.

MARTIAL ARTS WAY OF LIFE

'I started training in the martial arts of WTF Tae-kwondo ten years ago at the age of 37. At the time, I had no knowledge of the martial arts. As my children were growing up, I had more time on my hands and wanted to get fit. I saw Taekwondo advertised on a tree and I decided to go and see what it was like. I was very unfit, as I realised when my instructor said "20 press-ups" when I could not even do one! But I fell in love with Taekwondo and decided to stick with it.

'The instructor's wife was training at the time and became my partner. She was very patient with me as I was slow but with time, dedication and the will to learn, I eventually became fitter and achieved the goal of gaining the prestigious black belt. Since then, I have become an instructor with a club of my own. I have some very talented students and three black belts who have trained with dedication.

'You are never too old to learn a martial art. Providing you train hard, with an open mind and heart, and most of all enjoy what you do, then you can achieve your goals. Taekwondo has become a way of life for me and as a woman in a male dominated sport, it is an achievement.'

Mary Sellen, London.

'Through the years, martial arts has helped me in many ways. It has kept my mind occupied and as you delve deeper into each move and technique, you gain confidence to face all you have to do in everyday life.'

George Maughan,
Universal Golden Eagle Kenpo Karate.

THE HIGHS OF MARTIAL ARTS

'I started training in Tae Kwon Do at the age of 21 back in 1980 under Master Rhee Ki Ha, later moving on to the T.A.G.B. under their chief instructor, Master Hee Il Cho. I remember as a student being so impressed by Master Cho's performance, openness, teaching methods and all the articles about him in magazines. Today, more than ever, he is still the inspiration of many martial artists throughout the world. I was with the T.A.G.B for some ten years and then went on to follow Grandmaster Hee Il Cho to the formation of the I.T.F. Tae Kwon Do/A.I.M.A.A. programme after changes in 1993. I became chief instructor and the I.A.M.A.A. UK representative accumulating in me being selected from some of the country's top Tae Kwon Do instructors to be the first direct representative of Grandmaster Hee II Cho promoting the A.I.M.A.A in the UK. So far this has been my crowning glory and is worth more than any medal, trophy or title. To be respected for your qualities and held in high esteem by one of the top Grandmasters in the world today is truly a position to be proud of.'

> *Mr Ian H. Clode, 4th Dan chief instructor*
> *I.T.F. Tae kwon do/A.I.M.A.A.*

PRACTISE MAKES PERFECT

'Practise makes perfect! In fact, practise does not make perfect. Twenty-two years of Karate practise at varying degrees of intensity has demonstrated to me that perfect represents a transitory state of mind, which when reached challenges one to improve and do better. This of course makes practise the long term objective rather than a brief route to perfection.

'Martial arts, as with life, is dynamic. The test for the artist is whether or not he or she can adapt to all the apparent changes such as age, injury and personal circumstance, and the unapparent such as social conditions and mental state.

'Regardless of style, all the martial arts have the potential to provide a foundation for development that can assist the individual to reach physical and mental states that will enhance their lives in and outside the dojo.

'Without doubt, martial arts can be practised for the duration of one's life with the application of common sense and commitment. It is essential to listen to one's body as chronic injury will prevent consistent practise, prevent enjoyment and become a disincentive.

'Evolution is not just a programme on the plight of some unknown lizard; it is about change and development. So let perfection be the pleasure of practise.'

Philip J. Dyer, 3rd Dan Shotokan Karate.

'In 23 years of study, I have learnt 116 forms (Kata/kuen) of different styles and my technical knowledge has grown. I think the most important aspect in martial arts is the practise of forms. This is where the secret lies. I train forms and basics every single day. The modern schools of Kung Fu teach their students fighting and often neglect forms. This is a big mistake because students often become aggressive. The best kung fu student does not fight for glory but only for self-defence.'

D'aria Angelo, Instructor, Sporteam Voghera, Lee Kam Wing Martial Arts Sport Assoc. Italy branch.

HEALING ARTS

'A part of martial art tradition often overlooked in the west, but an important part of all traditional schools in Japan, is the study of traditional medicine (do-in, shiatsu, acupuncture and herbal remedies). When training as an instructor, it is your responsibility to ensure the safety of your students but sometimes accidents happen even in the best of dojos. So, you need to know how to heal the student so they can be back training as soon as possible.

'Traditional medicine also teaches you how to treat bodies which are tired from excessive exercise, muscle strain, back injuries and broken bones using herbal teas, balms and ointments. This method of medicine is over 5,000 years old and was studied by all members of the warrior class in Japan, China and India. It started because when in battle, the injured person may have been isolated from his fellow warriors and needing treatment. He needed medical knowledge to survive and return to his own country. Without this knowledge, a warriors training was considered incomplete!'

Prof. G. J. Wilson, 7th Dan National Coach,
Shinto Ryu Jiu-Jitsu, Japan.

TOURNAMENTS

'A true champion is not merited on one day's performance. A true champion is someone who can come up from nothing, to the heights of championship status to maintain consistency and to come back after defeat. That is a true champion! Do not be afraid to learn from the pain of defeat. It is important to experience what it is to lose. It is only through the backbreaking toil of training that you will learn about your weaknesses and your strengths, and ultimately about yourself and who you are. The grimacing may one day transform into the smile of success.'

Kevin Brewerton, World Semi-Contact Champion
(from Warrior Within,
Peterson Book Company 1992)

INFLUENCES

'It is not hard to see why so many martial artists, past and present, have been influenced by Bruce Lee. If it wasn't for his films, most of the traditional martial arts classes would not have the numbers they have now. Even the most ardent of traditionalists must acknowledge his drive and vision in the way he brought the world's attention to martial arts. If it wasn't for Bruce, the Jackie Chans and Van Dammes of this world would find it difficult convincing anyone to let them appear in front of a camera.'

Thomas Carruthers, Jeet Kune Do instructor.

NEVER-ENDING JOURNEY

'I began training in martial arts in 1972. I have studied Japanese, Korean and Chinese styles. I am a black belt in karate Shotokan, blue belt in judo, brown belt in Tae Kwon Do, red belt in Kung Fu Wu Tao and 4th level in Shaolin Chang. Throughout this period, I have also studied yoga and stretching.

'In 1989, I created my own personal style of martial art called Kar Kun Do which is the fusion of karate and kung fu, which I teach only to a few people. In March of 1994, I went to Hong Kong to find a traditional master and came across Lee Kam Wing, Seven Stars Praying Mantis kung fu master. Nowadays, I follow only this master because I have found the mantis style to be so complete and Lee Kam Wing is truly the master of my dreams.'

D'aria Angelo, Italy.

'Martial arts has been practised for hundreds of years, devised and passed on through generations of devoted human beings, reaching within themselves, discovering pure thoughts, strengths and self-esteem.'

M. R. Smith,
Chinese martial arts practitioner.

'Martial arts is like one straight road which stretches beyond view. You can not see the end of it but know that you must travel ever onwards, never once deviating from the path. To master martial arts, you will need great dedication to keep you on this road. There will be many temptations and distractions on route but you must keep going, focused like the hawk eyeing its prey.

'Back in 1983 when I first started martial arts, it didn't take me long to realise that the way ahead would be a difficult one. You are tested to the brink, not just physically but mentally and spiritually within training and in life itself. Challenges of a mental nature spring forth throughout this time and how you deal with them will reflect on your future.

'I train harder now than ever before; the effort I put in is far more concentrated. One has to stay hungry for training and knowledge, be ready for all the obstacles and this is the secret to longevity in the martial arts. Too many give up too soon for all kinds of reasons but it all boils down to lack of dedication and commitment in the end. Without these qualities, one cannot hope to progress in the martial arts.

'As for me, I look ahead on my road and still have no sight of the end but perhaps that's a good thing. Perhaps there is no end. As I journey forward, my feet grow older and my mind wiser as I learn from the environment which I come across. Every step forward adds to my knowledge. It is constantly accumulating. And, I have come to realise that it's far better to travel than arrive. While travelling, you are becoming more enlightened and it is this which enables you to master what you have.'

Sifu Mark Strange,
Chinese martial arts instructor.

Finally...

How martial arts will develop in the future depends upon the actions of the present and what we have learnt from the past. Tomorrow is undoubtedly unknown territory but if martial artists were to unite and share their visions and openly discuss the way forward, there would be good reason for increased optimism among the masses of practitioners all over the world.

Martial arts is somewhat like a child in the west. It has yet to grow and mature. Needless to say, the whole movement – no matter what style of martial art – has received more than its fair share of criticism over the years and has been subject to corruption and problems throughout. But it doesn't have to be this way. Rather than ignore trouble, the masses need to speak out in a united voice to stamp out all the problems. Students and instructors from all styles need to join forces to fight the negativity which eats away at the very core of martial arts.

The way ahead is relatively straight forward if you keep to

the fundamentals and that is to practise with positivity. Deep down, every true martial arts practitioner wants to get on with their development without the trials and tribulations. The way ahead depends upon a shared vision. Simply, it is to try and work together in harmony, to remember the values passed down to us and to convey the real meaning of martial arts practise to generations to come. We can but try.

> 'Without ascending the mountain, we cannot judge the height of heaven.
> Without descending into the valley, we cannot judge the depth of the earth.
> Without listening to the maxims of the ancient masters, we cannot know the excellence of learning.
> The words of saints though a thousand years old do not become useless.'
>
> *Wise Sage.*